THE OLD MAID, *and*

THE CABINET OF ANTIQUITIES

HONORÉ DE BALZAC

Published by Left of Brain Books

Copyright © 2021 Left of Brain Books

ISBN 978-1-396-32231-0

First Edition

Table of Contents

IN THE RUE DU CYGNE

Du Bousquier made no attempt to conceal this very serious deliberation, he passed his hand over his head, twisting his nightcap which concealed his disastrous baldness. Like all those who exceed their disastrous baldness. Like all those who exceed their aim, by finding more than they hoped for, Suzanne was astounded. To conceal her astonishment, she assumed the melancholy attitude of a wronged maid before her seducer; but inwardly she was laughing like a grisette at a junket.

LA VIEILLE FILLE

THE OLD MAID

TO MONSIEUR EUGENE-AUGUSTE-GEORGES-LOUIS MIDY DE
LA GRENERAYE SURVILLE, ENGINEER OF THE CORPS ROYAL
OF BRIDGES AND HIGHWAYS,

As a token of the affection of his brother-in-law

DE BALZAC

THE OLD MAID

Very many persons must have met in certain of the provinces of France a greater or less number of Chevaliers de Valois, for there is one in Normandy, another is to be found at Bourges, a third flourished in 1816 in the city of Alençon, and perhaps the Midi possesses one of its own. But the enumeration of this Valésienne tribe is here unimportant. All these chevaliers, among whom there were doubtless some who were Valois as Louis XIV. was Bourbon, were so little acquainted with each other that it was not worth while to mention their names to each other. All of them, moreover, permitted the Bourbons to remain upon the throne of France in perfect tranquillity, for it is somewhat too well established that Henri IV. became king owing to the want of a male heir in the first branch of the Orléans family, called Valois. If there be any Valoises in existence, they descend from Charles de Valois, Duc d'Angoulême, son of Charles IX. and Marie Touchet, whose male posterity came to an end, until the contrary is demonstrated, in the person of the Abbé de Rothelin; the Valois-Saint-Remy, who descended from Henri II., likewise became extinct in the famous Lamothe-Valois, implicated in the affair of the Diamond Necklace.

Every one of these chevaliers, if our information is reliable, was, like he of Alençon, an old gentleman, tall, dry, and without a fortune. He of Bourges had emigrated, he of Touraine had concealed himself, he of Alençon had fought in La Vendée and *Chouanned* a little. The latter had passed the greater part of his youth in Paris, where the Revolution surprised him at the age of thirty in the midst of his conquests. Accepted by the highest aristocracy of the province as a real Valois, this Chevalier de Valois d'Alençon was distinguished, like his homonyms, by his excellent manners, and had the appearance of a man accustomed to the best society. He dined out every day, and might be seen at play every evening. He had the reputation of being a witty man, thanks to one of his defects, a habit of relating a great number of anecdotes of the reign of Louis XV. and of the beginning of the Revolution. When these stories were heard for the first time, they seemed to be very well told. The Chevalier de Valois had, moreover, the virtue of not repeating his own bons mots and of never speaking of his love affairs; but his smiles and his agreeable manners were like delightful indiscretions. This good gentleman availed himself of the privilege of the old Voltaireans, of not going to mass, but his irreligion was regarded with the very greatest indulgence because of his devotion to the royal cause. One of his graces that was the most remarked was the manner, doubtless imitated from Molé, of taking snuff from an old gold snuff-box ornamented by a portrait of a Princess Goritza, a charming Hungarian, celebrated for her beauty in the latter days of the reign of Louis XV. Having had an attachment in his youth for this illustrious foreigner, he never spoke of her without emotion; he had fought a duel for her with Monsieur de Lauzun. Though fifty-eight years of age at this period, he acknowledged only fifty, and could very well permit himself this innocent deceit, for, among the advantages enjoyed by those who are both blond and spare is that of preserving that still-youthful figure which, in both men and women, delays the appearance of age. Yes, be it known, all the course of life, or all that elegance which is the expression of the life, resides in the figure. Among the number of the chevalier's properties, mention must be made of the prodigious nose with which Nature had endowed him. This nose divided vigorously a pale countenance into two sections which seemed to have no knowledge of each other, and of which only one flushed during the labor of digestion. This fact is worthy of remark at a time when physiology is so much concerned with the human mind. This incandescence took place on the left. Although the long and slender legs of Monsieur de Valois, his thin body and wan complexion did not give evidence of robust health, he nevertheless ate like an ogre, and pretended to have a malady known in the provinces as *foie chaud*—inflamed liver—doubtless as an excuse for his excessive appetite. The circumstance of his flushing supported this pretension; but, in a country where the repasts develop along the lines of thirty or forty courses, and last for four hours, the stomach of the chevalier seemed a blessing bestowed by Providence upon this good city. According to certain physicians, this flush on the left side indicates a prodigal heart. The gallantries of the chevalier confirmed these scientific assertions, the responsibility for which, very fortunately, does not weigh upon the historian. Notwithstanding these symptoms, Monsieur de Valois had a nervous, consequently a vivacious organization. If his liver was ardent, to make use of an old expression, his heart burned none the less. If some wrinkles might be discovered on his countenance, if his hair was silvered, an experienced observer would have seen there the stigmata of the passions and the furrows of pleasure. In fact, the characteristic *goose-feet* and the *palace steps* displayed those elegant lines so much prized at the court of Cythæra. Everything about the gallant chevalier betrayed the manners of a *ladies' man*; he was so exact in his ablutions that it was a pleasure to see his cheeks, they seemed to be refreshed with some marvellous water. That part of his skull which his hair refused to cover glittered like ivory. His eyebrows, like his hair, affected youthfulness by the regularity lent them by the comb. His skin, already so white, seemed to be still more whitened by some secret. Without using any perfumes, the chevalier exhaled, as it were, a perfume of youth which refreshed his surroundings. His hands of a gentleman, cared for like those of a fastidious woman, attracted attention by their pink and well-trimmed nails. In short, had it not been for his magisterial and superlative nose, he would have been merely spruce. It is necessary to summon courage to spoil this portrait by the admission of a weakness. The chevalier put cotton in his ears, and still wore in them two little rings representing heads of negroes in diamonds, admirably executed, moreover; but he considered himself sufficiently justified in this singular habit by asserting that, since he had had his ears pierced, his headaches had left him;—he had been subject to headaches. We do not present the chevalier as an accomplished man; but is it not well to pardon in old bachelors, whose hearts send so much blood to their faces, some admirable absurdities, founded perhaps upon some sublime secrets? Moreover, the Chevalier de Valois redeemed his negroes' heads by so many other graces that society should have considered itself sufficiently indemnified. He took, truly, a great deal of trouble to conceal his age and to give pleasure to his acquaintances. In the first place, there must be noticed the extreme care which he bestowed upon his linen, the sole distinction which persons of breeding can to-day have in their costume;—that of the chevalier was always of a most aristocratic fineness and whiteness. As to his coat, though it was of remarkable neatness, it was always somewhat worn, though without spots or wrinkles. The preservation of the garment seemed to be something extraordinary for those who noticed the fashionable indifference of the chevalier on this point; he did not go so far as to rub it with glass, a refinement invented by the Prince of Wales; but Monsieur de Valois brought to the observance of the most elegant English modes a personal foppishness which could scarcely be appreciated by the good people of Alençon. Does not the world owe some consideration to those who are at so much expense for it? Is there not in this the fulfilment of the most difficult precept of the Gospel, which commands that good shall be rendered for evil? This freshness of toilet, this care, became very well the blue eyes, the ivory teeth, and the blond aspect of the chevalier. Only, this Adonis in retreat had nothing virile in his appearance, and seemed to employ the adornment of the toilet to conceal the ruin occasioned by the military service of gallantry. To complete, his voice produced something like an antithesis in connection with the chevalier's blond delicacy. Without necessarily adopting the opinion of some observers of the human mind, and concluding that the chevalier had the voice appropriate to his nose, you might well have been surprised by its ample and redundant sound. Although it did not possess the volume of the colossal basses, the timbre of this voice was pleasant because of its full medium quality, similar to the tones of the *cor anglais*—a sort of hautboy—enduring and soft, strong and velvety. The chevalier had repudiated the absurd costume preserved by some of the monarchists, and had frankly modernized himself; he always appeared in a chestnut-colored coat with gilt buttons, in breeches half tight-fitting in *pou-de-soie* and with gold buckles, in a white waistcoat without embroidery, in a cravat worn tight without a shirt collar, the last vestige of the ancient French toilet which he had been the less inclined to renounce as he was thus able to display his neck of an abbé *in commendam.* His shoes were set off by square golden buckles, of which the present generation has no remembrance, and which were applied on varnished black leather. The chevalier showed two watch chains which hung in parallel lines from each of his fobs, another remnant of the eighteenth century which the *incroyables* had not disdained to adopt under the Directory. This costume of transition, which united two centuries, the chevalier wore with that grace of a marquis, the secret of which was lost from the French scene on the day when Fleury, the last pupil of Molé, disappeared. The private life of this old bachelor was apparently open to the inspection of all, but was, in reality, mysterious. He occupied a modest lodging—to say no more—in the Rue du Cours, on the second floor of a house belonging to Madame Lardot, the clear-starcher with the largest business in the city. This circumstance explains the excessive care bestowed upon his linen. Most unfortunately, Alençon had, one day, grounds for believing that the chevalier had not always conducted himself strictly as a gentleman should, and that he had privately married, in his old age, a certain Césarine, mother of an infant that had had the impertinence to come without being called.

"He had," said a certain Monsieur du Bousquier, "given his hand to her who had so long been lending him her smoothing-iron."

This dreadful calumny embittered all the more the declining years of the sensitive gentleman, because, as the present Scene will show, he was thus losing a hope that he had long cherished and for which he had made many sacrifices. Madame Lardot rented to Monsieur le Chevalier de Valois two chambers on the second floor of her house, for the moderate sum of a hundred francs a year. The worthy gentleman, who dined out every day, returned home only to sleep. His sole expense was thus his déjeuner, which consisted invariably of a cup of chocolate, accompanied with bread and butter and with the fruits of the season. He had a fire only during the most inclement winters, and then only at the hour when he rose. Between eleven o'clock and four he took his promenades, went out to read the journals, and made calls. At the period of establishing himself at Alençon he had nobly admitted his poverty, saying that his entire fortune consisted in an annuity of six hundred francs, the sole remnant which remained to him of his ancient opulence, and which was paid him quarterly by his former business agent who held the deeds of the annuity. In fact, a banker of the city counted out to him every three months, a hundred and fifty francs sent by a Monsieur Bordin, of Paris, the last of the procureurs of the Châtelet. Everyone was acquainted with these details, because of the profound secrecy which the chevalier always demanded of whomsoever received his confidence. Monsieur de Valois gathered the fruits of his misfortune;—his plate was laid regularly in all the most distinguished houses of Alençon, and he was invited to all the entertainments. His talents as a card-player, as a story-teller, as an agreeable man of good society, were so well appreciated, that it seemed as if everything were disarranged if the connoisseur of the city were absent. The masters of the households, the ladies, felt the need of his little approving grimace. When a young woman heard the old chevalier say at a ball: "You are admirably dressed!" she was happier at this eulogium than at the despair of her rival. Monsieur de Valois was the only one who could properly express certain phrases that had come down from former times. The words *my heart, my jewel, my little darling, my queen*, all the amorous diminutives of the year 1770, took on an irresistible grace in his mouth; finally, he had the privilege of superlatives. His compliments, of which he was, moreover, very sparing, acquired him the good-will of all the old women; he flattered everyone, even the men in official positions of whose good favors he did not stand in need. His conduct at play was of a distinction which would have made him remarked anywhere; he never complained, he praised his adversaries when they lost; he did not undertake the education of his partners by showing them how the hand could have been better played. When, during the deal, there arose those wearisome discussions, the chevalier drew out his snuff-box with a gesture worthy of Molé, looked at the Princess Goritza, lifted the lid worthily, gathered together his pinch; winnowed it, powdered it, fashioned it to an edge; then, when the cards were dealt, he had garnished the caverns of his nostrils and replaced the princess in his waistcoat pocket, always on the left side! A gentleman of the *fine* age—in opposition to the *grand* age— could alone have invented this transaction, half-way between a disdainful silence and the epigram which would not have been comprehended. He accepted the novices at play as partners, and knew how to make the most of them. His delightful evenness of temper caused a great many persons to say of him: "I admire the Chevalier de Valois!" His conversation, his manners, everything about him, seemed blond, like his person. He made a study of offending neither man nor woman. Indulgent for the bodily faults, as for mental defects, he listened patiently, with the aid of the Princess Goritza, to those who retailed to him the little unhappinesses of life in the provinces;— the badly cooked egg at déjeuner, the coffee in which the cream had turned, the absurd details of bodily health, the sudden awakenings from sleep, the dreams, the visits. The chevalier possessed a languorous look, a classic attitude for feigning compassion, which rendered him a delightful auditor: he placed an *Ah!*, a *Bah!*, a *What did you do?* with charming appositeness. He died without ever having been suspected of recalling to his memory the most affecting chapters of his romance with the Princess Goritza whilst these outpourings of silliness lasted. Has anyone ever thought of the services which an extinguished sentiment may render to society, of the extent to which love is sociable and useful? This may explain why, notwithstanding his constant winnings, the chevalier remained the spoiled child of the city,—for he never left a salon without carrying away about six francs of winnings. His losses, which, moreover, he announced loudly, were very small. All those who have known him, admit that they have never encountered anywhere, not even in the Egyptian museum at Turin, so gentle a mummy. In no country of the world did parasitism clothe itself in such graceful forms. Never did the most concentrated egotism show itself more obliging and less offensive than in this gentleman, it was worthy of a devoted friendship. If anyone came to request of Monsieur de Valois a little service which might have inconvenienced him, that one never left the good chevalier without being in love with him, without being above all convinced that he could do nothing in the affair, or that he would spoil it by interfering in it.

In order to explain the problematic existence of the chevalier, the historian, on whose throat, truth, that cruel debauchee, sets her grip, is obliged to say that lately, after the sadly glorious days of July, Alençon learned that the amounts won at play by Monsieur de Valois amounted quarterly to about a hundred and fifty crowns, and that the intelligent chevalier had had the courage to send himself his annuity, so that he might not appear to be without any resources in a country in which there is a demand for the positive. Many of his friends—after his death, be it understood!—have doggedly contested the truth of this statement, treated it as a fable, holding the Chevalier de Valois to have been a worthy and respectable gentleman calumniated by the liberals. Fortunately for the fine players, there are always to be found in the galleries, individuals who will sustain them. Ashamed at having to justify a wrong, these admirers deny it with intrepidity; do not accuse them of obstinacy, these men have the sentiment of their dignity: the government gives them the example of this virtue which consists in interring its dead in the night, without chanting the *Te Deum* of its defeats. If the chevalier had permitted himself this fine trick, which, moreover, would have procured him the esteem of the Chevalier de Gramont, a smile from the Baron de Fœneste, a grasp of the hand from the Marquis de Moncade, was he any the less the agreeable guest, the witty man, the equable player, the delightful story-teller who was the favorite of Alençon? In what, moreover, was his action, which is well within the domain of free will, contrary to the elegant manners of a gentleman? When so many individuals are obliged to pay out annuities to others, what is more natural than to give one voluntarily, to one's best friend? But Laius is dead.—At the end of fifteen years of this manner of living, the chevalier had amassed ten thousand and some hundred francs. On the return of the Bourbons, one of his old friends, Monsieur le Marquis de Pombreton, formerly lieutenant in the black musketeers, had, he said, returned to him twelve hundred pistoles which he had lent him to emigrate. This event made a sensation; it was, later, quoted against the jests invented by *Le Constitutionnel* concerning the manner of paying their debts employed by some of the *émigrés*. When any one spoke of this noble action of the Marquis de Pombreton before the chevalier, that poor man blushed even to the right cheek. Everyone then rejoiced for Monsieur de Valois, who consulted some moneyed men as to the best manner in which to invest the remnant of a fortune. Confiding in the fortunes of the Restoration, he inscribed his name on the register of creditors of the state at the period when the *Rentes* were held at fifty-six francs, twenty-five centimes. Messieurs de Lenoncourt, de Navarreins, de Verneuil, de Fontaine and la Billardière, whom he knew, he said, obtained for him a pension of a hundred écus from the king's privy purse and sent him the cross of Saint-Louis. It was never known by what means the old chevalier obtained these two solemn attestations of his title and his rank; but it is certain that the bestowal of the cross of Saint-Louis authorized him to take the grade of retired colonel, by reason of his services in the Catholic armies of the West. Not considering his fiction of the annuity, with which no one was any longer concerned, the chevalier had then an authenticated income of a thousand francs. Notwithstanding this amelioration in his circumstances, he made no change either in his manner of living or in his daily habits; only, the red ribbon was marvellously becoming on his chestnut-colored coat, and completed, so to speak, his physiognomy of a gentleman. Since 1802, the chevalier had been sealing his letters with a very antique gold seal, sufficiently badly engraved, but on which the Castérans, the d'Esgrignons, the Troisvilles, might see that he bore *party per pale France gemelles gules, gules five mascles or arranged in a cross, touching. The shield sommé with a chief sable, with a cross in pale, argent. For crest, a knight's helmet. For device:* VALEO. With these noble arms, the pretended bastard of the Valois should and could take his seat in any of the royal carriages of the world. Very many people have envied the pleasant life of this old bachelor, filled with parties of *boston*, of backgammon, of *reversi*, of whist and of piquet well played, of dinners well digested, of pinches of snuff taken gracefully, of tranquil promenades. Almost all Alençon believed this life to be free from ambition and from grave interests; but no man leads so simple a life as those envious of him believe. You will discover in villages the most forgotten of human molluscs, rotifera apparently dead, who have the collector's mania for lepidoptera or conchology, and who will take infinite trouble for I know not what butterflies or for the *concha Veneris*. Not only did the chevalier have his sea-shells, but, still more, he nourished an ambitious desire, cherished with a profundity worthy of Sixtus Fifth; he wished to marry some wealthy old maid, doubtless with the intention of making of this alliance a stepping-stone to attain the elevated spheres of the court. In this lay the secret of his pretensions to royalty and of his sojourn at Alençon.

One Wednesday, very early in the morning, about the middle of the spring of the year 16,—this was his manner of speaking,—at the moment when the chevalier donned his dressing-robe of old, green, flowered damask, he heard, notwithstanding the cotton in his ears, the light step of a young girl mounting the stairway. Presently three knocks were discreetly given on his door; then, without waiting for a summons, an attractive-looking young girl slipped like an eel into the old bachelor's chamber.

"Ah! it is you, Suzanne," said the Chevalier de Valois without discontinuing the operation he had commenced, which consisted in passing the blade of his razor backward and forward over a leathern strap. "What are you coming to do here, dear little jewel of mischief?"

"I came to tell you something that will perhaps give you as much pleasure as pain."

"Is it about Césarine?"

"Much I am troubled about your Césarine!" said she, with an air at once mutinous, grave and indifferent.

This charming Suzanne, whose pleasant adventure was destined to exert so great an influence on the destinies of the principal personages of this history, was one of Madame Lardot's workwomen. A word is necessary as to the arrangement of the house. The workrooms occupied the whole of the ground floor. The little courtyard served to hang out on cords the embroidered handkerchiefs, the collarettes, the *canezous*, the sleeves, the frilled shirts, the cravats, the laces, the embroidered gowns, all the fine linen of the best households in the city. The chevalier pretended to be able to determine, by the number of the canezous, or sleeveless gowns, of the wife of the receiver-general, the current of her intrigues; for there were to be seen frilled shirts and cravats in correlation with the canezous and collarettes. Although able to divine by this species of double appearance everything concerning the rendezvous of the city, the chevalier never committed an indiscretion, never did he utter an epigram capable of closing to him a single house—and he had wit!—Thus you may well take Monsieur de Valois for a man of superior parts, and one whose talents, like those of so many others, are lost in a restricted circle. Only, as he was, nevertheless, a man, the chevalier permitted himself certain incisive side glances that made the women tremble; nevertheless, they all loved him when they came to recognize how profound was his discretion, how much sympathy he really had for the pretty weaklings. The head workwoman, Madame Lardot's factotum, an old maid of forty-five, terrifyingly ugly, had her room directly opposite the chevalier's. Above them there was nothing but the garrets in which the lines was dried in winter. Each apartment, like that of the chevalier, consisted of two rooms lighted, one from the street and the other from the court. On the floor below the chevalier, lived an old paralytic, Madame Lardot's grandfather, an ex-corsair named Grévin, who had served under Admiral Simeuse in the Indies, and who was deaf. As to Madame Lardot, who occupied the other apartment on the first floor, she had such a weakness for people of condition that she might be considered as blind as far as the chevalier was concerned. For her, Monsieur de Valois was an absolute monarch who did everything for the best. Had one of her workwomen been guilty of a good fortune that might be attributed to the chevalier, she would have said: "He is such a nice man!" Thus, though this house was of glass, like all houses in the provinces, in all that concerned Monsieur de Valois it was as discreet as a cave of thieves. Born confidant of all the little intrigues of the workroom, the chevalier never passed before the door, which was usually open, without giving some small presents to his pets,—chocolate, bonbons, ribbons, laces, a gold cross, all kinds of pretty trifles of which the grisettes are so fond. Therefore the good chevalier was adored by these young girls. Women have an instinct which enables them to divine those men who love them solely because they wear petticoats, who are happy to be near them, and to whom it never occurs to stupidly demand a return for their gallantries. Women have in this respect the fine scent of dogs, who in the midst of a company, go straight to the man who has an affection for animals. The poor Chevalier de Valois had preserved, from his early life, that need of exercising a gallant protection which formerly distinguished the grand seigneur. Always faithful to the traditions of the houses of pleasure, he liked to give to women, the only beings who know how to receive gracefully, because they can always return. Is it not extraordinary that at a period when all the graduates issuing from their colleges set themselves to hunt out a symbol or to examine myths, no one has yet explained the young girls of the eighteenth century? Did they not represent the fifteenth century tournament? In 1550, the knights, the chevaliers, combated for their ladies; in 1750, they displayed their mistresses at Longchamp; to-day, they keep race horses; at every epoch the gentleman has endeavored to create for himself a mode of life which should be for himself alone. The shoes *á la poulaine* of the fourteenth century were the red heels of the eighteenth, and the luxury of mistresses was in 1750 an ostentation similar to that of the sentiments of knight errantry. But the chevalier could no longer ruin himself for a mistress! In the place of bonbons enveloped in bank notes, he offered gallantly a little bag of dry tarts. Let it be said for the glory of Alençon, these tarts were accepted more joyously than La Duthé ever received a dressing-case in silver or a carriage from the Comte d'Artois. All these grisettes had comprehended the fallen majesty of the Chevalier de Valois, and maintained for him a profound secrecy concerning their household familiarities. When they were questioned in certain houses in the city concerning the Chevalier de Valois, they spoke gravely of the gentleman, they made him older, he became a very respectable monsieur whose life was a flower of sanctity; but, in the house, they would all have climbed on his shoulders like parrakeets. He was very fond of hearing the secrets which the laundrywomen learned in the households, and they accordingly came in the mornings to retail to him the diversions of Alençon; he termed them his gazettes in petticoats, his living journals; never did Monsieur de Sartines have more intelligent spies, or cheaper ones, who would have preserved so much honor while displaying so much deceitfulness of mind. It will be noted that, during his déjeuner, the chevalier was amused like a true believer.

Suzanne, one of his favorites, clever, ambitious, had in her the quality of a Sophie Arnould, she was, moreover, as beautiful as the most beautiful courtesan that ever Titian invited to pose upon a black velvet to aid his brush in creating a Venus; but her countenance, though fine in the form of the eyes and the forehead, sinned in the lower part of the face by commonplace contours. It was the Norman type of beauty, fresh, brilliant, rounded, the flesh of Rubens, which should be married to the muscles of the Farnese Hercules, and not the Venus de Medici, that graceful spouse of Apollo.

"Well, my child, tell me your little story or your big one."

That which, from Paris to Pekin, would have made the chevalier remarkable, was his gentle, paternal manner with these grisettes; they recalled to him the young women he had known in former times, those illustrious queens of the Opéra, whose renown was European in extent during a good third of the eighteenth century. It is quite certain that the gentleman who had lived with that feminine nation, now forgotten like all other great things, like the Jesuits and the filibusters, like the abbés and the farmers of the king's revenue, had acquired an irresistible good nature, a graceful facility, an ease of manner quite destitute of egotism, all the incognito of Jupiter in the house of Alcmena, of the king who allows himself to be deceived by everyone, who throws to the devil the superiority of his thunderbolts and wishes to consume his Olympus in follies, in little suppers, in feminine wastefulness,—but far from Juno. Notwithstanding his dressing gown of old, green damask, notwithstanding the bareness of the chamber in which he received, and on the floor of which there was a wretched piece of tapestry in place of a carpet, greasy old armchairs, the walls covered with a public-house paper which presented here the profiles of Louis XVI. and the members of his family traced under a weeping-willow, there the sublime testament printed in the shape of an urn, in short, all the sentimentalities invented by royalism under the Terror; notwithstanding his ruins, the chevalier, shaving himself before an old toilet table ornamented with wretched lace, still represented the eighteenth century!—All the libertine graces of his youth reappeared, he seemed to be rich with three hundred thousand francs of debts and to have his berlin at the door. He was as grand as Berthier issuing orders during the retreat from Moscow, to the battalions of an army which no longer existed.

"Monsieur le chevalier," said Suzanne drolly, "it seems to me that I have nothing to relate to you, you have only to see."

And she posed herself in profile, in such a manner as to support her words with a demonstration like a lawyer's. The chevalier, who, be assured, was sufficiently shrewd, lowered, while still keeping the razor obliquely on his neck, his right eye upon the grisette, and feigned to understand.

"Good, good, my little dear, we will talk presently. But you are anticipating, it seems to me."

"But, monsieur le chevalier, should I wait till my mother beats me, till Madame Lardot turns me out? If I do not go promptly to Paris, I can never get married here, where the men are so absurd."

"What would you have, my child! society is changing; the women are victims, no less than the nobility, of the frightful disorder which is preparing. After the political overturnings, come the overturnings of manners and customs. Alas! woman will soon no longer exist—he took out his cotton in order to clear his ears;—she will have lost much in giving herself up to feeling; she will rack her nerves, and will no longer have this pleasant little enjoyment of our times, desired without shame, accepted without ceremony, and in which her whims are employed only—he polished his little negroes' heads— as a means of attaining her ends; she will make of it all a malady which will end in infusions of orange leaves.—He began to laugh.—In short, marriage will become something—he took his tweezers to remove superfluous hairs— exceedingly wearisome, and it was so cheerful in my time! The reigns of Louis XIV. and Louis XV., remember this, my child, were the farewells of the finest manners in the world."

"But, monsieur le chevalier," said the grisette, "it is a question of the morals and the honor of your little Suzanne, and I hope that you will not forsake her."

"What!" exclaimed the chevalier, finishing his coiffure, "I would rather lose my name!"

"Ah!" said Suzanne.

"Listen to me, little witch," said the chevalier, stretching himself out on a great couch which was formerly called *une duchesse*, and which Madame Lardot had succeeded in finding for him.

He drew the magnificent Suzanne to him, taking her legs between his knees. The pretty maid yielded, she so haughty in the street, she who had twenty times refused the fortune offered her by some of the men of Alençon, as much through honor as through contempt for their stinginess. Suzanne then presented her pretended sin so audaciously to the chevalier that that old sinner, who had sounded so many other mysteries in other existences very crafty in other ways, would have perceived the affair at a single glance. He knew well that no young girl makes a jest of a real dishonor; but he disdained to upset the scaffolding of this pretty falsehood by touching it.

"We are slandering ourselves," said the chevalier to her, smiling with inimitable subtlety, "we are as clever as the beautiful maid whose name we bear, we can get married without any fear; but we do not wish to vegetate here, we are thirsty for Paris, where charming creatures become rich when they are clever, and we are not a fool. We wish then to go to see if the capital of pleasures has reserved for us some young Chevaliers de Valois, a carriage, diamonds, a box at the Opéra. The Russians, the English, the Austrians, have brought with them millions, out of which Mamma has assigned a dot to us by making us pretty. Finally, we have some patriotism, we wish to aid France to recover her money from the pockets of these messieurs. Eh! eh! dear little lamb of the devil, all that is not bad. The world in which thou livest will cry out a little, perhaps, but success will justify everything. That which is very bad, my child, is to be without money, and that is the malady of both of us. As we have a good deal of wit, we have conceived the idea of making use of our pretty little honor to catch an old bachelor; but this old bachelor, my dear, knows the alpha and omega of feminine tricks,—which is to say, that thou mayst more easily put a grain of salt on a sparrow's tail than thou mayst make me believe that I have anything to do with thy affair. Go to Paris, little one, go there at the expense of the vanity of a bachelor, I will not hinder thee, I will aid thee, for the old bachelor, Suzanne, is the natural cash-box of a young girl. But do not drag me into it. Listen, my queen, thou who understandest life so well, thou wouldst do me much wrong and give me much trouble; wrong? thou couldst prevent my marriage in a country where they are particular; much trouble? in fact, thou wouldst be in an embarrassing position, which I deny, sly one! thou knowest, my dearie, that I no longer have anything, I am as poor as a church rat. Ah! if I should marry Mademoiselle Cormon, if I should become rich again, I should certainly prefer thee to Césarine. Thou hast always seemed to me as fine as gold with which to gild lead, and thou art made to be the love of some grand seigneur. I believe thee so clever that the little trick which thou playest me does not surprise me at all, I was expecting it. For a young girl, why it is throwing away the scabbard of thy sword. To act thus, my angel, it requires superior ideas. Therefore, thou hast my esteem!"

And he confirmed it on her cheek, in the manner of the bishops.

"But, monsieur le chevalier, I assure you that you are mistaken, and that—"

She blushed without having the courage to continue, the chevalier had, with one look, divined, penetrated her whole scheme.

"Yes, I hear thee, thou wishest that I should believe thee! Well, I believe it. But, take my advice, go to see Monsieur du Bousquier. Hast thou not been carrying the linen to Monsieur du Bousquier for the last five or six months? Well, I do not ask thee what has happened between you; but I know him, he has self-respect, he is an old bachelor, he is very rich, he has two thousand five hundred francs of income and does not expend eight hundred. If thou art as clever as I suppose, thou wilt see Paris at his expense. Go, my little dear, go and twist him up, above all, be as fine as silk; and at each word make a double turn and a knot; he is a man to dread scandal, and, if he has given thee occasion to put him in the prisoner's box—in short, thou comprehendest, threaten to apply to the ladies of the bureau of charity. Moreover, he is ambitious. Well, a man may attain to everything by means of his wife. Art thou not pretty enough, clever enough, to make thy husband's fortune? Eh! the devil, thou art capable of holding thy own against a lady of the court."

Suzanne, enlightened by the chevalier's last words, burned with desire to fly to Du Bousquier's house. But, not to leave too abruptly, she questioned the chevalier about Paris, whilst assisting him in dressing. The chevalier divined the effect of his instructions, and aided Suzanne's going out by asking her to tell Césarine to send him up the chocolate which Madame Lardot made for him every morning. Suzanne slipped away, to go to see her victim, whose biography here follows.

*

Du Bousquier, the descendant of an old family of Alençon, occupied a position midway between the bourgeois and the country gentleman. His father had exercised the judiciary functions of *lieutenant-criminel*. Left without means at the death of his father, Du Bousquier, like all the ruined provincials, went to Paris to seek his fortune. At the commencement of the Revolution, he had gone into commercial affairs. Notwithstanding the republicans, who are all very lofty concerning republican probity, the affairs of those times are not altogether clear. A political spy, a stock jobber, a contractor, a man who procured the confiscation of the property of the *émigrés,*—in collusion with the syndic of the commune—for the purpose of buying them in and selling them again, a minister and a general, all were equally interested in the business. From 1793 to 1799, Du Bousquier was a contractor to furnish supplies to the commissariat of the French armies. He had then a magnificent hôtel, he was one of the great lights of finance, he was in partnership with Ouvrard, kept open house, and led the scandalous life of the period, a life of Cincinnatus with full harvests gathered without trouble, with stolen rations, with little houses full of mistresses, and in which fine fêtes were given to the Directors of the Republic. The Citizen du Bousquier was one of the familiars of Barras, he was on the best terms with Fouché, very intimate with Bernadotte, and believed himself on the point of becoming minister by throwing himself headlong into the party which was secretly scheming against Bonaparte until Marengo. It required the charge of Kellermann and the death of Desaix to prevent Du Bousquier from becoming a great statesman. He was one of the superior employés of the undescribed government which Napoléon's good fortune caused to be shifted into the side scenes in 1793.—*See A Dark Affair.*—The victory so obstinately obtained at Marengo was the defeat of this party, which had its proclamations already printed for a return to the system of the Mountain, in case the First Consul had succumbed. Du Bousquier was so confident of the impossibility of his triumph that he had staked the greater part of his fortune on a decline in the market, and had kept two couriers on the battle field;—the first had started at the moment when Mélas was victorious; but, during the night, four hours later, the second came to announce the defeat of the Austrians. Du Bousquier cursed Kellermann and Desaix, he did not dare to curse the First Consul, who owed him millions. This alternative of millions to be gained and actual ruin deprived the contractor of all his faculties, for several days he was in a state of imbecility, he had abused himself so much by a life of excesses that this thunderbolt found him without strength to resist. The liquidation of his credits upon the state permitted him to cherish some hopes; but, notwithstanding his bribes, he encountered Napoléon's hatred for the contractors who had counted upon his defeat. Monsieur de Fermon, so jestingly called *Fermons la caisse*—Shut up the cash-box,—left Du Bousquier without a sou. The immorality of his private life, the relations of this contractor with Barras and Bernadotte, displeased the First Consul even more than his speculations on the Bourse; he struck him off the list of receivers-general on which, through a remnant of his credit, he had had himself inscribed for Alençon. Of all his fortune, Du Bousquier preserved only twelve hundred francs of annuity, invested in the national funds,—a purely accidental investment that preserved him from absolute poverty. His creditors, ignorant of the result of the liquidation, left him only an income of a thousand francs in consolidated funds, but they were all paid off with the moneys collected and by the sale of the Hôtel de Beauséant which Du Bousquier owned. Thus the speculator, after having narrowly escaped failure, preserved his business credit. A man who had been ruined by the First Consul, and with the immense reputation which he had previously acquired by his relations with the chiefs of the former government, by his manner of life, by his transient glory, excited great interest in the city of Alençon, where the royalist sentiment secretly predominated. Du Bousquier, furious against Bonaparte, retailing the scandals against the First Consul, the extravagances of Josephine, and the secret anecdotes of the ten years of the Revolution, was very well received. About this period, Du Bousquier, though he had well and duly attained to forty years, presented the appearance of a bachelor of thirty-six, of medium height, fat as a contractor, parading his calves of a sprightly procureur, with a strongly-marked physiognomy, having a flat nose, but with the nostrils garnished with hairs; black eyes with heavy eyebrows, and from which issued a glance like that of Monsieur de Talleyrand, but somewhat dulled; he still wore the republican short whiskers and kept his brown hair very long. His hands, enriched with a little tuft of hair on each phalanx, testified to the robustness of his physique by the prominence of the great blue veins. In fact, he had the chest of the Farnese Hercules, and shoulders that might sustain the Rente. Shoulders like these are, to-day, seen only at Tortoni's. This luxury of masculine life was admirably depicted by a phrase in use during the last century and which to-day is scarcely understood,—in the gallant speech of the last epoch, Du Bousquier would have passed for a true *payeur d'arréages*,— literally, payer of arrears. But, as with the Chevalier de Valois, there were indications to be perceived in Du Bousquier which contrasted with the general aspect of his person. Thus, the ex-contractor had not a voice appropriate to his muscles, not that his voice was that little, thin thread that sometimes issues from the mouths of these walruses with two feet; it was, on the contrary, a strong voice, but a smothered one, of which an idea cannot be given otherwise than by comparing it to the noise which a saw makes in soft and moist wood; in short, the voice of a broken-down speculator.

Du Bousquier continued to wear for a long time the costume in fashion at the period of his glory,—top-boots, white silk stockings, short breeches in ribbed cloth of a cinnamon color, waist-coat *á la* Robespierre and blue coat. Notwithstanding the titles which the First Consul's hatred gave him to the consideration of the leading royalists of the province, Monsieur du Bousquier was by no means received by the seven or eight families which composed the Faubourg Saint-Germain of Alençon, and whom the Chevalier de Valois visited. He had at first endeavored to marry Mademoiselle Armande, the sister of one of the most considerable nobles of the city, and of whom Du Bousquier hoped to make great use in his ulterior projects, for he dreamed of a brilliant revenge. He met with a refusal. He consoled himself by the compensation which was offered him by some ten rich families who had formerly been engaged in the manufacture of *point d'Alençon*, who possessed pasture lands or cattle, who were wholesale dealers in cloths, and among whom chance might deliver to him some good match. The old bachelor had, in fact, concentrated his hopes in the prospect of a fortunate marriage, which his divers capacities seemed, moreover, to promise him; for he was not wanting in a certain financial skill by which a number of persons profited. After the manner of a ruined gambler who directs the novices, he selected the speculations, he indicated the methods to be pursued, the chances of success and the manner of conducting them. He had the reputation of being a good administrator, he was frequently proposed for mayor of Alençon; but the memory of his underhand dealings under the Republican governments injured him, he was never received at the préfecture. All the governments which succeeded each other, even that of the Hundred Days, refused to make him mayor of Alençon, a post which was the object of his ambition, and which, if he had obtained it, would have brought about his marriage with an old maid in whom he had finally concentrated his hopes. His aversion to the Imperial government had at first thrown him into the royalist party, where he remained, notwithstanding the insults which he had received; but, when, on the first return of the Bourbons, his exclusion from the préfecture was still maintained, this last refusal inspired him with a hatred against the Bourbons as profound as it was secret, for he remained patiently faithful to his opinions. He became the head of the liberal party in Alençon, the invisible director of the elections, and he was exceedingly injurious to the Restoration through his hidden machinations and the perfidiousness of his secret practices. Du Bousquier, like all those who can no longer live but by using their wits, maintained his sentiments of hatred with all the quietness of a stream slight in appearance but inexhaustible; his hatred was like that of a negro, so peaceable, so patient, that it deceived the enemy. His vengeance, brooded over for fifteen years, was not glutted by any victory, not even by the triumph of the days of July, 1830.

It was not without design that the Chevalier de Valois had sent Suzanne to Du Bousquier. The liberal and the royalist had mentally divined each other, notwithstanding the knowing dissimulation with which they concealed their common hopes from the whole city. These two old bachelors were rivals. Each of them had conceived the idea of espousing the Demoiselle Cormon of whom Monsieur de Valois had spoken to Suzanne. Both of them, carefully concealing their plans, ostentatiously indifferent, waited for the moment when some happy chance should deliver to them this ancient spinster. Thus, even though these two celibates had not been separated by all the distance which was fixed between them by the two systems of which each was a living expression, their rivalry would still have made of them enemies. Epochs leave their color upon the men who traverse them. These two personages demonstrated the truth of this axiom by the opposition of the historic tints which appeared in their physiognomies, in their discourse, in their ideas and in their costumes. The one, abrupt, energetic, demonstrative and sudden in his manners, brief and rude in speech, gloomy in manner, in hair and in look, terrible in appearance, powerless in reality like an insurrection, well represented the Republic. The other, gentle and polite, elegant, well groomed, attaining his ends by the slow but infallible methods of diplomacy, always in good taste, was the image of the ancient courtliness. These two enemies met almost every evening on the same ground. The warfare was courteous and benign on the part of the chevalier, but Du Bousquier brought fewer formalities to it, while still regarding the conventionalities imposed by society, for he did not wish to be driven from the place. They alone thoroughly comprehended each other. Notwithstanding all the careful observation which the inhabitants of the provinces bring to bear on the little interests in the midst of which they live, no one suspected the rivalry of the two men. Monsieur le Chevalier de Valois occupied a superior position, he had never asked for the hand of Mademoiselle Cormon; whilst Du Bousquier, who had entered the lists after the check he had met with in the most noble household in the province, had been refused. But the chevalier supposed his rival to still have excellent chances when he dealt him an unforeseen blow so well driven home with such a tempered and finished blade as Suzanne. The chevalier had sounded the depths of Du Bousquier; and, as will be seen, he had not been deceived in any of his conjectures.

Suzanne departed with a light foot from the Rue du Cours, went by the Rue de la Porte-de-Séez and the Rue du Bercail to the Rue du Cygne, where five years previously, Du Bousquier had purchased a little provincial mansion, built in gray *chaussins,* which here take the place of the unhewn Norman granite or the Breton schist. The ex-contractor had established himself more comfortably than any other citizen, for he had retained some of the furniture of his former period of splendor; but provincial customs had gradually obscured the glory of the fallen Sardanapalus. The vestiges of his ancient luxury produced in his house somewhat the effect of a chandelier in a barn. Harmony, that bond of every work, human or divine, was here wanting in the great as in the small objects. Upon a handsome chest of drawers might be seen a covered water-pot, such as are found only in the outlying districts of Brittany. If a fine carpet covered the floor of his chamber, the window curtains displayed the rosettes of an ignoble printed calico. The chimney-piece, in badly-painted stone, made a discord with a handsome clock dishonored by the neighborhood of some miserable candlesticks. The stairway, by which everyone ascended without wiping his feet, was unpainted. Finally, the doors very badly set off by a country painter, offended the eye with their crude colors. Like the period itself which Du Bousquier represented, this household offered a confused collection of vulgar and of magnificent things. Considered as a man of leisure, Du Bousquier led the parasitical life of the chevalier; and he may always be considered rich who does not expend his income. For his only servant he had a species of country lout, sufficiently simple, who had been gradually trained to Du Bousquier's requirements, having been taught by him, like an ourang-outang, to rub up the rooms, dust the furniture, black the boots, brush the clothes, come after him in the evenings with a lantern when the night was dark and with sabots when it rained. Like some other beings, this domestic had in him the stuff for only one vice, he was a glutton. Frequently, when he gave state dinners, Du Bousquier made him discard his vest of blue checked cotton goods, with his distended pockets always filled with a handkerchief, a wooden-handled clasp knife, a fruit of some kind or broken pastry, and assume a domestic's garments to wait on the table. René then stuffed himself with the other servants. This obligation, which Du Bousquier had converted into a recompense, procured him the absolute devotion of his Breton domestic.

"Are you here, mademoiselle?" said René to Suzanne as he saw her enter; "this is not your day, we have no linen for Madame Lardot."

"You great dunce!" said Suzanne, laughing.

The pretty girl went upstairs, leaving René to finish a porringer full of buckwheat cakes cooked in milk. Du Bousquier, still in bed, was ruminating over his plans of attaining a fortune, for he could not but be ambitious, like all men who have sucked too dry the orange of pleasure. Ambition and gaming are inexhaustible. Thus, in a man with a good physical organization, the passions which proceed from the brain will always survive those which emanate from the heart.

"Here I am," said Suzanne, seating herself on the bed and sending the curtains sliding noisily along on their rings with a brusque, despotic movement.

"*Quésaco,* my dear?" said the old bachelor, sitting up in bed.

"Monsieur," said Suzanne gravely, "you must be surprised at seeing me come in this manner; but I find myself in circumstances which oblige me to take no heed of what may be said of me."

"What is it all about?" asked Du Bousquier, crossing his arms.

"But you do not understand me?" said Suzanne. "I know," she resumed, making a pretty little grimace, "how absurd it is for a poor girl to come to trouble a man for what you consider as merely trifles. But, if you knew me well, monsieur, if you appreciated all that I am capable of for a man who would become attached to me, as I would become attached to you, you would never have to repent of having married me. It is not in this place, for example, that I could be useful to you in great things; but, if we should go to Paris, you would see how I would assist a man of intelligence and of resources like you, at a time when the government is being remade from top to bottom, and when foreigners are the masters. In short, between ourselves, is that which is the matter a misfortune? is it not rather a happiness for which you would be willing to pay dearly some day? For whom would you interest yourself? for whom would you work?"

"For myself, to be sure," exclaimed Du Bousquier brutally.

"Old monster, you shall never be a father!" said Suzanne, giving to her speech the accent of a prophetic malediction.

"Come now, no foolishness, Suzanne," replied Du Bousquier; "I believe I am still dreaming."

"But how much of a reality do you require, then?" cried Suzanne, rising.

Du Bousquier rubbed his cotton nightcap around on his head with a rotary movement of mischief-making energy which indicated a prodigious fermentation in his ideas.

"Why, he believes it," said Suzanne to herself, "and he is flattered by it. *Mon Dieu,* how easy it is to catch them, these men!"

"Suzanne, what the devil is it that you want me to do? It is so extraordinary—I who thought—The fact is that—But no, no, that cannot be—"

"How, you cannot marry me?"

"Ah! as to that, no! I have engagements."

"Is it with Mademoiselle Armande or with Mademoiselle Cormon, who, both of them, have already refused you? Listen, *Monsieur du Bousquier*, my honor has no need of gendarmes to drag you to the mayor's office. I shall not want for husbands, and do not wish to have anything to do with a man who does not know how to appreciate what I am worth. Some day you may repent of the manner in which you have behaved, for nothing in the world, neither gold nor silver, will ever make me give to you that which is yours if you refuse to take it to-day."

"But, Suzanne, are you sure?—"

"Ah! monsieur," said the grisette, draping herself in her virtue, "for what do you take me? I will not recall to you the promises you have made me, and which have ruined a poor girl whose sole fault is to have as much ambition as love."

Du Bousquier was a prey to a thousand contradictory emotions, joy, mistrust, calculation. He had long been resolved to marry Mademoiselle Cormon, for the Charter, on which he had been meditating, offered to his ambition the magnificent political opening of a seat in the legislature. Now, his marriage with the spinster would give him such a high position in the city that he would certainly acquire great influence. Thus the storm raised by the malicious Suzanne plunged him into the greatest embarrassment. Were it not for this secret hope, he would have married Suzanne without even reflecting upon it. He would have placed himself frankly at the head of the liberal party in Alençon. After such a marriage, he would renounce the highest society to fall back into the bourgeois class of merchants, of rich manufacturers, of graziers, who would certainly carry him in triumph as their candidate. Du Bousquier already had visions of the Left. He made no attempt to conceal this very serious deliberation, he passed his hand over his head, twisting his nightcap which concealed his disastrous baldness. Like all those who exceed their aim, by finding more than they hoped for, Suzanne was astounded. To conceal her astonishment, she assumed the melancholy attitude of a wronged maid before her seducer; but inwardly she was laughing like a grisette at a junket.

"My dear child, I am not caught by any such *flams* as that, *I* am not!"

Such was the curt phrase by which the ex-contractor brought his deliberation to an end. Du Bousquier prided himself upon belonging to that school of cynical philosophers who are never willing to be *caught* by women, and who place them all in the same *suspicious* class. These strong souls, who are generally weak men, have one catechism with regard to all women. For them, all, from the queen of France down to the dressmaker, are essentially wantons, jilts, assassins, nay, even somewhat cheats, false at heart, and incapable of thinking of anything but trifles. For them, women are mischievous bayaderes who must be allowed to dance, to sing and to laugh as they list; they see in them nothing holy or great, for them, it is not the poetry of the senses, but gross sensuality. They are like those gourmands who take the kitchen for the dining-hall. Under this jurisprudence, if the woman is not constantly tyrannized over, she will reduce the man to a condition of slavery. In this respect, Du Bousquier was again the opposite of the Chevalier de Valois. As he uttered his phrase, he threw his nightcap on the foot of his bed, as Pope Gregory might have done with the taper which he overturned in fulminating an excommunication, and Suzanne thus perceived that the old bachelor wore a wig.

"You will remember, Monsieur du Bousquier," she replied majestically, "that in coming to you I have fulfilled my duty; you will remember that I have been obliged to offer you my hand and to ask for yours; but you will remember also that I have conducted myself with the dignity of a woman who respects herself,—I have not abased myself to weeping like a silly, I have not insisted, I have not tormented you. Now, you are aware of my situation. You know that I cannot remain at Alençon;—my mother will beat me; Madame Lardot gets on her high horse concerning principles, just as if she had to iron them, she will drive me away. Poor work-girl that I am, shall I go to the hospital? shall I go to beg my bread? No! sooner will I throw myself in the Brillante or in the Sarthe. But would it not be more simple for me to go to Paris? My mother could readily find a pretext for sending me there,—it might be an uncle who had sent for me, an aunt at the point of death, a lady who wished to be of advantage to me. It is only a question of having the money necessary for the journey and for all that you know—"

This piece of news had for Du Bousquier a thousand times more importance than for the Chevalier de Valois; but only he and the chevalier were in the possession of this secret, which will be revealed only in the dénoûment of this history. For the moment, it will be sufficient to say, that

Suzanne's falsehood threw this old bachelor's ideas into such confusion that he was quite incapable of making any serious reflection. Had it not been for this disturbance, and his inward joy,—for self-love is a sharper who never lacks for a dupe—he would have thought that an honest girl like Suzanne, whose heart was not yet corrupted, would have died a hundred times before provoking a discussion of this kind and asking him for money. He would have recognized in the grisette's look the cruel dastardliness of the gamester who would assassinate to secure his stake.

"You are going to Paris, then?" said he.

On hearing this phrase, Suzanne was conscious of a flash of cheerfulness that gilded her gray eyes, but the contented Du Bousquier saw nothing.

"Why, yes, monsieur!"

Then Du Bousquier began to make curious lamentations;—he had just completed the last payment on his house, he had to settle with the painter, the mason, the furniture-maker; but Suzanne allowed him to go on, she was waiting for the amount to be named. Du Bousquier offered a hundred écus. Suzanne executed what is known in the language of the side scenes as a false exit, she started toward the door.

"Well, where are you going?" said Du Bousquier, uneasy. "Here is a fine bachelor life!" said he to himself, "I hope that the devil may carry me away if I remember having ruffled anything about her but her neckerchief!—And, paf! she takes advantage of a little jest to draw a bill of exchange upon you point-blank!"

"Why, monsieur," said Suzanne, weeping, "I am going to see Madame Granson, the treasurer of the Maternal Society, who, to my knowledge, herself all but drew out of the river a poor girl in the same condition."

"Madame Granson?

"Yes," said Suzanne, "the relative of Mademoiselle Cormon, the president of the Maternal Society. By your leave, the ladies of the city have created here an institution which will prevent many poor creatures from destroying their infants, such as caused the death of one at Mortagne, just three years ago, the beautiful Faustine d'Argentan."

"Here, Suzanne," said Du Bousquier, handing her a key, "unlock the secretary yourself, take the bag which has been opened which still contains six hundred francs, it is all that I possess."

The ex-contractor showed by his downcast air with how little grace he sacrificed himself.

"The old wretch," said Suzanne to herself, "I will tell about his wig."

She made a comparison between Du Bousquier and the delightful Chevalier de Valois, who had given her nothing, but who had understood her, who had counselled her, and who treasured the grisettes in his heart.

"If you are playing me a trick, Suzanne," cried the other, seeing her hand in the drawer, "you—"

"But monsieur," said she, interrupting him with a royal impertinence, "you would not then give them to me if I asked them of you?"

Once recalled to the ways of gallantry, the ex-contractor felt one of the impulses of his better days, and uttered a grumble of acquiescence. Suzanne took the bag and went away, allowing herself to be kissed on the forehead by the old bachelor, who had the air of saying to himself: "This is a privilege which costs me dearly. It is better than being nagged at by a lawyer in the court of assizes, as the seducer of a girl accused of infanticide."

Suzanne concealed the bag in a species of game-bag in wicker-work, which she had on her arm, and cursed the avarice of Du Bousquier, for she wanted a thousand francs. Once bedeviled by a desire, and when she has once set foot in the ways of deceit, a girl will go far. As the lovely ironer wended her way along the Rue du Bercail, it occurred to her that the Maternal Society, presided over by Mademoiselle Cormon, would perhaps complete for her the sum at which she had estimated her expenses, and which, for a grisette of Alençon, was a considerable one. Moreover, she hated Du Bousquier. The old bachelor had appeared to dread the betrayal of his pretended crime to Madame Granson; therefore, Suzanne, at the risk of not receiving a liard from the Maternal Society, wished in leaving Alençon to entangle the ex-contractor in the inextricable meshes of a provincial scandal. In the grisette there is always a little of the mischievous spirit of a monkey. Suzanne accordingly entered Madame Granson's house, after having arranged a woeful countenance.

Madame Granson, the widow of a lieutenant-colonel of artillery, killed at Jena, possessed for her entire fortune a meagre pension of nine hundred francs, a hundred écus of income for herself, plus a son whose education and bringing-up had devoured all her savings. She occupied, in the Rue du Bercail, one of those melancholy ground-floor apartments which the passer-by in the principal street of one of the little towns takes in at one glance. The entrance was neither private door nor porte cochère, but opened at the top of three pyramidal steps into a passage which led to an interior court, at the farther end of which was a stairway covered by a wooden gallery. On one side of the passage was a dining-room and the kitchen; on the other, a salon of all work and the widow's bedchamber. Athanase Granson, a young man of twenty-three, lodged in an attic above the first floor of this house, brought to his poor mother's housekeeping the six hundred francs of a little post which the influence of his relative, Mademoiselle Cormon, had obtained for him in the office of the mayor of the city, where he was employed in the bureau of deeds of the civil establishment. From this description, anyone may imagine Madame Granson in her chilly salon with yellow curtains, upholstered in yellow Utrecht velvet, replacing after a visit the little mats which she kept before the chairs so that the polished red floor might not be soiled; then resuming her place in her armchair with cushions and her occupation at her worktable placed under the portrait of the lieutenant-colonel of artillery, between the two windows, a seat from which her eye embraced the Rue du Bercail and saw everything that was coming. She was a worthy woman, dressed with a bourgeois simplicity quite in keeping with her pale countenance, flattened, as it were, by anxiety. The rigorous modesty of poverty made itself manifest in all the accessories of this household, in which breathed, moreover, the upright and severe manners and customs of the provinces. At this moment, the son and the mother were together in the dining-room, where they were breakfasting on a cup of coffee with bread and butter and radishes. In order to understand the pleasure which Suzanne's visit would cause Madame Granson, it will be necessary to explain the secret interests of the mother and the son.

 *

Athanase Granson was a thin young man with a pale face, of medium height, with a hollow countenance in which his black eyes, sparkling with thought, appeared like two spots of coal. The somewhat irregular lines of his face, the sinuosity of the mouth, the chin brusquely brought forward, the regular outline of the marble forehead, an expression of melancholy caused by the consciousness of his poverty, repressing the capacity which he felt within himself, all indicated a man in whom talent was stifled. Thus, everywhere else than in the city of Alençon, his personal appearance alone would have secured him the assistance of superior men or of women who recognize genius in its disguises. If this were not genius, it was the form which it takes; if it were not the strength of a great mind, it was the light which it lends to the glance. Although he was capable of expressing the loftiest sensitiveness, the timidity which enveloped him destroyed in him even the graces of youth, even as the icy restraints of poverty suppressed all his audacity. The life of the provinces, without any issue, without approbation, without encouragement, described a monotonous circle within which perished that thought which was not yet even in the dawn of its day. Moreover, Athanase had that savage pride which poverty exalts in superior men, which makes them greater in their struggle with men and things, but which, from the first contact with life, interposes an obstacle to their preferment. Genius proceeds in two manners,—either it seizes its property, as did Napoléon and Molière, as soon as it perceives it; or it waits to be sought out when it has patiently revealed itself. The young Granson was of that class of men of talent who are ignorant of their own qualities and are easily discouraged. His mind was contemplative, he lived more in thought than in action. Perhaps he would have appeared incomplete to those who cannot conceive of genius without the passionate sparkling of the French race; but he was strong in the world of the intellect, and he would arrive, through a series of emotions hidden from the vulgar, at those sudden determinations which conclude them and cause the dunces to exclaim: "He is crazy." The contempt which the world bestows upon poverty was fatal to Athanase; the enervating atmosphere of a solitude with no current of refreshing air slackened the bow that was forever bent, and the soul became

28

wearied in this depressing and resultless struggle. Athanase was a man capable of taking his place among the most illustrious of France; but this eagle, imprisoned in a cage and without sustenance, was on the point of dying of hunger after having gazed with an ardent eye on the fields of the air and the Alps over which genius hovers. Although his researches in the city library attracted no attention, he buried his dreams of glory in his soul, for they might have been of injury to him; but he held still more profoundly buried the secret of his heart, a passion which hollowed his cheeks and yellowed his forehead. He was in love with his distant relative, that Demoiselle Cormon watched by the Chevalier de Valois and Du Bousquier, his unknown rivals. This love had been engendered by calculation. Mademoiselle Cormon was considered one of the richest persons in the city,—the poor youth had therefore been brought to love her by the desire for material happiness, by the wish, a thousand times formed, to smooth his mother's declining years, by that longing for the comfort necessary to men who live by their brains; but this very innocent point of departure dishonored his passion in his own eyes. He dreaded, moreover, the ridicule which the world would throw upon the love of a young man of twenty-three for a maid of forty. Nevertheless, his passion was a genuine one; for that which in these affairs would seem false everywhere else, is realized in the provinces. In fact, the manners and customs, being there without any chances, or accidents, or mysteries, render marriages necessary. No family would accept a young man of dissolute manners. However natural might appear in a capital the liaison of a young man like Athanase with a pretty girl like Suzanne, in the provinces it would scare away and render impossible in advance the marriage of a poor young man, while the fortune of a rich pretendant would rise superior to any such unfortunate antecedent. Between the depravation of certain liaisons and a sincere love, a man of heart and without fortune cannot hesitate;—he will prefer the unhappiness of virtue to the unhappiness of vice. But, in the provinces, the women with whom a young man can become enamored are rare;—a young girl, beautiful and rich, he will never obtain in a country in which everything is arranged by sordid calculation; a beautiful young girl, poor, he is forbidden to love,—that would be, as the provincials say, the marriage of thirst with hunger; finally, a monastical solitude is dangerous to youth. These considerations explain the fact that the life of the provinces is so largely based upon marriage. Thus the warm and vivacious geniuses, forced to rely upon the independence of poverty, should all leave those bleak regions in which thought is persecuted by a brutal indifference, in which no woman either can or is willing to make herself a Sister of Charity for a man of science or of art. Who could appreciate the passion of Athanase for Mademoiselle Cormon? It would not be the rich, those sultans of society who find in it their harems, nor the bourgeois, who follow the high road trodden by the conventional and commonplace, nor the women, who, not willing to comprehend anything of the passion of artists, attribute to them the *lex talionis* of their virtues, imagining that the two sexes are governed by the same laws. Here, perhaps, we should have to appeal to the young, distressed by the repression of all their first desires at the moment when all their powers are in tension, to the artists sickened by feeling their genius strangled in the grasp of poverty, to the talents which, at first persecuted and without support, frequently without friends, have ended by triumphing over the double anguish of the body and the mind, equally distressed. All these know but too well the sharp pains of the cancer which was devouring Athanase; they have been agitated by those long and cruel meditations in the presence of such noble ends for which there were no means to be found; they have endured those unknown miscarriages in which, the spawn of genius has fallen only on an arid strand. These know that the greatness of the desires is in proportion to the extent of the imagination. The higher they spring, the lower they fall; and how many are there who do not break their bonds in these falls! Their keen vision has discovered, like Athanase, the brilliant future which awaits them, and from which they believe themselves separated only by a gauze; this gauze, which offers no obstacle to their eyes, society changes into a wall of brass. Urged onward by a vocation, by the sentiment of art, they have thus sought many times to make a means of sentiments which society constantly materializes. What! the provinces scheme and arrange marriage with the object of creating happiness, and it shall be forbidden to a poor artist, to the man of science, to give it a double destination, to make it serve to preserve his intellectual labors by assuring him of an existence? Agitated by these thoughts, Athanase at first considered his marriage with Mademoiselle Cormon, as a manner of arranging his life which would be definite; he would be able to throw himself into the pursuit of glory, to render his mother happy, and he knew himself capable of faithfully loving Mademoiselle Cormon.

Presently his own will created, without his perceiving it, a real passion;—he set himself to studying the spinster, and, through the fascination which is exercised by habit, he ended by seeing in her only beauties, and forgetting the defects. In a young man of twenty-three the senses count for so much in his love! their flame produces a species of prism between his eyes and the woman. In this respect the grasp with which Chérubin seizes Marceline on the stage, is a stroke of genius in Beaumarchais. But if we reflect that, in the profound solitude in which his poverty secluded Athanase, Mademoiselle Cormon was the only figure that came into his vision, that she incessantly attracted his eye, that she appeared before him in full daylight, shall we not find this passion a natural one? This sentiment, so carefully concealed, necessarily strengthened itself from day to day. Desires, sufferings, hopes, meditations, enlarged in the calm and the silence the lake to which each hour brought its drop of water and which expanded itself in Athanase's soul. The more that the inward circle enlarged which the imagination aided by the senses described, the more imposing Mademoiselle Cormon became, the more the timidity of Athanase increased. His mother had discovered all. His mother, like a true woman of the provinces, considered ingenuously all the advantages the affair might offer. She said to herself that Mademoiselle Cormon might consider herself very happy to have for husband a young man of twenty-three, full of talent, who would be an honor to his family and to the country; but the obstacles which Athanase's want of fortune and Mademoiselle Cormon's age opposed to this marriage seemed to her insurmountable,—she could think of nothing but patience with which to overcome them. Like Du Bousquier, like the Chevalier de Valois, she had her own policy, she kept a keen watch on events, she waited for the propitious hour with that shrewdness which is given by self-interest and by maternity. Madame Granson did not mistrust the Chevalier de Valois; but she supposed that Du Bousquier, though once refused, still maintained his pretensions. A skilful and secret enemy of the former contractor, she was doing him an unsuspected bad turn for the sake of serving her son, to whom, however, she had as yet said nothing of her concealed processes. Therefore, the importance which Suzanne's falsehood would acquire when once confided to Madame Granson, may readily be imagined. What a weapon in the hands of the charitable lady, the treasurer of the Maternal Society! How she would go sweetly distributing the news while soliciting contributions for the chaste Suzanne!

At this moment, Athanase, thoughtfully leaning his elbow on the table, was turning his spoon in his empty bowl while contemplating with a wandering eye this poor room with its red tiled floor, its straw chairs, its buffet in painted wood, its red and white curtains like a chess-board, the walls covered with an old wine-shop paper, and which communicated with the kitchen by a glass door. As he had his back to the chimney, facing his mother, and as the chimney was nearly opposite the door, this pale face, strongly lit up by the light from the street, and framed in fine black locks, these eyes animated by despair and aflame with the morning's reflections, suddenly presented itself to Suzanne's glance. The grisette, in whom, generally, the instincts of poverty and of heart sufferings are innate, felt in this case that electric spark, springing from no one knows where, which cannot be explained, which certain keen intellects deny, but of which the sympathetic shock has been experienced by very many women and men. It is, all at once, a flame which lightens up the shadows of the future, a presentiment of the pure joys of partaken love, the certainty of comprehending one another. It is, above all, like the skilful and strong touch of a master hand upon the keyboard of the senses. The regard is fascinated by an irresistible attraction, the heart is moved, the melodies of happiness resound in the soul and in the ears, a voice cries: *It is he!* Then, very frequently, reflection comes to throw her douches of cold water on this boiling emotion,—and everything is over. In a moment, as rapid as a lightning flash, Suzanne received in her heart a whole broadside of ideas. A flash of true love burned up the ill weeds that had blossomed at the breath of libertinism and dissipation. She comprehended how much she would lose of sanctity, of grandeur, in defaming herself falsely. That which, the evening before, had been only a jest in her eyes, became a grave sentence passed upon her. She recoiled before her success. But the impossibility of any result, the poverty of Athanase, a vague hope of enriching herself and of returning from Paris with full hands to say to him: "I loved you!" fatality, if you wish, dried up this beneficent rain. The ambitious grisette requested with a timid air a moment's conversation with Madame Granson, who conducted her into her bedchamber. When Suzanne went out, she looked at Athanase again, she saw him still in the same attitude, and she suppressed her tears. As for Madame Granson, she was radiant with joy! She had at last a terrible weapon against Du Bousquier, she could deal him a mortal wound. Therefore she had promised to the poor seduced girl the support of all the charitable ladies, of all the contributors to the Maternal Society; she foresaw a dozen visits to make which would occupy all her day and during which there would gather around the head of the old bachelor a terrifying storm. The Chevalier de Valois, while foreseeing the turn which the affair would take, had not promised himself any such fine scandal as it was about to develop.

"My dear child," said Madame Granson to her son, "you know that we are going to dine with Mademoiselle Cormon, do take a little more care of your appearance. You are wrong to neglect your toilet, you are dressed too shabbily. Put on your fine shirt with a frill, your green broadcloth coat. I have particular reasons for asking it," she added meaningly. "Moreover, Mademoiselle Cormon is leaving to go to the Prébaudet, and there will be a great many people at her house. When a young man is of marriageable age, he should make use of all the means at his disposal to please. If the girls would tell the truth, *mon Dieu,* my child, you would be very much surprised to know what it is with which they fall in love. Frequently it is enough for a man to have passed by on horseback at the head of a company of artillerymen, or that he has appeared at a ball with very well-fitting clothes. Frequently a certain way of holding the head, a melancholy attitude, will cause a whole lifetime to be imagined, we invent for ourselves a romance around the hero,—he is often nothing but a fool, but the marriage is made. Watch Monsieur le Chevalier de Valois, study him, imitate his manners; see with what ease he appears in company, he has not a constrained air as you have. Talk a little; would not people say that you know nothing, you who know Hebrew by heart!"

Athanase listened to his mother with a surprised yet submissive air, then he rose, took his cap, and went his way to the mayor's office, saying to himself:

"Can my mother have divined my secret?"

He passed through the Rue du Val-Noble, in which Mademoiselle Cormon lived, a little pleasure which he allowed himself every morning, and he said to himself a thousand whimsical things:

"She certainly does not suspect that there is passing at this moment before her house a young man who would love her well, who would be faithful to her, who would never grieve her, who would leave her the entire disposition of her fortune, without meddling with it. *Mon Dieu!* what a fatality! in the same city, at only two steps from each other, two persons find themselves in the situation in which we are, and yet nothing can bring them together. If I should speak to her this evening?"

Meanwhile, Suzanne was returning to her mother's house, thinking of the poor Athanase; and, as many women have been able to desire it for men adored beyond human powers, she felt herself capable of making for him with her fair body a stepping-stone by means of which he might promptly attain his crown.

Now, however, it will be necessary to enter the household of that elderly spinster toward whom so many interests converge, and within whose walls the actors in this Scene are to meet this very evening, with the exception of Suzanne. This great and charming young woman, courageous enough to burn her ships like Alexander, at the outset of life, and to commence the struggle with a fault of deception, disappeared from the stage, after having introduced on it an element of great interest. Her desires were, moreover, gratified. She left her natal city a few days later, furnished with money and with some fine apparel, among which was a superb dress of green rep and a delicious green bonnet lined with pink which had been given her by Monsieur de Valois, a gift which she valued above all the others, even the money of the ladies of the Maternal Society. If the chevalier had come to Paris at the moment when she was in her glory, she would certainly have left everything for him. Much like the chaste Susannah of the Bible, of whom the elders had had but a glimpse, she established herself happy and full of hope at Paris, whilst all Alençon was deploring her misfortunes, for which the ladies of the two societies of Charity and of Maternity, manifested a lively sympathy. If Suzanne may be taken as a type of those fair Normans whom a learned physician has estimated as a third of those furnished for this consumption to the monstrous Paris, she remained in the most elevated and the most decent regions of this gay life. For an epoch in which, as Monsieur de Valois said, woman did not exist, she was only *Madame du Val-Noble;* formerly, she would have been the rival of the Rhodopes, the Impérias, the Ninons. One of the most distinguished writers of the Restoration took her under his protection; perhaps he will marry her; he is a journalist, and therefore rises superior to public opinion since he reconstructs it every six years.

In almost every prefecture of the second order in France there is to be found a salon in which meet the persons of considerable importance and those held in consideration who are, however, not the cream of society. The master and the mistress of the house are indeed counted among the eminent citizens, and are received wherever they please to go; there is not given in the city a reception, a diplomatic dinner, to which they are not invited; but the proprietors of châteaux, the peers who possess fine estates, the great people of the department, do not frequent their house but limit themselves to paying them an occasional visit, or to a dinner or a soirée accepted and returned. This miscellaneous salon, in which are to be met the lesser nobility with settled positions, the clergy, the magistrates, exercises a great influence. The spirit and the good sense of the country are to be found in this society, substantial and without vain show, where each one knows the amount of his neighbor's income, where there is professed a perfect indifference for luxury and for dress, considered as trivialities in comparison with a meadow property of ten or twelve acres in extent, the acquisition of which has been brooded over for years, and which has given rise to immense diplomatic combinations. Immovable in its prejudices, good or bad, this communion follows the same path, without looking either ahead or behind. It admits nothing from Paris without a long examination, refuses cashmeres as well as investments in State securities, derides all novelties, reads nothing and wishes to ignore everything,—science, literature, industrial inventions. It obtains the removal of a prefect who does not suit it, and, if the administration resists, it isolates him after the manner of the bees who cover with wax a snail that intrudes into their hive. In short, there the chatter frequently becomes solemn decrees. Also, although there are arranged here only card parties, the young women appear from time to time; they come here to seek for approbation of their conduct, a consecration of their importance. This superiority awarded to a certain house often offends the self-love of some of the natives of the country, who console themselves by computing the expense which it entails, and by which they profit. If there is not to be found any fortune sufficient to maintain an open house, the bigwigs choose for their reunions, as did the people of Alençon, the residence of some inoffensive person whose settled life, character or position allows society to preside in his house without offending either the vanities or the interests of each individual. Thus the upper society of Alençon had long been in the habit of holding its reunions in the house of the mature virgin whose fortune had been, unknown to her, the object of the scheming of

Madame Granson, her cousin twice removed, and of the two old bachelors whose secret hopes have been unveiled to the reader. This demoiselle lived with her maternal uncle, formerly grand vicar of the bishopric of Séez, her former tutor, and from whom she would inherit. The family which at this time was represented by Rose-Marie-Victoire Cormon had formerly been one of the most considerable in the province. Although plebeian, it came in contact with the nobility with which it had often been allied, it had formerly furnished intendants to the Ducs d'Alençon, many magistrates to the bench and several bishops to the Church. Monsieur de Sponde, the maternal grandfather of Mademoiselle Cormon, had been elected by the nobility to the États Généraux, and Monsieur Cormon, her father, by the third estate; but neither of them had accepted this mission. For something like a hundred years the daughters of the house had been in the habit of marrying nobles of the provinces, so that this family had planted so many young shoots in the duchy that it included all the family trees. There was no bourgeoisie that more resembled nobility.

Built under Henri IV. by Pierre Cormon, the intendant of the last Duc d'Alençon, the house in which Mademoiselle Cormon lived had always belonged to her family, and, of all her visible property, it was this which particularly stimulated the covetousness of her two elderly lovers. However, far from producing any revenue, this residence was a source of expense; but it is so difficult to find in a provincial town a dwelling-house centrally situated, without unpleasant surroundings, handsome outside, commodious inside, that all Alençon shared this envy. This old hôtel was situated precisely in the middle of the Rue du Val-Noble, corrupted into the Val-Noble, doubtless because of the undulation of the soil caused by the Brillante, a little stream which traverses Alençon. This building is noticeable because of the strongly characterized architecture which owed its origin to Marie de Médicis. Although built in granite, a stone very difficult to work, its angles, the casings of the windows and those of the doors are decorated with quoin work cut point-wise. It consists of a story above a ground floor; the roof, extremely elevated, presents salient windows with sculptured tympanums, handsomely set in the water gutter lined with lead and ornamented on the exterior with balustrades. Between each of these windows protrudes a gargoyle representing the fantastic mouth and throat of an animal without a body which vomits the water upon great stones pierced with five holes. The two gable ends are terminated by crotchets in lead, symbol of the bourgeois, for the nobles alone formerly had the right to have weathercocks. On the side of the court, at the right, are the carriage houses and the stables; at the left, the kitchen, the wood-house and the laundry. One of the leaves of the porte cochère remained open and was furnished with a little low door, with an opening and a bell, which permitted the passers-by to see, in the midst of a vast court, a mound of flowers the heaped-up earth of which was retained by a little privet hedge. Some perpetual roses, gilliflowers, scabiosa, lilies and Spanish genista composed this mound, around which were placed during the warm weather boxes of bay-trees, pomegranates and myrtle. A stranger would have divined the old maid by the excessive cleanliness of this court and its dependencies. The eye which presided over all this must be one unoccupied, ferreting, preserving less from force of character than through need of activity. Only an elderly demoiselle, obliged to find employment for her always empty days, would have all the grass pulled up between the paving stones, the tops of the walls cleaned, a perpetual sweeping maintained, the leathern curtains of the carriage-house forever closed. She alone was capable of introducing through idleness a species of Dutch cleanliness into a little province situated between Le Perche, Brittany and Normandy, a country in which a crass indifference to comfort is professed with pride. Never did either the Chevalier de Valois or Du Bousquier ascend the steps of the double stairway which surrounded the landing of the perron of this hotel without saying to themselves, one, that it was very suitable for a peer of France, and the other, that the mayor of the city should live there. A window opening down to the ground was at the top of this perron, and gave entrance into an antechamber lit by a second, similar window which opened on another perron on the side of the garden. This species of gallery paved with red tiles, wainscoted breast-high, was the hospital of the invalided family portraits—some of them had an eye damaged, others suffered from a shoulder in bad condition, this one held his hat in a hand which no longer existed, that one had a leg amputated. Here were deposited the cloaks, the sabots, the overshoes, the umbrellas, the hoods and the pelisses. It was the arsenal in which each habitué of the house left his baggage on his arrival, and resumed it when he departed. Thus, along each wall there was a bench for the domestics who came in armed with great lanterns, and there was a huge stove to combat the cold draughts that entered both from the court and the garden. The house was thus divided into two equal parts. On one side, on the court, was the main stairway, a large dining-room opening on the garden, then a pantry which communicated with the kitchen; on the other, a salon with four windows, and *en suite* two small apartments, one opening on the garden and forming a boudoir, the other, lit from the court and serving as a study. The first floor contained the complete apartments of a household and a domicile for the old Abbé de Sponde. The attics doubtless offered plenty of lodgings long inhabited by rats and mice, of which the high nocturnal revels were related by Mademoiselle Cormon to the Chevalier de Valois, in great surprise at the inutility of the measures employed against them. The garden, about half an acre in extent, is bordered by the Brillante, thus named because of the particles of mica which spangle its bed, but everywhere else rather than in the Val-Noble, where its scanty waters are charged with the dye-stuffs and the refuse thrown into them by the manufactures of the city. The shore opposite Mademoiselle Cormon's garden was encumbered, as in all the provincial towns through which a stream of water passes, with buildings in which were exercised various undesirable trades; but, fortunately, she had at that time opposite to her only quiet people, bourgeois, a baker, a scourer, some cabinet-makers. This garden, filled with ordinary flowers, ended naturally in a terrace forming a quay, at the end of which were a few steps by which to descend to the Brillante. On the balustrade of the terrace, imagine some great vases in blue and white faïence in which were gilliflowers; to right and to left, along the neighboring walls, might be seen two coverts of lime-trees trimmed squarely;—you may form some idea of the locality filled with a modest cheerfulness, a tranquil chasteness, the modest and bourgeois aspect offered by the opposite shore and its unpretentious buildings, the scarce waters of the Brillante, the garden, its two coverts stuck against the neighboring walls, and the venerable dwelling of the Cormons. What peace! what calm! nothing pompous, but nothing transitory,—there, everything seemed eternal. The ground floor was thus open to the reception of guests. There everything breathed the old, the unalterable province. The great square salon, with four doors and four windows, was modestly wainscoted with woodwork painted in gray. A single oblong mirror was placed over the chimney-piece, and the upper part of the pier represented the Day conducted by the Hours, painted in cameo. This species of painting infested all of the panels over the doors in which the artist had invented those eternal Seasons which, in a good proportion of all the houses in the centre of France, fill you with hatred for the detestable Amours occupied in harvesting, skating, sowing, or throwing flowers. Each window was adorned with curtains in green damask retained by cords with great tassels which outlined enormous baldaquins. The furniture, upholstered in tapestry, the painted and varnished wood-work of which was distinguished by the contorted forms so much the fashion in the last century, offered in its medallions La Fontaine's fables; but some of the edges of the chairs or the fauteuils had been repaired. The ceiling was divided into two portions by a great joist, from the middle of which hung an old chandelier in rock crystal, enveloped in a green covering. On the chimney-piece were two vases in Sèvres blue, old branched candlesticks attached to the pier of the wall and a clock of which the subject, taken from the last scene of the *Déserteur*, testified to the prodigious popularity of the work of Sedaine. This clock, in gilded copper, was composed of eleven personages, each one four inches in height,—at the back, the deserter issued from prison between soldiers; in the foreground, the young woman in a faint displayed all her grace. The hearth, the shovels and tongs were in a style analogous to that of the clock. The panels of the wood-work had for ornaments the most recent family portraits, one or two by Rigaud and three pastelles by Latour. Four card-tables, one for backgammon, one for piquet, crowded this very large apartment, the only one, moreover, that was floored with planks. The study completely wainscoted with old lacquer, red, black and gold, would certainly represent a few years later a fabulous price, of which Mademoiselle Cormon had no suspicion; but, had any one offered her a thousand écus a panel, she would not have disposed of a single one, for she had a fixed system of never parting with anything. In the provinces, they always believe in hidden ancestral treasures. The useless boudoir was hung with that old chintz which is so run after to-day by all the amateurs of the style called Pompadour. The dining-room, paved with black and white stones, without a ceiling, but with the rafters painted, was furnished with those formidable buffets with marble tops which are required by the pitched battles delivered to the stomachs in the provinces. The walls, painted in fresco, represented a trellis-work of flowers. The seats were in varnished cane and the doors in natural walnut. Everything completed admirably the patriarchal air which pervaded the interior as well as the exterior of this mansion. The genius of the provinces had here preserved everything; nothing was either new or ancient, young or decrepit. A cold exactitude made itself felt everywhere.

Tourists through Brittany and Normandy, through Maine and Anjou, must all have remarked in the capitals of these provinces, some mansion that resembled more or less the Hôtel of the Cormons'; for it is, in its kind, an archetype of the bourgeois mansions of a large part of France, and merits so much the more its place in this work that it explains customs and represents ideas. Who does not already feel how calm and filled with routine was life in this ancient dwelling? There was a library, but it was lodged a little below the level of the Brillante, well bound, well hooped, and the dust, far from damaging it, only enhanced its value. The works were there preserved with that care which is given, in these provinces deprived of vineyards, to productions full of their native flavor, exquisite, recommendable for their antique perfumes, and produced by the presses of Burgundy, Touraine, Gascony and the Midi. The cost of transportation is too considerable to permit of the importing of bad wines.

The basis of Mademoiselle Cormon's society was composed of about a hundred and fifty persons;—some of them had gone to the country, some of them were ill, some of them were travelling in the department on business affairs; but there were certain faithful ones who, with the exception of the reserved evenings, came every night,—just like people obliged by duty or by long custom to remain in the city. All these personages were of ripe age; few among them had travelled, almost all of them had remained in the province, and certain of them had dipped into Chouannerie. It was becoming possible to speak of this war without embarrassment since the rewards had been bestowed upon the heroic defenders of the good cause. Monsieur de Valois, one of the agents in the last feat of arms in which the Marquis de Montauran perished, delivered up by his mistress, in which the famous Marche-à-Terre, who at this time was peacefully engaged in the cattle business around Mayenne, distinguished himself, had been giving for the last six months the explanations of some good tricks played upon an old Republican named Hulot, the commandant of a demi-brigade stationed at Alençon from 1798 to 1800, and who had left some souvenirs in the country.—See *The Chouans.*

The ladies did not dress much, excepting on Wednesdays, the day on which Mademoiselle Cormon gave dinner parties, and on which the guests invited on the last Wednesday paid their digestion calls. On these days the assemblage was important; the company was numerous, invited guests and visitors arrayed themselves *in fiocchi;* some ladies brought their work, knitting or hand tapestry, some young persons worked without any shame at designs for the *point d'Alençon*, with the produce of which they supported themselves. Certain husbands brought their wives through policy, for there were very few young men; nothing could be whispered in the ear without exciting attention,—there was therefore no danger, either for a young woman or for a young wife, of hearing a love proposal. Every evening at six o'clock the long antechamber was filled with its furniture; each habitué brought either his cane or his cloak or his lantern. All these persons knew one another so well, the manners were so familiarly patriarchal, that if by chance the old Abbé de Sponde was under the covert and Mademoiselle Cormon in her chamber, neither Josette the femme de chambre, nor Jacquelin the domestic, nor the cook, notified them. The first comer waited for a second; then, when the habitués were in number sufficient for piquet, or whist, or boston, they began to play, without waiting for the Abbé de Sponde or Mademoiselle. If it were dark, at the sound of the bell Josette or Jacquelin came and lit the lights. When he saw the salon illuminated, the abbé made haste slowly to appear. Every evening the backgammon and the piquet table, the three tables for boston and that for whist were complete, which gave an average of about twenty-five or thirty persons, counting those who conversed; but there were frequently more than forty. Jacquelin then lit up the study and the boudoir. Between eight and nine o'clock the domestics began to arrive in the antechamber, coming for their masters; and, unless there were a revolution, there was no one left in the salon at ten o'clock. At this hour, the guests were going away in groups in the street, holding dissertations on the deals or continuing some observations on the meadow lands which were under inspection, on the divisions of inheritances, on the dissensions which arise among heirs, on the pretensions of aristocratic society. It was like the coming out from a theatre in Paris. Certain individuals, talking much of poetry, and understanding nothing about it, inveighed against provincial customs; but, rest your forehead upon your left hand, place one foot upon your andirons, support your elbow on your knee, then—if you have well realized the gentle and consistent atmosphere of this country, this mansion and its interior, the company and its interests, made larger by the smallness of the intellect, like gold beaten out between two sheets of parchment—ask yourself, what is human life. Seek to determine between him who engraved ducks on the Egyptian obelisks and him who has *bostoned* for twenty years with Du Bousquier, Monsieur de Valois, Mademoiselle Cormon, the president of the tribunal, the procureur du roi, the Abbé de Sponde, Madame Granson, *e tutti quanti*. If the exact and daily return of the same steps in the same path is not happiness, it simulates it so well that those who have been brought by the storms of an agitated life to reflect upon the blessings of quietness will say that happiness is there. To estimate the importance of Mademoiselle Cormon's salon, it will be sufficient to state that Du Bousquier, a born statistician of society, had calculated that the frequenters of it possessed a hundred and thirty-one votes in the electoral college and represented eighteen hundred thousand francs of income in landed property in the province. The city of Alençon was not, however, entirely represented by this salon, the high aristocratic society had its own; then the salon of the receiver-general was like an inn of the administration, for which the government was responsible, in which all society danced, intrigued, fluttered, loved and supped. These other two salons communicated by means of a few miscellaneous persons with the Cormon household, and *vice versa;* but the Cormon salon judged severely all that took place in the two other camps;—the luxury of the dinners was criticised, the ices of the balls were seriously considered, the conduct of the ladies was discussed, the toilets, the new inventions that were there produced.

*

Mademoiselle Cormon, a species of social partnership under which was comprehended an imposing coterie, naturally became the aim of two ambitious ones as profound as the Chevalier de Valois and Du Bousquier. For each of them, she represented the deputation, and, consequently, the peerage for the noble, a receiver-generalship for the ex-contractor. A dominating salon is established with as much difficulty in the provinces as in Paris, and this one was found already established. To espouse Mademoiselle Cormon would be to reign in Alençon. Athanase, the only one of the three pretenders to the hand of the spinster who no longer calculated anything, then was in love with her person as much as her fortune. To make use of the jargon of the day, was there not a singular drama in the situation of these four persons? Was there not to be found something grotesque in these three rivalries silently contesting around an old maid who did not suspect them, notwithstanding a frightful and perfectly legitimate desire to get married? But, although all these circumstances render the celibacy of this maid something extraordinary, it is not difficult to explain how and why, notwithstanding her fortune and her three lovers, she was still marriageable. In the first place, in accordance with the spirit of the traditions of her house, Mademoiselle Cormon had always desired to marry a gentleman; but, from 1789 to 1799, circumstances were very unfavorable to her aspirations. If she wished to become a lady of quality, she had a horrible fear of the Revolutionary tribunal. These two sentiments, equal in strength, compelled her to remain stationary by a law as true in æsthetics as in statics. This condition of uncertainty, moreover, is not unpleasing to maidens, so long as they think themselves young and in a condition to choose a husband. France is aware that the political system followed by Napoléon had for a result the making of many widows. Under this reign, the heiresses were in a very disproportionate number to the marriageable bachelors. Although the Consulate restored order at home, the troubles abroad rendered the marriage of Mademoiselle Cormon quite as difficult as in the past. If, on the one hand, Rose-Marie-Victoire refused to espouse an old man; on the other, circumstances and the fear of ridicule forbade her to marry a very young man,—now, the families married their children at a very early age, in order to withdraw them from the clutches of the conscription. Finally, through the obstinacy of a landed proprietor, neither would she have married a soldier; for she did not take a man in order to give him up to the Emperor, she wished to keep him for herself. From 1804 to 1815, it was then impossible for her to contest with the young girls who disputed among themselves for the eligible *partis,* thinned by the cannon. Outside of her predilection for the nobility, Mademoiselle Cormon had the whim, very excusable in itself, to wish to be loved for herself. You would not believe the lengths to which she had been led by this desire. She had employed all her ingenuity in setting a thousand traps for her adorers, so that she might discover their real sentiments. Her snares were so cunningly prepared that the unfortunates all fell into them, and each betrayed himself under the whimsical tests which she applied without awakening his suspicions. Mademoiselle Cormon did not study them, she spied on them. A word spoken lightly, a jest which she often misunderstood, was sufficient to cause her to reject these candidates as unworthy,—this one had neither heart nor delicacy, that one lied and was not a Christian; one wished to cut down her forests and coin money under the marriage canopy, another was not of a character to render her happy; in that one she suspected some hereditary gout; here, she was terrified by immoral antecedents; like the Church, she required a fine priest for her altars; then she wished to be married for her assumed ugliness and her pretended defects, as other women wish to be for the qualities which they have not and for hypothetical beauties. The ambition of Mademoiselle Cormon took its origin in the most delicate womanly sentiments,—she counted upon regaling her lover by revealing to him a thousand virtues after marriage, as other women discover the thousand imperfections which they have carefully concealed; but she was misunderstood; her nobility encountered only commonplace souls swayed only by calculations of material interests, and which comprehended nothing of the beautiful calculations of the feelings. The farther she advanced toward that fatal epoch so ingeniously denominated *the second youth,* the more her suspicions increased. She had the affectation of presenting herself under the most unfavorable aspect, and played her part so well that the latest enlisted ones hesitated to unite their fate to that of one whose virtuous hide-and-seek exacted a study that offered but little attraction to men who wish to find a virtue ready made for them. The constant fear of being married only for her fortune rendered her distrustful, suspicious beyond measure; she fell back upon the rich, and they could contract grand marriages; she feared the poor, to whom she refused the disinterestedness which she made of so much importance in a case like the present one,—so that her exclusions and the force of circumstances combined to thin out strangely the men thus selected, like gray peas picked over one by one. After each matrimonial failure the poor demoiselle, induced to view the men with contempt, naturally ended by seeing them in a false light. Her character necessarily contracted an intimate misanthropy which infused a certain tint of bitterness into her conversation and a slight severity into her glance. Her celibacy imparted a growing rigidity to her manners, for she essayed to perfect herself in despair of any sufficient cause. A noble vengeance! she polished for God the rough diamond rejected by man. Presently she had public opinion against her, for the public accepts it as indisputable that a free woman reflects upon herself in not marrying, in lacking for suitors or in refusing them. Each one infers that this refusal is founded on secret reasons, always misinterpreted. This one said that she had physical defects, that one ascribed to her hidden faults; but the poor girl was as pure as an angel, as sound as a child, and full of good intentions, for nature had destined her for all the pleasures, all the happinesses, all the fatigues of maternity.

Mademoiselle Cormon, however, did not find in her own person the auxiliary obliged to fulfil her desires. She had no other beauty than that so improperly called the *beauté du diable,* and which consists of a great freshness of youth which, theologically speaking, the devil could not have,—unless we explain this expression by the constant desire which he has to refresh himself. The feet of the heiress were large and flat; her leg, which she often allowed to be perceived by the manner in which, without any ill-intent, she lifted her dress when it had rained and when she issued from her own house or from Saint-Léonard, would not have been taken for the leg of a woman. It was a sinewy leg, with a little calf, prominent and thick, like that of a sailor. A good stout figure, the plumpness of a nurse, arms strong and fat, red hands, everything about her harmonized with the rounded forms, with the fat whiteness of the Norman beauties. Eyes of an undecided color and which seemed to be starting from her head, gave to her visage, the rounded contours of which had no nobility, an expression of surprise and of sheepish simplicity which was, moreover, appropriate to an old maid; if Rose had not been innocent she would have seemed to be. Her aquiline nose contrasted with the smallness of her forehead, for it is seldom that this form of nose does not indicate a good forehead. Notwithstanding her large red lips, the indication of great kindness of heart, this forehead revealed too few ideas for the heart to be directed by the intelligence—she was necessarily benevolent without gracefulness. Now, while Virtue is severely reproached for her defects, the qualities of Vice are treated with much indulgence. Her chestnut hair, of an extraordinary length, lent to the face of Rose Cormon that beauty which is the result of strength and abundance, the two principal characteristics of her person. At the period of her pretensions she had the little affectation of holding her head in three-quarter view in order to display a very pretty ear which was well set off by the blue-veined whiteness of her neck and of her temples, heightened by the great mass of her hair. Seen thus, in a ball dress, she might appear to be handsome. Her protuberant forms, her stature, her vigorous health, provoked from the officers of the Empire this exclamation:

"What a fine, well-shaped girl!"

But, with the progress of the years, the stoutness, encouraged by a sage and tranquil life, had insensibly so badly distributed itself over this body that it destroyed the early proportions. At this moment, no corset would be able to discover again the hips of the poor girl, who seemed to be cast all in one piece. The youthful harmony of her corsage no longer existed, and her excessive amplitude gave rise to fears that in stooping she would be carried over by her superior masses; but nature had endowed her with a natural counterweight which rendered unnecessary the mendacious precaution of a *tournure*. With her, everything was truthful. In becoming triple, her chin had diminished the length of her neck and spoiled the carriage of the head. Rose had no wrinkles, but folds; and the irreverent pretended that, to prevent chafing, she powdered her joints, after the manner in which children are treated. This plump person offered to a young man distracted by his desires, like Athanase, all those species of attractions which would naturally seduce him. The young imaginations essentially covetous and courageous, love to expand themselves over these beautiful living fields. It was the fat partridge enticing the knife and fork of the gourmand. There were very many elegant Parisians much in debt who would willingly have resigned themselves readily to contributing distinctly to the happiness of Mademoiselle Cormon. But the poor girl was already more than forty years old! At this period, after having long struggled to bring into her life all those interests which constitute a complete woman, and yet obliged to remain a virgin, she fortified herself in her virtue by the most severe religious observances. She had had recourse to religion, that grand consoler of well-guarded virginities! A confessor had been directing, with sufficient stupidity, Mademoiselle Cormon for the last three years in the ways of maceration; he recommended to her a strict discipline which, if we may believe modern medical science, produces an effect quite the contrary of that which this poor priest expected of it,—his hygienic knowledge not being very extensive. These absurd practices had begun to spread a monastic tint over the countenance of Rose Cormon, who was often enough in despair at seeing her white complexion assume those yellowish tones which announce maturity. The slight down with which the corners of her upper lip were ornamented took it upon itself to increase and manifested itself like a smoke. Her temples began to take on dappled tones! In short, the decline had commenced. It was an authentic piece of news in Alençon that Mademoiselle Cormon was troubled by too much blood; she made the Chevalier de Valois submit to receive her confidences, enumerating to him her foot baths and consulting with him as to refrigerators. The sly confidant would then draw out his snuff-box, and as matter of conclusion, contemplate the Princess Goritza:

"The best sedative," he said, "my dear demoiselle, would be a good and handsome husband."

"But in whom can you trust?" she would reply.

The chevalier then flicked away the grains of tobacco which had lodged in the folds of the *pou-de-soie* or on his waistcoat. This movement would have seemed very natural to anyone else; but it always inspired the poor girl with some misgivings. The violence of this passion without an object was so great that Rose no longer dared to look a man in the face, so much did she fear to allow to appear in her countenance the sentiment that tormented her. Through a caprice which was perhaps only a continuation of her former methods, although she felt herself attracted to those men who could still be acceptable to her, she was so much afraid of being accused of folly in appearing to make court to them, that she treated them with very little graciousness. The greater number of the persons of her society, being incapable of appreciating her motives, always so noble, explained her manner with her co-celibates as the vengeance for a refusal, experienced or anticipated. At the commencement of the year 1815, Rose attained that fatal age, which she would never admit, of forty-two. Her desire had by this time acquired an intensity that bordered on monomania, for she comprehended that all hopes of progeny would end by being lost; and that which, in her celestial ignorance, she desired above everything else, was children. There was not in all Alençon a single person who attributed to this virtuous maid a single desire for amorous license;—she loved *en bloc,* without imagining anything of love; she was a Catholic Agnès, incapable of inventing one of the ruses of the Agnès of Molière. For the last few months she had been counting upon a chance. The disbanding of the Imperial troops and the reconstruction of the Royal army brought about a certain movement in the destinies of a great number of men who were returning, some of them on half-pay, others with or without a pension, each one to his native province, all of them having the desire to better their evil fortune and to make a conclusion which, for Mademoiselle Cormon, might be a delicious commencement. It would be strange if, among those who returned to the neighborhood, there would not be found some brave and honorable soldier, able-bodied above all, of a convenient age, whose character would serve as a recommendation to Bonapartist opinions; perhaps even there might be met some who, to regain a lost position, would become Royalists. This thought sustained Mademoiselle Cormon a little longer, during the first months of the year, in the severity of her attitude. But the military men who came to reside in the city proved to be all either too old or too young, too Bonapartist or too reprehensible, in circumstances incompatible with the manners, the rank and the fortune of Mademoiselle Cormon, who each day fell deeper into despair. The superior officers had all taken advantage of their favorable positions under Napoléon to marry, and these turned Royalists, in the interest of their families. Mademoiselle Cormon might pray God to do her the grace to send her a husband that she might be Christianly happy,—it was doubtless written that she should die a virgin and martyr, for no man presented himself who had the appearance of a husband. The conversations which were held in her salon every evening constituted a sufficiently good detective service in the interests of society to inform her as to the manners, fortune and quality of every stranger that arrived in Alençon. But Alençon is not a city to allure the stranger, it is not on the highway to any capital, it has no happy fortunes to offer. The seafaring men who go from Brest to Paris do not even stop there. The poor maid finally comprehended that she was restricted to the natives,—thus it came that her eye assumed something as a fierce expression, to which the malicious chevalier replied by a shrewd glance as he drew out his snuff-box and contemplated the Princess Goritza. Monsieur de Valois knew that, in the feminine jurisprudence, a first constancy is a security for the future. But Mademoiselle Cormon, we must admit it, had but little wit;—she comprehended nothing of this business with the snuff-box. She redoubled her vigilance in combating the *spirit of evil*. Her rigid devotion and the most severe principles confined her cruel sufferings within the mysteries of private life. Every evening, when she found herself alone, she thought upon her lost youth, her faded freshness, the calls of nature thwarted, and, while sacrificing at the foot of the cross her passions, poems condemned to remain unpublished, she promised herself faithfully that, if by chance some man with good intentions should present himself, she would put him to no test and would accept him just as he was. In consulting only her own inclinations, after certain evenings more bitter than others, she would go so far in her imaginings as to marry a sub-lieutenant, a smoker whom she proposed to herself to render, by her cares, her complaisance and her sweetness, the best fellow in the world; she would go so far as to take him riddled with debts. But for these fantastic marriages in which she was pleased to play the sublime part of guardian angels, it required the silence of the night. In the morning, if Josette found Mademoiselle's bed very much disturbed, Mademoiselle had resumed all her dignity; after déjeuner she wished for a man of forty, a worthy landed proprietor, well preserved, a *quasi* young man.

The Abbé de Sponde was incapable of aiding his niece in any respect whatever in her matrimonial manœuvres. This worthy man, now about seventy years of age, attributed the disasters of the French Revolution to some design of Providence, zealous to chastise a dissolute Church. He had therefore thrown himself into that path so long abandoned which was formerly trodden by hermits in order to attain to Heaven,—he led an ascetic life, quietly, without outward display. He concealed from the world his charitable works, his continual prayers and mortifications; he was of the opinion that all priests should thus conduct themselves during the troublous times, and he preached the example. While always presenting to the world a calm and smiling visage, he had ended by detaching himself entirely from worldly interests,—he thought only of the unhappy, of the needs of the Church, and of his own salvation. He had left all the administration of his property to his niece, who paid over to him the revenues, and to whom he paid a small pension, so that he might dispense the surplus in secret alms and in gifts to the Church. All the affections of the abbé were concentrated in his niece, who regarded him as a father; but it was a father preoccupied, conceiving nothing of the agitations of the flesh, and thanking God that He had preserved his dear daughter in a state of celibacy; for he had, since his youth, adopted the theory of Saint John Chrysostom, who wrote that *the state of virginity was as much above the state of marriage as the angel was above the man.* Accustomed to respect her uncle, Mademoiselle Cormon did not dare to initiate him into the desires which inspired her with a longing for change. The good man, accustomed on his side to the course of the household affairs, would have relished but little the introduction of a master into the mansion. Preoccupied by the miseries which he soothed, lost in the abysses of prayer, the Abbé de Sponde frequently had moments of abstraction which the members of his society took for absences; but little of a talker, he preserved an affable and benevolent silence. He was a man with a tall figure, dry, with grave manners, and solemn, whose countenance expressed gentle sentiments, a great inward calm, and who, by his presence, gave to this household a certain saintly authority. He had a great affection for the Voltairean Chevalier de Valois. These two majestic remnants of the nobility and the clergy, although of different manners, recognized each other in their general traits. Moreover, the chevalier was as unctuous with the Abbé de Sponde as he was paternal with his grisettes.

There are those who would believe that Mademoiselle Cormon availed herself of all possible means for attaining her ends; that, among the legitimate artifices permitted to women, she would have recourse to the toilet, that she would bare her neck and shoulders, that she would display the negative coquetries of a magnificent array. But not at all! She was as heroic and motionless in her neck coverings as a soldier in his sentry box. Her dresses, her bonnets, her frippery, were all made by the milliners of Alençon, two humpbacked sisters who did not want for taste. Notwithstanding the arguments of these two artistes, Mademoiselle Cormon refused to adopt any of the trickeries of elegance; she wished to be substantial in everything, flesh and feathers, but perhaps the heavy fashion of her gowns well suited her physiognomy. Let him who will, mock at the poor girl! you will find her sublime, generous souls, who do not concern yourself with the form in which sentiment appears and who admire it wherever it exists! Perhaps there may be some light women who will endeavor to disparage the truthfulness of this recital, they will say that there does not exist in France a maid sufficiently stupid to be ignorant of the art of fishing for a man, that Mademoiselle Cormon is one of those monstrous exceptions which good sense forbids to present as a type; that the most virtuous and the most silly of girls who wishes to catch a gudgeon will still find a bait for her hook. But these criticisms will fall to the ground when we come to reflect that the sublime Catholic religion, Apostolic and Roman, is still maintained in Brittany and in the ancient duchy of Alençon. Faith, piety, do not admit of these subtleties. Mademoiselle Cormon walked in the way of salvation, preferring the unhappiness of her virginity, infinitely too much prolonged, to the unhappiness of a falsehood, to the sin of a ruse. In a maid armed with discipline, virtue could not make any accommodations; therefore love or calculation should very resolutely come to seek her. Moreover, let us have the courage to make a cruel observation at a time when religion is no longer considered but as a means by these, as merely poetical by those. Devotion causes a moral opthalmia. By a providential grace, it takes away from those on the road to eternity the sight of very many little terrestrial things. In a word, the devout women are stupid on a great many points. This stupidity proves, moreover, with what force they carry their spirit toward the celestial spheres, although the Voltairean Monsieur de Valois pretended that it was extremely difficult to decide whether the stupid females become devout naturally, or whether devotion has for its effect to render stupid the daughters of wit. Let it be understood, the purest Catholic virtue, with its loving acceptance of every cup of bitterness, with its pious submission to the commands of God, with its belief in the imprint of the Divine finger in all the potter's clay of life, is the mysterious light which will penetrate into the deepest recesses of this history to give them all their value, and which certainly will aggrandize them in the eyes of those who still possess the faith. Then, if there is stupidity, why should we not occupy ourselves with the unhappiness of stupidity, as we occupy ourselves with the unhappiness of genius? the one is a social element infinitely more abundant than the other. Thus,

Mademoiselle Cormon sinned in the eyes of the world by the divine ignorance of the virgins. She was not closely observing, and her conduct toward her suitors proved it sufficiently. At this very moment, a young girl of sixteen, who had not yet opened a single romance, would have read a hundred chapters of love in Athanase's eyes; whilst Mademoiselle Cormon saw in them nothing at all, she did not recognize in the tremulousness of his speech the strength of a sentiment which did not dare to manifest itself. Shamefaced herself, she did not divine the shame of another. Capable of inventing these refinements of sentimental grandeur which had been the first causes of her undoing, she did not recognize them in Athanase. This moral phenomenon will not appear extraordinary to those who are aware that the qualities of the heart are as independent of those of the mind as the faculties of genius are of the nobilities of the soul. Complete men are so rare that Socrates, one of the finest pearls of humanity, agreed with a phrenologist of his time that he was born to make a very sorry fellow. A great general may be capable of saving his country at Zurich and of having an understanding with the army contractors. A banker of doubtful probity may find himself a statesman. A great musician may conceive sublime melodies and compose a discord. A woman of sentiment may be perfectly dull. Finally, a devout woman may have a sublime soul, and not recognize the utterances of a beautiful soul beside her. The caprices produced by physical infirmities are also to be met with in the moral order. This good creature, who was in despair at having to prepare her confitures for only herself and her old uncle, had become almost absurd. Those who felt themselves moved with sympathy for her because of her good qualities, and some because of her defects, ridiculed her matrimonial failures. In more than one conversation it was asked what would become of such a fine property, and the savings of Mademoiselle Cormon and the estate of her uncle. For some time past she had been suspected of being in reality, notwithstanding appearances, *an original young woman.* In the provinces, it is not permitted to be original,—that would be to have ideas uncomprehended by others, and the equality of wits is demanded as well as the equality of manners. The marriage of Mademoiselle Cormon had become, ever since 1804, something so very problematical that *to marry like Mademoiselle Cormon* was a proverbial phrase in Alençon, equivalent to the most derisory of negations. If this mocking spirit were not one of the most imperative needs in France, this excellent lady would never have excited derision in Alençon. Not only did she receive everybody, she was charitable, pious and incapable of uttering an unkind word; but, still more, she was in accord with the general spirit and the manners of the inhabitants, who loved her as the purest symbol of their life; for she was thoroughly imbued with the habits of the province, she had never gone out of it, she partook of all its prejudices, she espoused its interests, she adored it. Notwithstanding her eighteen thousand francs of income from landed property, a considerable fortune in the provinces, she remained in unity with the houses of lesser wealth. When she went to her estate of the Prébaudet, she travelled in an old basket-work carriole, suspended on two long springs in white leather, drawn by a fat, short-winded mare, and scarcely closed in by two leathern curtains rusty with time. This carriole, known to the whole city, was cared for by Jacquelin as though it were the handsomest coupé in Paris; Mademoiselle clung to it, she had made use of it for twelve years, she called attention to this fact with the triumphant joy of happy avarice. The greater number of the inhabitants were grateful to Mademoiselle Cormon for not humiliating them by the luxury which she could have displayed; it is even to be believed that if she had sent for a calèche from Paris, they would have made more uncharitable remarks on it than on her failures to marry. The most brilliant carriage, moreover, would have carried her to the Prébaudet just like the old carriole. Now, the provinces, which always see the object, concern themselves very little with the beauty of the means, provided that they are efficient.

To complete the description of the domestic manners of this household, it is necessary to group around Mademoiselle Cormon and the Abbé de Sponde, Jacquelin, Josette and Mariette the cook, who occupied themselves in contributing to the happiness of the uncle and the niece. Jacquelin, a man of forty years of age, stout and short, ruddy-faced, dark-complexioned, with the appearance of a Breton sailor, had been in the service of the house for twenty-two years. He served at table, he took care of the mare, he gardened, he blacked the abbé's shoes, ran errands, sawed the wood, drove the carriole, went to the Prébaudet for the oats, hay and straw; in the evening he remained in the antechamber, sleeping like a dormouse. He was in love, it was said, with Josette, a maid of thirty-six, whom Mademoiselle Cormon would have sent away if she had married. Thus these two poor people saved their wages and

loved each other in silence, waiting for and desiring the marriage of
Mademoiselle as the Jews wait for the Messiah. Josette, born between Alençon
and Mortagne, was petite and fat; her face, which resembled a dirty apricot,
was not wanting either in expression or in intelligence; she had the reputation
of ruling her mistress. Josette and Jacquelin, certain of a dénoûment,
concealed a satisfaction which made it appear that these two lovers discounted
the future. Mariette, the cook, also in the service of the house for the last
fifteen years, knew how to prepare all the dishes held in honor in the country.

Perhaps it would be necessary to count for a good deal the great old
Norman brown-bay mare which drew Mademoiselle Cormon to her country-
place of the Prébaudet, for the five inhabitants of this house all bore for this
animal an insane affection. She was called Pénélope, and had been in service
for eighteen years; she was so well cared for, served with so much regularity,
that Jacquelin and Mademoiselle hoped to be able to use her for ten years
more. This beast was a perpetual subject of occupation and of conversation;
it seemed that the poor Mademoiselle Cormon, having no child on whom her
suppressed maternity could expend itself, transferred it all to this very
fortunate animal. Pénélope had prevented Mademoiselle Cormon from
having canaries, cats and dogs, that fictitious family which is assumed by
almost all individuals solitary in the midst of society.

These four faithful servitors—for the intelligence of Pénélope rose to the
level of that of these good domestics, while theirs was brought down to the
mute and submissive regularity of the animal—came and went every day in
the same occupations, with the infallibility of machinery. But, as they say in
their own tongue, they had eaten their white bread first. Mademoiselle
Cormon, like all persons nervously agitated by a fixed idea, became difficult
to please, changeable, less by character than through need of finding vent for
her activity. Not being able to occupy herself with a husband, with children
and the cares which they require, she devoted herself to minute things. She
would talk for hours about nothings, about a dozen napkins marked Z, which
she had found put before the O's.

"What is Josette thinking of?" she would cry. "Josette then takes care of
nothing."

For a whole week she asked if Pénélope had had her oats at two o'clock,
because Jacquelin had once been late. Her little imagination travailed over

trifles. A layer of dust forgotten by the duster, slices of bread badly toasted by Mariette, a delay by Jacquelin in closing the windows through which came the sun, the rays of which faded the colors of the furniture, all these great little things begat grave quarrels in which Mademoiselle flew into a passion. "Everything is changing, then!" she would cry, she no longer recognized her former servants; they were spoiled, she was too indulgent. One day Josette gave her the *Journée du chrétien* instead of the *Quinzaine de Pâques.* The whole city heard of this calamity that evening. Mademoiselle had been obliged to return from Saint-Léonard to her own house, and her sudden departure from the church, in which she had deranged all the chairs, gave rise to the gravest suspicions. She was therefore obliged to explain to her friends the cause of this accident.

"Josette," she had said mildly, "never let such a thing happen again!"

Mademoiselle Cormon was, without suspecting it, very well satisfied with these little disturbances which served as emunctories for her acrimony. The mind has its exigencies; it has, like the body, its gymnastics. These variations of humor were accepted by Josette and Jacquelin as the intemperatenesses of the atmosphere are by the agriculturist. These three worthy people said: "It is fine weather!" or "It rains!" without accusing Heaven. Sometimes, on rising in the morning, they would ask in the kitchen in what humor Mademoiselle would arise, as a farmer consults the mists of the dawn. Finally, necessarily, Mademoiselle Cormon had ended by contemplating herself in the infinite littlenesses of her life. Herself and God, her confessor and her washing-lyes, her confitures to make and the church services to attend, her uncle to care for, these had absorbed her feeble intelligence. For her, the atoms of life magnified themselves by virtue of a law of optics peculiar to individuals egotistical by nature or by chance. Her health, which was so perfect, gave a frightful importance to the least embarrassment which arose in her digestive organs. She lived, moreover, under the ferule of the medical science of our ancestors, and took yearly four medicines of precaution that would have demolished Pénélope, but which enlivened her. If Josette, in dressing her, found the slightest pimple on the still satiny shoulder blades of Mademoiselle, it was a subject for enormous perquisitions in the different alimentary boluses of the week. What a triumph if Josette recalled to her mistress a certain hare, too rich, which must have caused the eruption of that damned pimple. With what joy both of them would say:

"That must be it, it was the hare."

"Mariette put too much spice in it," resumed Mademoiselle, "I tell her all the time to *go softly* for my uncle and for me; but Mariette has no more memory than—"

"Than the hare," said Josette.

"That is true," replied Mademoiselle, "she has no more memory than the hare, that was well said by you."

Four times a year, at the commencement of each season, Mademoiselle Cormon went to pass a certain number of days at her country place of the Prébaudet. It was at this period the middle of May, an epoch at which Mademoiselle Cormon wished to see if her apple trees had *snowed* well, a rustic word which expresses the effect produced under these trees by the fall of their blossoms. When the circular heap of fallen petals resembles a layer of snow, the proprietor may hope for an abundant harvest of cider. At the same time that she thus estimated her casks, Mademoiselle Cormon inspected the reparations which the winter had rendered necessary; she gave directions concerning her garden and her orchard, from which she drew abundant provisions. Each season had its own special affairs. Mademoiselle gave before her departure a farewell dinner to her faithful friends, although she would find them again three weeks later. It was always a piece of news which spread through Alençon, this departure of hers. Her habitual associates, who were owing her a visit, then came to see her; her reception apartment was full; everyone wished her *bon voyage,* as though she were about to sail for Calcutta. Then, on the next morning, all the small dealers were on their doorsteps. Young and old looked at the carriole passing, and it seemed that they were receiving an item of news in repeating to each other:

"Mademoiselle Cormon is then going to the Prébaudet!"

Here some one would say:

"She has butter on her bread, she has!"

"Eh! my good fellow," the neighbor would reply, "that is a worthy woman; if good fortune always fell in such hands, the country would not see a beggar—"

Then another would say:

"Well, well, I should not be surprised if our full-grown vineyards were in blossom, there is Mademoiselle Cormon setting out for the Prébaudet. How comes it that she gets married so little?"

"I would marry her all the same," replied a joker; "the marriage is half made, there is one party who consents; but the other is not willing. Bah! it is for Monsieur du Bousquier that the oven is warm."

"Monsieur du Bousquier?—She has refused him."

That evening, at all the reunions, it was gravely said:

"Mademoiselle Cormon has gone."

Or:

"You have then let Mademoiselle Cormon go away?"

The Wednesday chosen by Suzanne for her scandalous disturbance was, as it happened, that very Wednesday of farewells, the day on which Mademoiselle Cormon drove Josette distracted by the multitude of packages to be taken. Therefore, during the morning, there had been said and had happened certain things in the city which gave the most lively interest to this farewell reunion. Madame Granson had been to sound the alarum in ten households, whilst the worthy spinster was deliberating upon the things necessary for her journey, and while the malicious Chevalier de Valois was occupied with a game of piquet in the house of Mademoiselle Armande de Gordes, sister of the old Marquis de Gordes and queen of the aristocratic salon. If there were no one who was not interested in seeing what kind of a countenance the seducer would assume during the evening, it was important for the chevalier and for Madame Granson to learn how Mademoiselle Cormon would take the news, in her double quality of nubile maid and president of the Maternal Society. As to the innocent Du Bousquier, he was taking a promenade on the Cours, beginning to suspect that Suzanne had tricked him;—this suspicion confirmed him in his opinion concerning women.

On these days of festival, the table was already laid in Mademoiselle's household at half-past three. At this period the fashionable world of Alençon dined on unusual occasions at four o'clock. They still dined under the Empire at two o'clock in the afternoon, as formerly; but they supped! One of the pleasures which Mademoiselle Cormon most relished, in which there was no malice, but which certainly was based on egotism, consisted in the inexpressible satisfaction which she felt in seeing herself arrayed like a mistress of the house who is about to receive her guests. When she was thus under arms, there slipped into the depths of her heart a ray of hope;—a voice said to her that nature had not so abundantly provided for her in vain, and that some enterprising man was about to present himself. Her desire was refreshed as she had refreshed her body; she contemplated herself in her double condition with a sort of intoxication, then this satisfaction continued when she descended to give her redoubtable glance over the salon, the cabinet and the boudoir. She walked through them with the ingenuous contentment of the rich man who reflects at each moment that he is rich and will never want anything. She looked at her everlasting furniture, her antiquities, her lacquers;—she said to herself that such beautiful things required a master. After having admired the dining-room, filled by an oblong table on which was laid a snowy cloth ornamented by twenty covers placed at equal distances from each other; after having verified the squadron of bottles which she had selected, and which all displayed honorable labels; after having minutely inspected the names of the guests written on little pieces of paper by the trembling hand of the abbé, the sole charge which he assumed in the household and which gave rise to grave discussions as to the seat of each diner,—then Mademoiselle went in all her finery to join her uncle who, at this hour, the finest of the day, was walking on the terrace, along the shore of the Brillante, listening to the chirping of the birds nestling in the covert without having to fear either hunters or children. During these waiting hours, she never accosted the Abbé de Sponde without putting to him some absurd questions, in order to lead the good old man into a discussion which might amuse him. We will explain, for this peculiarity should complete the description of the character of this excellent young woman.

Mademoiselle Cormon regarded it as one of her duties to converse; not that she was talkative, she had unfortunately too few ideas and was acquainted with too few phrases to discourse; but she thought thus to accomplish one of the social duties prescribed by religion, which commands us to make ourselves agreeable to our neighbors. This obligation cost her so much trouble that she had consulted her spiritual director, the Abbé Couturier, on this point of commonplace and worthy civility. Notwithstanding the humble observation of his penitent, who admitted to him the stress of inward labor to which her spirit was delivered in order to find something to say, this aged priest, so inflexible in discipline, had read to her the whole of a passage of Saint François de Sales on the duties of a woman of the world, on the decent cheerfulness of pious Christian women who should reserve their severity for themselves and show themselves pleasant and agreeable in their own houses and so act that their neighbor should not be wearied. Thus penetrated with her duties, and wishing at any price to obey her confessor, who had directed her to converse pleasantly, when the poor girl saw the conversation beginning to languish, she would sweat in her corset, so much did she suffer in essaying to emit ideas with which to reanimate the extinguishing discussions. She would then launch strange propositions, such as this: *No one can be in two places at the same time, unless he is a little bird,* by which, one day, she reanimated, not without success, a discussion upon the ubiquity of the apostles of which she comprehended nothing. These sorts of *re-entries* secured for her in her society the appellation of *the good Mademoiselle Cormon.* In the mouths of the fine wits of the society, this expression indicated that she was as ignorant as a carp, and a little bit simple-minded; but many individuals of a capacity equal to her own took the epithet literally and replied:

"Oh! yes, Mademoiselle Cormon is excellent."

Sometimes she put such absurd questions, still with the object of being agreeable to her guests and fulfilling her duties toward the world, that everybody broke out laughing. She asked, for example, what the government had done with all the taxes it had been receiving for so long; why the Bible had not been printed in the time of Jesus Christ, since it had been written by Moses. She was of the mental calibre of that *country gentleman* who, constantly hearing allusions to posterity in the House of Commons, rose to make that speech which became so celebrated: "Gentlemen, I am always hearing here of Posterity, I should like to know what that power has ever done for England?"

On these occasions, the heroic Chevalier de Valois brought to the assistance of the spinster all the resources of his so intelligent diplomacy on seeing the smiles which were exchanged between the pitiless demi-savants. The old gentleman, who loved to enrich the women, lent his wit to Mademoiselle Cormon by sustaining her paradoxically; he covered her retreat so well that sometimes she seemed not to have uttered any foolishness at all. She avowed seriously, one day, that she did not know what difference there was between bulls and oxen. The delightful chevalier arrested the bursts of laughter by replying that the oxen could be only the uncles of the *taures*—rustic term for heifers. Another time, hearing a great deal said about the breeding of domestic animals and the difficulties to be encountered in this business, a conversation that was frequently renewed in a country in which there was the superb stud-farm of the Pin, she understood that horses came from the *coverings,* and asked *why they did not make two coverings a year!* The chevalier drew the laughter upon himself.

"That is very possible," said he.

The company listened to him.

"The trouble," he resumed, "comes from the naturalists, who have not yet succeeded in persuading the mares to carry less than eleven months."

The poor girl knew no more what was a covering than she knew how to distinguish an ox from a bull. The Chevalier de Valois served an ingrate, for never did Mademoiselle Cormon comprehend a single one of his chivalrous services. When she saw the conversation revive, she concluded that she was not so stupid as she thought she was. Finally, one day, she became definitely established in her ignorance, like the Duc de Brancas; for the hero of the *Distrait* arranged himself in the ditch into which he had emptied, and there made himself so comfortable that when an effort was made to get him out, he asked what it was that was wanted with him. Since this date, comparatively recent, Mademoiselle Cormon had lost her fear, she had acquired an assurance which gave to her *re-entries* something of the solemnity with which the English accomplish their patriotic idiocies, and which is like the fatuity of stupidity. As she now approached her uncle with an authoritative step, she was meditating upon a question to put to him in order to draw him from that silence which always troubled her, for she thought him bored.

"Uncle," she said to him, leaning on his arm and pressing joyfully to his side—this was another of her fictions, she thought: "If I had a husband, I should be thus!"—; "uncle, if everything here below happens by the will of God, there is therefore a reason for everything?"

"Certainly," said the Abbé de Sponde gravely, for, cherishing his niece, he allowed her always to draw him from his meditations with an angelic patience.

"Then, if I remain unmarried, there is a supposition that God wills it so?"

"Yes, my child," said the abbé.

"However, since nothing prevents me from getting married to-morrow, His will may be destroyed by mine?"

"That would be true, if we knew the veritable will of God," replied the former prior of the Sorbonne. "Notice, my daughter, that you say *if?*"

The poor girl, who had hoped to draw her uncle into a matrimonial discussion through an argument *ad omnipotentem,* was disconcerted; but those who have an obtuse mind follow the terrible logic of children, which consists in going from answer to question, a logic that is frequently embarrassing.

"But, uncle, God has not made women for them to remain unmarried, for they should be either all maidens or all wives. There is injustice in the distribution of the positions in life."

"My daughter," said the good abbé, "you make the Church in the wrong, for it prescribes celibacy as the best means of attaining to God."

"But if the Church be right, and all the world were good Catholics, the human species would then come to an end, uncle."

"You have too much wit, Rose, it is not necessary to have so much to be happy."

Such a reply brought a smile of satisfaction to the lips of the poor girl, and confirmed her in the good opinion that she was beginning to have of herself. And it is in this manner that the world, that our friends and our enemies, are the accomplices of our defects! At this moment the interview was interrupted by the successive arrival of the guests. On these days of festival, this local event brought about little familiarities between the servants of the house and the invited friends. Mariette said to the president of the tribunal, a gourmand of a pronounced type, as she saw him pass:

"Ah Monsieur du Ronceret, I have cooked some *choux-fleurs au gratin* that will please you, for Mademoiselle knows how much you love them, and she said to me: 'Do not fail to have them, Mariette, Monsieur le Président is coming.'"

"That good Demoiselle Cormon!" replied the judge. "Mariette, have you seasoned them with gravy, instead of bouillon? It is more savory!"

The president did not disdain to enter into the council chamber in which Mariette issued her decrees, he surveyed it with the eye of the gastronomist and the judgment of a master.

"Good day, madame," said Josette to Madame Granson, who paid court to the femme de chambre; "Mademoiselle has thought of you, you shall have a dish of fish."

As to the Chevalier de Valois, he said to Mariette, with the light tone of a grand seigneur who stoops to familiarity:

"Well, my dear *cordon bleu,* to whom I will give the cross of the Legion of Honor, is there something very fine for which we shall reserve ourselves?"

"Yes, yes, Monsieur de Valois, a hare sent from the Prébaudet, it weighed fourteen pounds."

"Good girl!" said the chevalier, giving Josette a playful tap. "Ah! it weighs fourteen pounds!"

Du Bousquier had not been invited. Mademoiselle Cormon, faithful to the system which has been explained to you, treated this man of fifty badly, though the inexplicable sentiments she entertained for him were connected with the deepest recesses of her heart; although she had refused him, she sometimes repented of it, she had, at the same time, something like a presentiment that she would marry him and a feeling of terror that prevented her from wishing for this marriage. Her mind, stimulated by these ideas, was preoccupied with Du Bousquier. Without admitting it to herself, she was impressed by the herculean form of the Republican. Although they could not explain to themselves the contradictions of Mademoiselle Cormon, Madame Granson and the Chevalier de Valois had surprised some ingenuous glances, given surreptitiously, of which the significance had been sufficiently clear to induce both of them to endeavor to ruin the hopes, once disappointed already, of the ex-contractor, and which he certainly still cherished. Two of the guests, whose duties excused them in advance, were still waited for; one of them was Monsieur du Coudrai, the commissioner of mortgages; the other, Monsieur Choisnel, former intendant of the house of Gordes, the notary of the higher aristocracy, by whom he was received with a distinction which he merited by his virtues, and he was also possessed of a considerable fortune. When these two late comers arrived, Jacquelin said to them, as he saw them going into the salon:

"Everybody is in the garden."

The appetites were doubtless impatient, for, at the sight of the commissioner of mortgages, one of the most amiable men of the city, and who had the defect only of having married, for her fortune, an insupportable old woman and of perpetrating enormous puns at which he himself laughed the first, there arose the slight murmur that always welcomes the last comers on similar occasions. While waiting for the official announcement that dinner was served, the company promenaded on the terrace, along the Brillante, looking at the water plants, the mosaic of the river bed, and the picturesque details of the buildings grouped on the other shore, the old wooden galleries, the windows with their supports in ruins, the oblique shorings of some chambers jutting out over the river, the little gardens in which rags were drying, the work-shop of the cabinet-maker, in short, all those trifles of the little town to which the neighborhood of the water, a leaning weeping willow, some flowers, a rose bush, communicated I know not what grace, worthy the attention of the landscape painters. The chevalier was studying all the faces, for he had learned that his firebrand had very fortunately been thrown into the midst of the best circles in the city; but no one yet spoke aloud of this great piece of news, of Suzanne and of Du Bousquier. The inhabitants of the provinces possess in the highest degree the art of slowly distilling scandals; the moment for discussing this remarkable adventure had not yet arrived, it was necessary that each one should be reminded of it. Therefore, they whispered to each other:

"You have heard it?"

"Yes."

"Du Bousquier?"

"And the fair Suzanne."

"Mademoiselle Cormon knows nothing about it?"

"No."

"Ah!"

It was the *piano* of the scandal, the *rinforzando* of which would burst out when the guests came to discuss the first *entrée* of the dinner. Suddenly, Monsieur de Valois noticed Madame Granson who had mounted for this occasion her green bonnet with bouquets of auriculas and whose countenance was sparkling. Was it with eagerness to open the concert? Although such a piece of news was like a gold mine to be exploited in the monotonous lives of these personages, the observing and mistrustful chevalier thought that he recognized in this good woman the expression of a broader sentiment,—the joy caused by the triumph of a personal interest!—He immediately turned to examine Athanase, and surprised him in the significant silence of a profound concentration. Presently, a look cast by the young man upon the corsage of Mademoiselle Cormon, which bore a sufficient resemblance to two regimental kettle-drums, threw a sudden light into the chevalier's mind. This flash enabled him to perceive all the past.

"Ah! the deuce," he said to himself, "to what a sudden check am I exposed!"

Monsieur de Valois approached Mademoiselle Cormon to be able to give her his arm in conducting her to the dining-room. The maiden had for the chevalier a respectful consideration; for certainly his name and the position which he occupied among the aristocratic constellations of the department constituted him the most brilliant ornament of her salon. In her inmost conscience, for the last twelve years, Mademoiselle Cormon had desired to become Madame de Valois. This name was like a branch to which attached themselves the ideas which *swarmed* in her head concerning the nobility, the rank and the outward qualities of a desirable husband; but, if the Chevalier de Valois was the man selected by her heart, her mind, her ambition, this ancient ruin, though carefully prepared like the Saint-Jean of a procession, frightened Mademoiselle Cormon,—if she saw in him a gentleman, the maiden did not see in him a husband. The indifference which the chevalier affected for marriage, and above all, the pretended purity of his morals in a house full of grisettes, did Monsieur de Valois a great injury, quite contrary to all his prevision. This gentleman, who had judged so well in the matter of the annuity, had deceived himself in this. Without being conscious of it herself, the opinion of Mademoiselle Cormon concerning the too-discreet chevalier might be translated by this phrase: "What a pity that he is not a little of a rake!" Students of the human heart have observed the inclination of pious women for evil livers, in surprise at this taste, which they think opposed to Christian virtue. In the first place, what finer destiny would you give to the virtuous woman than that of purifying, in the manner of charcoal, the troubled waters of vice? But how is it that it has not been perceived that these noble creatures, compelled by the rigidity of their principles to refrain from infringing the conjugal fidelity, should naturally desire a husband of great practical experience? The evil livers are the great men in matters of love. Thus the poor maid sighed to find her chosen vessel broken into two portions. God alone would be able to solder together the Chevalier de Valois and Du Bousquier. In order to comprehend well the importance of the few words which the chevalier and Mademoiselle Cormon were about to exchange, it will be necessary to set forth two grave affairs which had taken place in the city, and concerning which opinions were divided. Du Bousquier, moreover, was mysteriously implicated in them. One of them concerned the Curé of Alençon, who had formerly taken the constitutional oath, and who at this period was overcoming the repugnance of the good Catholics by his manifestation of the highest virtues. He was indeed a Cheverus on a small scale, and so well appreciated that at his death the entire city wept. Mademoiselle Cormon and the Abbé de Sponde belonged to that little church, sublime in its orthodoxy, and which was at the court of Rome that which the *ultras* were to be at that of Louis XVIII. The abbé especially did not recognize the Church which, under compulsion, had any dealings with the constitutionals. This curé was not received in the Cormon household, the sympathies of which had been extended to the officiating priest of Saint Léonard, the aristocratic parish of Alençon. Du Bousquier, that rabid liberal concealed under the skin of a royalist, was aware of the necessity of rallying points for the discontented who constitute the available material for all oppositions, and he had already secured the sympathies of the middle classes for his curé. This was the second affair; under the secret inspiration of this rude diplomat, the idea of building a theatre had originated in the city of Alençon. The fanatics of Du Bousquier did not know their Mahomed, but they were none the less ardent in believing in the defense of their own idea. Athanase was one of the warmest partisans of the construction of a building for the drama, and, for the last few days, he had been arguing in the offices of the mayor in favor of a cause which all the young people had espoused. The elderly gentleman offered his arm to the spinster to promenade with her; she accepted it, not without thanking him by a happy look for this attention, and one to which the chevalier replied by indicating Athanase with a discreet air.

"Mademoiselle, you who bring so much good sense to the appreciation of the social conventionalities, and with whom that young man is connected by some ties—"

"Very distant ones" said she, interrupting him.

THE CORMON GARDEN

Presently, a look cast by the young man upon the corsage of Mademoiselle Cormon, which bore a sufficient resemblance to two regimental kettle-drums, threw a sudden light into the chevalier's mind. This flash enabled him to perceive all the past.

"Should you not," continued the chevalier, "make use of the ascendancy which you have over his mother and over him to prevent him from ruining himself? He is already not very religious, he follows the curé who took the oath; but that is nothing. Here is something much more grave,—is he not throwing himself in a senseless fashion into a way of opposition, without knowing what influence his present conduct may have upon his future! He is intriguing for the erection of the theatre; he is, in this business, the dupe of that disguised Republican, Du Bousquier—"

"Mademoiselle, you who bring so much good sense to the appreciation of the social conventionalities, and with whom that young man is connected by some ties—"

"Very distant ones" said she, interrupting him.

"Should you not," continued the chevalier, "make use of the ascendancy which you have over his mother and over him to prevent him from ruining himself? He is already not very religious, he follows the curé who took the oath; but that is nothing. Here is something much more grave,—is he not throwing himself in a senseless fashion into a way of opposition, without knowing what influence his present conduct may have upon his future! He is intriguing for the erection of the theatre; he is, in this business, the dupe of that disguised Republican, Du Bousquier—"

"*Mon Dieu!* Monsieur de Valois," she replied, "his mother told me that he was very clever, and he does not know enough to say *deuce,* he is set down before you like *two treys*—"

"Who—*qui ne, quine,* 'two fives'—thinks of nothing!" exclaimed the commissioner of mortgages. "I caught that on the fly, that one!—I present my respects—*devoirs, devoares,* term of play—to the Chevalier de Valois," he added, saluting that gentleman with all the emphasis which Henry Monnier attributes to Joseph Prudhomme, that admirable type of the class to which the commissioner of mortgages appertained.

Monsieur de Valois returned the dry and patronizing salutation of the noble who maintains his dignity; then he towed Mademoiselle Cormon away to some pots of flowers at a distance, to make the intruder comprehend that he did not wish to be watched.

"How could you expect," said the chevalier in a low voice, stooping to Mademoiselle Cormon's ear, "that the young men educated in these detestable Imperial lyceums should have any ideas? It is good manners and noble habits which produce great ideas and fine love-making. It is not difficult, in seeing him, to see that that poor youth will become altogether imbecile, and will die wretchedly. See how pale he is, how ghastly!"

"His mother pretends that he works much too hard," replied the old maid innocently; "he sits up at nights, but for what? to read books, to write. What kind of a condition can that bring a young man to, to write during the night?"

"But that will wear him out," resumed the chevalier, endeavoring to bring her thoughts back upon the grounds on which he hoped to see her hold Athanase in horror. "The customs in these Imperial lyceums are truly horrible."

"Oh! yes," said the ingenuous Mademoiselle Cormon. "Do they not take them out to walk with drums at their heads? Their masters have no more religion than have the pagans. And they put those poor children in uniform, exactly like soldiers. What ideas!"

"Behold their products," said the chevalier, indicating Athanase. "In my time, was a young man ever ashamed to look at a pretty woman? He, he lowers his eyes when he sees you! That young man terrifies me because he interests me. Tell him not to intrigue with the Bonapartists as he is doing for that theatrical building; when these little young people do not demand it insurrectionally, for this word is for me the synonym of constitutionally, the authorities will erect it. Then, tell his mother to watch over him."

"Oh! she will prevent him from visiting these people on half-pay and bad society, I am sure of it. I will speak to him," said Mademoiselle Cormon, "for he might lose his place at the mayor's office. And then what would he and his mother have to live on—? It is enough to make you shudder."

As Monsieur de Talleyrand said of his wife, the chevalier said to himself, looking at Mademoiselle Cormon:

"Will somebody find me any one more stupid! On the word of a gentleman! that virtue which takes away intelligence, is it not a vice? But what an adorable wife for a man of my age! What principles! what ignorance!"

You will understand that this monologue addressed to the Princess Goritza was made while preparing a pinch of snuff.

Madame Granson had guessed that the chevalier was speaking of Athanase. Eager to learn the result of this conversation, she followed Mademoiselle

Cormon, who walked toward the young man, projecting six feet of dignity in front of her. But, at that moment, Jacquelin came to announce that Mademoiselle was served. The spinster appealed by a look to the chevalier. The gallant commissioner of mortgages, who was beginning to see in the manners of the elderly gentleman that barrier which about this time the provincial nobles were raising between themselves and the bourgeoisie, was delighted to get the better of the chevalier; he was near Mademoiselle Cormon, he bent his arm in presenting it, she was forced to accept it. The chevalier hastened, through policy, to offer his to Madame Granson.

"Mademoiselle Cormon," said he to her, while walking slowly after all the rest of the guests, "my dear lady, takes the liveliest interest in your dear Athanase, but this interest is disappearing through the fault of your son,—he is irreligious and liberal, he is advocating this theatre, he frequents the company of the Bonapartists, he is interested in the constitutional curé. This conduct may cost him his situation in the mayor's office. You are aware with what care the king's government is purifying itself! Where will your dear Athanase, once dismissed, find other employment? Let him not get himself regarded with disfavor by the administration."

"Monsieur le chevalier," said the poor mother terrified, "how much gratitude do I not owe you! You are right, my son is the dupe of a wicked clique, and I will enlighten him."

The chevalier had at a single glance long ago penetrated the character of Athanase, he had recognized in him the element of republican conviction, so little malleable, to which at that age a young man sacrifices everything, intoxicated by that word *liberty* so ill defined, so little comprehended, but which, for those held in contempt, is a flag of revolt; and, for them, revolt is vengeance. Athanase would persist in his faith, for his opinions were interwoven with his griefs as an artist, with his bitter contemplations of the social state. He was ignorant that at thirty-six years of age, at the period when man has judged his fellows, the social relations and interests, the opinions for which he at first sacrificed his future, would become very much modified in his own mind, as in all men who are truly superior. To remain faithful to the Left in Alençon, that would be to earn Mademoiselle Cormon's aversion. In this the chevalier judged rightly. Thus this society, so peaceable in appearance, was inwardly as much agitated as could be diplomatic circles, in which craft, skill, passions, interests, are concerned in the gravest questions between empires. The guests finally sat down at this table laden with the first course, and each one began to eat as they eat in the provinces, without any shame at possessing a good appetite, and not as at Paris, where it seems that the jaws are moved by sumptuary laws which undertake to deny the laws of anatomy. In Paris, people eat with the tips of their teeth, they juggle away their pleasure; whilst in the provinces things pass off naturally, and existence concentrates itself perhaps a little too much upon that great and universal means of existence to which God has condemned his creatures. It was at the end of the first course that Mademoiselle Cormon made the most celebrated of her *re-entries*, for it was discussed for more than two years, and the incident is still related in the reunions of the small bourgeoisie of Alençon when her marriage is spoken of. The conversation, which had become very copious and animated at the moment when the penultimate *entrée* was attacked, had naturally turned on the affair of the theatre and on that of the curé who had taken the oath. In the first fervor of royalism which manifested itself in 1816, those who, later, were called the Jesuits of the country, wished to expel the Abbé François from his parish. Du Bousquier, suspected by Monsieur de Valois to be the supporter of this priest, the promoter of these intrigues, and on whose shoulders the gentleman had moreover thrown them with his usual address, was on the accused bench without any advocate to defend him. Athanase, the only guest frank enough to sustain Du Bousquier, was not in a position to enunciate his ideas before these potentates of Alençon, whom, moreover, he considered stupid. It is no longer any but the young people of the provinces who preserve a respectful countenance before those of a certain age, and who do not venture either to censure them or to contradict them too plainly. The conversation, attenuated by the virtues of some delicious ducks stuffed with olives, suddenly fell flat. Mademoiselle Cormon, zealous to contest with her own ducks, wished to defend Du Bousquier, who was represented as a pernicious contriver of intrigues, capable of *setting the mountains by the ears.*

"For my part," she said, "I thought that Monsieur du Bousquier concerned himself only with childish things."

In the actual condition of affairs, this speech had a prodigious success. Mademoiselle Cormon obtained a great triumph,—she made the Princess Goritza fall face down on the table. The chevalier, who was not expecting anything so very apropos from his Dulcinea, was so moved that he could not at first find any word sufficiently laudatory; he applauded noiselessly, as at the Italiens, simulating with the ends of the fingers a clapping.

"She is adorably *spirituelle,*" said he to Madame Granson. "I have always maintained that one day she would unmask her artillery."

"Oh! in intimacy, she is charming," replied the widow.

"In intimacy, madame, all women are brilliant," said the chevalier.

This Homeric laughter at last subsided, Mademoiselle Cormon asked the reason of her success. Then commenced the *forte* of the scandal. Du Bousquier was presented as a sort of celibate Père Gigogne, as a monster who, for the last fifteen years, had himself alone supplied the foundling asylum; the immorality of his habits was finally unveiled! they were worthy of the Parisian saturnalia, etc., etc. Conducted by the Chevalier de Valois, the most skilful *chef d'orchestre* of this species, the overture of the scandal was magnificent.

"I am not aware," said he, with a benevolent air, "of anything which could prevent a Du Bousquier from espousing a Mademoiselle Suzanne what's her-name; what did you call her? Suzette! Although I live at Madame Lardot's, I know these young girls only by sight. If this Suzon is a tall, handsome girl with an impertinent air, a gray eye, a fine figure, a little foot, whom I have scarcely noticed, but whose bearing struck me as very insolent, she is much superior in manners to Du Bousquier. Moreover, Suzanne has the nobility of beauty; as far as that goes, this marriage would be for her a mésalliance. You will remember that the Emperor Joseph had the curiosity to go and see, at Luciennes, the Du Barry; he offered her his arm for the promenade; the poor girl, surprised at such an honor, hesitated to take it; 'Beauty will always be the queen,' said the emperor to her. Notice that this was a German of Austria," added the chevalier. "But, believe me, Germany, which is here considered to be so very provincial, is a country of noble chivalry and of fine manners, especially in Poland and Hungary, where there are to be found—"

Here the chevalier stopped, fearing to be led into some allusion to his personal happiness; he merely took out his snuff-box again and confided the rest of the anecdote to the princess who had been smiling upon him for thirty-six years.

"That was a very delicate speech for Louis XV.," said Du Ronceret.

"But it is about the Emperor Joseph, I think," replied Mademoiselle Cormon with a little pretentious air.

"Mademoiselle," said the chevalier, seeing the president, the notary and the commissioner exchanging malicious glances, "Madame du Barry was the Suzanne of Louis XV., a circumstance sufficiently well known to wicked persons like ourselves, but with which the young ladies need not be acquainted. Your ignorance proves that you are a diamond without flaws; the corruptions of history do not attain to you."

The Abbé de Sponde looked graciously at the Chevalier de Valois and inclined his head in sign of laudatory approbation.

"Mademoiselle is not acquainted with history?" asked the commissioner of mortgages.

"If you mix up for me Louis XV. and Suzanne, how do you expect me to know your history?" replied Mademoiselle Cormon angelically, joyful at seeing that the dish which had contained the ducks was empty, and that the conversation was so completely revived that on hearing this last speech all the guests laughed with full mouths.

"Poor young thing!" said the Abbé de Sponde. "When a misfortune arrives, charity, which is a divine love, as blind as the pagan love, should no longer perceive the cause. Niece, you are president of the Maternal Society, this poor girl must be helped, she will find it difficult to marry."

"Poor child!" said Mademoiselle Cormon.

"Do you think that Du Bousquier will marry her?" asked the president of the tribunal.

"If he were an honest man, he would do so," said Madame Granson; "but truly, my dog has better manners."

"Azor is, however, a great purveyor"—*fournisseur,* purveyor, contractor,—said the commissioner of mortgages with a subtle air, endeavoring to pass from the pun to the bon mot.

At the dessert, the discussion still turned on Du Bousquier, who gave rise to a thousand pretty conceits which the wine rendered extravagant. Each one, led away by the commissioner of mortgages, replied to one pun by another. Thus Du Bousquier was a severe father—*père sévère,* persevering—a clownish father—*père manant,* permanent,—a father hooted at—*père sifflé, persiflé,* quizzed, bantered,—a green father—*père vert,*—a round father,—*père rond,* perron—a perforated father—*père foré*,—a father owed—*père dû, perdu*, lost—a hired bravo of a father—*père sicaire, persicaire*,—medical plant, persicaria.—He was neither *père*—father—nor *maire*—mother, mayor,—nor a *révérend père*; he played at *paire ou non*—father or not, even or odd;—neither was he a *père conscrit*—conscript father.

"This does not always make a *père nourricier*—foster father, nourishing father—," said the Abbé de Sponde with a gravity which arrested the laughter.

"Nor a *père noble*," replied the Chevalier de Valois.

The church and the nobility had descended into the arena of puns, while preserving their dignity.

"Hist!" said the commissioner of mortgages, "I hear the creaking of Du Bousquier's boots, which certainly are more than ever *à revers*—turned down."

It almost always happens that a man is ignorant of the reports which are spread concerning him—an entire city may be talking about him, calumniating him or lampooning him; if he have no friends, he will know nothing about it. Now, the innocent Du Bousquier, Du Bousquier who wished to be culpable and would have preferred that Suzanne had not lied, Du Bousquier was superb in ignorance; no one had spoken to him of Suzanne's revelations, and every one found it, moreover, inconvenient to question him concerning one of those affairs in which the interested party is sometimes possessed of secrets which oblige him to keep silent. Du Bousquier therefore seemed to be very exasperating and somewhat fatuous, when the company adjourned from the dining-room to take coffee in the salon, in which were several persons who had already arrived for the soirée. Mademoiselle Cormon, counselled by her modesty, did not dare to look at the terrible seducer; she had taken possession of Athanase, whom she was moralizing by retailing to him the most remarkable series of commonplaces of royalist politics and religious morality. Not possessing, like the Chevalier de Valois, a snuff-box adorned with a princess to enable him to endure these douches of silliness, the poor poet listened with a stupid air to her whom he adored, regarding her monstrous corsage which maintained that absolute repose which is the attribute of great masses. His desires produced in him something like an intoxication which transformed the little clear voice of the elderly maiden into a soft murmur and her flat ideas into suggestions full of spirit.

Love is a counterfeiter, who is continually changing copper sous into golden louis, and who often also makes of his louis mere copper sous.

"Well, Athanase, you will promise me?"

This final phrase struck the ears of the happy young man like those noises which rouse you suddenly from slumber.

"What, Mademoiselle?" he replied.

Mademoiselle Cormon rose brusquely, looking at Du Bousquier, who resembled at this moment that great god of Fable which the Republic placed upon its écus; she went toward Madame Granson and said to her in her ear:

"My poor friend, your son is an idiot! The lyceum has ruined him," she added, remembering the insistence with which the Chevalier de Valois had spoken of the evil education of the lyceums.

What a clap of thunder! All unknown to himself, the poor Athanase had had the opportunity to throw his firebrands upon the vine branches heaped up in the heart of the old maid; if he had listened to her, he could have made her comprehend his passion,—for, in the state of agitation in which Mademoiselle Cormon was, a single word would have sufficed; but that stupid avidity which characterizes youthful and true love had ruined him, as sometimes a child full of life kills itself through ignorance.

"What have you been saying to Mademoiselle Cormon?" asked Madame Granson of her son.

"Nothing."

"Nothing—I will explain it!" she said to herself, putting off serious affairs till to-morrow, for she attached but little importance to this speech, believing Du Bousquier completely ruined in the estimation of the spinster.

Presently the four tables were occupied by their sixteen players. Four persons were interested in piquet, the most costly game and one at which much money was lost. Monsieur Choisnel, the procureur du roi and two ladies went to play backgammon in the red-tinted study. The candlesticks were lighted; then the flower of Mademoiselle Cormon's society opened out before the fireplace, on the couches, around the tables, after each couple as they entered had said to her:

"You are then going to-morrow to the Prébaudet?"

"Why, it is necessary," she replied.

On the whole, the mistress of the house appeared preoccupied. Madame Granson was the first to perceive the unusual condition of the maiden,—Mademoiselle Cormon was thinking.

"Of what are you dreaming, cousin?" she said to her finally, finding her seated in the boudoir.

"I am thinking," she replied, "of that poor girl. Am I not president of the Maternal Society? I am going to fetch you ten écus."

"Ten écus!" exclaimed Madame Granson. "But you have never given as much as that."

"But, my dear, it is so natural to have children!"

This immoral sentence, delivered from the heart, stupefied the treasurer of the Maternal Society. Du Bousquier had evidently grown in the estimation of Mademoiselle Cormon.

"Truly," said Madame Granson, "Du Bousquier is not only a monster, he is still more, something infamous. When one has injured another, does he not owe him recompense? Is it not for him, rather than for us, to succor this girl, who, after all, seems to me to be a very bad case, for there were to be found in Alençon much better men than that cynical Du Bousquier? She must have been very loose in her morals to have had to do with him."

"Cynical! Your son, my dear, teaches you Latin words which are incomprehensible. Certainly I do not wish to excuse Du Bousquier; but explain to me how a woman is loose in morals in preferring one man to another?"

"My dear cousin, you should marry my son Athanase, there would be in that nothing which was not very natural; he is young and handsome, full of promise, he will be the glory of Alençon; only, everybody would think that you had taken so young a man in order to be very happy; the evil speakers would say that you had made your provision of happiness so that it would never fail; there would be jealous women who would accuse you of depravity; but what would that amount to? you would be well and truly loved. If Athanase appears to you to be an idiot, my dear, it is because he has too many ideas; extremes meet. He certainly sees things like a young girl of fifteen; he has not rolled in the impurities of Paris, *he* has not!—Well, change the expressions, as my poor husband used to say,—it is the same with Du Bousquier in connection with Suzanne. You would be calumniated, you would; but, in the affair of Du Bousquier, everything is true. Do you understand?"

"No more than if you were speaking Greek to me," said Mademoiselle Cormon, opening her eyes wide and exerting all the powers of her intelligence.

"Well, cousin, since it is necessary to put the dots on the *i*'s, Suzanne cannot be in love with Du Bousquier. And if the heart has nothing to do with this affair—"

"But, cousin, with what does one love then, if it is not with the heart?"

Here, Madame Granson said to herself that which the Chevalier de Valois had thought.

"This poor cousin is really too innocent, this goes beyond bounds!—Dear child," she resumed aloud, "it seems to me that children are not conceived solely by the spirit."

"Why, yes, my dear, for the Holy Virgin—"

"But, my child, Du Bousquier is not the Holy Ghost!"

"That is true," replied the spinster, "he is a man, a man whose appearance renders him sufficiently dangerous for his friends to persuade him to marry."

"You can, cousin, bring about this result."

"Eh! how?" said the old maid, with all the enthusiasm of Christian charity.

"Refuse to receive him until he has taken a wife; you owe it to good manners and to religion to display in these circumstances an exemplary reprobation."

"When I return from the Prébaudet, we will talk of this again, my dear Madame Granson; I will consult my uncle and the Abbé Couturier," said Mademoiselle Cormon, re-entering the salon, which at that moment was at its highest degree of animation.

The lights, the groups of well-dressed women, the solemn tone, the magisterial air of this assembly, rendered Mademoiselle Cormon no less proud than her society of this aristocratic quality. For many persons, nothing better would be seen at Paris in the best company. At this moment, Du Bousquier, who was playing at whist with Monsieur de Valois and two old ladies, Madame du Coudrai and Madame du Ronceret, was the object of suppressed curiosity. A few young women had come, who, under the pretext of watching the play, looked at him in so singular a manner, though surreptitiously, that the old bachelor finally began to suspect that there was something wrong in his costume.

"Can my wig be awry?" he said to himself, experiencing one of those capital anxieties to which the old bachelors are subject.

He took advantage of a bad deal which ended a seventh *rubber* to leave the table.

"I cannot touch a card without losing," he said, "I am decidedly too unlucky."

"You are lucky elsewhere," said the chevalier, throwing at him a sly look.

This speech naturally made the round of the salon, each one exclaiming over the exquisite tone of the chevalier, the Prince de Talleyrand of the country.

"There is no one but Monsieur de Valois who finds such things," said the niece of the Curé of Saint-Léonard.

Du Bousquier went to look at himself in the little oblong mirror above the *Déserteur,* and found nothing out of the way in his appearance. After innumerable repetitions of the same text varied in every way, about ten o'clock, the departures began from the little jetty of the long antechamber, not without several journeys of escort by Mademoiselle Cormon, who embraced her favorites on the perron. The groups went away, some toward the road to Brittany and the château, others toward the quarter which overlooks the Sarthe. Then commenced the discourses which, for twenty years, had re-echoed at this hour in this street. It was inevitably:

"Mademoiselle Cormon was looking very well this evening."

"Mademoiselle Cormon?—I thought there was something singular about her."

"How that poor abbé is breaking up! Did you see how he slept? He no longer knows where are his cards, he is so absent-minded."

"We shall have the grief of losing him."

"It is fine to-night, we shall have a beautiful day to-morrow!"

"A fine season for the apple trees to shed their blossoms."

"You beat us; but when you are on the side of Monsieur de Valois, you never do otherwise."

"How much did he win, then?"

"Why, this evening, he won three or four francs. He never loses."

"Yes; on my word, do you know that there are three hundred and sixty-five days in the year, and that, at that rate, his play is worth a farm to him!"

"Ah! what deals we had this evening!"

"You are very fortunate, monsieur and madame, here you are at your own door; while we, we have half the city to traverse yet."

"I do not sympathize with you, you could have a carriage, so as not to have to go on foot."

"Ah! monsieur, we have a daughter to marry who takes away one wheel, and the maintenance of our son at Paris carries off the other."

"You are still going to make of him a magistrate?"

"What would you have us do with young men?— And then there is no shame in serving the king."

Sometimes, a discussion concerning cider or flax, always conducted on the same lines and which returned at the same periods, was continued along the road. If some observer of the human mind had lived in this street, he could always have told what month it was by listening to this conversation. But, at this moment, it was exclusively concerned with amusing gossip, for Du Bousquier, who was walking alone ahead of the groups, was humming, without any suspicion of its appropriateness, the famous air, *Femme sensible, entends-tu le ramage?* etc.—Tender woman, dost hear the childish prattle?— For some of these, Du Bousquier was a very capable man, a man misjudged. The Président du Ronceret, since he had been confirmed in his office by a new royal appointment, had inclined toward Du Bousquier. For others, the ex-contractor was a dangerous man, of evil habits, capable of anything. In the provinces, as in Paris, men in public view resemble that statue in the beautiful allegory of Addison, for which two knights fight on arriving from opposite sides of the square in which it is set up,—one of them says it is white, the other maintains that it is black; then, when they are both on the ground, they see that it is white on the right and black on the left; a third knight comes to their aid and finds it red.

As he entered his own lodging, the Chevalier de Valois said to himself:

"It is time to spread the report of my marriage with Mademoiselle Cormon. The news shall come from the salon of the D'Esgrignons, it will go straight to Séez to the bishop's, will come back by the head curates to the Curé of Saint-Léonard, who will not fail to tell it to the Abbé Couturier; thus Mademoiselle

Cormon will receive this chain-shot under the water-line. The old Marquis d'Esgrignon will invite the Abbé de Sponde to dinner, in order to arrest a scandal which will injure Mademoiselle Cormon if I come out against her, will injure me if she refuse me. The abbé will be well and duly entrapped; then Mademoiselle Cormon will not hold out against a visit from Mademoiselle de Gordes, who will demonstrate to her the grandeur and the future of this alliance. The estate of the abbé is worth more than a hundred thousand écus, the savings of the niece must amount to more than two hundred thousand francs, she has her hôtel, the Prébaudet, and fifteen thousand francs of income. A word to my friend the Comte de Fontaine, and I become mayor of Alençon, deputy; then, once seated on the benches of the Right, we shall arrive at the peerage by crying: 'Closure!' or: 'Order!'"

On her return home, Madame Granson had a lively explanation with her son, who was not willing to recognize the connection which existed between his opinions and his love. This was the first quarrel which had troubled the harmony of this poor household.

The next morning, at nine o'clock, Mademoiselle Cormon, packed away in her carriole with Josette, and rising like a pyramid amid the ocean of her packages, ascended the Rue Saint-Blaise on her way to the Prébaudet, where she was to be surprised by the event which precipitated her marriage, and which could not be foreseen either by Madame Cranson, or Du Bousquier, or Monsieur de Valois, or Mademoiselle Cormon. Chance is the greatest of all artists.

The morning after her arrival at the Prébaudet, Mademoiselle Cormon was very innocently occupied, about eight o'clock in the morning, in listening during her déjeuner to the divers reports of her keeper and her gardener, when Jacquelin suddenly burst into the dining-room.

"Mademoiselle," said he distractedly, "monsieur your uncle has sent you a messenger, the son of the Mère Grosmort, with a letter. The lad left Alençon before daybreak, and he is already here. He has run almost like Pénélope! Shall he have a glass of wine?"

"What can have happened, Josette? My uncle, can he be?— "

"He would not have written," said the femme de chambre, divining her mistress's fears.

"Quick! quick!" exclaimed Mademoiselle Cormon after having read the first lines, "let Jacquelin harness Pénélope!—You must arrange, my girl, to have everything packed up again in a half hour," said she to Josette. "We shall return to the city—"

"Jacquelin!" cried Josette, excited by the feelings expressed in Mademoiselle Cormon's countenance.

Jacquelin, informed by Josette, arrived, saying:

"But, Mademoiselle, Pénélope is eating her oats."

"Eh! what difference is that to me? I wish to depart immediately."

"But, Mademoiselle, it is going to rain!"

"Well, we shall get wet."

"The house is on fire!" murmured Josette, piqued at the silence which her mistress maintained while finishing the letter, reading it and rereading it.

"At least, finish your coffee, do not get yourself all upset. Look how red you are!"

"Am I red, Josette?" said she, going to look at herself in a mirror from which the quicksilver was falling and which presented to her the reflection of her features doubly distorted. *"Mon Dieu!"* thought Mademoiselle Cormon, "if I should become ugly!—Come, Josette, come, my girl, help me to dress. I wish to be ready before Jacquelin has harnessed Pénélope. If you cannot get my packages in the carriage, I will leave them here, rather than lose a minute."

If you have well comprehended the excess of the monomania to which the desire for marriage had brought Mademoiselle Cormon, you will share her emotion. The worthy uncle announced to his niece that Monsieur de Troisville, formerly an officer in the Russian service, grandson of one of his best friends, wished to retire to Alençon, and had asked hospitality of him, recommending himself on the strength of the friendship which the abbé had entertained for his grandfather, the Vicomte de Troisville, chief of squadron under Louis XV. The former vicar-general, terrified, entreated his niece to return instantly to help him to receive their guest and to do the honors of the house, for the letter had been delayed, Monsieur de Troisville might be on their hands that very evening. On reading this letter, could there be any longer a question of the matters affecting the Prébaudet? At this moment, the keeper and the farmer, witnesses of the dismay of their mistress, kept very quiet while waiting for her orders. When they stopped her in the passage in order to obtain their instructions, for the first time in her life Mademoiselle Cormon, the despotic old maid, who saw into everything for herself at the Prébaudet, said to them: *"Whatever you like!"* which struck them with stupefaction; for their mistress carried her administrative care so far as to count her fruits and register them by species, so as to direct the consumption according to the number of each species.

"I think I am dreaming," said Josette, on seeing her mistress flying by way of the staircases like an elephant to whom God had given wings.

Presently, notwithstanding a driving rain, Mademoiselle departed from the Prébaudet, leaving her people the bridle on their necks. Jacquelin did not dare to take upon himself to increase the speed of the little habitual trot of the peaceable Pénélope, who, like the beautiful queen whose name she bore, had the appearance of taking as many steps backward as she did forward. Seeing this march, Mademoiselle ordered Jacquelin in a sharp voice to make the poor astonished mare gallop, with the whip if necessary; so much was she afraid of not having time to arrange the house suitably to receive Monsieur de Troisville! She calculated that the grandson of a friend of her uncle could not be more than forty years of age; a soldier should infallibly be a bachelor, she therefore promised herself, her uncle aiding, not to allow Monsieur de Troisville to issue from the dwelling in the same condition in which he would enter it. Although Pénélope galloped, Mademoiselle Cormon, occupied with her toilets and dreaming of a first bridal night, said several times to Jacquelin that he was not advancing. She fidgeted in the carriole without replying to Josette's questions, and talked to herself like one who is meditating great designs. Finally, the carriole reached the street of Alençon which is called the Rue Saint-Blaise when entering from the direction of Mortagne; but, toward the hôtel of the *More,* it takes the name of the Rue de la Porte-de-Séez, and becomes the Rue du Bercail leading into the road to Brittany. If the departure of Mademoiselle Cormon had made a great noise in Alençon, everyone can imagine the uproar which must be caused by her return on the day after her installation at the Prébaudet, and in a pouring rain which beat in her face without her appearing to notice it. Everyone remarked the wild gallop of Pénélope, the jeering air of Jacquelin, the early hour, the packages topsy-turvy, finally the animated conversation of Josette and of Mademoiselle, above all, their impatience. The lands of the house of Troisville were situated between Alençon and Mortagne. Josette knew the different branches of the Troisville family. A word dropped by Mademoiselle as they struck the pavements of Alençon had informed Josette of the facts in the present case; a free discussion had been established between the two women, and each of them had agreed that the expected De Troisville must be a gentleman between forty and forty-two years of age, a bachelor, neither rich nor poor. Mademoiselle saw herself Vicomtesse de Troisville.

"And my uncle who tells me nothing, who knows nothing, who inquires about nothing!— Oh! how much that is like my uncle! he would forget his nose if it were not attached to his face!"

Have you not observed that, under circumstances like these, the old maids become, like Richard III., intelligent, ferocious, courageous, promising, and, like tipsy clerks, no longer respect anything? The city of Alençon, informed in one moment from the upper end of the Rue Saint-Blaise to the gate of Séez, of this precipitous return, accompanied by grave circumstances, was immediately perturbed in all its viscera, public and domestic. The cooks, the tradespeople, the passers-by, carried this news from door to door; then it ascended into the higher regions. These words: "Mademoiselle Cormon has returned!" immediately burst like a bomb in every household. Jacquelin, at this moment, left the wooden bench, polished by a process unknown to the cabinetmakers, on which he had been seated, in the front of the carriole: he opened, himself, the great green gate, arched at the top, closed in sign of mourning, for, during the absence of Mademoiselle Cormon, the receptions did not take place. The faithful then alternately entertained the Abbé de Sponde. Monsieur de Valois paid his debt by inviting him to dinner at the house of the Marquis d'Esgrignon. Jacquelin called familiarly to Pénélope whom he had left standing in the middle of the street; the animal, accustomed to this proceeding, turned, of her own accord, passed through the gate, went round the court in such a manner as not to damage the flower bushes. Jacquelin resumed the bridle and led the carriage before the perron.

"Mariette!" cried Mademoiselle Cormon.

"Mademoiselle?" answered Mariette, who was occupied in closing the great gate.

"That gentleman has not come?"

"No, Mademoiselle."

"And my uncle?"

"Mademoiselle, he is at the church."

Jacquelin and Josette were at this moment standing on the first step of the perron and extending their hands to assist their mistress in descending from the carriage, she mounting on the shafts while holding on to the curtains. Mademoiselle threw herself into their arms; for, for the last two years, she had not been willing to risk herself on the iron step with a double joint, fixed in the shaft by a terrible arrangement with great iron pins.

When Mademoiselle Cormon was on the upper landing of the perron, she surveyed her courtyard with an air of satisfaction.

"Come, come, Mariette, leave the great gate and come here."

"There are great goings-on!" said Jacquelin to Mariette as the cook passed by the carriage.

"Now, my child, what provisions have you on hand?" said Mademoiselle Cormon, seating herself on the bench of the long antechamber, like a person exhausted with fatigue.

"Why, I have none at all," said Mariette, putting her fists on her hips. "Mademoiselle knows very well that, during her absence, Monsieur l'abbé always dines out; yesterday I went to get him at Mademoiselle Armande's."

"Where is he then?"

"Monsieur l'abbé? He is at church, he will not return before three o'clock."

"He thinks of nothing, my uncle! Could he not have told you to go to market? Mariette, go there now; without throwing away money, do not spare, get whatever there is that is nice, good and a delicacy. Go to inquire at the diligence office how you can get pâtés. I want some crawfish from the little streams of the Brillante. What o'clock is it?"

"Quarter to nine!"

"Mon Dieu! Mariette, do not lose any time gossiping! the gentleman expected by my uncle may arrive at any moment; if it became necessary to give him a déjeuner, we should be in a fine way!"

Mariette returned toward the sweating Pénélope, and looked at Jacquelin with an air which said: "Mademoiselle is going to put her hand on a husband this time."

"Now then, Josette, for our part," resumed the old maid "for we must see about Monsieur de Troisville's bed."

With what happiness this phrase was pronounced! *See about Monsieur de Troisville's*—pronounced Tréville's—*bed,* how many ideas in this word! The old maid was drowned in hope.

"Will you give him the green chamber?"

"That of Monseigneur the Bishop? No; it is too near mine," said Mademoiselle Cormon. "That will do for monseigneur, who is a holy man."

"Give him your uncle's apartment."

"It is so bare, that would be indecent."

"I know, Mademoiselle! we can set up in no time a bed in your boudoir, there is a fire-place there. Moreau can surely find in his store a bed that will match the chintz on the walls."

"You are right, Josette. Well, hurry to Moreau's; consult with him about everything that is necessary to be done, I authorize you. If the bed—the bed of Monsieur de Troisville!—can be set up this evening without Monsieur de Troisville perceiving it, in case Monsieur de Troisville should arrive here while Moreau is at work, I shall like it. If Moreau will not promise to do it, I will put Monsieur de Troisville in the green chamber, although Monsieur de Troisville will be there very near to me."

Josette went away, her mistress called her back.

"Explain everything to Jacquelin," she cried in a formidable voice and one full of fright; "let him go, himself, to Moreau's. My toilet! If I were surprised thus by Monsieur de Troisville, without my uncle to receive him!—Oh! my uncle, my uncle!—Come, Josette, you must dress me."

"But Pénélope?" said Josette, imprudently.

Mademoiselle Cormon's eyes flashed for the only time in her life:

"Always Pénélope! Pénélope here, Pénélope there! Is it Pénélope then who is the mistress?"

"But she is swimming in sweat and has not eaten her oats!"

"Well, let her burst!" exclaimed Mademoiselle Cormon;—"but let me get married," she thought.

On hearing this word, which appeared to her a homicide, Josette remained for a moment stupefied; then she flew down the perron at a gesture from her mistress.

"Mademoiselle has the devil in her, Jacquelin!" were Josette's first words.

Thus everything was in accord on this day to bring about the great dramatic stroke that decided the life of Mademoiselle Cormon. The city was already upside down in consequence of the five aggravating circumstances that had attended the sudden return of Mademoiselle Cormon, to wit: the driving rain; the gallop of Pénélope blown, sweating, and with hollow flanks; the early hour; the packages in disorder; and the singular appearance of the wild-looking spinster. But, when Mariette made her invasion of the public market to carry off everything from it, when Jacquelin came to the principal upholsterer of Alençon, Rue de la Porte-de-Séez, at two steps from the church, to get a bed, there was matter for the gravest conjectures. This strange adventure was discussed on the Cours, on the public promenade; it occupied everybody, and even Mademoiselle Armande, in whose house was the Chevalier de Valois. The city of Alençon had been agitated by such capital events, only two days apart, that some good women said: "Why, it is the end of the world!" This last piece of news was summed up in all the households by this phrase: "What has happened to the Cormons?" The Abbé de Sponde, questioned very adroitly when he came out from Saint-Léonard to go and promenade on the Cours with the Abbé Couturier, replied good-naturedly that he was expecting the Vicomte de Troisville, a gentleman who had been in the Russian service during the emigration, and who was returning to live in Alençon. From two o'clock to five, a species of labial telegraph was circulating through the city and apprising all the inhabitants that Mademoiselle Cormon had at last found a husband by correspondence, and that she was going to espouse the Vicomte de Troisville. Here it was said: "Moreau is already making the bed." There, the bed had six feet. The bed had four feet in the Rue du Bercail, at Madame Granson's. It was a simple couch at the Du Ronceret's where Du Bousquier was dining. The smaller bourgeoisie asserted that it cost eleven hundred francs. Generally, it was said that this *was selling the bear's skin.* Later, the price of carp had risen! Mariette had precipitated herself upon the market to sweep away everything. In the upper part of the Rue Saint-Blaise, Pénélope had foundered. This decease was put in doubt in the household of the receiver-general. Nevertheless, it was authentic at the préfecture that the animal had expired in entering the gate of the Hôtel Cormon, with such velocity had the old maid flown upon her prey. The saddler, who lived at the corner of the Rue de Séez, was hardy enough to come and ask if anything had happened to Mademoiselle Cormon's carriage, in order to see if Pénélope were dead. From the upper part of the Rue Saint-Blaise to the end of the Rue du Bercail, everyone learned that, thanks to Jacquelin's attentions, Pénélope, that silent victim of the intemperance of her mistress, was still living, but that she appeared to be suffering. On all the road to Brittany, the Vicomte de Troisville was a younger son without a sou, for the property of the Perche belonged to the Marquis de Troisville, peer of France, who had two children. This marriage was a piece of good fortune for the poor émigré, the viscount was just the thing for Mademoiselle Cormon; the aristocracy of the route to Brittany approved of the match, the old maid could not put her fortune to a better use. But, among the bourgeoisie, the Vicomte de Troisville was a Russian general who had fought against France, who was returning with a great fortune gained at the court of Saint-Petersburg; he was a *foreigner,* one of the *allies* held in hatred by the liberals. The Abbé de Sponde had secretly brought this marriage about. All those persons who enjoyed the privilege of entering Mademoiselle Cormon's house as they did their own, promised themselves to go and see her that evening. During all this transurban agitation, which almost caused Suzanne to be forgotten, Mademoiselle Cormon was not less agitated; she was experiencing entirely novel sentiments. When she surveyed her salon, her boudoir, the study, the dining-room, she was seized with a cruel apprehension. A species of demon called her attention sneeringly to all this ancient luxury; the handsome things which she had been admiring since her infancy were suspected, accused of being antiquated. In short, she was a victim of that fear which takes possession of almost all authors, at the moment they are reading a work which they think perfect to some critic, exacting or blasé;—the novel situations seem worn; the phrases the best turned, the most carefully licked, show themselves to be ambiguous or limping; the figures grin or contradict each other, the faults leap out and assert themselves. In the same manner the poor girl trembled to see upon the lips of Monsieur de Troisville a smile of disdain for this bishop's salon; she dreaded seeing him throw a cold glance upon this ancient dining-hall; in short, she feared that the frame would age the picture. If all these antiquities should throw a reflection of age upon her, herself? This question which she had put to herself, gave her gooseflesh. At this moment she would have given a quarter of all her savings to be able to renovate her house in an instant with the stroke of a fairy's wand. Who is the fatuous general who has not shivered on the eve of battle? The poor girl found herself between an Austerlitz and a Waterloo.

"Madame la Vicomtesse de Troisville," she said to herself, "what a fine name! Our property will at last go into a good family."

She was a prey to an irritation which made shudder her most delicate nervous fibres and their papillæ, so long smothered in fat. All her blood, whipped up by hope, was in movement. She felt herself strong enough to converse, if it were necessary, with Monsieur de Troisville. It is not necessary to speak of the activity with which were employed Josette, Jacquelin, Mariette, Moreau and his assistants. It was a hurrying of ants occupied with their eggs. Everything that a daily care rendered already so clean, was done over, brushed, washed, polished. The porcelains reserved for great days were brought to light. All the damask service, marked A, B, C, D, was drawn from the depths where it lay under a triple guard of wrappers defended by formidable lines of pins.

The most precious shelves of the library were interrogated. Finally, Mademoiselle sacrificed three bottles of the famous *liqueurs* of Madame Amphoux, the most illustrious of the distillers of beyond seas, a name dear to connoisseurs. Thanks to the devotion of her lieutenants, Mademoiselle Cormon was ready to present herself for the combat. All the different arms, the furniture, the artillery of the kitchen, the batteries of the pantry, the provisions, the munitions, the reserve corps, were ready all along the line. Jacquelin, Mariette and Josette received orders to appear on dress parade. The garden was raked over. The spinster regretted that she was not able to come to an agreement with the nightingales lodged in the trees in order to obtain from them their very best trills. Finally, about four o'clock, at the very moment when the Abbé de Sponde returned, when Mademoiselle was beginning to think that she had displayed her most coquettish table-service in vain, prepared the most delicate of dinners, the clic-clac of a postilion was heard in the Val-Noble.

"It is he!" she said to herself, receiving the strokes of the whip in her heart.

In fact, announced by so much tumult, a certain post cabriolet in which was seated a single man, had made so great a sensation in descending the Rue Saint-Blaise and turning the Rue du Cours, that some small boys and adult persons had followed it, and remained grouped around the door of the Hôtel Cormon to see its occupant enter. Jacquelin, who was on the scent also of his own marriage, had heard the clic-clac in the Rue Saint-Blaise, he had opened the great gate with double leaves. The postilion, who was one of his acquaintances, took pride in making a fine turn, and pulled up short at the perron. As for the postilion, you will understand that he went to be well and duly fuddled by Jacquelin. The abbé came to meet his guest, whose carriage was stripped with all the despatch which could have been exhibited by hurried robbers. It was put in the coach-house, the great gate was closed, and in a few minutes there was no trace of the arrival of Monsieur de Troisville. Never did two chemical substances unite with more promptitude than that with which the house of Cormon had absorbed the Vicomte de Troisville. Mademoiselle, whose heart was beating like that of a lizard caught by a herdsman, remained heroically seated on her couch, at the corner of the fire. Josette opened the door, and the Vicomte de Troisville, followed by the Abbé de Sponde, presented himself before the old maid.

"Niece, this is Monsieur le Vicomte de Troisville, the grandson of one of my friends at college.—Monsieur de Troisville, this is my niece, Mademoiselle Cormon."

"Ah! the good uncle, how well he puts the case!" thought Rose-Marie-Victoire.

The Vicomte de Troisville was, to describe him in two words, Du Bousquier well-bred. There was between them all the distance which separates the vulgar from the noble. If they had both been there, it would have been impossible for the most furious liberal to have denied aristocracy. The strength of the viscount had all the distinction of elegance; his form preserved a magnificent dignity; he had blue eyes and black hair, an olive complexion, and he did not appear to be older than forty-six. You would have said that he was a handsome Spaniard preserved in the ice of Russia. The manners, the walk, the attitude, everything announced a diplomat who had seen Europe. His dress was that of a man of the world when travelling. Monsieur de Troisville appeared to be fatigued, the abbé offered to have him shown to the chamber destined for him, and was stupefied when his niece opened the door of the boudoir transformed into a sleeping apartment. Mademoiselle Cormon and her uncle then left the noble stranger to arrange his affairs, with the aid of Jacquelin, who brought him all the baggage that he needed. The Abbé de Sponde and his niece went to promenade along the shores of the Brillante, while waiting for Monsieur de Troisville to finish his dressing. Although the abbé was, by a singular chance, more absent-minded than usual, Mademoiselle Cormon was no less preoccupied than he. Both of them walked along in silence. The maiden had never met a man so attractive as the Olympian Viscount. She could not say to herself in the German fashion: "There is my ideal!" but she felt herself taken possession of from head to foot, and she said to herself: "There is my affair!" Suddenly she flew to Mariette to learn if the dinner could be postponed a little without losing anything of its savor.

"Uncle, this Monsieur de Troisville is very agreeable," said she, on returning.

"But, my daughter, he has not yet said anything," replied the abbé, laughing.

"But that may be seen in his appearance, in his countenance. Is he a bachelor?"

"I know nothing about it," replied the abbé, who was thinking of a discussion upon Grace, on foot between the Abbé Couturier and himself. "Monsieur de Troisville wrote me that he wished to purchase a house here.—If he were married, he would not have come alone," he resumed with a careless air, for he did not admit that his niece could think of marriage.

"Is he rich?"

"He is the younger son of a younger branch," replied the uncle. "His grandfather had the command of squadrons; but the father of this young man made an unfortunate marriage."

"This young man!" repeated the old maid. "But it seems to me, uncle, that he is fully forty-five," she said, for she experienced a very great desire to compare their ages.

"Yes," said the abbé. "But to a poor priest of seventy, Rose, a man of forty appears young."

At this moment all Alençon knew that Monsieur le Vicomte de Troisville had arrived at Mademoiselle Cormon's house. The stranger presently rejoined his hosts, and began to admire the view of the Brillante, the garden and the house.

"Monsieur l'abbé," said be, "all my ambition would be to find a house similar to this."

The spinster wished to see a declaration in these words, and lowered her eyes.

"You should be very well satisfied with it, Mademoiselle?" resumed the Viscount.

"How should I not be satisfied with it! it has been in our family since the year 1574, the date at which one of our ancestors, intendant of the Duc d'Alençon, acquired this land and had it built," said Mademoiselle Cormon. "It is on piles."

Jacquelin having announced dinner, Monsieur de Troisville offered his arm to the happy maid, who endeavored not to lean upon it too strongly, she still feared so much to appear to be making advances!

"Everything here is in excellent harmony," said the viscount, seating himself at table.

"Our trees are full of birds which furnish us music very cheaply; no one disturbs them, and every night the nightingale sings," said Mademoiselle Cormon.

"I was speaking of the interior of the house," observed the viscount, who had not taken the trouble to study Mademoiselle Cormon and had not in the least recognized her lack of intelligence. "Yes, everything here is in harmony—*en rapport*—, the tones of the colors, the furniture, the general appearance."

"Nevertheless, it costs us a good deal, the taxes are very heavy," replied the excellent spinster, struck by the word *rapport*—returns, profits.

"Ah! the taxes are high here?" asked the viscount who, preoccupied by his own thoughts, did not notice the lack of sequence.

"I do not know," answered the abbé. "My niece has charge of the administration of our two fortunes."

"The taxes are mere trifles for those who are wealthy," resumed Mademoiselle Cormon who did not wish to appear avaricious. "As to the furniture, I will leave it as it is and will change nothing—unless I should marry: for then it would be necessary that everything here should be according to the taste of the master."

"Your principles are of the highest, Mademoiselle," said the viscount, smiling, "you will make a happy—"

"Never did anyone say anything so charming to me," thought the spinster.

The viscount complimented her on the service, on the management of the household, avowing that he had thought the province backward, and that he found it very comfortable.

"Whatever can that word mean, *bon Dieu?*" thought she. "Where is the Chevalier de Valois to reply to it? Comfortable! Are there several words in one? Come, courage," she said to herself, "it is perhaps a Russian word, I am not obliged to reply to it.—But," she went on aloud, feeling her tongue unloosened by the eloquence which almost all human creatures find in capital circumstances, "Monsieur, we have the most brilliant society here. It is in my house that the whole city has its reunions. You will be able to judge immediately, for some of our faithful friends have doubtless heard of my return, and will come to call on me. We have the Chevalier de Valois, a seigneur of the old court, a man of infinite wit and taste; then Monsieur le Marquis d'Esgrignon and Mademoiselle Armande, his sister—she bit her tongue here and changed her course;—a lady remarkable in her kind," she added. "She has resolved to remain unmarried so as to leave her entire fortune to her brother and her nephew."

"Ah!" said the viscount, "yes, the D'Esgrignons, I remember them."

"Alençon is very gay," resumed the maiden, now fairly launched. "There is a good deal of amusement, the receiver-general gives balls, the prefect is an agreeable man, Monseigneur the Bishop honors us sometimes with his visits—"

"Well, then," replied the viscount, smiling, "I have then done well in wishing to return, like the hare—*lievre,*—to die at home."

"I also," said she, "I am like the *lievre*—I will die where I am attached."

The viscount took the proverb thus rendered for a jest, and smiled.

"Ah!" said the spinster to herself, "everything is going well, he comprehends me, this one does!"

The conversation maintained itself on generalities. By one of those mysterious powers, unknown, indefinable, Mademoiselle Cormon found again in her brain, under the pressure of her desire to be agreeable, all the turnings of phrases of the Chevalier de Valois. It was like a duel, in which the devil himself seems to set the barrel of the pistol. Never was an adversary more fairly aimed at. The Vicomte de Troisville was too much a man of society to speak of the excellence of the dinner; but his silence was a eulogy. In drinking the excellent wines which were served him profusely by Jacquelin, he seemed to recognize friends and to find them again with a lively pleasure, for the veritable connoisseur does not applaud, he enjoys. He asked with some curiosity as to the price of land, houses, and sites; he caused Mademoiselle Cormon to give him a long description of the locality at the confluence of the Brillante and the Sarthe. He was surprised that the city was situated so far from the river; the topography of the country interested him greatly. The silent abbé allowed his niece to engross the conversation. Truly, Mademoiselle believed that she entertained Monsieur de Troisville, who smiled upon her graciously, and who made much more progress during this dinner than her most eager suitors had ever made in two weeks. Also, you may rely upon it that never was guest more covered with little cares, more enveloped in attentions. You would have said that it was a cherished lover, returned to the household of which he was the happiness. Mademoiselle foresaw the moment when the viscount would want some bread, she kept him constantly under observation; when he turned his head she supplied him adroitly with more of the dishes which he seemed to like; she would have stuffed him to bursting if he had been a gourmand; but what a delicious sample was not this of that which she counted upon doing for love! She did not commit the stupidity of depreciating herself, she set all her sails bravely, hoisted all her flags, posed as the queen of Alençon and praised her own confitures. In short, she fished for compliments, in speaking of herself, as if all her trumpeters were dead. She perceived that she pleased the viscount, for her desire had so well transformed her that she had become almost a woman. At the dessert, she heard, not without an inward ravishment, the comings and goings in the antechamber and the noises in the salon which announced that her habitual company was arriving. She caused her uncle and Monsieur de Troisville to remark in this zealousness a testimony of the general affection in which she was held, whereas it was only the effect of the burning curiosity which had taken possession of the entire city. Impatient to display herself in her glory, Mademoiselle Cormon directed Jacquelin to serve the coffee and the liqueurs in the salon, where the domestic went to display before the élite of the society the magnificence of a service of Dresden ware that issued from its cabinet only twice a year. All these circumstances were observed by all the company, in a mood to comment upon the slightest indication.

"Peste!" said Du Bousquier, "nothing but the liqueurs of Madame Amphoux, which are served only at the four high festivals!"

"It is evidently a marriage arranged a year ago by correspondence," said Monsieur le Président du Ronceret. "The postmaster has been receiving here, for the last year, letters stamped Odessa."

Madame Granson shuddered. Monsieur le Chevalier de Valois, although he had dined for four, pale even to the sinister side of his countenance, felt that he was about to betray his secret and said:

"Do you not think that it is cold to-day? I am frozen."

"It is the vicinity of Russia," said Du Bousquier.

The chevalier looked at him with an air which seemed to say: "Well done."

Mademoiselle Cormon appeared so radiant, so triumphant, that she was thought beautiful. This extraordinary brilliancy was not entirely due to feeling; all the blood in her body had been agitated since the morning, and her nerves were thrilling with the presentiment of a great crisis,—it required all these circumstances to enable her to resemble herself so little. With what happiness did she not make the solemn presentation of the viscount to the chevalier, of the chevalier to the viscount, of all Alençon to Monsieur de Troisville, of Monsieur de Troisville to those of Alençon! By a chance sufficiently explicable, the viscount and the chevalier, those two aristocratic natures, immediately met in unison; they recognized each other, and both of them considered themselves as men of the same sphere. They began to converse together, standing before the fireplace. A circle formed around them, and their conversation, although carried on *sotto voce,* was listened to in a religious silence. In order to have a just idea of this scene, it will be necessary to imagine Mademoiselle Cormon occupied in making the coffee of her pretended pretender, her back toward the chimney-piece.

MONSIEUR DE VALOIS.

"Monsieur le vicomte is about, it is said, to establish himself here?"

MONSIEUR DE TROISVILLE.

"Yes, monsieur, I am come here to look for a house"—Mademoiselle Cormon turns, a cup in her hand.—"And I require a large one, for"—Mademoiselle Cormon offers the cup—"my family."—*The eyes of the old maid grow dim.—*

MONSIEUR DE VALOIS.

"You are married?"

MONSIEUR DE TROISVILLE.

"For the last sixteen years, to the daughter of the Princess Sherbellof."

Mademoiselle Cormon fell, thunderstruck.—Du Bousquier, who saw her stagger, sprang forward, caught her in his arms, and the door was opened that he might pass through with this enormous burden. The fiery Republican, counselled by Josette, found strength to carry the spinster into her chamber, where he deposited her on her bed. Josette, armed with a pair of scissors, cut the corset lacings, tightened outrageously. Du Bousquier brutally threw drops of water upon the face of Mademoiselle Cormon and upon the corsage, which overflowed like an inundation of the Loire. The invalid opened her eyes, saw Du Bousquier, and modesty caused her to utter a cry in recognizing this man. Du Bousquier retired, allowing six women to enter, at the head of whom was Madame Granson, radiant with joy. What had the Chevalier de Valois done? Faithful to his system, he had covered the retreat.

"That poor Mademoiselle Cormon," said he to Monsieur de Troisville while looking over the assembly whose laughter was suppressed by his aristocratic glance, "is terribly troubled by fulness of blood; she was not willing to be bled before going to the Prébaudet—her country place—, and this is the effect of the turbulence of the blood in the spring of the year."

"She came in this morning in the rain," said the Abbé de Sponde, "she may have caught a little cold which has caused this little upsetting, to which she is subject. But it will not amount to anything."

"She said to me the day before yesterday that she had not had one for three months, adding that this would play her an ill trick some day," resumed the chevalier.

"Ah! you are married!" thought Jacquelin, looking at Monsieur de Troisville, who was drinking his coffee in little sips.

The faithful domestic shared the disappointment of his mistress, he understood her, he carried away the liqueurs of Madame Amphoux, offered to a bachelor but not to the husband of a Russian lady. All these little details were remarked, and furnished food for laughter. The Abbé de Sponde had known the motive of Monsieur de Troisville's journey, but, as one result of his distraction, he had said nothing about it, not knowing that his niece could conceive the slightest interest in Monsieur de Troisville. As to the viscount, preoccupied with the object of his journey, and, like a great many husbands, with but little zeal in speaking of his wife, he had not had any opportunity to declare himself married; moreover, he believed Mademoiselle Cormon informed of that fact. Du Bousquier reappeared and was questioned desperately. One of the six women descended and announced that Mademoiselle Cormon was much better, and that her doctor had arrived; but she must remain in bed, it appeared to be urgently necessary to bleed her. The salon was presently full. The absence of Mademoiselle Cormon permitted the ladies to entertain themselves with the tragi-comic scene, extended, commented upon, embellished, enriched, embroidered, festooned, colored, decorated, which had taken place and which on the morrow would occupy all Alençon with Mademoiselle Cormon.

"That good Monsieur du Bousquier, how he carried you! What a grasp!" said Josette to her mistress. "Truly, he was pale because of your trouble, he loves you still."

This phrase served to close this solemn and terrible day.

The next day, during the entire morning, the most minute circumstances of this comedy were retailed through all the houses of Alençon, and, let us say it to the shame of this city, they gave rise to universal laughter. The next day, Mademoiselle Cormon, whom the bleeding had much benefited, would have appeared sublime to the most abandoned laughers if they had been witnesses of the noble dignity, the sublime Christian resignation which animated her when she took the arm of her involuntary mystifier to go to déjeuner. Cruel jokers, who mocked at her, why did you not hear her saying to the viscount:

"Madame de Troisville will find it difficult to secure an apartment here which will suit her; do me the kindness, monsieur, to accept the use of my house during the entire time that you may require to arrange one in the city."

"But, mademoiselle, I have two daughters and two boys, we should inconvenience you greatly."

"Do not refuse me," she said, with a look full of contrition.

"I offered it to you in the answer which I sent you at a venture," said the abbé, "but you did not receive it."

"What! uncle, you knew?—"

The poor girl stopped short. Josette smiled. Neither the Vicomte de Troisville nor the uncle saw anything. After the déjeuner, the Abbé de Sponde took away the viscount, as had been agreed the evening before, to show him in Alençon the houses which he could acquire or the sites suitable for building.

Left alone in the salon, Mademoiselle Cormon said to Josette with a lamentable air:

"My child, I am at this moment the jest of the whole city."

"Well, Mademoiselle, get married!"

"But, my girl, I am not at all prepared to make a choice."

"Bah! if I were in your place, I would take Monsieur du Bousquier."

"Josette, Monsieur de Valois says that he is so republican!"

"They do not know what they are saying, your messieurs,—they pretend that he robbed the Republic, he did not then love it very much," said Josette as she went away.

"That girl has an astonishing wit," thought Mademoiselle Cormon, left alone, a prey to her perplexities.

She felt that a prompt marriage would be the only method of imposing silence on the city. This last check, so evidently mortifying, was of a nature to cause her to take an extreme course, for those who have but little intelligence find it difficult to issue from the paths, good or bad, in which they have become involved. Each of the two old bachelors had comprehended the situation in which Mademoiselle must find herself;—therefore each of them had resolved to go in the morning to inquire after her and, in the language of bachelors, *urge his point.* Monsieur de Valois judged that the circumstances required a most particular toilet, he took a bath, he adorned himself extraordinarily. For the first and the last time, Césarine saw him putting on with incredible skill the slightest touch of rouge. Du Bousquier, he, that gross Republican, animated by an active will, did not pay the least attention to his toilet, he hastened there the first. These little things decide the fortunes of men, as of empires. The charge of Kellermann at Marengo, the arrival of Blücher at Waterloo, the contempt of Louis XIV. for Prince Eugène, the Curé of Denain, all these great causes of fortunes or catastrophes, history enregisters; but no one profits by these lessons to take care to neglect nothing in the little details of his own life. Thus, see what happens! The Duchesse de Langeais—see the *History of the Thirteen*—turned nun for not having had ten minutes' patience; the Judge Popinot—see *The Interdiction*—postponed till the next day going to interrogate the Marquis d'Espard; Charles Grandet returned by way of Bordeaux instead of returning by way of Nantes,—and these events are called chances, fatalities! A suspicion of rouge to be applied killed the hopes of the Chevalier de Valois, this gentleman could perish only in this manner,—he had lived by the Graces, he should die by their hand. Whilst the chevalier was giving a last glance at his toilet, the gross Du Bousquier entered the salon of the desolated maid. This entrance came in combination with some considerations favorable to the Republican, traversing a deliberation in which the chevalier had, nevertheless, all the advantages.

"God wills it," said the old maid to herself when she saw Du Bousquier.

"Mademoiselle, you will not take my zeal amiss! I did not wish to trust to that great animal of a Réné to get news of you, and I have come myself."

"I am getting on perfectly well," she replied in a voice that betrayed emotion. "I thank you, Monsieur du Bousquier," she said after a pause and in an agitated voice, "for the trouble which you took and which I gave you yesterday—"

She remembered having been in Du Bousquier's arms, and this chance above all appeared to her to be a command from Heaven. She had been seen for the first time by a man, her girdle broken, her laces cut, her treasures violently thrust from their casket.

"I carried you with so willing a heart that I found you light."

Here, Mademoiselle Cormon looked at Du Bousquier as she had never yet looked at any man in the world. Much encouraged, the ex-contractor threw upon the spinster a glance that reached her heart.

"It is unfortunate," he added, "that that has not given me the right to guard you always for myself."—She listened with a ravished air.—"Fainting, there, on that bed, between us, you were dazzling; I have never seen in my life any one more beautiful, and I have seen a great many women!—The plump women have this advantage, that they are superb to see, they have only to show themselves, and they triumph!"

"You are mocking me," said the maid, "and that is not well when the whole city is perhaps putting an evil interpretation on that which happened to me yesterday."

"As true as my name is Du Bousquier, Mademoiselle, I have never changed my sentiments toward you, and your first refusal did not discourage me."

The old maid had lowered her eyes. There was a moment of silence cruel for Du Bousquier. But Mademoiselle Cormon took her decision, she lifted her eyelids, the tears trembled in her eyes, she looked at Du Bousquier tenderly.

"If that is true, monsieur," said she in a trembling voice, "permit me only to live a Christian life, never interfere with my religious habits, with my free choice of my spiritual directors, and I will give you my hand," said she, offering it to him.

Du Bousquier seized this good fat hand full of écus, and kissed it worshipfully.

"But," said Mademoiselle Cormon while allowing him to kiss her hand, "I ask one thing more."

"It is granted, and, if it is impossible, it shall be done"—a reminiscence of Beaujon.

"Alas!" resumed the old maid, "for the love of me, it is necessary for you to assume a sin which I know is very great, for falsehood is one of the seven capital sins; but you will confess it, will you not? We will both of us do penance"—They looked at each other tenderly.—"Moreover, perhaps it falls among those falsehoods which the Church calls officious—"

"Will she be like Suzanne?" thought Du Bousquier. "What good fortune!—Well, Mademoiselle?" said he aloud.

"It is necessary," she went on, "that you should take upon yourself—"

"What?"

"To say that this marriage has been arranged between us for the last six months—"

"Charming woman," said the ex-contractor, with the tone of a man who devotes himself, "these sacrifices are made only for a creature adored for ten years."

"Notwithstanding my severity, then?" she said to him.

"Yes, notwithstanding your severity."

"Monsieur du Bousquier, I have misjudged you."

She extended to him again her great red hand, which Du Bousquier kissed anew.

At that moment the door opened, the two fiancés looked to see who entered, and they perceived the delightful but tardy Chevalier de Valois.

"Ah!" said be entering, "you are then up, beautiful queen."

She smiled on the chevalier, and felt a pressure at her heart. Monsieur de Valois, remarkably young-looking and attractive, had the air of a Lauzun entering the apartments of Mademoiselle in the Palais-Royal.

"Eh! dear Du Bousquier," said he in a tone of raillery, so sure did he feel of success, "Monsieur de Troisville and the Abbé de Sponde are examining your house like a couple of surveyors."

"Upon my word," said Du Bousquier, "if the Vicomte de Troisville wants it, it is his for forty thousand francs. It has become of very little use to me!—If Mademoiselle will permit me?—It is necessary that this should be known—Mademoiselle, may I speak?—Yes?—Very well then, be the first, *my dear chevalier,* whom I inform"—Mademoiselle Cormon lowered her eyes—"of the honor," said the former contractor, "of the favor which Mademoiselle has done me, and of which I have kept the secret for more than six months. We shall be married in a few days, the contract is drawn up, we shall sign it to-morrow. You will understand that my house in the Rue du Cygne has become of but little use to me. I have been looking privately for a purchaser, and the Abbé de Sponde, *who knew of it,* has naturally conducted Monsieur de Troisville to it."

This great lie had such a coloring of truth that the chevalier was deceived by it. *My dear chevalier* was like the revenge taken by Peter the Great on Charles XII. at Pultowa for all his previous defeats. Du Bousquier thus avenged himself delightfully for a thousand little shafts which he had received in silence; but, in his triumph, he made a young man's gesture, he passed his hand through his small wig, and—he lifted it.

"I congratulate you both," said the chevalier with an agreeable air, "and I hope that you may end like the fairy stories: *They were very happy and had very* MANY CHILDREN!"

And he took a pinch of snuff.

"But, monsieur, you forget that—you wear a wig," he added mockingly.

Du Bousquier reddened, he had the wig ten inches from his skull. Mademoiselle Cormon lifted her eyes, saw the nudity of the skull and lowered her eyes through modesty. Du Bousquier threw upon the chevalier the most venomous glance that ever a toad shot at its prey.

"Scum of aristocrats who have despised me, I will crush you some day!" he thought.

The Chevalier de Valois felt that he had resumed all his advantages. But Mademoiselle Cormon was not the woman to comprehend the connection which the chevalier had made between his good wishes and the wig; moreover, had she comprehended, her hand no longer was at her own disposal. Monsieur de Valois perceived immediately that everything was lost. The innocent spinster, seeing these two men mute, wished to occupy them.

"Why do you not play piquet, both of you?" she said without any malice.

Du Bousquier smiled, and went, like the future master of the house, to get the piquet table. The Chevalier de Valois, whether because he had lost his head, or because he wished to remain there to study the causes of his disaster and to remedy it, allowed himself to be conducted, like a sheep led to the butcher's. He had received the most stunning blow that a man could experience, and a gentleman might well be at least bewildered. Presently the worthy Abbé de Sponde and the Vicomte de Troisville returned. Mademoiselle Cormon immediately rose, hastened into the antechamber, took her uncle to one side and confided to him her resolution. On learning that the house in the Rue du Cygne suited Monsieur de Troisville, she requested her future husband to do her the favor to say that her uncle knew that it was for sale. She did not dare to confide this falsehood to the abbé, through fear of some forgetfulness on his part. The lie prospered better than if it had been a virtuous action. In the course of the evening, all Alençon heard the great news. For the last four days the city had been agitated as in the disastrous days of 1814 and 1815. Some laughed, others accepted the marriage, these blamed it, those approved of it. The middle classes were happy over it, they saw in it a victory. The next day, in the houses of his friends, the Chevalier de Valois uttered this cruel speech:

"The Cormons are ending as they began; from intendant to contractor, it is all in the same line!"

The news of the choice made by Mademoiselle Cormon struck the poor Athanase to the heart, but he allowed to appear none of the terrible agitation to which he was a prey. When he heard of the marriage, he was in the house of the Président du Ronceret, where his mother was engaged at a game of boston. Madame Granson looked at her son in a mirror, she saw that he was very pale; but he had been so since the morning, for he had heard rumors of this marriage. Mademoiselle Cormon had been a card upon which Athanase had staked his life, and the chill presentiment of a catastrophe already enveloped him. When the soul and the imagination have aggrandized the misfortune, making of it a burden too heavy for the shoulders and for the brow; when a hope that has been long cherished, the realization of which would appease the insatiable vulture that devours the heart, finally fails, and when man has neither faith in himself, notwithstanding his strength, nor in the future, notwithstanding the divine power,—then he breaks. Athanase was one of the fruits of the Imperial education. Fatality, that religion of the Emperor, descended from the throne to the last ranks in the army, to the benches of the colleges. Athanase fixed his eyes upon Madame du Ronceret's cards in a stupor which might so readily pass for indifference, that Madame Granson thought she had been mistaken with regard to her son's sentiments.

MLLE. CORMON, DE VALOIS, AND DU BOUSQUIER

This great lie had such a coloring of truth that the chevalier was deceived by it. *My dear chevalier* was like the revenge taken by Peter the Great on Charles XII. at Pultowa for all his previous defeats. Du Bousquier thus avenged himself delightfully for a thousand little shafts which he had received in silence; but, in his triumph, he made a young man's gesture, he passed his hand through his small wig, and—he lifted it.

The apparent carelessness of Athanase explained his refusal to make for this marriage the sacrifice of his *liberal* opinions, an adjective which had been created for the Emperor Alexander, and which proceeded, I believe, from Madame de Staël by way of Benjamin Constant. Dating from this fatal evening, the unfortunate young man acquired the habit of going to walk in the most picturesque locality along the Sarthe, on one of the banks where the artists, who sketch Alençon, place themselves to secure the most favorable points of view. There are mills there. The river embellishes the meadows. The shores of the Sarthe are ornamented with trees handsome in form and well located. If the landscape be flat, it is not wanting in the sober graces which distinguish France, where the eye is neither fatigued by an Oriental sunlight nor saddened by too constant mists. This locality was a solitary one. In the provinces, no one pays any attention to a pretty view, either because everyone is blasé, or because there is no poetry in the souls. If there is to be found in the provinces a Mall, a plain, a promenade from which a rich and extended view may be had, that is the locality to which no one goes. Athanase had an affection for this solitude animated only by the river, where the meadows grew green again under the first smiles of the spring sun. Those who saw him seated there under a poplar and at whom he looked with his deep glance, said sometimes to Madame Granson:

"There is something troubling your son."

"I know what he is doing!" replied the mother, with a satisfied air, giving it to be understood that he was meditating a great work.

Athanase no longer interfered in political affairs, he no longer had any opinions; but he appeared on several occasions to be sufficiently gay, ironically gay, like those who insult in their single person a whole world. This young man, who kept himself outside of all the ideas, of all the pleasures of the province, interested very few people, he was not even an object of curiosity. If any one spoke of him to his mother, it was for her sake. There was not one soul that sympathized with that of Athanase; not a woman, not a friend, came to him to dry his tears, he dropped them in the Sarthe. If the magnificent Suzanne had passed that way, how many misfortunes would not have been prevented by this meeting, for these two creatures would have loved each other! She did come, however. Suzanne's ambition had been excited by the recital of an incident, sufficiently extraordinary in itself, which, about 1799, had commenced at the inn of the *More,* and the hearing of which had produced the greatest effect in her childish brain. A girl from Paris, as beautiful as an angel, had been commissioned by the police to win the affections of the Marquis de Montauran, one of the leaders sent by the Bourbons to take command of the Chouans; she had met him at the inn of the *More* on his return from his expedition to Mortagne,—she had seduced him and had delivered him up. This curious woman, this power of beauty over man, everything in the affair of Marie de Verneuil and the Marquis de Montauran, had dazzled Suzanne; from the day on which she attained the age of reason she was possessed by the desire to amuse herself with men. Some months after her flight, she then did not refuse to pass through her native city with an artist on their way to Brittany. She wished to see Fougères, where had taken place the dénoûment of the adventure of the Marquis de Montauran, and to traverse the theatre of this picturesque war, the tragedies of which, still but little known, had entertained her childish days. Then she wished to pass through Alençon with such brilliant surroundings and so completely metamorphosed that no one would recognize her. She counted upon providing for her mother, so as to place her beyond the reach of want, in a moment, and on delicately sending to the poor Athanase those funds which, in our age, are for genius that which was, in mediæval times, the armor and the war-horse which Rebecca procured for Ivanhoe.

A month passed away in the strangest alternatives relative to the marriage of Mademoiselle Cormon. There was a party of the incredulous who denied the marriage, and a party of believers who affirmed it. At the expiration of two weeks the party of the incredulous received a serious blow,—the house of Du Bousquier was sold for forty-three thousand francs to Monsieur de Troisville, who desired only a very simple house in Alençon; his intentions were to go to Paris later, after the death of the Princess Sherbellof,—he planned to wait peacefully for this heritage while occupying himself with the reëstablishment of his estate. This seemed to be positive. The incredulous did not allow themselves to be crushed. They pretended that, married or not, Du Bousquier had made an excellent bargain; his house had cost him only twenty-seven thousand francs. The believers were demoralized by this very direct statement of the incredulous. Choisnel, Mademoiselle Cormon's notary, had not yet heard the first word spoken relative to the marriage contract, said the incredulous again. The believers, firm in their faith, won on the twentieth day a signal victory over the incredulous. Monsieur Lepressoir, the notary of the liberals, came to Mademoiselle Cormon's house, where the contract was signed. This was the first of the numerous sacrifices which Mademoiselle Cormon was to make to her husband. Du Bousquier bore a profound hatred to Choisnel; he attributed to him the first refusal which he had received from Mademoiselle Armande, and the refusal of Mademoiselle Armande had, as he thought, brought about that of Mademoiselle Cormon. The former athlete of the Directory so ingratiated himself with the noble maiden, who thought that she had misjudged the fine soul of the ex-contractor, that she wished to expiate all her errors,—she sacrificed her notary to love! Nevertheless, she communicated the terms of the contract to him, and Choisnel, who was a man worthy of Plutarch, defended her interests in writing. This circumstance alone delayed the marriage. Mademoiselle Cormon received several anonymous letters. She learned, to her great astonishment, that Suzanne had been a girl as virginal as she could be herself, and that the seducer in the wig would never count for anything in similar adventures. Mademoiselle Cormon disdained anonymous letters; but she wrote to Suzanne, with the object of explaining the creed of the Maternal Society. Suzanne, who had doubtless heard of the future marriage of Du Bousquier, admitted her trick, sent a thousand francs to the association, and did an ill turn to the ex-contractor. Mademoiselle Cormon convoked the Maternal Society, which held an extraordinary sitting, and there was issued a decree making it known that the bureau would no longer succor the unfortunate about to fall, but only those who had fallen. Notwithstanding these underhand proceedings, which entertained the city with scandals distilled with every seasoning, the banns were published at the church and at the mayor's office. Athanase had to prepare the deeds. As a measure of public decency and general security, the fiancée went to the Prébaudet, where Du Bousquier, flanked by atrocious and sumptuous bouquets, presented himself in the morning and returned in the evening for dinner. Finally, on a rainy and melancholy day of June, at noon, the marriage between Mademoiselle Cormon and the Sieur du Bousquier, said the incredulous, was solemnized in the parish-church of Alençon, in the sight of all Alençon. The married couple went from their house to the mayor's, from the mayor's to the church, in a calèche, magnificent for Alençon, which Du

Bousquier had had secretly brought from Paris. The loss of the old carriole was, in the eyes of the whole city, a species of calamity. The saddler of the gate of Séez uttered piercing cries for he lost fifty francs of income which the repairs had brought him. Alençon saw with affright, luxury introduced into the city by the house of Cormon. Everyone feared an increase in the price of commodities, an augmentation in rents and the invasion of Parisian furniture. There were persons sufficiently pricked by their curiosity to give various ten sous to Jacquelin in order to be able to inspect more closely the caliche prejudicial to the economy of the country. The two horses purchased in Normandy also terrified greatly.

"If we buy our horses in this manner ourselves," said the society of the Roncerets, "we shall no longer sell them to those who come for them."

Although stupid, the reasoning appeared to be profound, in that it would prevent the country from securing money from strangers. For the provinces, the wealth of nations consists less in the active circulation of money than in a sterile heaping up. Finally, the murderous prophecy of the spinster was accomplished. Pénélope succumbed to the pleurisy with which she had been attacked forty days before the marriage, nothing could save her. Madame Granson, Mariette, Madame du Coudrai, Madame du Ronceret, the whole city, remarked that Madame du Bousquier had entered the church with *the left foot first!* a presage all the more horrible that already the phrase, *the Left,* had taken on a political significance. The priest who was to read the service opened the book by chance at the *De profundis.* Thus this marriage was accompanied by circumstances so fatal, so stormy, so overwhelming, that no one augured well of it. Everything went from bad to worse. There was no wedding festival, for the newly-married pair set out for the Prébaudet. Parisian customs were then to triumph over provincial customs! it was said. In the evening, Alençon commented upon all these idiocies; and there was a sufficiently general abandonment of restraint on the part of those who had counted upon one of those weddings of Gamache which are constantly taking place in the provinces, and which society considers as its due. The wedding of Mariette and of Jacquelin went off gayly,—they were the only two persons who contradicted the sinister prophecies.

Du Bousquier wished to employ the money he had made on his own house in restoring and modernizing the Hôtel Cormon. He had decided to pass two seasons at the Prébaudet, and conveyed thither his uncle De Sponde. This news spread terror in the city, where everyone foresaw that Du Bousquier was going to drag the country into the evil ways of comfort. This fear augmented when the inhabitants of the city perceived, one morning, Du Bousquier coming from the Prébaudet to the Val-Noble, for the purpose of overseeing the work, in a tilbury drawn by a new horse, having at his side René in livery. The first act of his administration had been to place all his wife's savings in Rentes, on the register of creditors of the state, which were at 67 francs, 50 centimes. In the space of a year, during which he constantly operated on a rising market, he had acquired a personal fortune almost as considerable as that of his wife. But these thunderous presages, these perturbing innovations, were exceeded by an event which was connected with this marriage, and which made it appear even more fatal. The very evening of the celebration, Athanase and his mother were seated, after their dinner, before a little fire of fagots, called *régalades,* and which the servant maid lit at dessert in the salon.

"Well, we will go this evening to the Président du Ronceret's, since we are without Mademoiselle Cormon," said Madame Granson. *"Mon Dieu!* I shall never become accustomed to calling her Madame du Bousquier, that name tears my lips."

Athanase looked at his mother with a melancholy and constrained air, he could no longer smile, and he wished, as it were, to recognize this ingenuous thought which soothed his wound without curing it.

"Mama," said he, resuming his childish voice, so soft was it, in resuming the childish word dropped for several years past; "my dear mama, do not let us go out yet, it is so pleasant here, before this fire!"

The mother heard without comprehending this supreme prayer of a mortal sorrow.

"Let us stay, my child," said she. "I certainly like better to talk with you, to listen to your projects, than to play a boston in which I may lose my money."

"You are beautiful this evening, I love to look at you. Then, moreover, I am in a train of thought which harmonizes with this poor little salon in which we have suffered so much."

"In which we shall suffer more, my poor Athanase, until your works succeed. For my part, I am made for poverty; but you, my treasure, to see your beautiful youth pass without any pleasure! with nothing but work in your life!

This thought is a suffering for a mother,—it torments me in the evening, and in the morning it wakes me. *Mon Dieu! Mon Dieu!* what have I done to Thee? for what crime dost Thou punish me?"

She left her sofa, took a little chair and embraced Athanase tightly, in such a manner as to bring her head on her son's chest. There is always grace in the love of a true motherhood. Athanase kissed his mother on her eyes, on her gray hair, on her forehead, with the sacred wish to place his soul wherever he placed his lips.

"I shall never succeed!" said he, endeavoring to deceive his mother regarding the fatal resolution which he was maturing in his brain.

"Bah! are you not discouraging yourself? As you say, thought is capable of everything. With ten bottles of ink, ten reams of paper and his strong will, Luther overturned Europe. Well, you will make yourself illustrious, and you will do good with the same means with which he did evil. Did you not say that? As for me, I listen to you, do you know it,—I understand you better than you think I do, for I carry you still in my womb, and the least of your thoughts I feel there as formerly I did the slightest of your movements."

"I shall not succeed here, indeed, mama; and I do not wish you to see the spectacle of my torments, of my struggles, of my anguish. Ah! mother, let me leave Alençon; I wish to go to suffer far away from you."

"I wish to be always at your side, I do," said the mother proudly. "Suffer without your mother, your poor mother who will be your servant if necessary, who will conceal herself so as not to injure you, if you ask it, your mother who will not then accuse you of pride? No, no, Athanase, we will never separate."

Athanase embraced his mother with the ardor of a dying man who embraces life.

"I wish it, however," he went on. "Without that, you will ruin me.— This double pain, yours and mine, will kill me. It would be better that I should live, would it not?"

Madame Granson looked at her son with a haggard eye.

"This is then what you were brooding over! They were right when they told me of it. Then you must go away."

"Yes."

"You will not depart without telling me everything, without giving me warning. You must have a wardrobe, some money. I have some louis sewed in my under petticoat, I must give them to you."

Athanase wept.

"That is all that I wished to say to you," he said. "Now I will conduct you to the president's. Let us go—"

The mother and son went out. Athanase left his mother on the steps of the door of the house in which she was going to pass the evening. He looked a long time at the light which escaped through the chinks of the shutters; he flattened himself against them, he experienced the most frenzied of joys when, at the expiration of a quarter of an hour, he heard his mother saying:

"Great independence in hearts!"

"Poor mother, I have deceived her!" he exclaimed as he reached the banks of the Sarthe.

He arrived before the fine poplar under which he had meditated so much during the last forty days, and to which he had brought two large stones for a seat. He contemplated this beautiful nature, then illuminated by the moon, he saw again in a few hours all his future of glory,—he passed through cities agitated by his name; he heard the applause of the crowd; he breathed the incense of fêtes, he adored all his life seen in vision, he mounted radiant through radiant triumphs, he set up his statue, he evoked all his illusions to say adieu to them in a last Olympian banquet. This magic had been possible for a moment; now, it was flown forever. In this supreme moment he clasped his beautiful tree, to which he had become attached as to a friend; then he put the two stones in the two pockets of his coat and buttoned it. He had come out purposely without a hat. He went to see again the deep spot which he had long before selected; he slid into it resolutely, endeavoring to make no noise, and he made very little. When, about half-past nine, Madame Granson returned home, her maid said nothing to her of Athanase, she handed her a letter; Madame Granson opened it and read these few words:

"My good mother, I have gone, do not be vexed with me!"

"He has done a fine thing!" she cried. "And his linen! and the money! He will write to me, I will go to find him. These poor children, they always think themselves more clever than father and mother."

And she went to bed tranquil.

The Sarthe had risen on the preceding morning in a flood foreseen by the fishers. These floods of troubled waters bring down with them eels carried along by the current. Now, one of these fishermen had set his traps in the very pool into which the poor Athanase had thrown himself, thinking that no one would ever find him. About six o'clock in the morning the fisher brought up this young body. The two or three friends whom the poor widow had, employed a thousand precautions to prepare her to receive this dreadful remnant of mortality. The news of this suicide, as may well be imagined, produced a great sensation in Alençon. The evening before, the poor young man of genius had not a single protector; the day after his death, a thousand voices exclaimed: "I would have helped him so willingly!" It is so convenient to pose as charitable *gratis!* This suicide was explained by the Chevalier de Valois. That gentleman related, in a spirit of revenge, the ingenuous, the sincere, the beautiful love of Athanase for Mademoiselle Cormon. Madame Granson enlightened by the chevalier, recalled a thousand little circumstances, and confirmed Monsieur de Valois's recital. The story became touching; some women wept over it. The grief of Madame Granson was concentrated, mute, and but little comprehended. There are for mourning mothers two sorts of sorrows. Frequently, the world knows the secret of their loss; their son, appreciated, admired, young or handsome, pursuing a fine course and in the way to fortune, or already glorious, excites universal regret; the world associates itself with the mourning and attenuates it in aggrandizing it. But there is the sorrow of mothers who alone know what their son was, who alone have received his smiles, who alone have recognized the treasures of this life too soon cut off; this sorrow hides its crape, the color of which makes pale that of other griefs; but it does not assert itself, and fortunately there are but few women who know what heart string is forever broken. Before Madame du Bousquier had returned to the city, the wife of the President du Ronceret, one of her good friends, had already been to throw this corpse upon the roses of her joy, to inform her of what love she had refused; she distilled in the sweetest manner a thousand drops of wormwood upon the honey of her first month of marriage. When Madame du Bousquier re-entered Alençon, she encountered by chance Madame Granson on the corner of the Val-Noble— the glance of the mother, dying of grief, reached the heart of the old maid. It was at once a thousand maledictions in a single one, a thousand sparks of fire in a single ray. Madame du Bousquier was terrified at it, this glance predicted for her, invoked for her, unhappiness. The very evening of the catastrophe, Madame Granson, one of those most opposed to the curé of the city, and who followed the officiating minister of Saint-Léonard, shuddered in reflecting on the inflexibility of the Catholic doctrines professed by her own sect. After having herself put her son in his shroud, while thinking of the mother of the Saviour, Madame Cranson took her way, her soul rent by its terrible anguish, to the house of the curé who had taken the oath. She found this modest priest occupied in storing away the hemp and the flax which he gave to all women to spin, to all the poor girls of the city, so that the workwomen should never lack for work, a most intelligent charity that saved more than one household incapable of stooping to beggary. The curé left his hemp and led Madame Granson considerately into his apartment, where the heart-broken mother recognized in the cure's supper, the frugality that pervaded her own household.

"Monsieur l'abbé," said she, "I came to entreat you—"

She broke into tears without being able to complete her sentence.

"I know what brings you," replied the holy man, "but I trust in you, madame, and in your relative, Madame du Bousquier, to conciliate Monseigneur at Séez. Yes, I will pray for your unhappy child; yes, I will say masses; but let us avoid all scandal and give no occasion for the wicked of the city to assemble in the church—I alone, without any clergy, at night—"

"Yes, yes, whatever you like, provided that it be in consecrated ground!" said the poor mother, taking the hand of the priest and kissing it.

Accordingly, about midnight, a bier was carried clandestinely to the parish church by four young men, the most cherished comrades of Athanase. There were assembled a few female friends of Madame Granson, a group of women in black and veiled; with the seven or eight young men who had received some of the confidences of this talent now extinct. Four large wax tapers lit up the bier covered with crape. The curé, assisted by a discreet choir boy, celebrated a mortuary mass. The body of the suicide was carried noiselessly to a corner of the cemetery, where a cross of blackened wood, without inscription, indicated the grave to the mother. Athanase lived and died in the shadows. No voice was lifted to accuse the curé, the bishop kept silence. The piety of the mother redeemed the impiety of the son.

A few months later, one evening, the poor woman, irrational with grief, and moved by one of those inexplicable thirsts which inspire the unhappy to bury their lips in their bitter cup, was seized with a desire to go and see the spot where her son had drowned himself. Her instinct perhaps told her that there might be thoughts for her to gather under this poplar; perhaps also she desired to see the scene which her son had last beheld. There are mothers who would have died at this sight; others there yield themselves up to a holy adoration. The patient dissectors of human nature cannot repeat too often the truths against which education, laws and philosophical systems are vain. Let us assert it frequently,—it is absurd to endeavor to submit all sentiments to identical formulas; in each man they combine with the personal elements which are peculiar to him, and assume his characteristics.

Madame Granson saw a woman approaching from a distance, who exclaimed upon the fatal spot:

"It was there!"

Only one person wept there as did the mother,—this creature was Suzanne. Arrived that morning at the inn of the *More,* she had been informed of the catastrophe. If the poor Athanase had lived, she would have been able to do that which noble natures, penniless, frequently dream of doing, and that which the rich never think of doing, she would have sent several thousand francs with a message: *Money due your father by a comrade who restores it to you.* This angelic ruse had been invented by Suzanne during her journey.

The courtesan perceived Madame Granson, and fled precipitately, after having said to her:

"I loved him!"

Suzanne, faithful to her nature, did not leave Alençon without transforming into water-lilies the orange flowers that crowned the bride. She was the first to declare that Madame du Bousquier would never be aught but Mademoiselle Cormon. She avenged with a stab of the tongue Athanase and the dear Chevalier de Valois.

Alençon was witness of a continued suicide, pitiable in a very different manner, for Athanase was promptly forgotten by society, which wishes to, and should, promptly forget its dead. The poor Chevalier de Valois died while still living, he committed suicide every morning during fourteen years. Three months after the marriage of Du Bousquier, society noticed, not without astonishment, that the chevalier's linen was becoming yellowed and that his hair was carelessly combed. Disheveled, the Chevalier de Valois no longer existed! Several ivory teeth deserted without the observers of the human heart being able to discover to what body they had belonged, if they were of the foreign legion or native, vegetable or animal, whether age had wrested them from the chevalier or whether they were forgotten in the drawer of his toilet table. The cravat rolled over on itself, quite indifferent to elegance! The negroes' heads grew paler in growing dirtier. The wrinkles of the visage deepened, darkened, and the skin became like parchment. The uncared-for finger nails were sometimes bordered with an edge of black velvet. The waistcoat appeared furrowed with forgotten droppings from the nose which were there diffused like autumn leaves. The cotton in the ears was but rarely renewed. Melancholy sat on this brow, and insinuated its yellowish tones into the bottoms of the wrinkles. In short, the progress of ruin, so skilfully kept in restraint, fissured this handsome edifice and proved how much power the soul has over the body, since the blond man, the cavalier, the *jeune premier,* perished when hope failed. Up to this time, the nose of the chevalier had always presented itself under a gracious form; never had there fallen from it either humid black pastilles or drops of amber; but the nose of the chevalier stuffed with tobacco which overflowed at the nostrils, and dishonored by the droppings which profited by the little channel situated in the middle of the upper lip: this nose, which no longer cared to appear agreeable, revealed the excessive care which the chevalier had formerly taken of himself and made manifest, by the extent of it, the grandeur, the persistence, of this man's designs upon Mademoiselle Cormon. He was demolished by a pun of Du Coudrai, whose dismissal, moreover, he procured. This was the first vengeance wreaked by the benign chevalier; but this pun was a murderous one and surpassed by a hundred cubits all the puns of the commissioner of mortgages. Monsieur du Coudrai, seeing this nasal revolution, had named the chevalier *Nérestan*—a personage of romance,—*nez restant,* only the nose remaining.—Finally, the anecdote followed the example of the teeth; then the bons mots became rare; but the appetite survived, the gentleman saved only his stomach in this shipwreck of all his hopes; if he prepared but indifferently his pinches of snuff, he still continued to eat terrifically. You will comprehend the extent of the disaster which this event brought about in the ideas when you learn that Monsieur de Valois held communion less frequently with the Princess Goritza. One day, he came to the house of Mademoiselle Armande with the calf of his leg in front of his tibia. This bankruptcy of the graces was horrible, I swear it to you, and agitated all Alençon. This *quasi* young man become an old one, this personage who, under the enfeeblement of his soul, passed from fifty to ninety years of age, terrified society. Then he delivered up his secret,—he had waited, watched Mademoiselle Cormon; he had, patient hunter, levelled his weapon for ten years, and he had missed the game. In fact, the powerless Republic had triumphed over the valiant aristocracy, and in the very midst of the Restoration! Form triumphed over spirit, mind was vanquished by matter, diplomacy by insurrection. A last misfortune! an offended grisette revealed the secrets of the chevalier's mornings, he was known as a libertine. The liberals gave him credit for all the foundlings of Du Bousquier, and the Faubourg Saint-Germain of Alençon accepted them very proudly; it laughed over it and said: "That good chevalier, what would you have him do?" It had compassion on the chevalier, took him to its bosom, brought back his smiles, and a fearful hatred gathered around the head of Du Bousquier. Eleven persons passed over to the D'Esgrignons and left the salon Cormon.

This marriage had, above all, the effect of defining parties in Alençon. The house of D'Esgrignon there represented the higher aristocracy, for the returned Troisvilles joined them. The house of Cormon represented, under the skilful influence of Du Bousquier, that fatal opinion which, without being really liberal or resolutely royalist, gave birth to the 221, on the day when the combat was defined between the most august, the greatest, the only real power, *royalty,* and the falsest, the most changeable, the most oppressive power, the power called *parliamentary,* exercised by the elective assemblies. The salon Du Ronceret, secretly allied to the salon Cormon, was courageously liberal.

*

On his return from the Prébaudet, the Abbé de Sponde suffered continuously, but he concealed everything in his soul and said nothing to his niece. Only to Mademoiselle Armande did he open his heart, to her he admitted that, folly for folly, he would have preferred the Chevalier de Valois to *Monsieur du Bousquier*. Never would the dear chevalier have had the bad taste to vex a poor old man who had but few days remaining. Du Bousquier had destroyed everything in the dwelling. The abbé said, with thin tears in his dimmed eyes:

"Mademoiselle, I have no longer the covert in which I have taken my walks for fifty years! My well-beloved linden-trees have been cut down! At the moment of my death, the Republic appears to me again under the form of a horrible overturning in my household!"

"It is necessary to forgive your niece," said the Chevalier de Valois. "Republican ideas are the first error of youth, which seeks for liberty, but which finds the most frightful of despotisms, that of the powerless rabble. Your niece is not punished where she has sinned."

"What shall I become, in a house in which dance naked women, painted on the walls? Where shall I find again the linden-trees under which I read my breviary?"

Like Kant, who could not govern his thoughts when the fir tree which he had been in the habit of contemplating during his meditations was cut down, so the good abbé could not obtain the same uplifting in his prayers when he paced through alleys without shade. Du Bousquier had planted an English garden!

"This was better," said Madame du Bousquier without believing it; but the Abbé Couturier had authorized her to do a great many things to please her husband.

This restoration deprived the old house of all its glory, its cheerfulness, its patriarchal air. Like the Chevalier de Valois, whose carelessness might be accepted as an abdication, the bourgeois majesty of the salon Cormon no longer existed when it was white and gold, furnished with ottomans in mahogany and hung with blue silk. The dining-room, decorated in the modern taste, resulted in the dishes being less hot, the dining was no longer so good as it had been, Monsieur du Coudrai pretended that he felt his puns arrested in his throat by the figures painted on the walls, which looked him straight in the eye. In the exterior, the province still asserted itself; but the interior of the house revealed the contractor of the Directory. It was everywhere the bad taste of the exchange broker,—the columns in stucco, the glass doors, the Greek profiles, the dry mouldings, a mixture of all styles, a magnificence quite inappropriate. The city of Alençon criticised for two weeks this luxury, which appeared to it unheard-of; then, a few months later, it was proud of it, and several rich manufacturers renewed all their furniture and made for themselves fine salons. Modern furniture began to show itself in the city. Astral lamps were seen! The Abbé de Sponde was one of the first to perceive the secret unhappinesses which this marriage would inevitably bring into the private life of his well-beloved niece. The character of noble simplicity which had regulated their common existence was lost from the first winter, during which Du Bousquier gave two balls a month. To hear the violins and the profane music of mundane festivals in this saintly household! the abbé prayed on his knees while this festivity lasted! Then the political system of this grave salon was slowly perverted. The grand vicar read Du Bousquier's character,—he shuddered at his imperious tone; he perceived tears in his niece's eyes when she lost the control of her fortune, and when her husband left her only the care of the linen, of the table and of those things which are the usual portion of women. Rose had no longer any orders to give. The will of Monsieur alone was considered by Jacquelin, now coachman only; by René, the groom; by a *chef* brought from Paris, for Mariette was no longer anything but kitchen maid. Madame du Bousquier had now only Josette to rule over. Is it known how much it costs to renounce the delightful habit of power? If the triumph of the will is one of the intoxicating pleasures in the lives of great men, it is the whole of life for limited souls. It is necessary to have been a minister and to have been disgraced to appreciate the bitter grief which took possession of Madame du Bousquier, when she was now reduced to the most complete helotism. She often rode in a carriage against her will, she saw people who were not agreeable to her; she no longer had the management of her dear money, she who had seen herself free to expend whatever she liked, and who had then expended nothing. Does not every limit imposed inspire the desire to overleap it? Do not the keenest sufferings arise from the thwarting of free will? These commencements were like roses. Each concession made to the marital authority was then counselled by the love which the poor girl bore her husband. Du Bousquier at first behaved admirably toward his wife; he was excellent, he gave her valid reasons for each new encroachment. That chamber, so long deserted, heard in the evenings the voices of husband and wife seated at the corners of the fire. Thus, during the first two years of her married life Madame du Bousquier showed herself very well satisfied. She had that little resolute, artful air which distinguishes young wives after a marriage of love. Her fullness of blood no longer tormented her. This showing put the scoffers to confusion, denied all the rumors which were current regarding Du Bousquier, and disconcerted the students of the human heart. Rose-Marie-Victoire feared so greatly, by displeasing her husband, by running counter to him, to lose his affection, to be deprived of his company, that she would have sacrificed everything to him, even her uncle. Her foolish little joys deceived the poor Abbé de Sponde, whose personal sufferings were easier to bear when he thought his niece was happy. Alençon at first was of the abbé's opinion. But there was a man more difficult to deceive than the whole city! the Chevalier de Valois, having taken refuge on the sacred mountain of the high aristocracy, passed his days in the house of the D'Esgrignons; he listened to the backbiting and the scandal, he thought night and day how not to die unavenged. He had beaten down the man of the puns, he wished to stab Du Bousquier to the heart. The poor abbé comprehended the treacherous nature of the first and last love of his niece, he shuddered in divining the hypocritical nature of his nephew and his perfidious practices. Although Du Bousquier restrained himself while thinking of his uncle's inheritance, and did not wish to cause him any grief, he dealt him nevertheless a last blow which brought him to the tomb. If you are willing to explain the word *intolerance* by the phrase *firmness of principles,* if you are not willing to condemn in the Catholic soul of the former grand vicar the stoicism which Walter Scott makes you admire in the Puritan soul of the father of Jeanie Deans, if you are willing to recognize in the Roman church the *Potius mori quam fœdari,* which you admire in Republican opinions, you will comprehend the grief experienced by the great Abbé de Sponde when he saw in the salon of his nephew the apostate priest, renegade, relapsed heretic, the enemy of the Church, the curé abettor of the constitutional oath. Du Bousquier, whose secret ambition was to regulate the whole country, wished, as the first test of his power, to reconcile the officiating minister of Saint-Léonard with the curé of the parish, and he attained his object. His wife thought that it was accomplishing a work of peace when, according to the immovable abbé, it was treason. Monsieur de Sponde saw himself left alone in his faith. The bishop came to Du Bousquier's house and appeared to be satisfied with the cessation of hostilities. The virtues of the Abbé François overcame everything, excepting the Catholic Roman capable of exclaiming with Corneille:

"My God, how many virtues Thou makest me to hate!"

The abbé died when orthodoxy expired in the diocese.

In 1819, the inheritance of the Abbé de Sponde increased the territorial revenue of Madame du Bousquier to twenty-five thousand francs, without including either the Prébaudet or the house in the Val-Noble. It was about this time that Du Bousquier returned to his wife the capital of the savings which she had delivered over to him; he caused her to employ it in the acquisition of property contiguous to the Prébaudet, and thus rendered this estate one of the most considerable in the department, for the lands belonging to the Abbé de Sponde adjoined those of the Prébaudet. No one knew the personal fortune of Du Bousquier, he invested his capital with the Kellers of Paris, where he went four times a year. But, at this period he passed for the richest man in the department of the Orne. This skillful man, the eternal candidate of the liberals, to whom seven or eight hundred votes were constantly lacking in all the electoral contests waged under the Restoration, and who ostensibly repudiated the liberals in seeking for his election as a ministerial royalist, without being able to overcome the repugnance of the administration, notwithstanding the support of the congregation and of the magistracy; this malevolent Republican, mad with ambition, took it into his head to contest with royalism and aristocracy in this country at the moment when they were triumphing there. Du Bousquier secured the support of the priesthood by the deceitful appearance of a well-feigned piety,—he accompanied his wife to mass, he gave money to the convents of the city, he supported the congregation of the Sacred Heart, he took sides with the clergy on every occasion on which the clergy was at issue with the city, the department, or the state. Secretly sustained by the liberals, protected by the Church, remaining a constitutional royalist, he kept the aristocracy of the department constantly in view with the purpose of ruining it, and he ruined it. Attentive to all the errors committed by the most eminent of the nobility and by the government, he brought about, the bourgeoisie aiding him, all the ameliorations which the nobility, the peerage and the minister should have inspired and directed, but which they hindered in consequence of the silly jealousy which pervades the ruling powers in France. The constitutional opinions supported him in the affair of the curé, in the erection of the theatre, in all the questions of improvement foreseen by him, and he caused them to be proposed by the liberal party, with which he associated himself in the most animated of the debates in the name of the good of the country. Du Bousquier developed the industries of the department. He aided the prosperity of the province through hatred of the families living on the road to Brittany. He thus prepared his vengeance against the proprietors of châteaux, and above all against the D'Esgrignons, in whose heart he was one day on the point of planting a poisoned dagger. He contributed funds to revive the manufacture of point d'Alençon; he restored the business of linen-cloths, the city had a spinning-mill. In thus identifying himself with all the interests of the masses, in winning their affection, in doing that which royalty did not do, Du Bousquier did not hazard a farthing. Having his fortune to support him, he could afford to wait for that realization of his projects which enterprising but more hampered men are frequently obliged to abandon to fortunate successors. He posed as a banker. This Laffitte in a small way advanced funds to all the new inventions, taking his securities. He managed his own affairs very well in attending to public affairs; he was the organizer of insurance, the patron of new lines of public vehicles; he suggested petitions to the administration for the necessary roads and bridges. Thus forewarned, the government saw an encroachment upon its authority. The conflict began in an unfortunate manner, for the public benefit required that the prefecture should yield. Du Bousquier incited the nobility of the province against the nobility of the court and against the peerage. Finally, he brought about the frightful support of a strong party of constitutional royalism to the struggle which the *Journal des Débats* and Monsieur de Chateaubriand were sustaining against the throne, an ungrateful opposition based upon ignoble interests, and which was one of the causes of the triumph of the bourgeoisie and of journalism in 1830. Thus Du Bousquier, like the class that he represented, had the happiness of seeing the funeral procession of royalty go by, without receiving any testimonials of sympathy in the province disaffected by the thousand causes which are incompletely enumerated here. The old republican, burdened with masses, and who for fifteen years had concealed his sentiments in order to satisfy his *vendetta*, himself tore down the white flag at the mayor's amid the applause of the people. No man in France beheld the new throne elevated in August, 1830, with eyes fuller of joyful vengeance. For him, the coming into power of the younger branch was the triumph of the Revolution. For him, the triumph of the tricolor flag was the resurrection of the Mountain, which, this time, was going to beat down the gentlefolks by methods surer than that of the guillotine, in that their action would be less violent. The abolition of hereditary privileges in the peerage, the National Guard which brought to the same camp bed the grocer of the corner and the marquis, the abolition of the majorats insisted upon by a bourgeois advocate, the Catholic Church deprived of its supremacy, all the legislative innovations of August, 1830, were for Du Bousquier the most intelligent applications of the principles of 1793. Since 1830, this man has been receiver-general. He has relied, for his success, upon his relations with the Duc d'Orléans, father of the king Louis-Philippe, and with Monsieur de Folmon, formerly intendant of the dowager duchess of Orléans. He is reputed to have eighty thousand francs of income. In the estimation of the country, *Monsieur* du Bousquier is a man of property, a respectable man, steadfast in his principles, full of integrity, considerate. Alençon owes to him its association with the industrial movement which constitutes the first link of the chain by which some day Brittany will perhaps attach itself to that which is called modern civilization. Alençon, which in 1816 did not own two respectable carriages, in the course of ten years saw traversing its streets calèches, coupés, landaus, cabriolets and tilburys, without any astonishment. The bourgeois and the landed proprietors, terrified at first to see the price of articles increasing, recognized later that this augmentation had a financial counter effect on their incomes. The prophetic phrase of the Président du Ronceret: *Du Bousquier is a very strong man!* was adopted by the country. But, unfortunately for his wife, this phrase contains a horrible contradiction. The husband bears no resemblance to the public man, the politician. This great citizen, so liberal in public, so kindly, animated by so much love for his country, is a despot at home and perfectly devoid of conjugal love. This man so deeply astute, hypocritical, calculating, this Cromwell of the Val-Noble, carried himself in his household as he did toward the aristocracy, whom he caressed that he might cut their throats. Like his friend Bernadotte, he covered his hand of iron with a glove of velvet. His wife gave him no children. Suzanne's assertion, the insinuations of the Chevalier de Valois, were thus justified. But the liberal bourgeoisie, the constitutional royalist bourgeoisie, the country gentlemen, the magistracy, and "the priest party," to quote *Le Constitutionnel,* gave the blame to Madame du Bousquier. She had been so old when Monsieur du Bousquier married her! they said. Moreover, how fortunate for that poor wife, for at her age it was so dangerous to have children! If Madame du Bousquier confided with tears her periodical despairs to Madame du Coudrai, to Madame du Ronceret, these ladies said to her:

"But you are crazy, my dear, you do not know what it is that you desire; a child would be the death of you!"

Then, a great many men who, like Monsieur du Coudrai, attached their hopes to Du Bousquier's triumph, caused their wives to sing his praises. The old maid was constantly tortured by these cruel phrases:

"You are very happy, my dear, in having espoused a capable man; you will escape the misfortunes of those wives who are married to men without energy, incapable of taking care of their fortune, of bringing up their children."

"Your husband makes you the queen of the country, fair lady. He will never leave you in any entanglement, not he! he is the leader of everything in Alençon."

"But I should like," said the poor wife, "that he would take less trouble for the public, and that he—"

"You are very hard to please, my dear Madame du Bousquier, all the women envy you your husband."

Misjudged by the world, which had begun by putting her in the wrong, this Christian woman found within herself an ample field for the exercise of her virtues. She lived in tears, and did not cease to present to the world a placid countenance. For a pious soul, was it not a crime, this thought which forever pecked at her heart: "I loved the Chevalier de Valois, and I am the wife of Du

Bousquier!" The love of Athanase also appeared before her in the form of a remorse, and pursued her in her dreams. The death of her uncle, whose distress had been made manifest, rendered her future still more mournful, for she reflected constantly on the sufferings which he must have experienced in seeing the great change in the political and religious doctrines of the house of Cormon. Frequently misfortune falls with the rapidity of the lightning, as with Madame Granson; but with the former spinster it diffused itself like a drop of oil which does not leave the material until it has slowly steeped it.

The Chevalier de Valois was the malicious artisan of Madame du Bousquier's misfortune. He had it at heart to undeceive her mistaken religion; for the chevalier, so expert in love, had fathomed Du Bousquier married as he had fathomed Du Bousquier bachelor. But the astute Republican was a difficult man to surprise,—his salon was naturally closed to the Chevalier de Valois, as to all those who, in the first days of his marriage, had renounced the house of Cormon. Then he was impervious to ridicule, he was possessed of an immense fortune, he reigned in Alençon, he was concerned about his wife, just as Richard III. was concerned to see the horse expire by the aid of which he had gained the battle. In order to please her husband, Madame du Bousquier had broken off with the house of D'Esgrignon, which she no longer visited; but, when her husband left her alone, during his visits to Paris, she took the opportunity to make a visit to Mademoiselle Armande. Now, two years after her marriage, just at the time of the death of the Abbé de Sponde, Mademoiselle Armande accosted Madame du Bousquier as they came out of Saint-Léonard, where they had heard a funeral mass for the abbé. The generous spinster thought that in these circumstances she should offer some consolation to the heiress in tears. They walked together, conversing on the dear deceased, from Saint-Léonard to the Cours; and from the Cours they reached the forbidden hôtel into which Mademoiselle Armande enticed Madame du Bousquier by the charm of her conversation. The poor heartbroken woman perhaps loved to speak of her uncle to one whom her uncle had loved so much. Then she wished to greet the old marquis, whom she had not seen for nearly three years. It was half-past one, there she found the Chevalier de Valois, who had come to dinner, and who, in saluting her, took her hands:

"Well, dear lady, virtuous and well-beloved," said he to her in a voice of emotion, "*we* have lost our sainted friend; we have shared your mourning; yes, your loss is as keenly felt here as in your own house,—more so," he added, with an allusion to Du Bousquier.

After a few words of funeral oration, to which each one contributed his phrase, the chevalier took Madame du Bousquier's arm gallantly and placed it on his own, pressed it in a very adoring manner and led her into the embrasure of a window.

"Are you at least happy?" he said in a paternal voice.

"Yes," she replied, lowering her eyes.

On hearing this *yes*, Madame de Troisville, the daughter of the Princess Sherbellof and the old Marquise de Castéran came to join the chevalier, accompanied by Mademoiselle Armande. All the ladies went to walk in the garden while waiting for dinner, without Madame du Bousquier, dulled by her grief, perceiving that the ladies and the chevalier had on foot a little conspiracy of curiosity. "We have her now, let us learn the answer to the enigma!" was a phrase written in the looks which they exchanged with each other.

"In order that your happiness might be complete," said Mademoiselle Armande, "you should have children, a fine boy like my nephew—"

A tear glistened in Madame du Bousquier's eyes.

"I have heard that it is you who are the only one culpable in this, that you were afraid of child-bearing?" said the chevalier.

"I!" said she ingenuously, "I would buy a child with a hundred years of hell!"

On the question thus presented there arose a discussion conducted with excessive delicacy by Madame la Vicomtesse de Troisville and the old Marquise de Castéran, which so entrapped the poor old maid that she revealed without suspecting it, the secrets of her household. Mademoiselle Armande had taken the arm of the chevalier and had withdrawn to a little distance, in order to allow the three wives to talk marriage. Madame du Bousquier was then undeceived with regard to the thousand deceptions of her marriage, and, as she had remained as stupid as ever, she amused her confidantes with delicious simplicity. Although, at first the mendacious marriage of Mademoiselle Cormon had excited the laughter of the whole city, early initiated into the secrets of Du Bousquier's manœuvres, nevertheless Madame du Bousquier gained the esteem and sympathy of all the women. As long as Mademoiselle Cormon had thrown herself headlong on marriage without succeeding in getting married, everyone derided her; but, when each one learned of the exceptional situation in which she was placed by the severity of her religious principles, everyone admired her. *That poor Madame du Bousquier* replaced *that good Demoiselle Cormon.* The chevalier thus succeeded in rendering Du Bousquier odious and ridiculous for some time, but the ridicule ended by dying out; and, when everyone had said his speech about him, the scandal ceased. Then, at fifty-seven years of age, the silent Republican seemed to very many people to be entitled to retirement. This circumstance envenomed the hatred which Du Bousquier bore to the house of D'Esgrignon to such a degree that it rendered him pitiless on the day of vengeance. Madame du Bousquier received orders to never set foot in that house again. As a return for the trick which the Chevalier de Valois had played him, Du Bousquier, who had just established the *Courrier de l'Orne,* caused the following announcement to be inserted in it:

"A certificate of a thousand francs of Rente will be given to anyone who can demonstrate the existence of one Monsieur de Pombreton, before, during, or after the emigration."

Although her marriage was essentially negative, Madame du Bousquier saw in its certain advantages: was it not much better to interest herself in the most remarkable man in the city than to live alone? Du Bousquier was still preferable to the dogs, the cats, the canaries, adored by celibates; he entertained for his wife a sentiment more real and less interested than is that of servants, confessors and legacy-hunters. Later, she came to see in her husband the instrument of divine wrath, she recognized in all her desires for marriage innumerable sins; she considered herself as thus justly punished for the misfortunes which she had caused Madame Granson, and for the premature death of her uncle. Obeying that precept of religion which commands you to kiss the rod with which correction is administered to you, she praised her husband, she approved of him publicly; but, in the confessional or in the evening at her prayers, she often wept in asking forgiveness of God for the apostasy of her husband, who believed the contrary of that which he said, who wished for the destruction of the aristocracy and the Church, the two religions of the house of Cormon. Finding all her own sentiments thwarted and frustrated, but obliged by duty to contribute to the happiness of her husband, to injure him in nothing, and attached to him by an undefinable affection which perhaps was due to habit, her life was a perpetual contradiction. She had married a man whose conduct and whose opinions she hated, but with whom she was obliged to concern herself with a compulsory tenderness. Frequently, she rose to the highest heavens when Du Bousquier ate her confitures, when he pronounced the dinner good; she watched to see that his slightest desires were satisfied. If he forgot the wrapper of his newspaper upon the table, instead of throwing it away, Madame said:

"René, leave that there, monsieur has not put it there without a purpose."

If Du Bousquier went on a journey, she was anxious about his cloak, his linen; she took the most minute precautions for his material happiness. If he went to the Prébaudet, she consulted the barometer from the day before to know whether the weather would be fine. She watched for indications of his wishes in his looks, after the manner of a dog which, even while sleeping, hears and sees his master. If the gross Du Bousquier, vanquished by this ordered love, seized her round the waist, kissed her on the forehead and said to her: "You are a good wife!" tears of pleasure would fill the eyes of the poor creature. It is probable that Du Bousquier considered himself obliged to make these indemnifications which gained for him the respect of Rose-Marie-Victoire, for Catholic virtue does not command a dissimulation quite as complete as was that of Madame du Bousquier. But frequently the pious woman was struck dumb on hearing the conversation in her own house between hateful individuals who concealed themselves under the mask of constitutional royalist opinions. She shuddered in foreseeing the ruin of the Church; sometimes she risked a stupid phrase, an observation which Du Bousquier cut short with a look. The contradictions of this existence thus pulled in opposite directions, ended by stupefying Madame du Bousquier, who found it more simple and more worthy to concentrate her intelligence without any outward display, resigning herself to the leading of a purely animal life. She had thenceforth all the submission of a slave, and regarded it as a meritorious work to accept the abasement in which her husband placed her. The accomplishment of the marital will never brought from her the slightest murmur. This timid ewe followed from this time the path indicated to her by the shepherd; she forsook no more the lap of the Church, and delivered herself up to the most severe religious practices, without thinking either of Satan, or of his pomps, or of his works. She thus presented an example of an assemblage of the purest Christian virtues, and Du Bousquier became certainly one of the most fortunate men in the kingdom of France and Navarre.

"She will be stupid till her very last breath," said the cruel commissioner now out of office, but he dined at her house, nevertheless, twice a week.

This history would be strangely incomplete if it did not mention the coincidence of the death of the Chevalier de Valois with that of the mother of Suzanne. The chevalier perished with the monarchy, in August, 1830. He went to join the cortége of Charles X. at Nonancourt, and escorted him piously as far as Cherbourg with all the Troisvilles, the Castérans, the D'Esgrignons, the Verneuils, etc. The old gentleman had taken with him fifty thousand francs, the amount of his savings and of his income; he offered it to one of the faithful friends of his masters to transmit it to the king, alleging his own approaching death, saying that this sum had been drawn from the bounties of his majesty, that, in fact, the fortune of the last of the Valoises belonged to the crown. It is not known whether the fervor of his zeal vanquished the repugnance of the Bourbon, who left his fair kingdom of France without carrying away a farthing of it, and who certainly should have been affected by the chevalier's devotion; but it is certain that Césarine, the sole heir of Monsieur de Valois, received scarcely six hundred francs of income. The chevalier returned to Alençon cruelly affected by both grief and fatigue, and he expired just as Charles X. landed on foreign soil.

Madame du Val-Noble and her protector, who now feared the vengeance of the liberal party, were happy to have a pretext to take refuge incognito in the village in which Suzanne's mother died. At the sale which took place after the decease of the Chevalier de Valois, Suzanne, wishing to have some souvenir of her first and her good friend, bid his snuff-box up to the excessive price of a thousand francs. The portrait of the Princess Goritza was worth in itself this sum. Two years later, a young man of fashion who was making a collection of handsome snuff-boxes of the last century obtained from Suzanne that of the chevalier, remarkable for its marvelous workmanship. This jewel, the confidant of the most beautiful love in the world and the joy of a long old age, thus ended by being exposed in a species of private museum. If the dead knew what was done after them, the face of the chevalier would at this time have reddened on the left cheek.

Should this history have no other effect than that of inspiring, in the possessors of certain venerated relics a sacred fear, and of causing them to have recourse to a codicil to determine immediately the fate of these precious souvenirs of a vanished happiness by bequeathing them to fraternal hands, it would have rendered the greatest service to the loving and chivalrous portion of the public; but it contains a much loftier moral!—Does it not demonstrate the necessity of a new education? Will it not evoke, from the very enlightened solicitude of the ministers of public instruction, the establishment of chairs of anthropology, a science in which Germany excels us? The modern myths are still less comprehended than the ancient myths, though we are devoured by the myths. Myths crowd upon us from every side, they serve all purposes, they explain everything. If they are, according to the humane school, the torches of history, they will save empires from all revolutions, provided only that the professors of history cause the interpretations which they furnish to be carried even among the departmental masses! If Mademoiselle Cormon had been lettered, if there had existed in the department of the Orne a professor of anthropology, in fact, if she had read Ariosto, would the frightful unhappiness of her married life ever have occurred? She would perhaps have searched out the reason that the Italian poet shows us Angelica preferring Medoro, who was a blond Chevalier de Valois, to Roland whose mare was dead and who knew no better than to go mad. Would not Medoro become the mythical figure of the courtiers of feminine royalty, and Roland the myth of the disorderly revolutions, furious, powerless, which destroy everything without producing anything? We publish, declining all responsibility for it, this opinion of a pupil of Monsieur Ballanche.

No information has come to us concerning the fate of the little negroes' heads in diamonds. You may see to-day Madame du Val-Noble at the Opéra. Thanks to the early education given her by the Chevalier de Valois, she has almost the air of a woman *comme il faut*, while being only a woman *comme il en faut*—a woman of the world, a lady;—a woman who is necessary.

Madame du Bousquier is still living; is not that to say that she is still suffering? When she had attained the age of sixty, a period at which women permit themselves frank avowals, she said in confidence to Madame du Coudrai, whose husband recovered his position in August, 1830, that she could not endure the idea of dying a maid.

Paris, October, 1836.

THE PROVINCIALS IN PARIS

THE CABINET OF ANTIQUITIES

TO MONSIEUR LE BARON DE HAMMER-PURGSTALL, AULIC COUNCILLOR, AUTHOR OF THE "HISTORY OF THE OTTOMAN EMPIRE."

DEAR BARON,

You have been so warmly interested in my long and vast history of French manners and customs in the nineteenth century, and you have bestowed such encouragement on my work, that you have thus given me the right to attach your name to one of the fragments which form a part of it. Are you not one of the gravest representatives of the conscientious and studious Germany? Would not your approbation command that of others and protect my enterprise? I am so proud of having obtained it, that I have endeavored to merit it in continuing my labors with that intrepidity which has characterized your studies and your exhaustive research of documents without which the literary world would have been deprived of the monument reared by you. Your sympathy for the labors with which you have been acquainted and have applied to the interests of the most brilliant oriental society has often sustained the ardor of my night watches, occupied by the details of our modern society;—will you not be happy to know it, you whose ingenious benevolence may be compared to that of our own La Fontaine?—I trust, dear Baron, that this testimony of my veneration for you and your work will find you at Dobling, and may serve to recall to you, as well as to all of yours, of your most sincere admirers and friends.

DE BALZAC.

VICTURNIEN LEAVES THE PREFECTURE

At this moment, the well-known tilbury of the Comte d'Esgrignon was seen descending the upper part of the Rue Saint-Blaise, and coming from the prefecture. This tilbury was driven by the count, accompanied by a charming, unknown young man.

THE CABINET OF ANTIQUITIES

In one of the least important prefectures of France, in the centre of the city, at the corner of a street, is a house; but the names of this street and this city must not be given here. Everyone will appreciate the reasons for this discreet restraint, imposed by the conventionalities. A writer touches so many wounds in constituting himself the annalist of his own time!—The house was known as the Hôtel d'Esgrignon; but we will assume that D'Esgrignon is an arbitrary name, without any more reality than have the Belvals, the Floricours, the Dervilles of the theatre, the Adalberts or the Monbreuses of romances. In short, the names of the principal personages will also be changed. Here, the author will endeavor to assemble contradictions, to pile up anachronisms, in order to conceal the truth under a heap of improbabilities and absurdities; but, whatever he may do, it will always assert itself, as a vine, badly rooted up, grows again in vigorous shoots in a cultivated vineyard.

The Hôtel d'Esgrignon was simply the house in which lived an old gentleman named Charles-Marie-Victor-Ange Carol, Marquis d'Esgrignon or des Grignons, according to the ancient titles. The bourgeois and commercial society of the city had epigrammatically named his dwelling a hôtel, and, for the last twenty years, the greater number of the inhabitants had acquired the habit of saying seriously the *Hôtel d'Esgrignon* when designating the dwelling of the marquis.

The name of Carol—the brothers Thierry would have spelled it Karawl— was the glorious name of one of the most powerful of the chiefs that had come down from the North in ancient times to conquer and feudalize the Gauls. Never had the Carols stooped their heads, neither before the communes, nor before royalty, nor before the Church, nor before financial power. Having had formerly the charge of defending a French March, their title of marquis was at once a duty and an honor, and not the simulacrum of a supposed charge; the fief of Esgrignon had always been their property. A true nobility of the provinces, ignored for more than two hundred years at court, but pure of any base alliance, sovereign in the country, respected by the natives superstitiously and as much as a Holy Virgin who cures the toothache, this house had been preserved in the depths of its province as the charred piles of some bridge built by Cæsar are preserved at the bottom of a river. For thirteen hundred years the daughters had been regularly married without dowry or placed in convents; the younger sons had constantly accepted their mothers' portions, had become soldiers, bishops, or had married at court. A younger son of the house of Esgrignon had been an admiral, was created duke and peer of France, and died without issue. Never had the Marquis d'Esgrignon, the head of the elder branch, been willing to accept the title of duke.

"I hold the marquisate of Esgrignon on the same conditions that the king holds the state of France," he said to the Constable de Luynes, who was at that time, in his eyes, only a very inferior companion.

You may safely reckon that during the troublous times there had been D'Esgrignons decapitated. The French strain had been preserved, noble and proud, until the year 1789. The then Marquis d'Esgrignon would not emigrate,—he was obliged to defend his March. The respect which he had inspired in the country people preserved his head from the scaffold; but the hatred of the true *sans-culottes* was sufficiently powerful to cause him to be considered as an *émigré* during the time that he was obliged to remain in hiding. The district formally dishonored the lands of Esgrignon in the name of the sovereign people, the forests were sold by the nation, notwithstanding the personal protests of the marquis, then at the age of forty. Mademoiselle d'Esgrignon, his sister, being a minor, saved some portions of the fief by the intercession of a young intendant of the family, who demanded the legal division of the estate before the death of the owner, in his client's name,—the château and some farms were given her by the liquidation decreed by the Republic. The faithful Chesnel was obliged to purchase in her name, with the funds which the marquis furnished him, certain portions of the domain to which his master attached a peculiar value, such as the church, the manse and the gardens of the château.

The slow and rapid years of the Terror having passed, the Marquis d'Esgrignon, whose character had secured the respect of the country, wished to return to inhabit his château with his sister, Mademoiselle d'Esgrignon, in order to improve the property, to the saving of which Maître Chesnel, his ex-intendant, now become notary, had devoted himself. But alas! the château, pillaged, unfurnished, was it not too vast, too costly for a proprietor all of whose valuable rights had been suppressed, whose forests had been cut to pieces and who, for the moment, could not draw a budget of more than nine thousand francs from the lands preserved from his ancient domains?

When the notary brought back the marquis, in the month of October, 1800, to the old feudal château, he could not repress a profound emotion on seeing him stand motionless in the midst of the court, before his filled up moats, looking at his towers razed to the level of the eaves. The Frank contemplated, in silence and alternately, Heaven and the place where formerly had been the pretty weather-vanes of the Gothic towers, as if to ask God the reason for this social overturning. Chesnel alone could contemplate the profound grief of the marquis, then known only as the Citizen Carol. This grand D'Esgrignon remained silent a long time, he breathed in the patrimonial sentiment in the air and uttered the most melancholy interjections.

"Chesnel," said he, "we will return here later, when the troubles are over; but, until the edict of pacification is issued, I shall not live here, since *they* forbid me to re-establish my arms."

He indicated the château, turned, mounted his horse again, and departed with his sister, who had come in a shabby carriole of wicker-work belonging to the notary. In the city, there was no longer any Hôtel d'Esgrignon. The noble house had, been demolished, on its site were erected two manufactories. Maître Chesnel employed the marquis's last bag of louis in purchasing, at the corner of the public place, an old house with gable ends, weather-cocks, a tower, a dove-cote, in which had formerly been established the seignorial bailiwick, afterward the presidial, and which had been the property of the Marquis d'Esgrignon. For the sum of five hundred louis, the tenant who had acquired this under the national sale ceded the ancient edifice to the legitimate proprietor. It was then that, half jestingly, half seriously, this dwelling acquired the name of the *Hôtel d'Esgrignon*.

In 1800, some of the *émigrés* returned to France, the erasure of the names inscribed on the fatal lists was obtained readily enough. Among the nobles who were the first to return to the city were the Baron de Nouastre and his daughter,—they were quite ruined. Monsieur d'Esgrignon generously offered them an asylum, in which the baron died two months later, devoured by grief. Mademoiselle de Nouastre was twenty-two years of age, the Nouastres were of the purest blood of the nobility, the Marquis d'Esgrignon married her in order to continue his line; but she died in child-bed, killed by the unskilfulness of the physician, and leaving, very fortunately, a son to the D'Esgrignons. The poor old man—although the marquis was then only fifty-three, adversity and the crushing griefs of his life had always given more than twelve months to the year,—this old man then lost the joy of his last years when he saw expire the prettiest of human creatures, a noble woman in whom were revived all the graces, now imaginary, of the feminine figures of the sixteenth century. He received one of those terrible blows whose effects are felt in every moment of life. After having remained standing some moments by the bed, he kissed the forehead of his wife, extended before him like a saint, with her hands joined; he drew out his watch, broke the spring and went to suspend it over the chimney-piece. It was eleven o'clock in the morning.

"Mademoiselle d'Esgrignon, let us pray God that this hour be not fatal to our house. My uncle, Monseigneur the Archbishop, was massacred at this hour; my father also died at this hour—"

He kneeled down by the side of the bed, leaning his head upon it; his sister followed his example. Then, at the expiration of a moment, both rose,— Mademoiselle d'Esgrignon melted into tears, the old marquis looked at the child, the chamber and the dead with a dry eye. To his firmness of a Frank this man joined a Christian courage.

All this took place in the second year of our century. Mademoiselle d'Esgrignon was twenty-seven years of age; she was beautiful. A certain parvenu, who had been a contractor for the armies of the Republic, a native of the district, possessed of six thousand écus of income, persuaded Maître Chesnel, after having overcome his reluctance, to advocate his marriage with Mademoiselle d'Esgrignon. The brother and the sister were equally incensed at such assurance. Chesnel was in despair at having allowed himself to be seduced by the Sieur du Croisier. From that day forward, he no longer found either in the manners or in the words of the Marquis d'Esgrignon that species of caressing benevolence which may be taken for friendship. Henceforth, the marquis was grateful to him. This gratitude, noble and genuine, was a source of perpetual grief to the notary. He is of those sublime hearts to whom gratitude seems to be an enormous payment, and who prefer the gentle equality of sentiment which is given by the harmony of thoughts and the voluntary commingling of souls. Maître Chesnel had tasted the pleasure of this honorable friendship; the marquis had elevated him to his own level. For the old noble, this goodman was less than a child and more than a servant, he was the voluntary vassal, the serf attached by all the bonds of the heart to his suzerain. There was no longer a question of the notary, everything was equalized by the continual exchange of a sincere affection. In the eyes of the marquis, the official character which the notaryship gave to Chesnel was of no significance, his servitor seemed to him to be disguised as a notary. In the eyes of Chesnel, the marquis was a being who always belonged to a divine race; he believed in the nobility, he remembered without any shame that his father had opened the doors of salons and said: "Monsieur le Marquis is served." His devotion to the ruined noble house did not take its origin in a faith, but in an egotism, he considered himself as making a part of the family. His chagrin was profound. When he ventured to speak of his error to the marquis, notwithstanding the fact that the marquis had forbidden it:

"Chesnel," the old noble answered him in a grave tone, "you never permitted yourself such injurious suppositions before the late troubles. What are then these new doctrines, if they have spoiled you?"

Maître Chesnel enjoyed the confidence of the whole city, he was everywhere held in high consideration; his probity, his large fortune, contributed to give him importance; he conceived from this time a decided aversion to the Sieur du Croisier. Although the notary was but little rancorous by nature, he communicated his dislike to a considerable number of families. Du Croisier, a malevolent man and one capable of brooding over a vengeance for twenty years, conceived for the notary and for the D'Esgrignon family one of those concealed and capital hatreds that are to be encountered in the provinces. This refusal injured him greatly in the eyes of the malicious provincials among whom he had come to establish himself, and over whom he wished to acquire authority. It was a catastrophe so real that the effects were not long in making themselves manifest. Du Croisier was also refused by an old maid to whom he had addressed himself as a last hope. Thus, the ambitious plans which he had at first formed were thwarted by the refusal of Mademoiselle d'Esgrignon, an alliance with whom would have given him the entrance to the Faubourg Saint-Germain of the province; then the second refusal brought him so much into disesteem that he could only with difficulty maintain himself in the second society in the city.

In 1805, Monsieur de la Roche-Guyon, the eldest of one of the most ancient families in the country, which had formerly allied itself to the D'Esgrignons, made a request through Maître Chesnel for the hand of Mademoiselle d'Esgrignon. Mademoiselle Marie-Armande-Claire d'Esgrignon refused to listen to the notary.

"You should have divined that I am a mother, my dear Chesnel," she said to him, as she finished putting to bed her nephew, a beautiful child of five years.

The old marquis rose to meet his sister as she returned from the cradle; he kissed her hand respectfully; then, as he seated himself again, he found his speech to say:

"You are a D'Esgrignon, my sister!"

The noble maiden trembled and wept. Monsieur d'Esgrignon, the father of the marquis, in his old age had married the granddaughter of a farmer of the revenue, ennobled under Louis XIV. This marriage was considered as a horrible misalliance by the family, but without importance, since the only issue from it had been a daughter. Armande was well acquainted with this fact. Although her brother had always been very kind to her, he had always regarded her as an outsider, and this speech legitimatized her. But did not her answer complete admirably the noble conduct which she had followed for eleven years, during which, from the date she came of age, each of her actions had been marked by the purest devotion? She had a sort of worship for her brother.

"I shall die Mademoiselle d'Esgrignon," she said simply, to the notary.

"There is no finer title for you," replied Chesnel, who thought to pay her a compliment.

The poor lady blushed.

"You have made a stupid speech, Chesnel," replied the old marquis, at once flattered by the phrase used by his ancient servitor and pained at the trouble it gave his sister. "A D'Esgrignon might espouse a Montmorency,—our blood is not so mixed as theirs has been. The D'Esgrignons *bear or, two bends gules,* and nothing, for nine hundred years, has been changed in their arms; they are as they were on the first day. Hence our motto: *Cil est nostre,* which was taken at the tourney of Philippe-Auguste, as well as the knight armed *or* for a supporter on the right and the lion *gules* on the left."

"I do not remember to have ever met a woman who affected my imagination as much as did Mademoiselle d'Esgrignon," said Blondet, to whom contemporary literature is, among other things, indebted for this history. "I was, to tell the truth, very young, I was a child, and perhaps the image which she has left in my memory owes the vividness of its colors to the disposition which at that age draws us toward marvelous things. When I saw her in the distance coming on the Cours, where I was playing with other children, and where she brought Victurnien, her nephew, I experienced a sensation which was similar in many respects to the sensations produced by galvanism upon corpses. Young as I was, I felt myself as if endowed with a new life. Mademoiselle Armande had hair of a tawny yellow, her cheeks were covered with a very fine down with silvery reflections which I took delight in seeing by placing myself in such a manner that the outlines of her face were illuminated by the light, and I gave myself up to the fascinations of those emerald eyes which dreamed, and which set me on fire when they fell upon me. I feigned to roll on the grass before her in play, but I endeavored to approach her small feet to admire them more nearly. The soft whiteness of her skin, the fineness of her features, the purety of the lines of her forehead, the elegance of her slender figure, surprised me without my perceiving the elegance of her figure, or the beauty of her forehead, or the perfect oval of her visage. I admired her as we pray at that age, without knowing too much why. When my eager looks had at length attracted her attention, and when she said in her melodious voice, which seemed to me to possess more volume than any other voice: 'What are you doing there, little one? Why do you look at me?' I came up to her, I twisted about, I bit my fingers, I reddened and said: 'I do not know.' If by chance she passed her white hand through my hair and asked me my age, I ran away and replied at a distance: 'Eleven years!' When I read *The Thousand and One Nights* and saw a queen or a fairy appearing, I gave to her the features and the gait of Mademoiselle d'Esgrignon. When my drawing-master made me copy the heads from the antique, I remarked that these heads had the hair arranged like that of Mademoiselle d'Esgrignon. Later, when these foolish ideas had disappeared one after the other, Mademoiselle Armande, to whom the men on the Cours respectfully gave place, watching the movement of her long dark skirt until it was out of sight, Mademoiselle Armande remained vaguely in my memory as a type. Her exquisite form, the roundness of which was sometimes revealed by a gust of wind, and which I was able to divine notwithstanding the fulness of her dress, this form appeared to me in my young man's dreams. Then, still later, when I reflected gravely upon some mysteries of human thought, I believed that I remembered that my respect had been inspired in me by the sentiments expressed upon the countenance and in the attitude of Mademoiselle d'Esgrignon. The admirable calm of that head which inwardly was so ardent, the dignity of the movements, the sanctity of duties fulfilled, affected me and imposed upon me. Children are more sensitive than is supposed to the invisible effects of ideas,—they never deride a person really imposing, true grace touches them, beauty attracts them, because they are beautiful and there exist mysterious bonds between things of the same nature. Mademoiselle d'Esgrignon was one of my religions. To-day, my unbridled imagination never climbs the corkscrew staircase of an ancient manor house without depicting Mademoiselle Armande there as the genius of feudality. When I read the old chronicles, she appears before my eyes with the features of celebrated women, she is alternately Agnès, Marie Touchet, Gabrielle; I ascribe to her all the love lost in her heart, and which she never expressed. This heavenly figure, of which glimpses are seen through the cloudy illusions of childhood, comes now in the midst of the shadows of my dreams."

Remember this portrait, faithful mentally as well as physically! Mademoiselle d'Esgrignon is one of the most instructive figures of this history,—she will instruct you in the truth that the purest virtues may, through lack of intelligence, become injurious.

In the course of the years 1804 and 1805, two-thirds of the families that had emigrated returned to France, and almost all of those of the province in which Monsieur d'Esgrignon dwelt replanted themselves in the paternal soil. But there were some defections. A few of the gentlemen took service, either in the armies of Napoléon or at his court; others allied themselves with certain parvenus. All those who went over to the Imperial movement reconstituted their fortunes and recovered their property through the munificence of the Emperor, many of them remained at Paris; but there were eight or nine noble families that remained faithful to the proscribed nobility and to their ideas under the fallen monarchy,—the Roche-Guyons, the Nouastres, the Verneuils, the Castérans, the Troisvilles, etc., some of them poor, some of them rich; but the greater or less quantity of gold was not considered,—the ancient name, the preservation of the race, was everything for them, exactly as for an antiquary the weight of the medal is of but little importance in comparison with the purity of the letters and the head, and the antiquity of the coin. These families took for their head the Marquis d'Esgrignon,—his house became their place of assembly. There, the Emperor and King was never anything but Monsieur de Buonaparte; there, the sovereign was Louis XVIII., then at Mittau; there, the department was always the province, and the prefecture an intendant's office. The admirable conduct, the loyalty of a gentleman, the courage of the Marquis d'Esgrignon procured for him the sincerest homage; in the same manner as his misfortunes, his constancy, his inalterable attachment to his opinions, entitled him to universal respect in the city. This admirable ruin had all the majesty of great things destroyed. His chivalrous delicacy was so well known that in many cases he was selected as sole arbitrator by disputants. All those of superior education who were attached to the Imperial system, and even the authorities, had as much consideration for his prejudices as they displayed regard for his person. But a considerable portion of the new society, the individuals who, under the Restoration were to be called *the liberals,* and at the head of which was, secretly, Du Croisier, derided the aristocratic oasis into which no one was allowed to enter without being of gentle birth and irreproachable. Their animosity was so much the more bitter that many honest people, worthy country gentlemen, some high officials of the administration, were obstinate in considering the salon of the Marquis d'Esgrignon as the only one in which there was good company. The prefect, a chamberlain of the Emperor, endeavored to be received there,—he humbly sent there his wife who was a Grandlieu. The excluded ones had then, in their hatred of this little Faubourg Saint-Germain of the provinces, given the name of the *Cabinet of Antiquities* to the salon of the Marquis d'Esgrignon, whom they called Monsieur Carol, and to whom the collector of taxes always addressed his notifications with this parenthesis,—"ci-devant des Grignons.—" This antique manner of writing the name was only a childish spite, since the spelling "D'Esgrignon" had been adopted.

"For my part," said Émile Blondet, "if I collect my childish remembrances, I must admit that the phrase 'Cabinet of Antiquities' always made me laugh, notwithstanding my respect, should I say my love, for Mademoiselle Armande. The Hôtel d'Esgrignon looked upon two streets, at the corner of which it was situated, so that the salon had two windows on one of these streets and two windows on the other, the most frequented streets in the city.

The market place was at five hundred steps from the hôtel. This salon was therefore like a glass cage, and no one went backward and forward in the city without glancing at it. This apartment always seemed to me, I being then a lad of twelve, to be one of those rare curiosities which later we find, when we dream, on the borders of the real and the fantastic, without the possibility of determining whether they are more on one side or the other. This salon, formerly the audience chamber, was situated over a basement of cellars lit by openings with iron railings, in which were formerly confined the criminals of the province, but in which at this time was carried on the marquis's cooking. I do not know if the high and magnificent chimney-piece of the Louvre, sculptured so marvelously, caused me any more astonishment than I felt in seeing for the first time the immense chimney of this salon, embroidered like a melon, and over which was a great equestrian portrait of Henri III.—under whom this province, an ancient duchy in appanage, was reunited to the crown,—executed in high relief and framed with gildings. The ceiling was formed by chestnut rafters which inclosed recesses ornamented in the interior with arabesques. This magnificent ceiling had been gilded at its angles, but the gilding had almost disappeared. The walls, hung with Flemish tapestries, represented the Judgment of Solomon in six tableaux framed with gilded thyrses in which disported Cupids and satyrs. The marquis had had the salon floored. Among the remnants of the châteaux which had been sold from 1793 to 1795, the notary had procured some consoles in the style of the age of Louis XIV., some furniture upholstered in tapestry, tables, clocks, chimney-pieces, branched candlesticks, which completed marvelously well this grandiose salon out of proportion to the whole house, but which, fortunately, had an antechamber equally lofty, the ancient waiting-room of the presidial court, with which communicated the chamber of deliberations, now converted into a dining-room. Under these ancient ceilings, tinsel furnishing of a vanished time, there were to be seen, in the first line, eight or ten dowagers, some of them with shaking heads, others withered and black as mummies; these straight, those inclined, all of them arrayed in gowns more or less fantastically in opposition to the fashion of the day; powdered heads with curls, caps with bows of ribbons, yellow laces. The most absurd or the most serious paintings have never represented anything like the incoherent poetry of these women, who return in my dreams and grimace in my souvenirs whenever I encounter an old woman whose face or whose dress recalls to me some of their features. But, whether unhappiness has initiated me into the secrets of the unfortunate, whether it is that I have comprehended all human sentiments, above all, regrets and old age, never have I been able to find anywhere, either among the dying or the living, the paleness of certain gray eyes, the frightful vivacity of certain black eyes. In fact, neither Maturin nor Hoffmann, the two most sinister imaginations of these times, has ever terrified me as did the automatic movements of these busked figures. The rouge of the actors has never surprised me,—I have seen the rouge inveterate, 'the rouge of birth,' said one of my comrades, quite as malicious as I could be. There were moving there visages flattened but furrowed by wrinkles which resembled the heads carved on nut-crackers in Germany. I saw through the windows humped bodies, limbs badly attached, of which I never undertook to explain the physical economy or the contexture; jaw bones very square and very apparent, enormous bones, luxuriant hips. When these women came and went they seemed to me no less extraordinary than when they kept their mortuary immobility, when they would play cards. The men of this salon presented the gray and faded colors of old tapestries, their life was crippled by indecision; but their costumes resembled much more nearly the costumes of the day; only their white hair, their withered countenances, their complexions of wax, their ruined foreheads, the paleness of their eyes, gave them all a resemblance to the women, which destroyed the reality of their costumes. The certainty of finding these personages invariably at table or seated at the same hours, completed, in my eyes, their indescribably theatrical, pompous, supernatural air. Never since, have I entered those celebrated store-rooms in Paris, London, Vienna or Munich, where the old guardians display to you the splendors of past times, without peopling them with the figures of the Cabinet of Antiquities. We often proposed to each other, scholars of from eight to ten years of age, to go on a pleasure party to see these rarities in their glass cage. But, as soon as I perceived the pleasant, gentle Mademoiselle Armande, I trembled, then I admired with a sentiment of jealousy that delightful child, Victurnien, in whom we all involuntarily recognized a nature superior to our own. This young and fresh creature, in the midst of this cemetery resuscitated before its time, struck us as something indescribably strange. Without defining our ideas to ourselves, we felt ourselves bourgeois and small before this proud court."

The catastrophes of 1813 and 1814, which crushed Napoléon, restored life to the guests of the Cabinet of Antiquities, and above all, the hope of recovering their ancient importance; but the events of 1815, the misfortunes of the allied occupation, then the oscillations of the government postponed the hopes of these personages, so well described by Blondet, until the fall of Monsieur Decazes. This history therefore assumes a consistent form only about 1822.

In 1822, notwithstanding the benefits which the Restoration brought to the *émigrés*, the fortune of the Marquis d'Esgrignon had not augmented in any degree. Of all the nobles affected by the Revolutionary laws, none was more maltreated than he. The major portion of his revenues consisted, before 1789, in rights of domain resulting, as with several great families, from the tenure of his fiefs, which the seigneurs were zealous in dividing so as to increase the product of their *lods et ventes,*—taxes on sales of inheritances. The families who found themselves in these circumstances were ruined without any hope of redress, the ordinance by which Louis XVIII. restored to the *émigrés* the properties not sold could restore them nothing; and, later, the law of indemnity could not indemnify them. Everyone knows that their suppressed rights were re-established, for the profit of the state, under the very name of *domaines.* The marquis necessarily belonged to that fraction of the royalist party which would have no transactions with those whom he named, not the revolutionists, but the rebels, known in more parliamentary language as liberals or constitutionals. These royalists, surnamed *ultras* by the opposition, had for chiefs and heroes the courageous orators of the right, who, from the very first royal sitting endeavored, like Monsieur de Polignac, to protest against the Charter of Louis XVIII., regarding it as an evil edict, forced through by the necessities of the moment, and which royalty should certainly revise. Thus, far from associating himself with that renovation in manners which Louis XVIII. wished to bring about, the marquis remained immovable, at the order arms of the purists of the right, waiting for the restitution of his immense fortune, and not admitting even the thought of that indemnity which preoccupied the ministry of Monsieur de Villèle, and which was to consolidate the throne in extinguishing the fatal distinctions, then maintained, notwithstanding the laws, between property. The miracles of the

Restoration of 1814, those greater ones of the return of Napoléon in 1815, the prodigies of the second flight of the house of Bourbon and of its second return, this almost fabulous phase of contemporary history, surprised the marquis at the age of sixty-seven. At this age, the most haughty characters of our times, less crushed than worn out by the events of the Revolution and the Empire, had in the depths of the provinces converted their activity into passionate, unshakable ideas; they were almost all of them fixed in the soft and enervating habits of the life which is habitual there. Is it not the greatest misfortune which can afflict a party to be represented by old men, when its ideas are already taxed with senility? Moreover, when in 1818 the legitimist throne appeared to be solidly established, the marquis asked himself what opening there was for a septuagenarian at court; what charge, what post could he fill there? The proud and noble D'Esgrignon therefore contented himself, and should so have contented himself with the triumph of the monarchy and of religion, while waiting for the results of this victory, unhoped for, disputed, which was simply an armistice. He continued therefore to enthrone himself in his salon, so well named the Cabinet of Antiquities. Under the Restoration, this sobriquet of gentle mockery became envenomed as the vanquished of 1793 found themselves the victors.

This city was no more preserved than the greater number of other cities from the hatreds and rivalries engendered by party spirit. Contrary to the general expectation, Du Croisier had finally espoused the wealthy old maid who had at first refused him, and although he had for rival in this suit the spoiled child of the aristocracy of the city, a certain chevalier whose illustrious name will be sufficiently concealed in designating him, in accordance with an ancient custom followed by the city, by his title only; for he was there the CHEVALIER as at the court the Comte d'Artois was MONSIEUR. Not only had this marriage given rise to one of those wars by land and sea such as are waged in the provinces, but it had still more accelerated that separation between the higher and lower aristocracy, between the bourgeois elements and the nobles, reunited for the moment under the pressure of the great Napoléonic authority; a sudden division that did so much injury to our country. In France, that which is the most national quality, is vanity. The great mass of wounded vanities there has created the thirst for equality; whilst, later, the most ardent innovators will find equality impossible. The royalists wounded the liberals in the most sensitive portions of their hearts. In the provinces specially, the two parties lent themselves to all sorts of horrors and slandered each other shamelessly. The blackest actions were then committed in political matters in order to secure the favor of public opinion, to capture the suffrages of that imbecile audience that offers its arms to whoever is sufficiently skilful to provide them with weapons. These contests formulated themselves in certain individuals. Those who hated each other as political enemies, became presently personal enemies. In the provinces, it is difficult not to engage in a hand to hand struggle over questions or interests which, in the capital, present themselves as generalities, theoretical, and which, thenceforth dignify the champions sufficiently for Monsieur Laffitte, for example, or Casimir Perier, to respect the man in Monsieur de Villèle or in Monsieur de Peyronnet. Monsieur Laffitte, who caused the ministers to be fired upon, would have concealed them in his hôtel if they had come there the 29th of July, 1830. Benjamin Constant sent his work on religion to the Vicomte de Chateaubriand, accompanying it with a flattering letter in which he admitted having received some favors from the minister of Louis XVIII. In Paris, men are systems; in the provinces, the systems become men, and men with enduring passions, always face to face, spying on each other's privacy, censuring each other's discourses, watching each other like two duelists ready to plunge six inches of steel in their sides at the least inattention, and endeavoring to make each other inattentive,—in short, absorbed in their hatred like gamblers without pity. The epigrams, the calumnies, are there directed at the man under pretext of aiming at the party. In this warfare, conducted courteously and without rancor by the Cabinet of Antiquities, but waged by the Hôtel du Croisier even with the poisoned weapons of savages, the fine mockery, all the advantages of wit, were on the side of the nobles. Of this be assured—of all possible wounds, those made by the tongue and the eye, mockery and contempt, are incurable. The chevalier, from the moment when he entrenched himself on the sacred mountain of the aristocracy, while forsaking the salons of mixed company, directed all his witticisms against the salon of Du Croisier; he stirred up the fire of the war without knowing just how far the spirit of vengeance might lead the salon of Du Croisier against the Cabinet of Antiquities. Only those of pure blood entered the Hôtel d'Esgrignon, loyal gentlemen and women sure of each other; there, no indiscretions were committed. The discourses, the ideas good or bad, just or false, fine or absurd, gave no opening to ridicule. The liberals were obliged to direct their attacks against the political actions in order to ridicule the nobles; whilst the intermediaries, the administrative officials, all those who paid court to the superior powers, produced in the liberal camp deeds and proposals which furnished abundant food for laughter. This inferiority, keenly felt, redoubled again among the adherents of Du Croisier their thirst for vengeance. In 1822, Du Croisier placed himself at the head of the industries of the department, as the Marquis d'Esgrignon was at the head of the nobility. Each of them thus represented a party. Instead of proclaiming himself openly a man of the true left, Du Croisier had ostensibly adopted the opinions which were formulated one day by the 221. He was thus able to reunite under him the magistrates, the administration, and the finance of the department. The salon of Du Croisier, a power at least equal to that of the Cabinet of Antiquities, more numerous, younger, more active, swayed the department; whilst the other remained tranquil and, as it were, annexed to the party in power which these adherents frequently embarrassed, for they encouraged its faults, they even exacted some which were fatal to the monarchy. The liberals, who had never been able to elect one of their candidates in this department rebellious to their commands, were aware that after his nomination Du Croisier would sit in the left centre, the nearest possible to the real left. The correspondents of Du Croisier were the brothers Keller, three bankers, of whom the eldest was illustrious among the nineteen of the left, a phalanx illustrated by all the liberal journals, and which was connected by alliance with the Comte de Gondreville, a constitutional peer who enjoyed the favor of Louis XVIII. Thus the constitutional opposition was always ready to turn over at the last moment its votes, evidently pledged to a fictitious candidate, to Du Croisier, if he could gain enough royalist votes to obtain a majority. Each election, in which the royalists repelled Du Croisier, a candidate whose conduct was admirably divined, analyzed, judged by the leading royalists who were sustained by the Marquis d'Esgrignon, augmented still more the hatred of the man and of his party. That which most excites factions against each other is the uselessness of a trap carefully prepared.

In 1822, the hostilities, very lively during the first four years of the Restoration, seemed to have moderated. The salon of Du Croisier and the

Cabinet of Antiquities, after having recognized each other's strength and weakness, awaited doubtless the effects of chance, that Providence of parties. The commonplace spirits contented themselves with this apparent calm which deceived the throne; but those who were on more intimate terms with Du Croisier were aware that, with him as with all other men whose interests in life are no longer other than those which reside in the brain, the passion of vengeance is implacable, especially when it is based upon political ambition. At this period, Du Croisier, who formerly had turned red or pale at the name of the D'Esgrignons or of the chevalier, who shuddered in pronouncing or in hearing pronounced the phrase Cabinet of Antiquities, affected the gravity of the savage. He smiled upon his enemies, hated, watched from hour to hour still more closely. He appeared to have assumed the rôle of living tranquilly, as if he despaired of victory. One of those who abetted the calculations of this chilled rage was the president of the tribunal, Monsieur du Ronceret, a country gentleman who had aspired to the honors of the Cabinet of Antiquities, without having succeeded in obtaining them.

The small fortune of the D'Esgrignons, carefully administered by the notary Chesnel, scarcely sufficed for the support of this worthy gentleman, who lived as a noble, but without the least ostentation. Although the preceptor of the Comte Victurnien d'Esgrignon, the hope of the house, was a former Oratorian donated by Monseigneur the Bishop, and though he lived in the hôtel, still be required some salary. The wages of a female cook, those of a femme de chambre for Mademoiselle Armande, of the old valet de chambre of monsieur le marquis and of two other domestics, the board of four instructors, the expenses of an education in which nothing was neglected, entirely absorbed the revenues, notwithstanding Mademoiselle Armande's economy, notwithstanding the sage administration of Chesnel, notwithstanding the affection of the domestics. The old notary was able to make no repairs in the ruined château, he waited for the expiration of the leases to secure an augmentation of revenue, brought about either by the new methods of agriculture, or by the decline in monetary values, and which was to bear fruit at the expiration of the contracts signed in 1809. The marquis was not initiated into the details of the household or of the administration of his property. The revelation of the excessive care taken in order *to make the two ends of the year meet,* to employ the phrase used by housekeepers, would have been a thunderstroke for him. Everyone, seeing him drawing near the end of his career, hesitated to enlighten him. The grandeur of the house of D'Esgrignon, to which no one paid any attention either at the court or in the state; which, outside the gates of the city and a few localities in the department, was entirely unknown, revived in the eyes of the marquis and his adherents in all its former splendor. The house of D'Esgrignon was to assume a new degree of brilliancy in the person of Victurnien, on the day when the despoiled nobles entered again into the possession of their property, and even when this fine heir should appear at court to take service under the king, to espouse later, as did the D'Esgrignons formerly, a Navarreins, a Cadignan, a D'Uxelles, a Beauséant, a Blamont-Chauvry, in short, a maiden uniting all the distinctions of nobility, wealth, beauty, intelligence and character. All those who came in the evenings to this house, the chevalier, the Troisvilles—pronounced Trévilles,—the La Roche-Guyons, the Castérans—pronounced Catérans,— the Duc de Verneuil, having long been in the habit of considering the grand marquis as a very great personage, encouraged him in his ideas. There was nothing mendacious in this belief, it would have been quite justified if it were possible to efface the last forty years of the history of France. But the most dignified of consecrations, the most undeniable of rights, as Louis XVIII. had endeavored to assert them in dating the Charter in the twenty-first year of his reign, exist only when ratified by universal consent,—there was wanting to the D'Esgrignon the support of the then actual political language, money, that great reliance of the modern aristocracy; there was wanting to them also the continuation of *the historic,* that renown which maintains itself at the court as well as on the battle-fields, in the salons of diplomacy as in the tribune, in the support of a literary work as in the case of an adventure, and which is like a consecrated oil poured on the head of each new generation. A noble family, inactive and forgotten, is a maid stupid, ugly, poor and honest, the four cardinal degrees of misfortune. The marriage of a Demoiselle de Troisville with General Montcornet, far from enlightening the Cabinet of Antiquities, all but caused a rupture between the Troisvilles and the salon D'Esgrignon, which declared that the Troisvilles *were making a mess of themselves.*

But there was one person among all this company who did not share these illusions. Is it necessary to say that this was the old notary, Chesnel? Although his devotion, sufficiently demonstrated by this history, was absolute to this great family now reduced to three persons, although he accepted all these ideas as worthy and genuine, he had too much good sense and conducted too well the business affairs of the greater number of families of the department not to be acquainted with the immense revolution in men's minds, not to recognize the great change produced by industrial processes and by modern habits. The former intendant perceived that the Revolution had passed from the devouring action of 1793, which had armed men, women and children, set up scaffolds, cut off heads and gained European battles, to the tranquil action of ideas consecrated by events. After the clearing of the ground and the sowing, comes the harvest. For him, the Revolution had established the ideas of the new generation, he touched its facts at the bottom of a thousand old wounds, he found them irrevocably accomplished. This king's head struck off, this queen executed, this partition of the property of the nobles, constituted in his eyes solemn engagements which united too many interests for those interested ever to allow the results to be attacked. Chesnel saw clearly. His fanaticism for the D'Esgrignons was entire without being blind, and this rendered it still finer. The faith which enables a young monk to see the angels of Paradise is much inferior to the power of the old monk who shows them to him. The former intendant resembled the old monk, he would have given his life to defend a worm-eaten shrine. Every time that he endeavored to explain, with a thousand precautions, to his former master *the new ideas,* sometimes in making use of a derisory tone, sometimes in affecting surprise or pain, he met with the smile of the prophet on the lips of the marquis, and in his soul the conviction that these follies would pass away like all the others. It has occurred to no one to remark how much events have aided these noble champions of ruins in persisting in their beliefs. What could Chesnel reply when the old marquis made an imposing gesture and said: "God has swept away Buonaparte, his armies and his new great vassals, his thrones and his vast conceptions! God will deliver us from the rest!" Chesnel bowed his head sadly without daring to reply: "God will not wish to sweep away France!" They were both of them fine,—one, maintaining himself against the torrent of facts, like an ancient and moss-grown granite boulder upright in an Alpine abyss; the other, observing the course of the waters and meditating how to utilize them. The good and venerable notary sighed when he remarked the irreparable ravages made by these beliefs in the spirit, in the manners and in the future ideas of the Comte Victurnien d'Esgrignon.

Idolized by his aunt, idolized by his father, this youthful heir was in every meaning of the word a spoiled child, who, moreover, justified the paternal and maternal illusions, for his aunt was truly a mother to him; but, no matter how tender and foreseeing an unmarried woman may be, there will always be wanting in her some undefinable quality of maternity. The second sight of a mother is not to be acquired. An aunt, as chastely united to her nursling as was Mademoiselle Armande to Victurnien, may love him as much as a mother could, be as attentive, as good, as delicate, as indulgent as a mother; but she will not be severe with the precautions and the appropriateness of the mother; her heart will not have those sudden forewarnings, those anxious hallucinations of mothers, in whom the nervous or mental attachments, by which the child is still connected with them, still vibrate, though broken, and who, always in communication with him, receive the shocks of every pain, thrill at every happiness, as with an event of their own life. If nature has considered the woman as a neutral ground, speaking physically, she has not forbidden her in certain cases to identify herself completely with her work,— when the mental maternity is united with the natural maternity we may then perceive those admirable phenomena, unexplained rather than inexplicable, which establish the preferences awarded to maternity. The catastrophe of this history, then, proves once more this well-known fact,—a mother cannot be replaced. A mother foresees misfortune long before an unmarried woman like Mademoiselle Armande admits it, even when it has arrived. The one foresees the disaster, the other remedies it. The factitious maternity of a virgin, moreover, has adorations too blind to permit her to reprimand a beautiful boy.

The habits of life, the experience in affairs, had given to the old notary an observing and perspicacious mistrust which caused him to have maternal presentiments. But he was of so little consideration in this house, especially since the species of disgrace into which he had fallen, in consequence of the marriage proposed by him between a D'Esgrignon and Du Croisier, that from that time he promised himself to follow blindly the family doctrines. A simple soldier, faithful to his post and ready to give up his life, his advice could never be listened to, even at the height of the storm; unless chance should place him, like the king's beggar in *The Antiquary,* on the sea-shore when the lord and his daughter were there surprised by the rising tide.

Du Croisier had perceived the possibility of a frightful vengeance in the contradictory character of the education given this young noble. He hoped, according to the fine expression of the author who has just been quoted, "to drown the lamb in its mother's milk." This hope had been the cause of his silent resignation and brought to his lips his smile of the savage.

The dogma of his supremacy was instilled into the Comte Victurnien from the first moment that an idea could enter his brain. Excepting the king, all the seigneurs of the kingdom were his equals. Below the nobility, there were for him only interiors, individuals with whom he had nothing in common, toward whom he was under no obligations; enemies vanquished, conquered, of whom he need take no heed, whose opinions should be indifferent to a gentleman, and who all owed him respect. These opinions Victurnien unfortunately carried to extremes, incited thereto by the rigorous logic which leads children and young people to the final consequences of good as of evil. He was, moreover, confirmed in his beliefs by his outward advantages. A child of a wonderful beauty, he became the most accomplished young man that a father could desire for a son. Of medium height but well-shaped, he was slender, delicate in appearance, but muscular. He had the sparkling blue eyes of the D'Esgrignons, their curved nose finely modeled, the perfect oval of their face, their light hair, their whiteness of skin, their elegant gait, their graceful extremities, fine and tapering fingers, the distinction of those articulations of the wrist and the ankle, beautiful and delicate lines which indicate race in men as in horses. Skilful, quick at all bodily exercises, he was an admirable shot with the pistol, expert at arms as a Saint George, and rode like a paladin. In short, he flattered all the pride which parents take in the external graces of their children, which are, moreover, founded upon a reasonable idea, upon the very great influence of beauty. A privilege, like that of nobility, beauty cannot be acquired, it is everywhere recognized, and is often more valuable than fortune or talent, it needs only to show itself to triumph, all that is asked of it is to exist. In addition to these two great privileges, nobility and beauty, fortune had endowed Victurnien D'Esgrignon with an ardent mind, with a marvellous aptitude at comprehending everything, and with a fine memory. His instruction had been from that time perfect. He was much better informed than are usually the young nobles of the provinces, who become very distinguished sportsmen, smokers and proprietors, but who treat very cavalierly sciences and letters, the arts and poetry, all those talents whose superiority offends them. These gifts of nature and this education should suffice to realize one day the ambitions of the Marquis d'Esgrignon,—he saw his son marshal of France, if Victurnien decided for the army, ambassador, if diplomacy tempted him, minister, if administration appealed to him; everything in the state belonged to him. In short, flattering thought for a father, if the count had not been a D'Esgrignon he would have succeeded by his own merit. This fortunate youth, this gilded adolescence, had never encountered any opposition to his wishes. Victurnien was the king of the household, no one restrained the desires of this little prince, who, naturally, became as egotistical as a king's son, as opinionated as the most unruly cardinal of the Middle Ages, impertinent and audacious, vices which were deified by everyone in seeing in them only the essential qualities of a noble.

The chevalier was a man of those good old times in which the gray musketeers ravaged the theatres of Paris, mauled the watchmen and the sheriffs, played a thousand pages' tricks, and found only a smile on the lips of the king, provided only that the thing was droll. This charming seducer, an ancient ladies' man, contributed greatly to the unfortunate denoûment of this history. This amiable old man, who found no one to comprehend him, was very happy to encounter this admirable budding Faublas who recalled to him his own youth. Without appreciating the difference in the times, he instilled the principles of the encyclopedic roués into this young mind, narrating to him anecdotes of the reign of Louis XV., glorifying the customs of 1750, relating the orgies in the houses of pleasure and the follies committed for the courtesans, and the excellent tricks played upon creditors, in short, all the morality which has supplied the comedy of Dancourt and the epigrams of Beaumarchais. Unfortunately, this corruption, concealed under an excessive elegance, adorned itself with a Voltairean wit. If the chevalier sometimes went too far, he brought in as a corrective the laws of good company, which a gentleman should always obey. Victurnien comprehended of all these discourses only that which flattered his passions. He saw, in the first place, his old father laughing in company with the chevalier. The two old men considered the inborn pride of a D'Esgrignon as a sufficiently strong barrier against all unseemly things, and no one in the household imagined that a D'Esgrignon could permit himself anything contrary to honor. HONOR, that great monarchical principle, erected in the hearts of all this family like a beacon light, enlightened the slightest actions, animated the slightest thoughts of the D'Esgrignons. This fine maxim, which in itself should have preserved the nobility: "A D'Esgrignon should not permit himself such or such a thing, he bears a name which makes the past a guarantee for the future," was like a refrain with which the old marquis, Mademoiselle Armande, Chesnel and all the friends of the family had cradled the childhood of Victurnien. Thus good and evil found themselves face to face, and equal in strength, in this young soul.

When, at the age of eighteen, Victurnien made his appearance in the city, he observed in the outer world some slight contradictions to the life of the interior of the Hôtel d'Esgrignon, but of these he did not seek the causes. The causes were in Paris. He did not yet know that those whom he saw so courageous in thought and in speech in the evenings in his father's house were very circumspect in the presence of the enemies with whom their interests obliged them to come in contact. His father had conquered his own right to freedom of speech. No one thought it worth while to contradict an old man of seventy, and moreover, everybody granted willingly to a man who had been violently despoiled, his right to fidelity to the ancient order of things. Deceived by appearances, Victurnien conducted himself in such a manner as to make enemies of all the bourgeoisie of the city. In the hunting field he made difficulties, carried a little too far by his impetuosity, which were terminated only by grave legal proceedings, compromised by Chesnel with sums of money, and of which no one dared to speak to the marquis. You may imagine his astonishment if the Marquis d'Esgrignon had learned that his son had been sued for having hunted in his estates, in his domains, in his forests, under the reign of a son of Saint Louis! That which might ensue was too much feared to acquaint him with these vexations, said Chesnel. The young count permitted himself some other escapades, treated as little love affairs by the chevalier, but which ended by costing Chesnel various dowries given to young girls seduced by imprudent promises of marriages,—other actions, entitled in the Code *corruption of minors,* which, in consequence of the brutality of the new administration of justice would have conducted the young count no one knows where, without the prudent intervention of Chesnel. These victories over the bourgeois justice emboldened Victurnien. Accustomed to extricating himself from these evil courses, the young count did not recoil before any jest. He considered the tribunals as scarecrows for people who had no advantages like his own. That which he would have blamed in the plebeians, was an excusable amusement for himself. This character, this conduct, this inclination to despise the new laws while obeying only the maxims of the Code of nobles, were studied, analyzed, dissected by some skilful individuals belonging to Du Croisier's party. These persons made use of them as arguments to convince the people that the calumnies of liberalism were in fact revelations, and that a return to the ancient order of things in all its purity would be found to be the base of the ministerial policy. What a piece of good fortune for them to have a half proof of the truth of their assertions! The Président du Ronceret lent himself admirably, as did the procureur du roi, to all the circumstances that were not incompatible with the duties of the magistracy; he lent himself designedly even beyond due bounds, happy to excite the liberal party over a too great concession. He thus excited the popular passions against the house of D'Esgrignon while seeming to serve it. This traitor had planned to show himself incorruptible at some time, when he should have the support of some serious event, and should be sustained by public opinion. The evil dispositions of the young count were perfidiously encouraged by two or three youths among those who composed his suite, who acquired his good graces by making court to him, who flattered him and encouraged his ideas by endeavoring to confirm him in his belief in the superiority of the noble, at a period when the noble would not have been able to preserve his power save by using it during a half century with extreme prudence. Du Croisier hoped to reduce the D'Esgrignons to the last extremity, to see their château demolished, their lands put up at auction, and sold piecemeal, in consequence of their weakness for this young scatterbrain whose follies would compromise everything. He did not go farther; he did not believe, as did the Président du Ronceret, that Victurnien would otherwise come under the grasp of the law. The vengeance of these two men was moreover well seconded by the excessive self-love of Victurnien, and by his love for pleasure. The son of the Président du Ronceret, a young man of seventeen, who filled exceedingly well the rôle of an agent to lure him on, was one of the companions and the most perfidious courtier of the count. Du Croisier took this new species of spy into his pay, equipped him admirably for the chase to run down the virtues of this handsome and noble youth; he directed him mockingly in the art of stimulating the evil dispositions of his prey. Fabien du Ronceret was in fact of an envious and intelligent nature, a young sophist who was allured by the prospect of such a deception, and who found in it that superior amusement which is so wanting for intelligent people in the provinces.

Between eighteen and twenty-one years of age, Victurnien cost the poor notary nearly eighty thousand francs, without either Mademoiselle Armande or the marquis being informed of it. The civil actions that had been compromised accounted for more than half of this sum, and the extravagance of the young man had dissipated the rest. Of the ten thousand francs of income which the marquis enjoyed, five thousand were necessary for the maintenance of the household; the support of Mademoiselle Armande, notwithstanding her economy, and that of the marquis, required more than two thousand francs; the allowance of the handsome heir presumptive, therefore, did not amount to a hundred louis. What were two thousand francs on which to make a suitable appearance? His dressing alone consumed this income. Victurnien had all his linen, his coats, his gloves, his perfumery, brought from Paris. Victurnien had wished to have a fine English horse to ride, a horse for a tilbury and a tilbury. Monsieur du Croisier had an English horse and a tilbury. Should the nobility allow itself to be crushed out by the bourgeoisie? Then the young count had wished to have a groom in the livery of his house. Flattered at setting the style for the city, for the department, for the youth, he had entered that world of whims and of luxuries which comports so well with handsome and brilliant young people. Chesnel furnished everything, not without making use, as did the ancient parliaments, of the right of remonstrance, but with an angelic mildness.

"What a pity so worthy a man should be so wearisome," said Victurnien to himself every time that the notary applied the necessary funds to some crying necessity.

A widower and childless, Chesnel had adopted the son of his former master in the innermost recesses of his heart; he enjoyed seeing him drive through the high street of the city, perched upon the double cushion of his tilbury, whip in hand, a rose in his buttonhole, handsome, well dressed, envied by all. When, in some pressing need, loss at cards at the Troisvilles', at the Duc de Verneuil's, at the prefecture or in the house of the receiver-general, Victurnien came, his voice calm, his look unquiet, his gestures wheedling, to seek his Providence, the old notary, in a modest house in the Rue du Bercail, he had taken the city merely in showing himself.

"Well, what is it, monsieur le comte? what has happened to you?" asked the old man in an altered voice.

Oh great occasions, Victurnien sat down, assumed a melancholy and thoughtful air, he allowed himself to be questioned while putting on little affectations. After having caused the greatest anxiety to the worthy man, who began to fear the consequences of a dissipation so long sustained, he admitted some peccadillo liquidated by a thousand-franc note. Chesnel, in addition to his income from his profession, possessed about twelve thousand francs of revenue. This fund was not inexhaustible. The eighty thousand francs that had been devoured had constituted his savings, reserved for the day when the marquis should send his son to Paris, or to bring about some fine marriage. Clear-seeing when Victurnien was not present, Chesnel lost, one by one, the illusions cherished by the marquis and his sister. In recognizing in this young man a total want of enlightenment in his conduct, he desired to marry him to some noble damsel, intelligent and prudent. He asked himself how a young man could think so justly and conduct himself so badly, when he saw him doing one day the contrary of that which he had promised the day before. But there is never anything good to be expected from young people who admit their faults, repent of them, and recommence them. The men of great character admit their faults only to themselves, they punish themselves for them. As for the feeble, they fall back in the rut, finding the edges too difficult to climb over. Victurnien, in whom similar tutors had in concert with his companions and his habits, weakened the spring of the secret pride of great men, had unexpectedly arrived at the feebleness of the voluptuous ones, at the very period of his life when, in order to exercise itself, his strength would have had need of that régime of obstacles and poverty which formed such men as Prince Eugène, Frederick II., and Napoléon. Chesnel perceived in Victurnien that unconquerable fury for enjoyment which should be the appanage of men endowed with great faculties who feel the necessity of counterbalancing fatiguing exercise by equal compensation in pleasure, but which conducts to ruin individuals capable only of voluptuousness. The worthy man was terrified at moments; but at other moments, the judicious sallies and the broad intelligence which rendered this young man so remarkable, reassured him. He said to himself that which the marquis said when the report of some escapade came to his ear: "Youth must have its day!" When Chesnel complained to the chevalier of the propensity of the young count for making debts, the chevalier listened to him with a mocking air while taking a pinch of snuff.

"Explain to me then what is the public debt, my dear Chesnel," he replied to him. "Well, the deuce! if France has debts, why should not Victurnien have them? To-day, as always, the princes have debts, all gentlemen have debts. Perhaps you would like Victurnien to bring you his savings? You know what our great Richelieu did, not the cardinal, he was a wretch who killed the nobles, but the marshal, when his grandson, the Prince de Chinon, the last of the Richelieus, showed him that he had not expended his pocket-money at the University?"

"No, monsieur le chevalier."

"Well, he threw the purse out of the window, to a street sweeper, saying to his grandson: 'You are not then taught here how to be a prince?'"

Chesnel bowed his head, without saying a word. Then, in the evening, before retiring, the worthy old man reflected that these doctrines were dangerous in a period when the correctional police existed for everybody,—he saw in them the germ of the ruin of the great house of D'Esgrignon.

Without these explanations, which depict one aspect of provincial life under the Empire and the Restoration, it would have been difficult to understand the scene with which this story commences, and which took place near the end of the month of October of the year 1822, in the Cabinet of Antiquities, one evening, after the play, when the noble habitués, the old countesses, the young marchionesses, the simple baronesses, had settled their accounts. The old gentleman was walking up and down the length of his salon, in which Mademoiselle d'Esgrignon herself was going to extinguish the candles on the card tables; he was not walking alone, the chevalier was with him. These two débris of the preceding century were talking of Victurnien. The chevalier had been charged to make some overtures to the marquis on his account.

"Yes, marquis," said the chevalier, "your son is losing here his time and his youth, you should, in fact, send him to the court."

"I have always thought that, if my great age forbade me from going to the court, where, between ourselves I do not know what I should do, seeing what is taking place and in the midst of the new people whom the king is receiving, I should at least send my son to present our homage to His Majesty. The king should give something to the count, something like a regiment, a post in his household, in short, enable him at least to gain his spurs. My uncle the archbishop suffered a cruel martyrdom, I have warred without deserting the camp like those who thought it their duty to follow the princes,—in my opinion, the king was in France, his nobility should surround him. Ah! well! no one thinks of us, whilst Henri IV. would already have written to the D'Esgrignons: *Come, my friends! we have gained the cause.* At least we are something better than the Troisvilles, and here are two Troisvilles named peers of France, another is deputy of the nobility—he takes the great electoral colleges for the assemblies of his order. Truly, we are no more thought of than if we did not exist! I have been waiting for the visit which the princes should have made here; but the princes are not coming to us, it is then necessary to go to them."

"I am delighted to learn that you think of bringing our dear Victurnien out in the world," said the chevalier skilfully. "This city is a hole in which he should not bury his talents. All that he can hope to find here is some Norman woman or other, very stupid, very badly educated and rich. What would he make of her?—his wife? Ah! Good Lord!"

"I hope that he will not marry until he has received some honorable charge in the kingdom or from the crown," said the old marquis. "But there are grave difficulties."

These are the only difficulties which the marquis perceived as attending his son's entry upon his career:

"My son," he said, after a pause accented by a sigh, "the Comte d'Esgrignon cannot present himself like a barefooted beggar, he must be fitted out. Alas! we no longer have, as we had two centuries ago, our gentlemen in attendance. Ah! chevalier, this demolition from top to bottom, it still appears to me as it did on the day after the first stroke of the hammer given by Monsieur de Mirabeau. To-day, it is only a question of having money, that is all that I see clearly in the benefits of the Restoration. The king does not ask you if you are a descendant of the Valois, or if you are one of the conquerors of Gaul, he asks you if you pay a thousand francs of taxes. I should not then be willing to send the count to court without some twenty thousand écus—"

"Yes, with that bagatelle, he can make a gallant display," said the chevalier.

"Well," said Mademoiselle Armande, "I have asked Chesnel to come here this evening. Would you believe it, chevalier, that, ever since the day on which Chesnel proposed to me to marry that wretch of a Du Croisier—"

"Ah! that was indeed an indignity, mademoiselle," exclaimed the chevalier.

"Unpardonable!" said the marquis.

"Well," resumed Mademoiselle Armande, "my brother has never been able to bring himself to ask anything whatever of Chesnel."

"Of your former domestic?" replied the chevalier. "Ah! marquis, but you would do Chesnel an honor, an honor for which he would be grateful to his last moment."

"No," replied the gentleman, "I do not consider the thing dignified."

"It is a fine question of dignity! the thing is necessary," said the chevalier, shrugging his shoulders slightly.

"Never!" exclaimed the marquis, answering with a gesture which decided the chevalier to risk a great stroke in order to enlighten the old man.

"Well," said the chevalier, "if you do not know it, I will tell you, myself, that Chesnel has already given something to your son, something like—"

"My son is incapable of having accepted anything whatever from Chesnel," cried the old man, straightening himself up and interrupting the chevalier. "He could have asked of you, of you, twenty-five louis—"

"Something like a hundred thousand francs," continued the chevalier.

"The Comte d'Esgrignon owes a hundred thousand francs to a Chesnel!" cried the old man, evidently deeply affected. "Ah! if he were not an only son he would set out this evening for the Indies with a captain's brevet! To be indebted to usurers with whom you settle by paying heavy interest, good! but Chesnel, a man to whom you are attached!"

"Yes, our adorable Victurnien has eaten up a hundred thousand francs, my dear marquis," replied the chevalier, shaking off the grains of snuff fallen on his waistcoat; "that is but little, I admit. At his age, I!—Well, let us leave our souvenirs, marquis. The count is in the provinces, all things considered, that is not bad, he will do well; I see in him the extravagances of men who, later, accomplish great things—"

"And he is sleeping up-stairs without having said anything to his father," exclaimed the marquis.

"He is sleeping with the innocence of a child who has as yet made only five or six little bourgeoises unhappy, and for whom it is now necessary to provide duchesses," replied the chevalier.

"But he will bring upon himself a *lettre de cachet!*"

"*They* have suppressed the *lettres de cachet,*" said the chevalier. "When an attempt was made to constitute an especial form of justice, you know what an outcry was made. We have not been able to maintain the *prévôt's* courts which Monsieur *de* Buonaparte called *commissions militaires.*"

"Well, then, what is going to become of us when we have wild sons, or those that are too bad subjects.—we can then no longer lock them up?" asked the marquis.

The chevalier looked at the despairing father, and did not venture to reply to him: "We shall be obliged to educate them well—"

"And you have said nothing of this to me, Mademoiselle d'Esgrignon," resumed the marquis, turning to his sister.

These words always indicated irritation, he usually called her *my sister.*

"But, monsieur, when a lively and vigorous young man remains idle in a city like this, what would you expect him to do?" said Mademoiselle d'Esgrignon, who did not understand her brother's anger.

"Eh! the deuce! make debts," replied the chevalier; "he plays, he has little adventures, he hunts, all that costs terribly to-day."

"Come," resumed the marquis, "it is time to send him to the king. I will spend the morning to-morrow in writing to our relations."

"I have some acquaintance with the Ducs de Navarreins, de Lenoncourt, de Maufrigneuse, de Chaulieu," said the chevalier, who nevertheless knew himself to be quite forgotten.

"My dear chevalier, there is no need of so many preparations to present a D'Esgrignon at court," said the marquis, interrupting him.—"A hundred thousand francs!" he said to himself, "that Chesnel has a great deal of assurance. These are the effects of those cursed troubles. Master Chesnel protects my son. And it is necessary that I should ask him—No, my sister, you shall arrange this affair. Chesnel shall take his securities upon our property for the entire amount. Then we will reprimand this young scapegrace, for he will end by ruining himself."

To the chevalier and Mademoiselle d'Esgrignon these words appeared very simple and natural, however absurd they might have seemed to any other hearers. Far from that, these two persons were very much affected by the expression, almost one of great pain, which was depicted on the old gentle man's features. At this moment, Monsieur d'Esgrignon was under the influence of some sinister premonition, he almost estimated his epoch justly. He went to sit down at the corner of the fire, forgetting Chesnel, who was to appear and of whom he wished to ask nothing.

The Marquis d'Esgrignon had at this period the physiognomy which somewhat poetic imaginations would have desired for him. His head, almost bald, still retained some silky white hairs on the back thereof falling in flat locks but curling at the extremities. His fine forehead, full of nobility, the forehead which is admired in the head of Louis XV., in that of Beaumarchais and in that of the Maréchal de Richelieu, did not present either the square amplitude of that of the Maréchal de Saxe, or the little hard, compressed, too full circumference of Voltaire; but a gracious, convex form finely modeled, with smooth and handsome temples. His brilliant eyes sparkled with that courage and that fire which age does not diminish. He had the nose of the Condés, the amiable mouth of the Bourbons from which issue only intelligent and kindly words, such as the Comte d'Artois always used. His cheeks, modeled more sloping than foolishly round, were in harmony with his thin body, his fine legs and his dimpled hand. His neck was enclosed in a cravat arranged like that of the marquises seen in all the engravings which ornament the works of the last century, and which you remark on a Saint-Preux as on a

Lovelace, on the heroes of the bourgeois Diderot as on those of the elegant Montesquieu—see the first editions of their works.—The marquis always wore a great white waistcoat embroidered with gold, on which glittered the ribbon of commander of the order of Saint-Louis; a blue coat with great skirts, the flaps turned up and embroidered with fleur-de-lys, a singular costume which the king had adopted; but the marquis had in no wise abandoned the French breeches, or the stockings in white silk, or the buckles. After six o'clock in the evening he appeared in his full dress. He read only *La Quotidienne* and *La Gazette de France,* two journals which the constitutional sheets accused of obscurantism, of a thousand enormities, monarchical and religious, and which the marquis himself found to be full of heresies and of revolutionary ideas. However exaggerated may be the organs of any opinion, they are always much milder than the zealous partisans of that side; in the same manner as the depicter of this magnificent personage will certainly be accused of having exceeded the limits of truth, whereas he has softened down some tones too crude and has repressed some too extravagant details in his model.

The Marquis d'Esgrignon had placed his elbows on his knees and held his head between his hands. During all the time that he was meditating, Mademoiselle Armande and the chevalier looked at each other without expressing their thoughts. Was the marquis grieved to be indebted for his son's future to his former intendant? Did he doubt the welcome which the young count would receive? Did he regret having made no preparations for the entrance of his heir into the brilliant world of the court, while remaining in the depths of his province where he had been detained by his poverty, for how could he have appeared at court? He sighed deeply as he raised his head.

This sigh was one of many breathed at this time by the true and loyal aristocracy, that of the provincial gentlemen, then so neglected, like the greater number of those who had seized their swords and resisted during the storm.

"What have they done for the Du Guénics, for the Fontaines, for the Bauvans, who never submitted?" he said to himself in a low voice. "To those who have combated the most courageously, they have thrown some miserable pensions, some lieutenancy of the king in a fortress, on the frontiers!"

Evidently, the marquis doubted royalty. Mademoiselle d'Esgrignon was endeavoring to reassure her brother as to the outcome of this journey, when there was heard on the little, dry pavement of the street, outside the windows of the salon, a step which announced Chesnel. Presently the notary appeared in the doorway, the old valet de chambre of the count, Joséphin, opening for him without announcing.

"Chesnel, my boy—"

The notary was sixty-nine years of age, gray-headed, a square, venerable visage, breeches of an amplitude which would have merited an epic description from Sterne; milled stockings, shoes with silver clasps, a coat in the shape of a chasuble, and the great waistcoat of a tutor.

"—You have been very presumptuous to lend money to the Comte d'Esgrignon! You deserve that I should return it to you instantly and that we should never see you, for you have given wings to his vices."

There was a moment of silence as at court when the king publicly reprimands a courtier. The old notary maintained a humble and contrite attitude.

"Chesnel, this youth makes me anxious," resumed the marquis kindly; "I wish to send him to Paris to serve the king. You will make arrangements with my sister that he may appear there in a suitable manner—. We will settle our accounts—."

The marquis retired, gravely saluting Chesnel with a familiar gesture.

"I thank monsieur le marquis for his favors," said the old man, remaining standing.

Mademoiselle Armande rose to accompany her brother; she had rung, the valet de chambre was at the door, a light in his hand, to conduct his master to bed.

"Sit down, Chesnel," said the elderly maiden, returning.

Mademoiselle Armande, by her feminine delicacy, removed all the asperities of the intercourse of the marquis with his former intendant, although under this asperity Chesnel was conscious of a superb affection. The attachment of the marquis for his ancient servitor constituted a passion like that of a master for his dog, which leads him to quarrel with any one who kicks his animal,—he regards him as an integral part of his existence, as a thing which, without being altogether himself, represents him in that which he holds the dearest, the feelings.

"It was time to make monsieur le comte leave this city, mademoiselle," said the notary sententiously.

THE MARQUIS TO THE NOTARY

"Chesnel, my boy—"
The notary was sixty-nine years of age, gray-headed, a square, venerable visage, breeches of an amplitude which would have merited an epic description from Sterne; milled stockings, shoes with silver clasps, a coat in the shape of a chasuble, and the great waistcoat of a tutor.
"—You have been very presumptuous to lend money to the Comte d'Esgrignon!"

"Yes," she replied. "Has he permitted himself any new escapade?"

"No, mademoiselle."

"Well, then, why do you accuse him?"

"Mademoiselle, I do not accuse him. No, I do not accuse him. I am very far from accusing him. I shall, moreover, never accuse him, whatever he may do!"

The conversation languished. The chevalier, a being with a fine gift of comprehension, began to yawn like a man assailed by slumber. He excused himself gracefully for leaving the salon and departed, having as much desire to sleep as he had to go to drown himself,—the demon of curiosity opened his eyes widely and with his delicate hand removed the cotton which the chevalier had in his ears.

"Well, Chesnel, is there anything new?" asked Mademoiselle Armande anxiously.

"Yes," replied Chesnel, "it is a question of things of which it is impossible to speak to monsieur le marquis,—he would be struck down with an apoplexy."

"Tell it, then," she replied, leaning her handsome head on the back of the seat and dropping her arms by her sides, like a person who waits for the death stroke without defending himself.

"Mademoiselle, monsieur le comte, who has so much intelligence, is the sport of some small individuals who are watching for a great vengeance,—they wish to see us ruined, humiliated! The president of the tribunal, the Sieur du Ronceret, has, as you know, the greatest pretensions to aristocracy."

"His grandfather was procureur," said Mademoiselle Armande.

"I know it," said the notary. "Now, you have not received him here; neither does he go to the house of the Messieurs de Troisville, nor to that of the Duc de Verneuil, nor to that of the Marquis de Castéran; but he is one of the pillars of the salon Du Croisier. Monsieur Fabien du Ronceret, with whom your nephew can come in contact without compromising himself too much—he must have companions,—well, this young man is the adviser in all his follies, he and two or three others who are of the party of your enemies, of the enemies of monsieur le chevalier, of those who breathe only vengeance against you and against all the nobility. All hope to ruin you through your nephew, to see him fall in the mire. This conspiracy is managed by that sycophant of a Du Croisier, who pretends to be royalist; his poor wife is ignorant of everything, you know her, I would have discovered this sooner if she had had ears to understand the evil. During a certain length of time these young fools were not in the secret, no one was permitted to be; but, through laughing too much, the ringleaders compromised themselves, the simpletons understood, and, since the last escapades of the count, certain words have escaped them when they were drunk. These words have been brought to me by some people who were grieved to see so handsome, so noble and so charming a young man ruin himself through pleasure. At this moment, he is pitied; in a few days, he will be,—I do not dare—"

"Despised, say it, say it, Chesnel!" cried Mademoiselle Armande sorrowfully.

"Alas! how would you prevent the best people in the city, those who do not know what to do from morning till evening, from regulating the actions of their neighbor? Thus, the losses of monsieur le comte at play have been figured up. Behold, within the last two months, thirty thousand francs thrown away, and every one asks where he obtained them. When they speak of it before me, I recall them to the proprieties! ah! but—'Do you think,' I said to them this morning, 'that if the valuable rights and the lands of the house of D'Esgrignon have been taken, that all their treasures have been plundered? The young count has the right to conduct himself as he pleases; and, so long as he does not owe you a sou, you have not a word to say.'"

Mademoiselle Armande extended her hand, on which the old notary deposited a respectful kiss.

"Good Chesnel!—My friend, how shall we find the funds for this journey? Victurnien cannot go to court without maintaining himself there according to his station."

"Oh Mademoiselle, I have borrowed on the Jard."

"What! you no longer had anything! *Mon Dieu!*" she cried, "what shall we do to recompense you?"

"Accept the hundred thousand francs which I hold at your disposition. You understand that the loan has been effected secretly, so as not to affect you unfavorably. In the eyes of the city, I belong to the house of D'Esgrignon."

A few tears came into the eyes of Mademoiselle Armande; Chesnel, seeing them, took a fold of the dress of this noble maiden and kissed it.

"That will not amount to anything," he resumed, "it is necessary that young people should sow their wild oats. An acquaintance with the fine salons of Paris will change the young man's course of ideas. And here, truly, your old friends have the most noble hearts, they are the most worthy people in the world, but they are not amusing. Monsieur le comte, to entertain himself, is obliged to descend, and he will finish by vulgarizing himself."

The next day, the old travelling carriage of the house of D'Esgrignon saw the daylight, and was sent to the coachmakers to be renovated. The young count was solemnly notified by his father, after the déjeuner, of the intentions formed concerning him,—he would go to court to demand some service from the king; on the journey he could decide on some particular career. The navy or the army, the ministries or the embassies, the king's household, he had only to choose, everything would be open to him. The king would doubtless be grateful to the D'Esgrignons for having asked nothing of him, for having reserved the favors of the crown for the heir of the house.

During his period of follies, the young D'Esgrignon had acquired some knowledge of the Parisian world and formed his judgment of real life. As it was a question for him of leaving the province and the paternal mansion, he listened gravely to the address of his worthy father, without replying to him that no one now entered either the navy or the army as formerly; that to become sub-lieutenant of cavalry without passing through special military schools, it was necessary to have served as a page; that the sons of the most illustrious families went to Saint-Cyr and the École Polytechnique, neither more nor less than the sons of plebeians, after public competitions in which the gentlemen ran a fair chance of being surpassed by the serfs. By enlightening his father he would not obtain the funds necessary for a sojourn in Paris, he therefore allowed the marquis and his aunt Armande to believe that he would certainly have to ride in the king's carriages, to appear in the rank which the D'Esgrignons attributed to themselves at the present time, and to come in contact with the greatest seigneurs. The marquis, concerned at being able to give his son but one domestic to accompany him, offered him his old valet, Joséphin, a man in whom he had confidence, who would take care of him, who would watch faithfully over his affairs, and whom the poor father would dispense with, hoping to replace him by a young domestic.

"Remember, my son," he said to him, "that you are a Carol, that your blood is a blood pure of any misalliance, that your arms have for motto: *It is ours!* that it permits you to go everywhere with your head high, and to pretend to queens. Return thanks to your father, as I do to mine. We owe it to the honor of our ancestors, sacredly preserved, to be able to look everything in the face,—and to have to bend the knee only before a mistress, before the king and before God. This is the greatest of your privileges."

The good Chesnel had been present at the déjeuner, he had not taken any part in the heraldic recommendations, or in the letters to the reigning powers of the day; but he had passed the night in writing to one of his old friends, one of the most ancient notaries of Paris. The factitious and real paternity of Chesnel for Victurnien would be uncomprehended if we omitted to give this letter, comparable perhaps to the discourse of Dædalus to Icarus. Are we not obliged to go back to mythology to find comparisons worthy of this antique man?

MY DEAR AND WORTHY SORBIER,

"I remember with delight having made my first exercise of arms in our honorable career under your father, when you had an affection for me, poor little clerk that I was. It is to these clerical souvenirs, so soothing to our hearts, that I appeal to ask of you the only service which I have asked of you in the course of our long life, agitated by political catastrophes to which I have perhaps been indebted for the honor of becoming your colleague. This service, I ask of you, my friend, on the borders of the tomb, in the name of my white hairs, which will fall with grief if you do not yield to my prayers. Sorbier, it is not a question either of me or of mine. I have lost poor Madame Chesnel and have no children. Alas! it is a question of more than my family, if I had one; it concerns the only son of Monsieur le Marquis d'Esgrignon, of whom I have had the honor of being intendant from the day I left the office in which his father had placed me, at his expense, with the intention of enabling me to make my fortune. This household, in which I have been nourished, has experienced all the misfortunes of the Revolution. I have been able to save some of its property, but what is that in comparison with the lost opulence? Sorbier, I should not know how to express to you the degree of attachment which I have for this great house, which I have seen on the point of falling into the abyss of the present times,—proscription, confiscation, old age and childlessness. How many misfortunes! Monsieur le marquis married, his wife died in giving birth to the young count, there remains to-day living only this noble, dear and precious parent. The destinies of this house are centered in this young man, he has made some debts in amusing himself here. What is to be expected in the provinces with a miserable hundred louis? Yes, my friend, a hundred louis, behold the state of the great house of D'Esgrignon. In this extremity, his father has felt the necessity of sending him to Paris to claim at the court the king's favor. Paris is a place very dangerous for youth. It requires, in order to live there wisely, that dose of reason which makes notaries of us. I should moreover be in despair to know this poor child living in such privations as we have experienced. Do you remember the pleasure with which you shared my piece of bread in the parterre of the Théâtre-Français, when we stayed there a day and a night, to see the representation of the *Mariage de Figaro?* Blind that we were! We were happy and poor, but a noble could not be happy in indigence. The indigence of a noble is a thing unnatural. Ah! Sorbier, when one has had the happiness to have, with his own hand, arrested in its fall one of the finest genealogical trees in the kingdom, it is so natural to become attached to it, to love it, to water it, to wish to see it blossom again, that you will not be in the least astonished at the precautions I take, and to hear me claim the assistance of your enlightenment in bringing our young man to good fortune. The house of D'Esgrignon has set aside the sum of a hundred thousand francs for the expenses of the journey of monsieur le comte. You will see him, there is not in Paris a young man who can be compared with him! You will interest yourself in him as in an only son. And I am certain that Madame Sorbier will not hesitate to second you in the moral tutelage with which I invest you. The allowance of Monsieur le Comte Victurnien is fixed at two thousand francs a month; but you will begin by remitting him ten thousand for his first expenses. Thus, the family has provided for a sojourn of two years, unless in the case of a journey abroad, for which we will then see about taking other measures. Associate yourself, my old friend, in this work, and hold the purse-strings a little tightly. Without admonishing monsieur le comte, submit all the considerations to him, restrain him as much as you can, and arrange it so that he will not anticipate his month's allowance, without valid reasons, for he must not be driven to despair in circumstances in which his honor is engaged. Inform yourself of his proceedings, of whatever he does, of his associates; watch over his liaisons. Monsieur le chevalier has informed me that a dancer of the Opéra is often less costly than a woman of the court. Acquire some information on this point, and send me an answer. Madame Sorbier could, in case you are too much occupied, learn what becomes of the young man, where he goes. Perhaps the idea of constituting herself the guardian angel of so charming and so noble a youth will appeal to her! God will be grateful to her for having accepted this saintly mission. Her heart will perhaps tremble in learning how many dangers threaten Monsieur le Comte Victurnien in Paris; you will see him,—he is as handsome as youthful, as intelligent as confiding. If he allies himself with some dangerous woman,

Madame Sorbier could, better than you, warn him of all the dangers which he runs. He is accompanied by an old domestic who can tell you many things. Interrogate Joséphin, whom I have told to consult you in delicate conjunctures. But why should I say more to you? We have been clerks and scamps together, recall to yourself our escapades, and bring to this affair some return of your youth, my old friend. The sixty thousand francs will be remitted to you in a draft on the Treasury by a monsieur of our city, who is going to Paris." Etc.

If the old couple had followed Chesnel's instructions, they would have been obliged to have hired three spies to watch the Comte d'Esgrignon. Nevertheless, there was ample wisdom in the choice of the depositary. A banker pays out funds, so long as he has them in his strongbox, to him who has a letter of credit on him; whilst at each new need of money the young count would be obliged to pay a visit to the notary, who certainly would make use of the right of remonstrance. Victurnien feared to betray his joy in learning that he would have two thousand francs a month. He knew nothing of Paris. With this sum, he believed that he would be able to live royally.

The young count departed on the second day, accompanied with the benedictions of all the habitués of the Cabinet of Antiquities, embraced by the dowagers, overwhelmed with good wishes, followed outside of the city by his old father, by his aunt and by Chesnel, who, all three of them, had their eyes full of tears. This sudden departure furnished for several evenings subject for conversation in the city, it especially moved the malignant hearts of the salon Du Croisier. After having sworn the ruin of the D'Esgrignons, the former contractor, the president and their adherents saw their prey escape them. Their hope for vengeance was based upon the vices of this heedless youth, henceforward beyond their reach.

*

A natural inclination of the human mind, which often makes a profligate of the daughter of a pious woman, a devout woman of the daughter of a woman of light manners, the law of contraries, which is doubtless *the resultant* of the law of similarities, drew Victurnien toward Paris by a desire to which he would have yielded sooner or later. Brought up in an ancient household in the provinces, surrounded by gentle and peaceful faces that smiled upon him, by grave servitors, affectionate toward their masters and in harmony with the antique colors of this dwelling, this youth had never seen any but worthy friends. Excepting only the secular chevalier, all those who surrounded him had formal manners, decent and sententious speech. He had been caressed by those ladies in gray skirts, in embroidered mittens, whom Blondet has described for you. The interior of the paternal mansion was embellished by an ancient luxury which inspired only the least extravagant of thoughts. Finally, instructed by an abbé whose religion was genuine, full of that amenity of the old men whose knowledge embraces two centuries, who bring into ours the dried roses of their experience and the faded flower of the customs of their youth, Victurnien, whom everything should have fashioned for serious habits, whom everything counselled to continue the glory of an old historic house, holding his life as a great and beautiful thing, Victurnien gave ear to the most dangerous ideas. He saw in his rank a stepping-stone that would serve him to rise above other men. By sounding this much worshipped idol in the paternal dwelling, he had been made aware of the hollowness of it. He had become the most dreadful of social beings and the one most commonly encountered, a consistent egotist. Encouraged by the aristocratic religion of self to follow his whims, adored by the first who had had care of his infancy and by the first companions in his youthful follies, he had become accustomed to estimating everything solely by the amount of pleasure it would give him, and to see faithful friends repairing the consequences of his excesses,—a pernicious complaisance that should end by ruining him. His education, however fine and pious it had been, had the defect of having too much isolated him, of having concealed from him the general trend of the life of his epoch, which certainly is not the trend of a provincial town,—his true destiny should have led him higher. He had contracted the habit of not valuing the fact at its social value, but its relative one; he considered his actions good in proportion to their utility. Like the despots he enacted the law for the circumstance; a system which is to the actions of vice that which fantasy is to works of art, a perpetual cause of irregularity. Endowed with a quick and piercing glance, he saw rapidly and justly, but he acted quickly and badly. Something indescribably incomplete, which cannot be explained and which is to be met with in very many young persons, affected his conduct. Notwithstanding his active thought, so sudden in its manifestations, as soon as the sensation was experienced, the brain, obscured, seemed no longer to exist. He should have been the astonishment of sages; he was capable of surprising fools. His desires, like the beginning of a tempest, rapidly covered all the clear and lucid spaces of his brain; then, after the dissipations against which he found himself without any powers of resistance, he fell into a state of enfeeblement of the head, the heart, and the body, into complete prostrations in which he was half imbecile,—a character to drag a man down into the mire when he is delivered up to himself, to conduct him to the highest offices in the state when he is sustained by the hand of a friend without compassion. Neither Chesnel, nor the father, nor the aunt, had been able to sound this soul which was poetical in so many of its tendencies, but which was attainted with a frightful weakness at its heart.

When Victurnien was at the distance of some leagues from his natal city, he did not experience the slightest regret,—he no longer thought of his old father who cherished him as though he were ten generations in one, or of his aunt, whose devotion was almost devoid of reason. He longed for Paris with a fatal violence, he had always transported himself there in thought as into a fairy world, and he had made it the scene of his most beautiful dreams. He counted upon lording it there as in the city and in the department where the influence of his father's name prevailed. Filled, not with pride, but with vanity, his enjoyments aggrandized themselves with all the grandeur of Paris. The journey was rapidly made. As with his thoughts, his carriage made an immediate transition from the narrow horizon of his province to the enormous world of the capital. He stopped at a fine hotel in the Rue de Richelieu, near the Boulevard, and hastened to take possession of Paris as a famished horse rushes into a meadow. But it was not long before he had distinguished the difference between the two localities. Surprised, rather than intimidated by this change, he recognized, with the quickness of his discernment, how small a thing he was in the midst of this Babylonian encyclopedia, how insane he would be to set himself against the torrent of the new manners and ideas. A single fact sufficed for him. The evening before, he had presented his father's letter to the Duc de Lenoncourt, one of the French seigneurs the most in favor with the king. He had found him in his magnificent hôtel, in the midst of aristocratic splendors; the next day he met him on the boulevard, on foot, an umbrella in his hand, lounging, without any distinction, without his blue ribbon which formerly a chevalier of the orders never omitted in his dress. This duke and peer, first gentleman of the king's bed chamber, had not been able, notwithstanding his exquisite politeness, to repress a smile when reading the letter of the marquis, his relative. This smile had informed Victurnien that there was more than sixty leagues between the Cabinet of Antiquities and the Tuileries; there was a distance of several centuries.

At every epoch the throne and the court have been surrounded by favorite families which have no resemblance either in names or characters with those of other reigns. In this sphere, it would seem that it is the fact and not the individual which is perpetuated. If history were not there to prove this observation, it would be incredible. The court of Louis XVIII. thus brought into relief certain men who were almost strangers to those who ornamented that of Louis XV.,—the Rivières, the Blacas, the D'Avarays, the Dambrays, the Vaublancs, Vitrolles, D'Autichamp, La Rochejaquelein, Pasquier, Decazes, Lainé, De Villèle, La Bourdonnaye, etc. If you compare the court of Henri IV. with that of Louis XIV., you will not find five great houses existing,—Villeroi, favorite of Louis XIV., was the grandson of a parvenu secretary under Charles IX. The nephew of Richelieu is already almost nothing there. The D'Esgrignons, almost princely under the Valois, all-powerful under Henry IV., had no chance at the court of Louis XVIII., who did not even think of them. To-day, names as illustrious as those of sovereign houses, like the Foix-Graillys, the D'Hérouvilles, through want of money, the sole power in these days, are in an obscurity which is equivalent to extinction. As soon as Victurnien had formed his opinion of this world, and he judged it only in this light, feeling himself injured by the Parisian equality, a monster which under the Restoration finished devouring the last portion of the social state, he determined to reconquer his station by the use of the arms, dangerous though rusty, which the age had left to the nobility,—he took to imitating the proceedings of those to whom Paris accords its costly attention, he felt that it was necessary to have horses, handsome carriages, all the accessories of modern luxury. As was said to him by De Marsay, the first dandy whom he met in the first salon in which he was introduced, it was necessary for him to *establish himself at the level of his period.* Unfortunately for him, he fell in with the crowd of Parisian roués, the De Marsays, the Ronquerolles, the Maxime de Trailles, the Des Lupeaulx, the Rastignacs, the Vandenesses, the Ajuda-Pintos, the Beaudenords, the la Roche-Hugons and the Des Manervilles whom he met at the houses of the Marquise d'Espard, the Duchesses de Grandlieu, de Garigliano, de Chaulieu, the Marquises d'Aiglemont and De Listomère, Madame de Sérizy, at the Opéra, at the embassies, everywhere where he was received because of his fine name and his apparent fortune. At Paris, a name of the higher nobility, recognized and adopted by the Faubourg Saint-Germain, which knows all its provinces by heart, is a passport which opens all the doors that turn on their hinges with so much difficulty for those unknown or for the heroes of the secondary society. Victurnien found all his relatives agreeable and hospitable so long as he did not appear as soliciting anything,— he had perceived immediately that the method to obtain nothing was to ask for something. At Paris, if the first impulse is to appear as a protector, the second, much more durable, is to have contempt for the protected one. The arrogance, the vanity, the pride, all the good as well as the evil qualities of the young count, induced him to assume, on the contrary, an aggressive attitude. The Ducs de Verneuil, d'Hérouville, de Lenoncourt, de Chaulieu, de Navarreins, de Grandlieu, de Maufrigneuse, the Princes de Cadignan and de Blamont-Chauvry, therefore took pleasure in presenting to the king this charming scion of an old family. Victurnien went to the Tuileries in a magnificent equipage bearing the arms of his house; but his presentation demonstrated to him that the people gave the king too many cares for him to think of his nobles. He perceived at once the state of helotism to which the Restoration, equipped with its eligible old men and its aged courtiers, had condemned the youthful nobility. He comprehended that there was no place suitable for him, either at the court, or in the State, or in the army, in short, anywhere. He therefore threw himself into the world of pleasure. Introduced at the Elysée-Bourbon, at the Duchesse d'Angoulême's, at the Pavilion Marsan, he met everywhere with the testimonials of a superficial politeness due to the heir of an old family which was remembered when it was seen. To be remembered was indeed a good deal. In the distinction with which Victurnien was received, there was the possibility of a peerage and a fine marriage; but his vanity prevented him from declaring his true position, he continued under the appearances of his fictitious opulence. He was at first so complimented on his style, so happy at his first success, that a mortification experienced by many young people, the mortification of abdicating, counselled him to keep up his appearances. He took a little apartment in the Rue du Bac, with a stable, a coach-house and all the accompaniments of the elegant life to which he found himself immediately condemned.

This establishing of himself required fifty thousand francs, and the young count obtained them, in spite of all the precautions of the sage Chesnel, by a combination of unforeseen circumstances. The letter from Chesnel arrived duly at the office of his friend, but his friend was deceased. On seeing a business letter, Madame Sorbier, a widow with very little poetry about her, sent it to the successor of the defunct. Maître Cardot, the new notary, informed the young count that the order on the treasury was valueless if drawn in the name of his predecessor. In reply to the so carefully meditated epistle of the old provincial notary, Maître Cardot wrote a note of four lines concerning, not Chesnel, but the money. Chesnel drew up the order in the name of the young notary who, but little susceptible to the sentimentality of his correspondent and delighted to put himself at the orders of the Comte d'Esgrignon, gave to Victurnien all that he asked. Those who are acquainted with Parisian life are aware that it does not require very many articles of furniture, carriages, horses and much elegance to use up fifty thousand francs; but they should consider that Victurnien had immediately some twenty thousand francs of debts among his tradesmen and furnishers, who at first did not wish for cash payments, his fortune having been promptly exaggerated by public opinion and by Joséphin, a species of Chesnel in livery.

A month after his arrival Victurnien was obliged to go to his notary to draw some ten thousand francs; he had simply been playing whist at the Ducs de Navarreins, de Chaulieu, de Lenoncourt, and at the club. After having at first gained some thousands of francs, he had immediately lost five or six thousand, and he felt the necessity of having a purse for play. Victurnien had the spirit which pleases in the world and which permits the youths of good family to take their stations at any elevation. Not only was he immediately admitted on an equality into the society of this fine youth, but he was even envied. When he saw himself the object of envy, he experienced an intoxicating satisfaction but little calculated to inspire him with desire for reform. He was, in this respect, quite devoid of reason. He did not wish to think of the means, he drew upon his money bags as if they would always fill themselves, and he forbade himself to reflect on the results of this system. In this dissipated world, in this whirlpool of festivals, the actors are admitted on the scene in their brilliant costumes, without any inquiry as to their means,—nothing is in worse taste than to discuss them. Everyone should perpetuate his riches as nature perpetuates hers, in secret. The failures are talked about, there is a mocking anxiety over the fortune of those who are not known, but it goes no farther. A young man like Victurnien, supported by all the powers of the Faubourg Saint-Germain, and to whom his protectors themselves attribute a fortune superior to that which he has, were it only to get rid of him, all that very finely, very elegantly, by a word, by a phrase; in short, a marriageable count, a handsome man, with good ideas, intelligent, whose father still possesses the estates of his old marquisate and the hereditary château, this young man is cordially welcomed in all the houses where there are young wives afflicted with ennui, mothers accompanied by marriageable daughters, or beautiful dancers without dowries. The world, then, enticed him smilingly to the front seats of her theatre. The seats which the marquises of former times occupied on the stage still exist in Paris, where names change, but not things.

Victurnien found again in the society of the Faubourg Saint-Germain, wherein one expresses one's self with extreme reserve, the chevalier's double in the person of the Vidame de Pamiers. The Vidame was a Chevalier de Valois elevated to the tenth power, surrounded by all the prestige of fortune and enjoying the advantages of a lofty station. This dear vidame was the depository of all confidences, the gazette of the faubourg; discreet nevertheless, and, like all gazettes, saying only what can be published. Victurnien heard again the transcendent doctrines of the chevalier set forth. The vidame advised D'Esgrignon, without the least ambiguity, to take some women of good style, and related to him what he had done at his age. That which the Vidame de Pamiers had permitted himself at that time is so very far from modern customs, in which the soul and passion play so large a part, that it is unnecessary to repeat it to readers who would not believe it. But this excellent vidame did still better, he said, as a conclusion, to Victurnien:

"I will give you a dinner to-morrow at the chop-house. After the opera, where we will go to digest, I will conduct you to a house where you will find some persons who have the greatest desire to see you."

The vidame gave him a delicious dinner at the *Rocher de Cancale,* where he found three guests only; De Marsay, Rastignac and Blondet. Émile Blondet was a compatriot of the young count, a writer who was connected with aristocratic society by his liaison with a charming young woman who had come from Victurnien's province, that Demoiselle de Troisville who had married the Comte de Montcornet, one of Napoléon's generals who had gone over to the Bourbons. The vidame professed a profound disesteem for dinners in which the number at table exceeded six. According to him, in those cases, there was no longer any conversation, or cooking, or wines appreciated with justness and knowledge.

"I have not yet informed you where I am going to take you this evening, my dear boy," he said, taking Victurnien by the hands and tapping on them. "You will go to see Mademoiselle des Touches, where will be assembled informally all the pretty young women who have any pretensions to wit. Literature, art, poetry, in short, talents, are there held in honor. It is one of our old depositories of wit, but varnished with monarchic morality, the livery of these times."

"It is sometimes as tedious and wearisome as a pair of new boots, but there are to be found women to whom you can talk only there," said De Marsay.

"If all the poets who come there to clean off their muses resembled our companion here," said Rastignac, slapping Blondet familiarly on the shoulder, "it would be amusing. But the ode, the ballad, the meditations with cheap sentiments, the romances with wide margins, infest a little too much the wits and the sofas."

"Provided that they do not spoil the wives and that they corrupt the young girls," said De Marsay, "I do not hate them."

"Messieurs," said Blondet, smiling, "you are trespassing on my literary field."

"Keep silent, you have stolen from us the most charming woman in the world, you happy scamp!" exclaimed Rastignac, "we can well take from you your least brilliant ideas."

"Yes, the rogue is happy," said the vidame, taking Blondet by the ear and twisting it. "But Victurnien may perhaps be happier this evening—"

"Already!" exclaimed De Marsay. "He has been here a month, scarcely has he had time to shake off the dust of his old manor, to dry the brine in which his aunt had preserved him; scarcely has he had an English horse nearly correct, a tilbury in the fashion, a groom—"

"No, no, he has no groom," said Rastignac, interrupting De Marsay; "he has a species of little peasant whom he has brought *from his town,* and whom Buisson, the tailor who best understands liveries, declares incapable of wearing a waistcoat."

"The fact is," said the vidame gravely, "that you should have modelled yourself upon Beaudenord, who has over you all, my little friends, the advantage of possessing the real English tiger—"

"Behold then, messieurs, the true position of the gentlemen in France!" exclaimed Victurnien. "For them, the great question is to have a tiger, an English horse and knick-knacks—"

"Bless us!" said Blondet, indicating Victurnien,

'The good sense of Monsieur sometimes terrifies me.'

Well then, yes, young moralist, there you are. You have not even any more, like the dear vidame, the glory of the extravagances which made him famous fifty years ago! We have our debauchery in the second story Rue Montorgueil. There is no longer any war with the cardinal nor any field of the Cloth of Gold. In short, you, Comte d'Esgrignon, you sup with a Sieur Blondet, younger son of a miserable provincial judge, to whom you would not give your hand down there, and who in the course of ten years may sit beside you among the peers of the kingdom. After that, believe in yourself, if you can!"

"Well," said Rastignac, "we have passed from the fact to the idea, from brutal force to intellectual force, we are speaking—"

"Let us not speak of our disasters," said the vidame, "I am resolved to die gaily. If our friend has not yet a tiger, he is of the race of the lions, he has no need of one."

"He cannot dispense with one," said Blondet, "he is too recently arrived."

"Although his elegance is still new, we will adopt him," replied De Marsay. "He is worthy of us, he understands his epoch, he has wit, he is noble, he is agreeable, we will love him, we will serve him, we will push him—"

"Where?" said Blondet.

"You inquisitive one!" replied Rastignac.

"With whom is he going to set up housekeeping this evening?" asked De Marsay.

"With a whole seraglio," said the vidame.

"*Peste!* why is it then," De Marsay went on, "that the vidame should require us to be so strict in keeping our word with the Infanta? I should be very unhappy if I were not acquainted with her—"

"I have, however, been as presumptive as he," said the vidame, indicating De Marsay.

After the dinner, which was very agreeable, and maintained on a sustained plane of charming scandal and pretty corruption, Rastignac and De Marsay accompanied the vidame and Victurnien to the Opéra so as to follow them to Mademoiselle des Touches'. These two roués went there at the hour when, as they calculated, there would be finished the reading of a tragedy, which they considered as the thing the most unwholesome to take between eleven o'clock and midnight. They came to spy on Victurnien, and to vex him with their presence,—veritable schoolboy's malice, but sharpened by the rancour of the jealous dandy. Victurnien had that effrontery of a page which contributes greatly to ease of manner; so that, when watching the newcomer make his entrance, Rastignac was surprised at his prompt initiation into the good manners of the moment.

"That little D'Esgrignon will go far, will he not?" he said to his companion.

"That depends," replied De Marsay, "but he makes a good start."

The vidame presented the young count to one of the duchesses, the most charming, the most frivolous of that period, and whose adventures did not make any sensation till five years later. In all the splendor of her glory, suspected already of some lightness of conduct, but without any proof, she was then enjoying all the prominence which Parisian slander lends to a woman as to a man,—slander never attacks the mediocrities, who are furious at living peacefully. This lady was, in fact, the Duchesse de Maufrigneuse, a Demoiselle d'Uxelles, whose father-in-law was still living, and who was not Princesse de Cadignan till later. A friend of the Duchesse de Langeais, a friend of the Vicomtesse de Beauséant, two splendors that had been extinguished, she was intimate with the Marquise d'Espard, with whom at this moment she disputed the fragile royalty of fashion. A number of important kinsfolk long protected her; but she was one of that species of women who, without anyone being able to discover on what, where, or how, would devour the revenues of the earth and those of the moon if they could get them. Her character was only indicating itself as yet, De Marsay alone had sounded it. When he saw the vidame bringing Victurnien up to this delightful person, this formidable dandy leaned over to Rastignac's ear.

"My dear fellow, he will be," he said, *"uist!* hissed like a punchinello by a hackney coachman."

This horribly vulgar word predicted admirably the incidents of this passion. The Duchesse de Maufrigneuse came to dote upon Victurnien after having studied him seriously. A loving one who had seen the angelic glance with which she thanked the vidame would have been jealous of such an expression of friendship. Women are like horses set loose in a wide steppe when they find themselves, like the duchess with the vidame, in a field in which there is no danger,—they are then natural, they love, perhaps, to give thus specimens of their secret tendernesses. It was a discreet glance, from eye to eye, impossible to repeat in any mirror, and which no one caught.

"How she has prepared herself!" said Rastignac to De Marsay. "What a toilet of a virgin, what swanlike grace in her neck of snow, what a glance of an inviolate Madonna, what a white dress, what a young girl's girdle! Who would have said that you had passed by that way?"

"But she is thus precisely because of that," replied De Marsay, with an air of triumph.

The two young men exchanged a smile. Madame de Maufrigneuse caught this smile and divined the subject of their conversation. She darted at the two roués one of those glances with which the French were unacquainted before the peace, and which have been imported by the English with the shapes of their silverware, their harness, their horses and their piles of Britannic ice which refresh a salon when there are assembled in it a certain number of "ladies." The two young men became as serious as two clerks who wait for a donation at the end of the reproof which a director is administering to them. In becoming enamored of Victurnien, the duchess had resolved to play that rôle of the romantic Agnès which several women have imitated to the misfortune of the youth of the day. Madame de Maufrigneuse had concluded to improvise the character of an angel, as she meditated taking up with literature and science about the age of forty, instead of taking up with religion. She made it a point to resemble no one. She created for herself dresses and rôles, bonnets and opinions, toilets and original lines of action. After her marriage, while she was still almost a young girl, she had played the part of a knowing and almost perverted woman,—she had allowed herself to make compromising repartees in the company of superficial people, but which proved her ignorance to the true connoisseurs. As the date of this marriage prevented her from concealing from general knowledge one single year of her age, and as she had reached the age of twenty-six, she had invented the plan of making herself immaculate. She appeared to be scarcely attached to the earth, she agitated her great sleeves as if they were wings. Her glance took its flight to Heaven at the slightest word, at an idea, at a look a little too ardent. The Madonna of Piola, that great Genoese painter, assassinated through jealousy at the moment when he was on the point of making another Raphael, this Madonna, the most chaste of all and which can scarcely be seen under its glass in a little street of Genoa, this celestial Madonna is a Messalina compared with the Duchesse de Maufrigneuse. The women asked themselves how this heedless young thing had become, in one single change of toilet, this veiled seraphic beauty which seemed, according to an expression then in vogue, to have a soul as white as the last fall of snow upon the highest Alps; how she had so promptly resolved the Jesuitical problem of freely displaying a throat whiter than her soul while concealing it under gauze; how she could be so entirely ethereal while directing her glances in a manner so assassinating. She had the air of promising a thousand voluptuousnesses by this almost lascivious glance of the eye when by an ascetic sigh, full of aspirations toward a higher life, her mouth appeared to say that she would not realize one of them. Some ingenuous young men—there were some at this period in the Garde Royale—

asked themselves if, even in the most intimate moments possible, any one would *thou* this species of White Lady, a sidereal vapor fallen from the Milky Way. This system, which triumphed for several years, was very profitable to those women who had their elegant bosoms lined with a strong philosophy, and who concealed great exigencies under these little airs of the sacristy. Not one of these celestial creatures was ignorant of the amount of profit in good love which they would make from the desire of every well-born man to bring them back to earth. This fashion permitted them to remain in their Empyrean, semi-Catholic and semi-Ossianic; they could and would ignore all the vulgar details of life, which solved a great many questions. The application of this system divined by De Marsay will explain his last speech to Rastignac, whom he saw to be almost jealous of Victurnien.

"Young man," he said to him, "remain where you are,—our Nucingen will make your fortune, whilst the duchess would ruin you. She is too expensive a woman."

Rastignac allowed De Marsay to depart without asking him anything more,—he knew his Paris. He knew that the woman the most precious, the most noble, the most disinterested in the world, who could be persuaded to accept nothing more important than a bouquet, would become as dangerous for a young man as the girls from the Opéra of former times. In fact, the girls of the Opéra have passed into the mythological period. The present customs of the theatres have made of the dancers and the actresses something as amusing as a declaration of Women's Rights, puppets who go about in the morning as virtuous and respectable mothers of families, before showing their legs in the evening in tights in a man's part. From the depths of his study in the provinces, the good Chesnel had well divined one of the rocks on which the young count might shipwreck himself. The poetic aureole assumed by Madame de Maufrigneuse dazzled Victurnien, who was padlocked in from the very first hour, attached to this young girl's girdle, caught fast by these curls twisted by the hands of fairies. This youth already so corrupted believed in this humbug of virginity in muslin, in this smooth expression prepared in deliberation like a law in the two Chambers. Is it not sufficient for him who is to believe in the falsehoods of a woman to believe in them? The rest of the world has for two lovers the value of the figures in a tapestry. The duchess was, without compliment, one of the ten prettiest women in Paris, admitted, recognized. You know that there are in the world of lovers as many *prettiest women in Paris* as there are *finest works of the epoch* in literature. At Victurnien's age, the conversation which he held with the duchess could be maintained without too much fatigue. Sufficiently young, and sufficiently little informed of the ways of Parisian life, he had no need of being on his guard, or of watching carefully his slightest words and his looks. That religious sentimentalism, which betrays itself in each conversationalist in very absurd mental reservations, excludes the pleasant familiarity, the spiritual ease of the ancient French conversations,—now, we love through two clouds. Victurnien had precisely enough of the innocence of the department to remain in a very suitable and unfeigned ecstasy which pleased the duchess, for the women are no more the dupes of the comedies played by men than of their own. Madame de Maufrigneuse estimated, not without some affright, the error of the young count as equivalent to six good months of pure love. She was as delicious to see as a clove, extinguishing the light of her glances under the golden fringe of her lashes, so that the Marquise d'Espard, coming to bid her good-night, began by whispering in her ear: "Good! very good! my dear!" Then the beautiful marchioness left her rival to wander over the modern map of the country of Tenderness, which is not so altogether a ridiculous conception as some persons think. This map is re-engraved from century to century with other names and always leads to the same capital. In an hour of public tête-à-tête, in a corner, on a divan, the duchess led D'Esgrignon up to Scipionesque generosities, to Amadisian devotions, to abnegations of the Middle Ages which were then beginning to display their daggers, their machicolations, their coats-of-mail, their hauberks, their peaked shoes, and all their romantic baggage in painted cardboard. She was, moreover, admirable in ideas unexpressed, but thrust into Victurnien's heart like needles in a pin-cushion, one by one, in an inattentive and discreet manner. She was marvellous in reticences, charming in hypocrisies, prodigal of subtle promises which dissolved on examination like ice in the sun after having revived hope, in fine, very perfidious in desires conceived and inspired. This beautiful meeting ended in the running noose of an invitation to come to see her, given with those dissembling graces which printed writing will never depict.

"You will forget me!" she said, "you will see so many women eager to pay court to you instead of enlightening you.—But you will come back to me disabused.—Would you have come, ere now?—No, as you like.—For my part, I will say quite frankly that your visits will give me much pleasure. People with souls are so rare, and I believe you have one.—Come, say farewell; we shall end by being talked about if we talk together any longer."

Literally, she flew away. Victurnien did not remain long after the departure of the duchess; but he remained, however, long enough to allow his ravishment to be perceived by that attitude of happy people, which partakes at once of the calm discretion of inquisitors and the concentrated beatitude of devotees who issue with full absolution from the confessional.

"Madame de Maufrigneuse attained her end with sufficient rapidity this evening," said the Duchesse de Grandlieu, when there were but six persons remaining in the salon of Mademoiselle des Touches,—Des Lupeaulx, a maître des requêtes much in favor, Vandenesse, the Vicomtesse de Grandlieu, Canalis and Madame de Sérizy.

"D'Esgrignon and Maufrigneuse are two names which should hang up together," replied Madame de Sérizy, who had pretensions as a maker of phrases.

"For the last few days, she has thrown herself with new zest into Platonism," said Des Lupeaulx.

"She will ruin that poor innocent," said Charles de Vandenesse.

"How do you mean?" asked Mademoiselle des Touches.

"Oh! morally and financially, there is no doubt about it," said the viscountess, rising.

This cruel speech had cruel realities for the young Comte d'Esgrignon. The next morning he wrote a letter to his aunt in which he painted his début in the lofty world of the Faubourg Saint-Germain in the lively colors which are reflected by the prism of love. He detailed the welcome which he had everywhere received in such a manner as to gratify his father's pride. The marquis caused this long letter to be read to him twice and rubbed his hands on hearing the recital of the dinner given by the Vidame de Pamiers, an old acquaintance of his, and of the presentation of his son to the duchess; but he lost himself in conjectures without being able to comprehend the presence of the younger son of a judge, of the Sieur Blondet, who had been public prosecutor during the Revolution. There was a fête that evening in the Cabinet of Antiquities,—the success of the young count afforded matter for discussion. They were so discreet concerning Madame de Maufrigneuse that the chevalier was the only man in whom they confided. This letter was without a financial postscript, without that disagreeable conclusion relative to the sinews of war, which every young man adds in a similar case. Mademoiselle Armande communicated the letter to Chesnel. Chesnel was happy over it, without raising the slightest objection. It was clear, as the chevalier and the marquis said, that a young man beloved by the Duchesse de Maufrigneuse was destined to be one of the heroes of the court, where, as formerly, success of all kinds was obtained through the women. The young count had not made a bad choice. The dowagers related all the gallant stories concerning the Maufrigneuses from Louis XIII. down to Louis XVI., they spared the preceding reigns; in short, they were enchanted. Madame de Maufrigneuse was much praised for having taken an interest in Victurnien. The assembly of the Cabinet of Antiquities was worthy of being listened to by a dramatic author who wished to depict the real comedy. Victurnien received charming letters from his father, from his aunt, from the chevalier who asked to be remembered to the vidame, with whom he had visited Spa, at the period of the journey made in 1778 by a celebrated Hungarian princess. Chesnel wrote also. All these pages glowed with the adulation to which this unfortunate youth had been habituated. Mademoiselle Armande seemed to enter largely into the pleasures of Madame de Maufrigneuse. Happy in the approval of his family, the young count threw himself vigorously into the perilous and costly path of dandyism. He had five horses, he was moderate,—De Marsay had fourteen. He returned to the vidame, to De Marsay, to Rastignac, and even to Blondet, the dinner he had been given. This dinner cost five hundred francs. The provincial was fêted by these messieurs, on the same scale, grandly. He played a great deal, and unluckily, at whist, the game then in fashion. He organized his idleness in such a manner as to be occupied. Victurnien went every morning, from noon to three o'clock, to the house of the duchess; from there, he joined her again in the Bois de Boulogne, he on horseback, she in a carriage. If these two charming partners arranged some equestrian parties, they took place on fine mornings. In the evening, society functions, balls, fêtes, theatres, occupied the young count's hours. Victurnien shone everywhere, for everywhere he threw about the pearls of his wit, he judged men, things and events with words of discretion,—you would have said a fruit tree which bore nothing but flowers. He led that wearisome life in which there is perhaps even more dissipation of mind than of money, in which the finest talents are buried, in which perish the most incorruptible probities, in which the best-tempered wills become enfeebled. The duchess, this creature so white, so frail, so angelic, found pleasure in the dissipated life of bachelors; she liked to attend first representations, she loved the curious, the unexpected. She was not acquainted with the chop-house,—D'Esgrignon arranged for her a charming party at the *Rocher de Cancale* with the society of the agreeable roués with whom she frequented while moralizing them, and who displayed a gaiety, a wit, an entertaining quality equal to the price of the supper. This party led to others. Nevertheless, this was for Victurnien an angelic passion. Yes, Madame de Maufrigneuse remained an angel untainted by the corruptions of the earth,—an angel at the Variétés before those farces half for the people and half obscene which made her laugh, an angel in the midst of the cross fire of delightful pleasantries and scandalous chronicles which enlivened the fine assemblies, a languid angel at the Vaudeville in a closed box, an angel when watching the attitudes of the ballet-dancers at the Opéra and when criticising them with all the science of an old man of the ancient theatrical faction of the *coin de la reine*, an angel at the Porte Saint-Martin, an angel at the little theatres of the boulevard, an angel at the masked ball where she amused herself like a schoolboy; an angel who wished that love should subsist on privations, on heroism, on sacrifices, and who made D'Esgrignon change a horse whose color displeased her, who wished him to maintain the style of an English lord with an income of a million. She was an angel at play. Certainly no bourgeoise woman would have ventured to say angelically as she did to D'Esgrignon: "Make the stakes for me!" She was so divinely foolish when she committed a folly that it was worth while selling your soul to the devil to entertain this angel in her appreciation of terrestrial joys.

At the end of his first winter, the young count had drawn from Monsieur Cardot, who scrupulously refrained from using the right of remonstrance, the trifle of thirty thousand francs in excess of the sum sent by Chesnel. An extremely polite refusal of the notary to a new demand apprised Victurnien of this debit, and he was all the more vexed at the refusal as he had lost six thousand francs at the club and he required the money to pay. After having taken offence at the refusal of Maître Cardot, who had had thirty thousand francs' worth of confidence in him, and who while writing fully to Chesnel, made a great parade of this pretended confidence to the favorite of the beautiful Duchesse de Maufrigneuse, D'Esgrignon was obliged to ask him what steps to take, as it was a question of a debt of honor.

"Draw some bills of exchange on your father's banker, carry them to his correspondent, who will doubtless discount them, then write to your family to remit the funds to this banker."

In the distress in which he found himself, the young count heard an inward voice which suggested to him the name of Du Croisier, whose disposition toward the aristocracy, before whom he had seen him cringing, was entirely unknown to him. He therefore wrote a very easy and indifferent letter to this banker in which he informed him that he had drawn upon him a bill of exchange for ten thousand francs, the funds for which would be remitted to him on the receipt of his letter by Monsieur Chesnel or by Mademoiselle Armande D'Esgrignon. Then he wrote two affecting letters to Chesnel and to his aunt. When it is a question of ruining themselves, young men give evidence of great address, of singular skill, they have surprising good fortune. Victurnien discovered in the course of the morning the address of the Parisian bankers, the Kellers, who were connected with Du Croisier, De Marsay giving it to him. De Marsay knew all about Paris. The Kellers remitted to D'Esgrignon, without discount, without a word said, the amount of the bill of exchange,—they were indebted to Du Croisier. This gambling debt was nothing in comparison with the state of things in the apartment; it rained bills around Victurnien.

"Well, you concern yourself with that?" said Rastignac one morning to D'Esgrignon, laughing. "You will settle them, my dear fellow? I did not think you so bourgeois."

"My dear boy, it is quite necessary to think of them, I have them to the amount of some twenty and odd thousand francs."

De Marsay, who had come to get D'Esgrignon for a steeple-chase, drew out an elegant little pocket-book, took from it twenty thousand francs and presented them to him.

"Behold," said he, "the surest way of not losing them. I am to-day doubly delighted at having won them yesterday from my honorable father, my Lord Dudley."

This French grace seduced D'Esgrignon entirely, he believed in friendship, he did not pay his bills, and made use of this money for his pleasures. De Marsay, to use an expression of the language of dandies, saw with an indescribable pleasure, D'Esgrignon *sinking in the mud,* he took pleasure in placing his hand on his shoulder with all the feline amenities of friendship to press him down and to make him disappear all the sooner, for he was jealous of the display with which the duchess allied herself with D'Esgrignon when she had demanded privacy from him. He was, moreover, one of those rude banterers who take pleasure in evil as the Turkish women do in the bath. Therefore, when he had carried off the prize of the race, and when the bettors had assembled in an inn where they were taking déjeuner, and where there were to be found several good bottles of wine, De Marsay said laughingly to D'Esgrignon:

"Those bills over which you were worrying were certainly not yours."

"Eh! was he worrying?" asked Rastignac.

"And whose were they then?" asked D'Esgrignon.

"You do not then know the duchess's position?" said De Marsay, assuming a lofty air.

"No," replied D'Esgrignon, interested.

"Well, then, my dear," replied De Marsay, "listen,—thirty thousand francs with Victorine, eighteen thousand francs with Houbigant, an account with Herbault, with Nattier, with Nourtier, with the little Latours, in all, a hundred thousand francs."

"An angel," said D'Esgrignon, lifting his eyes to heaven.

"Behold the account for her wings," cried Rastignac boisterously.

"She owes all that, my dear fellow," replied De Marsay, "precisely because she is an angel; but we have all met angels in these situations," said he, looking at Rastignac. "The women are sublime in this, that they understand nothing about money, they do not have anything to do with it, it does not concern them; they are invited to the *banquet of life,* according to the expression of I-know-not-what poet wrecked in a hospital."

"How is it that you know that, whilst I do not know it?" said D'Esgrignon ingenuously.

"You will be the last to know it, as she will be the last to learn that you have debts."

"I thought that she had a hundred thousand francs of income," said D'Esgrignon.

"Her husband," replied De Marsay, "has separated from her and lives with his regiment, where he practises economy, for he has some little debts also, our dear duke! Where do you come from? Learn then to compute like us, the accounts of your friends. Mademoiselle Diane—I loved her for her name!—Diane d'Uxelles was married with sixty thousand francs of income of her own, her household has for the last eight years been conducted on a basis of two hundred thousand francs of income; it is clear that at this moment her estates are all mortgaged beyond their actual value; it will be necessary some fine morning to cast the die, and the angel will be put to flight by—must it be said? by the sheriff's officers who will have the impudence to levy on an angel as they would collar one of us."

"Poor angel!"

"Eh! the deuce! it costs very dearly to remain in the Parisian paradise; it is necessary to whiten your skin and your wings every morning," said Rastignac.

As it had occurred to D'Esgrignon to confide his embarrassment to his dear Diane, he experienced something like a shiver in reflecting that he already owed sixty thousand francs and that he had bills for ten thousand more coming in. He returned, sufficiently melancholy. His ill-disguised preoccupation was observed by his friends, who said to each other at dinner:

"That little D'Esgrignon is going down! he has not the Parisian style, he will blow out his brains. He is a little fool—" Etc.

The young count was promptly consoled. His valet de chambre handed him two letters. In the first place, a letter from Chesnel which smelled musty with the fidelity which chides, and the consecrated phrases of probity; he respected it, he would keep it for the evening. Then, a second letter in which he read with an infinite pleasure the Ciceronian phrases in which Du Croisier, on his knees before him like Sganarelle before Géronte, entreated him to spare him in the future the affront of depositing in advance the funds for the bills of exchange which he would deign to draw on him. This letter ended by a phrase which resembled so much a strong-box open and full of écus for the service of the noble house of D'Esgrignon, that Victurnien made the gesture of Sganarelle, of Mascarille and of all those who feel the prickings of conscience to the ends of their fingers. Confident that he had an unlimited credit at the Kellers, he gaily unsealed Chesnel's letter; he expected four pages full, filled and overflowing with remonstrances, he saw already the usual words of prudence, honor, line of conduct, etc., etc. He was seized with something like a vertigo in reading these words:

"MONSIEUR LE COMTE,
"There remains to me, of my entire fortune, only two hundred thousand francs; I entreat you not to exceed them, if you will do me the honor of accepting them from the most devoted of the servitors of your family, who presents to you his respects.

"CHESNEL."

"There is a man for Plutarch," said Victurnien to himself, throwing the letter on the table.

He had a feeling of self-contempt, he felt himself little before so much grandeur.

"Come, it is necessary to reform," he thought.

Instead of dining at the restaurant, where he expended at each dinner between fifty and sixty francs, he economized by dining at the house of the Duchesse de Maufrigneuse, to whom be related the anecdote of the letter.

"I should like to see that man," said she, making her eyes shine like two fixed stars.

"What would you do with him?"

"Why, I would give him charge of my business affairs."

Diane was divinely arrayed, she wished to do honor with her toilet to Victurnien, who was fascinated by the lightness with which she spoke of her affairs, or, more exactly, her debts. The handsome couple went to the Italiens. Never had that beautiful and seductive woman appeared more seraphic or more ethereal. No one in the audience would have believed in the debts, the amount of which had been stated that very morning by De Marsay to D'Esgrignon. None of the cares of earth touched this sublime forehead, filled with feminine pride most nobly enshrined. In her, a thoughtful air seemed to be the reflection of earthly love nobly suppressed. The greater number of the men bet that Victurnien was in it at his own expense, against the women who were sure of the defeat of their rival, and who admired her as Michael Angelo admired Raphael, *in petto!* Victurnien loved Diane, according to these, because of her hair, for she had the most beautiful blond hair in France; according to those, her principal merit lay in her whiteness, for she was not very well-formed, only well-dressed; according to others, D'Esgrignon loved her for her foot, the only beautiful thing about her, her figure was flat. But that which depicts surprisingly the actual manners of Paris,—on one side, the men said that the duchess furnished Victurnien's luxury; on the other, the women gave it to be understood that Victurnien paid, as Rastignac said, for the wings of this angel. As they returned, Victurnien, on whom the debts of the duchess weighed much more heavily than his own, had on his lips twenty times an interrogation that should open this chapter; but twenty times it was lost before the attitude of this divine creature in the light of the lanterns of her coupé, seducing with those voluptuousnesses which, with her, seemed always to be wrested violently from her Madonna-like purity. The duchess did not commit the fault of speaking of her virtue, or of her condition of an angel, like the women of the provinces who have imitated her; she was much more skilful, she made him think of it, for whom she committed such great sacrifices. She would give at the end of six months, the air of a capital sin to the most innocent kissing of the hand, she managed the apparent extortion of her good graces with so consummate an art that it was impossible not to believe her more of an angel after than before. It is only the Parisiennes who are clever enough to be able always to give a new attraction to the moon and to make the stars romantic, to be able always to roll in the same sack of charcoal and always to come out of it whiter than ever. Therein is the highest state of civilization, intellectual and Parisian. The women from the other side of the Rhine or the channel believe in these foolish stories when they retail them; whereas the Parisiennes make their lovers believe in them so as to make them happier in flattering all their vanities, temporal and spiritual. Some persons have wished to diminish the merit of the duchess in pretending that she was herself the first dupe of her sorcery. Infamous calumny! The duchess believed in nothing but herself.

At the commencement of the winter, between the years 1823 and 1824, Victurnien had at the Kellers a debit account of two hundred thousand francs, of which neither Chesnel nor Mademoiselle Armande knew anything at all. In order to conceal better the source on which he drew, be caused Chesnel to send him from time to time two thousand écus; he wrote lying letters to his poor father and to his aunt, who lived in happiness, deceived as are the greater number of happy people. A single individual was in the secret of the horrible catastrophe which the fascinating allurement of Parisian life had prepared for this grand and noble family. Du Croisier, when he passed in the evening before the Cabinet of Antiquities, rubbed his hands with joy, he hoped to attain his ends. His ends were no longer the ruin, but the dishonor of the house of D'Esgrignon, he had at this time the instinctive sense of his vengeance, he scented it! At last he was sure of it when he knew the young count's debts to amount to a burden under which this young soul must succumb. He began by assassinating that one of his enemies who was the most antipathetic to him, the venerable Chesnel. This good old man lived in the Rue du Bercail in a house with very high roofs, with a little paved court, along the walls of which the rose bushes grew as high as the first story. Behind it was a little provincial garden, enclosed with damp and sombre walls, divided into beds by box-wood borders. The gate, neat and gray, had that grated opening armed with bells which announced, as clearly as the scutcheons: "Here breathes a notary." It was half-past five o'clock in the evening, the hour at which the old man was digesting his dinner. Chesnel was in his old black leather armchair, before his fire; he had put on that armor of painted cardboard, imitating a boot, with which he protected his legs from the heat. The good man had the habit of placing his feet on the bar and of poking the fire as he digested, he always ate too much,—he loved good cheer. Alas! without this petty defect would he not have been more perfect than it is permitted to man to be? He had just taken his cup of coffee, his old housekeeper had retired, carrying away the tea-board which had served for this purpose for twenty years; he was waiting for his clerks before going out for his engagements; he was thinking, do not ask of whom or of what. Rarely did a day pass away without his saying to himself: "Where is he? what is he doing?" He believed him to be in Italy with the beautiful Maufrigneuse. One of the most soothing enjoyments of men who possess a fortune acquired, and not inherited, is the remembrance of the pains it has cost and the thought of the future which they will give to their écus,—they enjoy all the tenses of the verb. Thus this man, all whose sentiments were bound up in an only attachment, had double pleasure in reflecting that his lands, so carefully selected, so well cultivated, so painfully acquired, would increase the domains of the house of D'Esgrignon. At his ease in his old armchair he swelled with pride in his hopes,—he contemplated alternately the edifice reared by his tongs in the burning coals and the edifice of the house of D'Esgrignon restored by his cares. He congratulated himself on the course which he had given to his life when he imagined the young count happy. Chesnel was not wanting in intelligence, his soul did not act singly in this great devotion, he had his own pride, he resembled those nobles who rebuild the pillars in the cathedrals and inscribe their own names on them,—he would inscribe his in the memory of the house of D'Esgrignon. They should speak of the old Chesnel. At this moment, his aged housekeeper entered with all the signs of excessive fright.

"Is it a fire, Brigitte?" asked Chesnel.

"It is something like that," she replied. "Here is Monsieur du Croisier who wishes to speak to you—"

"Monsieur du Croisier," repeated the old man, so cruelly touched, even to the heart, by the cold blade of suspicion, that he dropped his tongs. "Monsieur du Croisier here," he thought, "our deadly enemy!"

Du Croisier entered with the manner of a cat which smells the milk in a pantry. He bowed, took the armchair which the notary pushed toward him, seated himself in it very gently, and presented an account of two hundred and twenty-seven thousand francs, interest included, amounting to the total of the sums advanced to Monsieur Victurnien in bills of exchange drawn upon and paid by him, and of which he required a settlement under penalty of immediate procedure with the utmost rigor against the heir presumptive of the house of D'Esgrignon. Chesnel handled these fatal letters one by one, requesting secrecy from the enemy of the family. The enemy promised to keep silence, if he were paid within forty-eight hours,—he was pressed for money, he had advanced to the manufacturers. Du Croisier set forth that series of pecuniary falsehoods which deceive neither the borrowers nor the notaries. The eyes of the good man were troubled, he retained his tears with difficulty, he could pay only by mortgaging his property for the remainder of its value. On learning the difficulty which attended his repayment, Du Croisier was no longer pressed, he was no longer in need of money, he suddenly proposed to the old notary to purchase his property from him. This sale was signed and consummated in two days. The poor Chesnel could not support the thought of knowing the son of the house imprisoned for debts, for five years. A few days later, there remained therefore to the notary nothing but his business, his debts due to it, and his house. Chesnel walked about, stripped of his property, under the black walnut ceiling of his cabinet, looking at the chestnut rafters with carved fillets, looking at his vine arbor through the window, thinking no longer of his farms or of his dear country place of the Jard, not at all.

"What will become of him? He must be recalled, married to a rich heiress," he said to himself, his eyes troubled and his head heavy.

He did not know how to approach Mademoiselle Armande, or in what terms to inform her of this news. He who had just discharged the amount of the debts in the name of the family, trembled to have to speak of these things. In going from the Rue du Bercail to the Hôtel d'Esgrignon the good old notary was palpitating like a young girl flying from the paternal roof to return to it only as a mother and despairing. Mademoiselle Armande had just received a letter charming in hypocrisy, in which her nephew appeared to be the happiest man in the world. After having been to take the waters and to Italy with Madame de Maufrigneuse, Victurnien sent the journal of his travels to his aunt. Love breathed through every phrase. At one time, a ravishing description of Venice and an enchanting appreciation of the masterpieces of Italian art; at another, divine pages upon the Duomo of Milan, upon Florence; here, the description of the Apennines contrasted with that of the Alps; there, villages, like that of Chiavari, where happiness ready-made is to be found around you, fascinated the poor aunt, who saw floating across these countries of love an angel whose tenderness lent to these beautiful things an illuminated air. Mademoiselle Armande inspired this letter in long breaths, as should a discreet maiden, ripened in the fire of restrained, compressed passions, a victim of desires offered as a holocaust upon the domestic altar with a constant joy. She had not the angelic air of the duchess, she resembled at this time those statuettes, straight, thin, lank, yellowish in color, which the marvellous artists of the cathedrals have placed in some angles, at the feet of which the dampness permits the bindweed to grow and to crown them some fine day with a beautiful blue flower. At this moment the bell-flower expanded in the eyes of this saint,—Mademoiselle Armande loved whimsically this beautiful couple, she found nothing to condemn in the love of a married woman for Victurnien, she would have blamed it in any other; but here the crime would have been not to love her nephew. The aunts, the mothers and the sisters have a particular jurisprudence for their nephews, their sons and their brothers. She saw herself then in the midst of the palaces built by fairies on the two banks of the Grand Canal. She was there in Victurnien's gondola, and he told her how happy he had been to feel in his hand the beautiful hand of the duchess, and to be loved while sailing over the bosom of this amorous queen of the Italian seas. At this very moment of angelic beatitude Chesnel appeared at the end of the alley! Alas! the gravel creaked under his shoes, like that which falls from the hourglass of Death, and which he treads under his unshod feet. This sound and the sight of Chesnel in a state of dreadful desolation gave to the spinster that cruel emotion which is caused by the recall of the senses sent by the soul into the realms of imagination.

"What is the matter?" she exclaimed, as if struck to the heart.

"Everything is lost" said Chesnel. "Monsieur le comte will dishonor the house, if we do not stop it."

He showed the bills of exchange, he depicted the tortures which he had experienced for the last four days, in a few words, simple yet energetic and affecting.

"The unhappy one, he is deceiving us!" cried Mademoiselle Armande, whose heart dilated under the affluence of the blood which surged into it in great waves.

"Let us say our *mea culpa*, mademoiselle," replied the old man in a strong voice, "we have accustomed him to following his own will; he required a severe guide, and that could be neither you who are a maiden, nor I to whom he would not listen,—he has had no mother."

"There are terrible fatalities for the noble races which are falling," said Mademoiselle Armande, her eyes full of tears.

At this moment, the marquis appeared. The old man returned from his walk reading the letter which his son had written him on his return, describing his journey from the aristocratic point of view. Victurnien had been received by the greatest Italian families, at Genoa, at Turin, at Milan, at Florence, at Venice, at Rome, at Naples; he had been indebted for their flattering welcome to his name and also perhaps to the duchess. In short, he had made a magnificent display, and such as a D'Esgrignon should have done.

"You are going to do foolish things, Chesnel," he said to the old notary.

Mademoiselle Armande made a sign to Chesnel, an eager and terrible sign, equally understood by both. This poor father, this flower of feudal honor, must be allowed to die in his illusions. A compact of silence and of devotion between the noble notary and the noble maid was concluded by a simple inclination of the head.

"Ah! Chesnel, it was not altogether in this manner that the D'Esgrignons went into Italy in the fifteenth century, when the Maréchal Trivulce, in the service of France, served under a D'Esgrignon who had Bayard under his orders,—other times, other pleasures. The Duchesse de Maufrigneuse is, however, well worth the Marquise de Spinola."

The old man, posed upon his genealogical tree, balanced himself with a complacent air as if he had had the Marquise de Spinola, and as if he possessed the modern duchess. When the two afflicted ones were alone, seated on the same bench, united in the same thoughts, they exchanged for a long time only vague, insignificant words, while contemplating this happy father who went away gesticulating as if he were speaking to himself.

"What will become of him?" said Mademoiselle Armande.

"Du Croisier has given orders to the Messieurs Keller to remit him no more sums without authority," replied Chesnel.

"He has debts," Mademoiselle Armande went on.

"I fear so."

"If he has no more resources, what will he do?"

"I do not dare to answer to myself."

"But it is necessary to snatch him from this life, to bring him back here, for he will come to want for everything."

"And to fail in everything," answered Chesnel lugubriously.

Mademoiselle Armande did not yet comprehend, she could not comprehend the meaning of this speech.

"How can we get him away from that woman, from that duchess, who perhaps will draw him on?" she asked.

"He will commit crimes to remain with her," said Chesnel, endeavoring to arrive by supportable transitions at an insupportable idea.

"Crimes!" repeated Mademoiselle Armande. "Ah! Chesnel, this idea could only come from you," she added, throwing upon him a crushing look, the look by which a woman can overwhelm the gods. "Gentlemen commit no other crimes than those called high treason, and then their heads are struck off on a black cloth, like kings'."

"The times are very much changed," said Chesnel, shaking his head, from which Victurnien had caused the last gray locks to fall. "Our martyr king did not die like Charles of England."

This reflection calmed the magnificent anger of the noble maid; she shuddered, without yet accepting Chesnel's idea.

"We will decide to-morrow," she said, "it requires reflection. We have our property, in case of misfortune."

"Yes," replied Chesnel, "you are joint proprietor with monsieur le marquis, the greater part belongs to you, you can mortgage it without saying anything to him."

During the evening, the players, male and female, of whist, of reversi, of boston, of backgammon, remarked some agitation in the features, usually so calm and so pure, of Mademoiselle Armande.

"Poor sublime child!" said the old Marquise de Castéran, "she must suffer still. A woman never knows to what she commits herself in making the sacrifices which she has made to her house."

It was decided the next day with Chesnel that Mademoiselle Armande should go to Paris, to snatch her nephew from his perdition. If any one could bring about the carrying off of Victurnien, would it not be the woman who had for him the heart of a mother? Mademoiselle Armande, resolved to go and see the Duchesse de Maufrigneuse, wished to make everything known to this woman. But it required some pretext to justify this journey in the eyes of the marquis and of the city. Mademoiselle Armande risked all her modesty as a virtuous maid in allowing a belief to be spread in some malady that required a consultation of skilful and celebrated physicians. God knows if it were talked about! Mademoiselle Armande saw a very different honor from her own in peril! She set out, Chesnel brought her his last bag of louis, she took it, without even noticing it, as she took her white capote and her knit mittens.

"Generous woman! What kindness!" said Chesnel as he assisted her into the carriage, with her femme de chambre, who resembled a gray Sister of Charity.

Du Croisier had calculated his vengeance as the people in the provinces calculate everything. There is nothing in the world like savages, peasants and provincials for studying their affairs to the bottom in every sense of the word; thus, when they proceed from ideas to deeds, you will find the thing completed. The diplomats are but children compared with these classes of mammiferous animals, who have plenty of time before them, that element which is wanting to those who are obliged to think of many things, obliged to arrange everything, to prepare everything in the important human affairs. Had Du Croisier so well fathomed the heart of the poor Victurnien that he foresaw the facility with which he would lend himself to his vengeance, or did he indeed profit by a chance discerned during several years? There is certainly one detail which proves a certain skilfulness in the manner in which the blow was prepared. Who notified Du Croisier? Was it the Kellers? was it the son of the president Du Ronceret, who was finishing his law studies at Paris? Du Croisier wrote to Victurnien a letter to announce to him that he had forbidden the Kellers to advance him any funds henceforth, at the moment when he knew the Duchesse de Maufrigneuse to be in the last embarrassment, and the Comte d'Esgrignon devoured by a distress as frightful as it was knowingly concealed. This unfortunate young man was displaying all his intelligence in feigning opulence! This letter, which informed the victim that the Kellers would remit him nothing without security, left, between the formulas of an exaggerated respect and the signature, a sufficiently wide space. By cutting off this portion of the letter it was easy to make of it an order for a considerable sum. This infernal letter extended to the second sheet, the back of which was blank, it was enclosed in an envelope. When this letter arrived, Victurnien was rolling in the abysses of despair. After two years of a life the most happy, the most sensual, the least reflective, the most luxurious, he saw himself face to face with an inexorable wretchedness, an absolute impossibility of obtaining money.

The journey had not been completed without some pecuniary embarrassments. The count had extorted with great difficulty, the duchess aiding, several sums from the bankers. These sums, represented by bills of exchange, rose before him in all their rigor, with the implacable summons of the Bank and of commercial jurisprudence. Through his last pleasures this unfortunate youth felt the point of the sword of the Commander. In the midst of his suppers he heard, as did Don Juan, the heavy sound of the statue ascending the stairs. He experienced those indescribable shudders which are given by the *sirocco* of debts. He reckoned upon a chance. He had always gained at the lottery of fortune for the last five years, his purse had always been refilled. He said to himself that after Chesnel, had come Du Croisier, that after Du Croisier, there would appear another gold mine. Moreover, he won heavy sums at play. Gambling had already served him in many unfortunate places. Often, in a mad hope, he went to lose at the *Salon des Etrangers* the gains which he had made at the club or in society at whist. His life, for the last two months, had resembled the immortal finale of the *Don Juan* of Mozart! This music should make shiver certain young men who have come to the situation in which Victurnien was struggling. If anything could demonstrate the immense power of music, is it not this sublime translation of disorder, of the difficulties which spring from a life exclusively voluptuous, this frightful picture of a determination to spend one's self without reflection on debts, duels, deceivings, on evil fortunes? Mozart is, in this work, the successful rival of Molière. This terrible finale, eager, vigorous, despairing, joyous, filled with horrible phantoms and with goblin women, signalized by a last attempt which sets fire to the wines of the supper and by a furious defence; all this infernal poem, Victurnien played it alone! He saw himself alone, abandoned, friendless, before a stone on which was engraved, as at the end of a book of enchantment, the word FINIS. Yes! everything with him was coming to an end. He saw in advance the cold and mocking look, the smile, with which his companions would receive the recital of his disaster. He knew that among all those who hazarded important sums upon the green cloth which Paris spreads at the Bourse, in the salons, in the clubs, everywhere, no one would dispense a bank note to save a friend. Chesnel must be ruined. Victurnien had devoured Chesnel. All the Furies were in his heart and were dividing it among them while he smiled at the duchess at the Italiens, in that box where their happiness excited the envy of the whole auditorium. Finally, to depict the depth to which he had fallen in the abyss of doubt, of despair and of unbelief, he who loved life to the point of becoming base in order to preserve it, that angel made it so beautiful for him! well, he looked at his pistols, he went so far as to contemplate suicide, he, this voluptuous evil liver, unworthy of his name. He who would not have endured the appearance of an insult, he addressed to himself those horrible reproofs which we can only take from ourselves. He left Du Croisier's letter open on his bed,—it was nine o'clock when Joséphin handed it to him, and he had slept on his return from the Opéra, although his furniture might be seized; but he had come from the voluptuous retreat where the duchess and he met for some hours after the fêtes at court, after the most brilliant balls, the most splendid soirées. Appearances were very skilfully preserved. This retreat was a garret, common in appearance, but which the peris of India had decorated, and in which Madame de Maufrigneuse was obliged to stoop, in entering, her head crowned with feathers or flowers. On the eve of perishing, the count had wished to bid adieu to this elegant nest, constructed by him who had made of it a poem worthy of his angel, and in which, henceforth, the enchanted eggs, broken by misfortune, would no longer hatch out in white doves, in brilliant finches, in pink flamingoes, in a thousand fantastic birds which still hover around our heads in the last days of our life. Alas! in three days he would have to fly, the last limit of time for the bills of exchange given the usurers had expired. There passed through his head an atrocious idea,—to fly with the duchess, to go to live in some unknown corner, in the depths of North or South America, but to fly with a fortune, and leaving the creditors face to face with their own claims. To realize this plan, it would be sufficient to cut off the bottom of this letter signed by Du Croisier, to make an order on the Kellers out of it, and to carry it to them. There was a frightful combat, in which there were tears shed and in which the honor of his race triumphed, but conditionally. Victurnien wished to be sure of his fair Diane, he subordinated the execution of his plan to her consent to their flight. He went to the house of the duchess, in the Rue du Faubourg-Saint-Honoré; he found her in one of those coquettish négligés which cost her as much care as money, and which permitted her to begin her rôle of angel at eleven o'clock in the morning.

Madame de Maufrigneuse was somewhat thoughtful,—the same anxieties were devouring her, but she supported them with courage. Among the diverse organizations which the physiologists have noted among women, there is one which has in it something indescribably terrible, which comprises a vigor of soul, a clearness of perception, a promptitude of decision, a lightness, or rather a fixed opinion on certain things which would terrify a man. These faculties are concealed under an exterior of the most graceful weakness. These women, alone among women, present the reunion, or rather the conflict of two beings, which Buffon recognized as existing only among men. Other women are entirely womanly; they are entirely tender, entirely motherly, entirely devoted, entirely null or wearisome; their nerves are in accord with their blood and their blood with their head; but women like the duchess are capable of attaining to all that sensitiveness has of the most elevated, and of giving proofs of the most egotistic lack of sensitiveness. One of the glories of Molière is to have admirably depicted, on one side only, these feminine natures in the greatest figure which he has carved all in marble,—Célimène! Célimène, who represents the aristocratic woman, as Figaro, that second edition of Panurge, represents the people. Thus, overwhelmed under the burden of enormous debts, the duchess had commanded herself, absolutely as Napoléon forgot and resumed at will the burden of his thoughts, to think of this avalanche of cares only for a single moment, and for the purpose of taking a definite decision. She had the faculty of separating herself from herself and of contemplating the disaster from the distance of several steps, instead of allowing herself to be buried underneath it. This was certainly grand, but dreadful in a woman. Between the hour of her awakening in which she had recovered all her faculties and the hour in which she had begun her toilet, she had contemplated the danger in all its extent, the possibility of a frightful fall. She meditated: either flight to foreign countries; or to go to the king and declare her indebtedness to him; or to seduce a Du Tillet or a Nucingen, and pay, by gambling on the Bourse: in the money which he would give her, the bourgeois banker would be sufficiently intelligent to bring only the profits, and to never speak of the losses, a delicacy which would gloss over all. These various methods, this catastrophe, all had been deliberated over coolly, calmly, without trepidation. In the same manner as a naturalist takes the most magnificent of lepidoptera, and fastens it to the cotton with a pin, Madame de Maufrigneuse had removed her love from her heart in order to think of the necessities of the moment, ready to resume her beautiful passion on its immaculate cushion of down when she had saved her duchess's coronet. None of those hesitations which Richelieu confided only to Father Joseph, which Napoléon concealed at first from all the world; she but said to herself: "This, or that." She was at the corner of her fire, ordering her toilet to go to the Bois, if the weather permitted, when Victurnien entered.

Notwithstanding his suppressed capabilities and his lively spirit, the count was at this moment as this woman should have been,—his heart was palpitating, he was sweating under his harness of a dandy, he did not dare as yet to place his hand upon a corner stone which, removed, would bring down the pyramid of their mutual existence. It cost him so much to acquire a certainty! The strongest men like to deceive themselves concerning certain things in which the known truth would humiliate them, would give offence to themselves. Victurnien forced his own uncertainty to appear by dropping a compromising phrase.

"What is the matter with you?" had been the first word of Diane de Maufrigneuse at the sight of her dear Victurnien.

"Why, my dear Diane, I am in such a state of perplexity that a man at the bottom of the water, and at his last gurgle, is happy in comparison with me."

"Bah!" said she, "trifles, you are a child. Come now, tell us?"

"I am ruined with debts, and have come to the foot of the wall."

"Is that all?" said she, smiling. "All monetary affairs arrange themselves in one manner or another, there is nothing irreparable but the disasters of the heart."

Put at his ease by this quick comprehension of his position, Victurnien unrolled the brilliant tapestry of his life during the last thirty months, but on the wrong side and with talent, moreover, above all, with spirit. He displayed in his recital that poetry of the moment which is not wanting in persons in a great crisis, and knew how to varnish it with an elegant scorn for things and men. This was aristocratic. The duchess listened as she knew how to listen, her elbow supported on her knee which was raised very high. She had her foot on a stool. Her fingers were delicately grouped around her pretty chin. She kept her eyes attached to the eyes of the count, but myriads of sentiments passed under their blue like the flashes of a storm between two clouds. Her forehead was calm, her mouth serious with attention, serious with love, the lips following the lips of Victurnien. To be listened to thus, do you see, was to believe that divine love emanated from that heart. Thus, when the count had proposed flight to this soul attached to his soul, he was compelled to exclaim:

"You are an angel!"

The beautiful Maufrigneuse responded without having yet spoken.

"Good, good," said the duchess, who, instead of being possessed by the love which she expressed, was absorbed in profound combinations which she kept to herself; "it is not a question of that, my friend."—The *angel* was no more *than that.*—"Let us think of ourselves. Yes, we will go, the sooner the better. Arrange everything,—I will follow you. It will be fine to leave Paris and the world. I will go to work to make my preparations in such a manner that nothing can be suspected."

This phrase, *I will follow you!* was uttered as La Mars would have uttered it at that period in such a manner as to thrill two thousand spectators. When a Duchesse de Maufrigneuse offers in such a phrase such a sacrifice to love, she has paid her debt. Is it possible to speak to her of ignoble details? Victurnien could all the more readily conceal the methods which he proposed to employ as Diane was very careful not to question him,—she remained the guest, crowned with roses, as De Marsay said, at the banquet which every man prepared for her. Victurnien was unwilling to go away without this promise being sealed,—he needed to replenish his courage from his happiness in order to bring this resolution to the point of committing an action which would be, he said to himself, wrongly interpreted; but he counted, and this was his determining reason, upon his aunt and his father to suppress the affair, he even counted again upon Chesnel to invent some business transaction. Moreover, *this affair* was the only means of raising a loan upon the family estates. With three hundred thousand francs the count and the duchess would go to live happily, concealed in a palace at Venice; there, they would forget the universe! They pictured their romance to themselves in advance.

The next day, Victurnien drew up an order for three hundred thousand francs, and carried it to the Kellers. The Kellers paid it, they held, at that moment, some funds of Du Croisier; but they notified him by letter that he should not draw upon them again without advising them. Du Croisier, very much surprised, demanded his account, it was sent to him. This statement explained everything to him,—his vengeance was complete.

When Victurnien had received *his* money, he carried it to Madame de Maufrigneuse, who locked up in her secretary the bank notes and wished to bid adieu to the world by going to the Opéra for the last time. Victurnien was thoughtful, absent-minded, anxious; he was beginning to reflect. He thought that his seat in the duchess's box might cost him clear, that he would have done better, after having placed the three hundred thousand francs in security, to have hastened by post and fallen at the feet of Chesnel in confessing his troubles to him. Before going out, the duchess could not prevent herself from throwing upon Victurnien an adorable look in which shone the desire to again bid farewell to that nest which she loved so much! The too young count lost a night. The next day at three o'clock he was at the Hôtel de Maufrigneuse, and came to take the orders of the duchess to depart in the middle of the night.

"Why should we go?" said she. "I have thought seriously of this plan. The Vicomtesse de Beauséant and the Duchesse de Langeais have disappeared. My flight would have the appearance of something very vulgar. We will make head against the storm. That will be much finer. I am sure of success."

Victurnien was bewildered, it seemed to him that his skin was dissolving and that his blood was flowing away in every direction.

"What is the matter with you?" exclaimed the beautiful Diane, perceiving a hesitation which the women never forgive.

To all the whims of women, men who are skilful should at first assent, and then suggest to them contrary reasons by leaving them in full exercise of their right to change indefinitely their ideas, their resolutions and their sentiments. For the first time, Victurnien grew angry, the anger of feeble and poetic men, a storm commingled with rain, with lightning, but without any thunder. He treated very badly this angel upon whose faith he had hazarded more than his life, the honor of his house.

"See now," said she, "where we find ourselves after eighteen months of tenderness! You are odious, perfectly odious. Go away. I do not wish to see you any more. I thought that you loved me, you do not love me at all."

"I do not love you?" he asked, overwhelmed by this reproach.

"No, monsieur."

"What again!" he exclaimed. "Ah! if you knew what I have just done for you!"

"And what have you done so much for me, monsieur?" she said; "as if one should not do everything for a woman who has done so much for you!"

"You are not worthy of knowing it," cried Victurnien in a rage.

"Ah!"

After this sublime *ah!* Diane inclined her head, rested it in her hand, and remained cold, motionless, implacable, as should be the angels, who partake of none of the human sentiments. When Victurnien saw this woman in this terrible attitude, he forgot his danger. Had he not abused the most angelic creature in the world? he desired her forgiveness, he threw himself at the feet of Diane de Maufrigneuse and kissed them; he implored her, he wept. The unhappy man remained there two hours committing a thousand follies,—he met always with a cold visage and with eyes in which at moments tears appeared, great silent tears, immediately dried, that the unworthy lover might not wipe them away. The duchess assumed one of those sorrows which render women august and sacred. Two more hours succeeded these first two. The count finally secured Diane's hand, he found it cold and without soul. This beautiful hand, full of treasures, resembled supple wood,—it expressed nothing; he had seized it; she had not given it. He no longer lived, he no longer thought. He would not have seen the sun. What to do? what to resolve? what action to take? On these occasions, in order to preserve his self-possession, a man should be constituted like that convict who, after having spent the night in stealing the golden medals of the Bibliothèque Royale, comes in the morning to request his honest brother to melt them for him, hears him say: "What is it you want?" and replies to him: "Make me some coffee." But Victurnien fell into a dull stupor the obscurities of which enveloped his mind. Against these gray mists passed before him, like those figures which Raphael has depicted against black backgrounds, the images of the voluptuousness to which he would be compelled to bid adieu. Inexorable and scornful, the duchess played with the end of her scarf, throwing irritated glances upon Victurnien, she coquetted with her worldly souvenirs, she spoke to her lover of his rivals, as if this anger had decided her to replace by one of them a man capable of thus denying in a moment eighteen months of love.

"Ah!" she said, "it would not be that dear charming little Félix de Vandenesse, so faithful to Madame de Mortsauf, who would allow himself to make such a scene,—he is a lover, he is! De Marsay, that terrible De Marsay, whom everybody thinks such a tiger, is one of those strong men who are rude with men, but who keep all their delicacy for women. Montriveau broke under his foot the Duchesse de Langeais, as Othello killed Desdemona, in an access of rage which at least attested the excess of his love,—it is not mean like a quarrel! there is some pleasure in being broken so! The blond men, little, fine and weakly, love to torment women, they can only rule over these poor feeble creatures; they fall in love so as to have a reason for thinking themselves men. The tyranny of love is their only chance for power."

She did not know why she had placed herself under the control of a blond man. De Marsay, Montriveau, Vandenesse, those fine dark men, had a flash of sunlight in their eyes.

It was a deluge of epigrams which flew whistling like bullets. Diane launched three darts in one word,—she humiliated, she pricked, she wounded, herself alone, as much as ten savages could wound their victim bound to a stake, when they wished to make him suffer the most.

In a fury of impatience the count exclaimed: "You are mad!" and rushed away, God knows in what a state! He drove his horse as if he had never driven before. He ran into the vehicles, he collided with a boundary stone in the Place Louis XV., he went without knowing where. His horse, finding itself not directed, ran by the Quai d'Orsay to his stable. In turning the Rue de l'Université, the cabriolet was stopped by Joséphin.

"Monsieur," said the old man with a terrified air, "you cannot go home, the officers of justice have come to arrest you—"

Victurnien attributed this arrest to the order which could not yet have reached the procureur du roi, and not to his actual bills of exchange which had been circulating for the last few days under the form of regular judgments and which the hands of the commercial police were bringing out with an accompaniment of spies, bailiff's men, judges of the peace, commissaries of police, gendarmes, and other representatives of social order. Like the greater number of criminals, Victurnien no longer thought of anything but his crime.

"I am lost!" he exclaimed.

"No, monsieur le comte, drive on, go to the hotel of the *Bon la Fontaine*, in the Rue de Grenelle. You will find there Mademoiselle Armande who has arrived, the horses are put to her carriage, she is waiting for you, and will take you away."

In his trouble, Victurnien seized this branch offered to his grasp, in the midst of his shipwreck; he hastened to this hotel, found it, embraced there his aunt, who wept like a Magdalen,—you would have said that she was an accomplice in the faults of her nephew. Both of them took their places in the carriage, and a few moments later they were outside of Paris, on the road to Brest. Victurnien, overwhelmed, remained in a profound silence. When the aunt and the nephew spoke, they were both victims of the fatal mistake which had thrown Victurnien without reflection into the arms of Mademoiselle Armande,—the nephew thought of his crime, the aunt thought of the debts and the bills of exchange.

"You know all, aunt," said he.

"Yes, my poor child, but we are here. In this moment, I do not reproach you, take courage again."

"It will be necessary for me to conceal myself."

"Perhaps—Yes, that is an excellent idea."

"If I could enter Chesnel's house without being seen, by arranging our arrival in the middle of the night!"

"That will be better, we shall be more free to hide everything from my brother. Poor angel, how he suffers!" she said, caressing this unworthy child.

"Oh! now I understand dishonor, it has chilled my love."

"Unhappy child, so much happiness and so much misery!"

Mademoiselle Armande held the burning head of her nephew on her bosom, she kissed this forehead damp with sweat notwithstanding the cold, as the holy women must have kissed the forehead of Christ when placing Him in His shroud. Following out his excellent scheme, this prodigal son was introduced by night into the peaceable house in the Rue du Bercail; but chance willed it so that in coming there he threw himself, according to the proverbial expression, into the wolf's mouth. Chesnel had, the evening before, been negotiating for the sale of his business with the head clerk of Monsieur Lepressoir, the notary of the liberals, as he himself was the notary of the aristocracy. This young clerk belonged to a family sufficiently wealthy to be able to advance Chesnel an important sum on account, a hundred thousand francs.

"With a hundred thousand francs," the old notary was saying to himself at this moment, rubbing his hands, "we can liquidate a great many bills. The young man has usurious debts, we will shut him up here. I will go down there myself, to bring these dogs to reason."

Chesnel, the honest Chesnel, the virtuous Chesnel, the worthy Chesnel, called *dogs* the creditors of his beloved child, the Comte Victurnien.

The future notary was leaving the Rue du Bercail as the calèche of Mademoiselle Armande entered it.

The curiosity natural to every young man who might have seen in this city, at this hour, a calèche stopping at the door of the old notary, was sufficiently aroused to make the head clerk halt in the corner of a door-way, whence he perceived Mademoiselle Armande.

"Mademoiselle Armande d'Esgrignon, at this hour! What is happening then to the D'Esgrignons?" he said to himself.

At the appearance of Mademoiselle, Chesnel received her mysteriously, concealing the light which he held in his hand. When he saw Victurnien, at the first word which Mademoiselle Armande said in his ear, the good man comprehended everything; he looked out in the street, found it silent and peaceful, he made a sign, the young count sprang from the calèche into the court. All was lost, Victurnien's retreat was known to Chesnel's successor.

"Ah! monsieur le comte!" exclaimed the ex-notary when Victurnien was installed in a chamber which opened into Chesnel's cabinet, and into which no one could penetrate without passing over the good man's body.

"Yes, monsieur," replied the young man, comprehending the exclamation of his old friend, "I did not listen to you, I am at the bottom of an abyss where I must perish."

"No, no," said the good man, looking triumphantly at Mademoiselle Armande and the count. "I have sold out my business. It is a long time that I have been working and that I have been thinking of retiring. I shall have to-morrow, at noon, a hundred thousand francs, with which a great many things can be arranged. Mademoiselle," said he, "you are fatigued, take your carriage again and go home to bed. Business to-morrow."

"He is safe?" she replied, indicating Victurnien.

"Yes," said the old man.

She embraced her nephew, left some tears on his forehead, and departed.

"My good Chesnel, what use will your hundred thousand francs be in the situation in which I am?" said the count to his old friend when they began to talk business. "You are not acquainted, I believe, with the extent of my misfortunes."

Victurnien explained his case. Chesnel was thunderstruck. Had it not been for the strength of his devotion, he would have succumbed under this blow. Two streams of tears issued from his eyes, which might be thought to have been dried up. He became a child again for some moments. For some moments he was devoid of reason, like a man who should see his house burning and, through a window, the cradle of his children flaming and hear their hair crackle as it consumed. He *rose on his feet,* Amyot would have said, he seemed to grow larger, he lifted his old hands, he waved them in despairing and insane gestures.

"May your father die without ever knowing anything, young man! It is enough to be a forger, do not be a parricide! Fly? No, you would be condemned by default. Unhappy child, why did you not counterfeit my signature? I, I would have paid, I would not have carried the paper to the procureur du roi! I can do no more. You have driven me into the deepest hole of hell. Du Croisier! what will become of it? what to do? If you had killed some one, that might still be excused; but a forgery! a forgery! And time, time which is slipping away," said he, indicating his old clock with a menacing gesture. "It will require a false passport, now,—one crime begets another. We must—" said he, making a pause, "we must, before all, save the house of D'Esgrignon."

"But," cried Victurnien, "the money is still in the house of Madame de Maufrigneuse."

"Ah!" exclaimed Chesnel. "Well, there is some hope, a very feeble one,—can we persuade Du Croisier, buy him? He shall have, if he wishes, all the property of the house. I am going there, I am going there to awaken him, to offer him everything. Moreover, it was not you who committed the forgery, it shall be me. I will go to the galleys, I have passed the age of the galleys, they can only put me in prison."

"But I wrote the body of the draft," said Victurnien, without any surprise at this senseless devotion.

"Imbecile!—Pardon, monsieur le comte. We must state it to have been written by Joséphin," cried the maddened old notary. "He is a good fellow, he could have had charge of everything. It is all over, the world is crumbling," repeated the old man, crushed and sitting down. "Du Croisier is a tiger, we must be careful not to waken him. What o'clock is it? Where is the draft? At Paris, it can be redeemed at the Kellers, they will agree to it. Ah! it is an affair in which everything is dangerous, a single false step will ruin us. In any case, it requires money. Come now, no one knows that you are here, live buried in the cellar if necessary. For my part, I am going to Paris, I will hurry there, I hear the mail-coach from Brest coming."

In a moment the old man regained the faculties of his youth, his agility, his vigor; he made himself up a package for the journey, took some money, put a six pound loaf of bread in the little chamber and locked in it his adopted child.

"Make no noise," said he to him, "stay there till my return, without any light at night, or else you go to the bagnio! Do you understand me, monsieur le comte? yes, to the bagnio, if, in a town like this, anyone knows that you are there."

Then Chesnel left his house after having directed his housekeeper to say that he was ill, to receive no one, to send everyone away, and to postpone all business for three days. He went to seduce the director of the post, related to him some romance, for he had the genius of a skilful romancer,—he secured a place, in case there was one, without a passport, and made him promise secrecy as to this precipitate departure. The mail-post very fortunately arrived empty.

He arrived on the following night, at Paris, and the next morning at nine o'clock he was at the Kellers,—there he learned that the fatal draft had been returned three days before to Du Croisier; but, while obtaining this information he had said nothing compromising. Before leaving the bankers, he asked them if, by refunding the money, they could return this paper. François Keller replied that the document belonged to Du Croisier, who alone had the power to keep it or return it. The old man, in despair, went to the house of the duchess. At that hour, Madame de Maufrigneuse received no one. Chesnel was conscious of the value of time, he seated himself in the antechamber, wrote a few lines and succeeded in getting them to Madame de Maufrigneuse by seducing, by fascinating, by interesting, by commanding the most insolent, the most intractable domestics in the world. Although she was still in bed, the duchess, to the great astonishment of her household, received in her chamber the old man in black breeches, in milled stockings, in shoes with clasps.

"What is it, monsieur?" said she, arranging herself in her disorder; "what does he wish of me, the ingrate?"

"It is, madame la duchesse," exclaimed the good man, "that you have a hundred thousand écus of ours."

"Yes," she said. "Which means?"

"This sum is the result of a forgery which will take us to the galleys, and which we have committed for love of you," said Chesnel quickly. "How is it that you did not suspect it, you who are so brilliant? Instead of scolding the young man, you should have questioned him, and saved him by stopping him in time. Now, God grant that the misfortune be not irreparable! We are going to have need of all your influence with the king."

At the first words which explained the affair to her, the duchess, ashamed of her conduct toward so passionate a lover, feared to be suspected of complicity. In her desire to show that she had kept the money without touching it, she forgot all the conventionalities and moreover did not consider that this notary was a man,—she threw off her eiderdown coverlet with a violent movement, hastened to her secretary, passing before the notary like one of those angels who traverse the vignettes of Lamartine, and returned to her bed in great confusion after having handed the hundred thousand écus to Chesnel.

THE RUE DU BERCAIL

The notary returned to the Rue du Bercail after three days of absence. Although it was eleven o'clock at night, he was too late. Chesnel saw gendarmes at his door, and, when he reached the threshold, he saw in his court the young count arrested. Certainly, if he had had the power, he would have killed all those officers of justice and the soldiers.

"You are an angel, madame," said he.—She was obliged to be an angel for everyone!—"But this will not be all," resumed the notary, "I count upon your support to save us."

"Save you! I will succeed in it, or I will perish. It is necessary to love greatly not to recoil before a crime. For what woman has any one done such a thing as that? Poor child! Go, do not lose any time, dear Monsieur Chesnel. Rely upon me as upon yourself."

"Madame la duchesse! madame la duchesse!"

The old notary could say nothing but these words, so much was he affected. He wept, he had an inclination to dance, but he was afraid of losing his senses, he restrained himself.

"We two, we will save him," he said as he went out.

Chesnel went immediately to see Joséphin, who opened for him the secretary and the table of the young count, in which there were, very fortunately, some letters from Du Croisier and the Kellers which might become useful. Then he took a place in a diligence, which departed immediately. He paid the postilions so liberally that the heavy vehicle went as fast as the mail-coach, for he met two other travellers in as much of a hurry as he, and they came to an agreement to take their meals in the coach. The road was, as it were, devoured. The notary returned to the Rue du Bercail after three days of absence. Although it was eleven o'clock at night, he was too late. Chesnel saw gendarmes at his door, and, when he reached the threshold, he saw in his court the young count arrested. Certainly, if he had had the power, he would have killed all those officers of justice and the soldiers, but he could only throw himself upon Victurnien's neck.

"If I do not succeed in suppressing this affair, you must kill yourself before the act of accusation is drawn up," he said to him in his ear.

Victurnien was in such a state of stupor that he looked at the notary without understanding him.

"Kill myself?" he repeated.

"Yes! If you have not the courage to do it, my child, count upon me," said Chesnel to him, grasping his hand.

He remained, notwithstanding the pain which this sight caused him, planted upon his two trembling legs, looking at the son of his heart, the Comte d'Esgrignon, the heir of this great house, walking between the gendarmes, between the commissioner of police of the city, the judge of the peace and the officer of the court. The old man did not recover his resolution and his presence of mind until this troop had disappeared, until he no longer heard the sound of their steps and silence was restored.

"Monsieur, you will catch cold," said Brigitte to him.

"The devil take you!" exclaimed the exasperated attorney.

Brigitte, who had never heard anything like this in the twenty-nine years that she had served Chesnel, dropped her candle; but, without paying any attention to her terror, her master, who did not hear his housekeeper's exclamation, began to run toward the Val-Noble."

"He is crazy," she said to herself. "After all, there is reason. But where is he going? it is impossible for me to follow him. What will become of him? is he going to drown himself?"

Brigitte awakened the head clerk, and sent him to watch the shores of the river, which had acquired a fatal notoriety since the suicide of a young man full of promise, and the recent death of a young girl seduced. Chesnel went to Du Croisier's hôtel. There was no longer any hope but there. Crimes of forgery can only be prosecuted on private complaints. If Du Croisier were willing to compromise, it was still possible to make the complaint pass for a misunderstanding, Chesnel still hoped to be able to buy off this man.

During this evening there had been many more people than usual at the reception of Monsieur and Madame du Croisier. Although this affair should have been kept secret between the president of the tribunal, Monsieur du Ronceret, Monsieur Sauvager, first deputy to the procureur du roi, and Monsieur du Coudrai, the former commissioner of mortgages, superseded for having voted wrongly, Mesdames du Ronceret and du Coudrai had confided it under promise of secrecy to one or two intimate female friends. The news had therefore spread in the mixed society, half noblesse and half bourgeoisie, which met at Monsieur du Croisier's house. Everyone felt the gravity of such an affair, and did not dare to speak of it openly. The attachment of Madame du Croisier to the upper nobility was, moreover, so well known, that scarcely did anyone venture to whisper about the misfortune that had overtaken the D'Esgrignons in asking for further details. The principals interested, awaited, to discuss it, the hour at which the good Madame du Croisier effected her retreat to her bedchamber, where she performed her religious duties far from the eyes of her husband. At the moment when the lady of the house disappeared, the adherents of Du Croisier, who were acquainted with the secrets and the plans of this great industrial leader, counted themselves, they saw still in the salon some persons whom their opinions or their interests rendered suspicious; they therefore continued to play. Toward half-past eleven, there remained only intimate friends, Monsieur Sauvager, Monsieur Camusot, the juge d'instruction and his wife, Monsieur and Madame du Ronceret, their son Fabien, Monsieur and Madame du Coudrai, Joseph Blondet, eldest son of an old judge, in all, ten persons.

It is related that Talleyrand, on a fatal night, at three o'clock in the morning, playing cards in the house of the Duchesse de Luynes, interrupted the game, placed his watch on the table, asked the players if the Prince de Condé had any other child than the Duc d'Enghien.

"Why do you ask a thing that you know so well?" replied Madame de Luynes.

"It is because, if the prince has no other child, the house of Condé is ended."

After a moment of silence, the game was resumed. It was a similar action, that of the president Du Ronceret, whether it were that he was acquainted with this detail of contemporary history, or whether it be that the little spirits resemble the great ones in the expressions of political life. He looked at his watch and said, interrupting the boston:

"At this moment Monsieur le Comte d'Esgrignon is arrested, and that house so proud is forever dishonored."

"You have then placed your hand on the youth?" exclaimed Du Coudrai joyously.

All the others present, excepting the president, the first deputy and Du Croisier, manifested a sudden astonishment.

"He has just been arrested in the house of Chesnel, where he was in hiding," said the first deputy, assuming the air of a capable but unappreciated man who should have been minister of police.

This Monsieur Sauvager, first deputy, was a young man of twenty-five, thin and tall, with a long and olive-tinted face, with black and crisp hair, his eyes sunken and bordered underneath with large brown circles, repeated above by his eyelids wrinkled and swarthy. He had the nose of a bird of prey, a tightly closed mouth, cheeks flattened by study and hollowed by ambition. He presented the type of those secondary beings ever on the watch for events, ready to do anything to succeed, but in keeping within the limits of the possible and within the restraints of legality. His important air revealed admirably his servile loquacity. The secret of the young count's hiding-place had been revealed to him by Chesnel's successor, and it did credit to his penetration. This news seemed to have greatly surprised the juge d'instruction, Monsieur Camusot, who, upon Sauvager's requisition, had issued the warrant of arrest so promptly executed. Camusot was a man of about thirty years of age, little, already fat, blond, with flabby flesh, with a livid complexion such as have almost all the magistrates who live shut up in their cabinets or in their halls of audience. He had little eyes of a clear yellow, full of that mistrust which passes for shrewdness.

Madame Camusot looked at her husband as if to say to him: "Was I not right?"

"So the affair will come off?" said the juge d'instruction.

"Could you doubt it?" replied Du Coudrai. "Everything is settled, since the count is held."

"There is the jury," said Monsieur Camusot. "For this affair, monsieur le préfet will know how to make it up so that, with the challenges ordered by the prosecution and those of the accused, there will remain in it only those in favor of acquittal. My advice would be to come to an agreement," he said, addressing Du Croisier.

"Come to an agreement!" said the president, "but the case is in the hands of justice."

"Acquitted or condemned, the Comte d'Esgrignon will be none the less dishonored by it," said the first deputy.

"I am the civil prosecutor," said Du Croisier, "I shall employ Dupin the elder. We shall see how the house of D'Esgrignon will get out of his claws."

"It will know how to defend itself, and select an advocate from Paris, it will oppose to you Berryer," said Madame Camusot. "Diamond cut diamond."

Du Croisier, Monsieur Sauvager and the president Du Ronceret all looked at the juge d'instruction with the same thought in their minds. The tone and the manner in which the young wife had thrown her proverb into the faces of the eight persons who were plotting the ruin of the house of D'Esgrignon, caused them emotions which each of them concealed as know how to dissimulate the people of the provinces, accustomed by their continual coherency to all the ruses of monastic life. The little Madame Camusot remarked the changes in the countenances, which composed themselves again when they scented the probable opposition of the judge to Du Croisier's designs. When she saw her husband revealing his inmost thoughts, she had wished to sound the depth of these hatreds, and to discover by what interests Du Croisier had attached to himself the first deputy, who had acted so precipitately and so contrary to the views of the authorities.

"In any case," said she, "if in this affair there are celebrated advocates brought from Paris, it promises us some very interesting sittings of the court of assizes; but the case will come to an end between the tribunal and the royal court. It is to be believed that the government will do secretly all that it can to save a young man who belongs to the great families, and who has the Duchesse de Maufrigneuse for a friend. Therefore, I do not believe that we shall have any scandal at Landerneau."

"How you go on, madame!" said the president severely. "Do you believe that the tribunal which prepares the case and which first tries it will be influenced by any considerations foreign to justice?"

"The event proves the contrary," said she maliciously, glancing at the first deputy and the president, who threw cold looks at her.

"Explain yourself, madame," said the deputy. "You speak as if we had not done our duty."

"Madame's words have no value," said Camusot.

"But have not those of monsieur le président prejudged a question which depends upon the preliminary examination," she replied, "and yet the examination is still to be made and the tribunal has not yet pronounced its decision?"

"We are not at the Palais," replied the deputy sharply, "and, moreover, we know all that."

"Monsieur le procureur du roi is still ignorant of it," she replied, looking at him ironically. "He will return from the Chamber of Deputies in all haste. You have cut out work for him, he will speak for himself doubtless."

The deputy knit his heavy tufted eyebrows, and the listeners saw on his forehead some belated scruples. There was then a complete silence during which nothing was heard but the throwing down and taking up of the cards. Monsieur and Madame Camusot, who saw themselves very coolly treated, departed to allow the conspirators to talk at their ease."

"Camusot," said his wife to him in the street, "you have gone ahead too fast. Why did you make those people suspect that you will not lend yourself to their plans? They will play you some ill trick."

"What can they do against me? I am the only juge d'instruction."

"Can they not slander you secretly and procure your removal?"

At this moment the couple were jostled by Chesnel. The old notary recognized the juge d'instruction. With the clearness of men accustomed to affairs, he comprehended that the destiny of the house of D'Esgrignon was in the hands of this young man.

"Ah! monsieur," exclaimed the good man, "we are going to have need of you. I only want to say to you one word—Pardon me, madame," he said to the wife of the judge as he took her husband apart.

Like a good conspirator, Madame Camusot watched in the direction of the house of Du Croisier in order to break off the tête-à-tête in case any one came out of it; but she judged rightly that the enemy was occupied in discussing the incident which she had thrown athwart their plans. Chesnel drew the judge into a dark corner, by the side of the wall, and bent to his ear.

"The influence of the Duchesse de Maufrigneuse, that of the Prince de Cadignan, of the Ducs de Navarreins, of Lenoncourt, the keeper of the seals, the chancellor, the king, all are secured you if you are for the house of D'Esgrignon," he said to him. "I have just arrived from Paris, I know all, I have hastened to explain all to the court. We count upon you, and I will keep the secret for you. If you are our enemy, I will depart to-morrow again for Paris and place in the hands of His Grace a complaint of legitimate suspicion against the tribunal, several members of which were doubtless this evening at Du Croisier's house, have drunk there, have eaten there, contrary to the laws, and who, moreover, are his friends."

Chesnel would have made the Father Eternal intervene if he had had the power; he left the Judge, without waiting for his reply, and hastened like a young deer toward the house of Du Croisier. Summoned by his wife to reveal

to her the confidences of Chesnel, the judge obeyed and was assailed by that
"Was I not right, my dear?" which the women say also when they are wrong,
but less sweetly. When they had arrived at their house, Camusot had confessed
the superiority of his wife and recognized the happiness of belonging to her,
an avowal which doubtless prepared a happy night for the two spouses.
Chesnel met the group of his enemies issuing from Du Croisier's, and feared
to find him abed, which he would have considered a misfortune, for he was in
one of those circumstances which demand promptitude.

"Open in the name of the king!" he exclaimed to the domestic who was
closing the vestibule.

He had just brought the king before a little ambitious judge, he had kept
this word upon his lips, he was becoming confused, he raved. The door was
opened. The notary threw himself into the antechamber like lightning.

"My lad," he said to the domestic, "a hundred écus for you if you can
awaken Madame du Croisier, and send her to me immediately. Say to her
whatever you like."

Chesnel became calm and cool as he opened the door of the brilliant salon
in which Du Croisier was walking up and down alone with great strides. These
two men measured each other for a moment with a look which had in its
depths twenty years of hatred and aversion. One had his foot on the heart of
the house of D'Esgrignon, the other advanced with the strength of a lion to
wrest it from him.

"Monsieur," said Chesnel, "I humbly salute you. Your complaint has been
lodged?"

"Yes, monsieur."

"Since when?"

"Since yesterday."

"No other act than the warrant of arrest has been issued?"

"I think so," replied Du Croisier.

"I have come to treat."

"Justice is notified, public vengeance will have its course, nothing can arrest
it."

"We will not concern ourselves with that, I am at your orders, at your feet."

The aged Chesnel fell upon his knees and extended his supplicating hands
toward Du Croisier.

"What do you require? Will you have our estate, our château? Take all, withdraw the complaint, leave us only life and honor. In addition to all that I offer you, I will be your servitor, you will dispose of me as you like."

Du Croisier left the old man on his knees and sat down in an armchair.

"You are not vindictive, you are good, you are not so offended at us as not to lend yourself to an arrangement," said the old man. "Before day break, the young man will be free."

"The whole city knows of his arrest," said Du Croisier, critically enjoying his vengeance.

"That is a great misfortune; but if there are neither judgment nor proofs, we will well arrange everything."

Du Croisier reflected, Chesnel believed him occupied with his self-interests, he had the hope of holding his enemy by this great spring of human actions. At this supreme moment, Madame du Croisier appeared.

"Come, madame, help me to move your dear husband," said Chesnel, still on his knees.

Madame du Croisier assisted the old man to rise, manifesting the most profound surprise. Chesnel explained the affair. When the noble daughter of the servitors of the Ducs d'Alençon learned of the matter in question, she turned with tears in her eyes toward Du Croisier.

"Ah! monsieur, can you hesitate? the D'Esgrignons, the honor of the province!" she said to him.

"Much question there is of that!" exclaimed Du Croisier, rising and resuming his agitated walk.

"And of what, then, is there question?—" said Chesnel, astonished.

"Monsieur Chesnel, it is a question of France! it is a question of the country, it is a question of the people, it is a question of teaching messieurs your nobles that there is justice, law, a bourgeoisie, a lesser nobility which is worth them and which holds them! You do not ravage ten fields of grain for a rabbit, you do not carry dishonor into families by seducing poor girls, you should not despise people who are your equals, you do not deride them for ten years, without these deeds accumulating, enlarging, producing avalanches, and without these avalanches falling, crushing, burying messieurs the nobles. You wish to return to the ancient order of things, you wish to tear up the social compact, this Charta in which our rights are inscribed—"

"And after that?" said Chesnel.

"Is it not a sacred mission to enlighten the people?" cried Du Croisier. "They will open their eyes to the morality of your party when they see the nobles going, like Pierre and Jacques, to the court of assizes. It will be said that the poor people who are honorable are worth more than the great people who dishonor themselves. The court of assizes shines for everybody. I am here the defender of the people, the friend of the laws. You have yourself thrown me twice on the side of the people, at first in refusing my alliance, then in outlawing me from your society. You shall reap what you have sown."

This opening terrified Chesnel, as well as Madame du Croisier. The wife acquired a horrible knowledge of the character of her husband, this was a light that illumined for her not only the past but also the future. It appeared to be impossible to make this colossus capitulate; but Chesnel did not recoil before the impossible.

"What! monsieur, you would not forgive? you are not then a Christian?" said Madame du Croisier.

"I forgive as God forgives, madame, on conditions."

"What are they?" said Chesnel, who thought he perceived a ray of hope.

"The elections are approaching, I want the votes of which you dispose."

"You shall have them," said Chesnel.

"I wish," Du Croisier went on, "to be received, my wife and I, familiarly, every evening, with friendliness, in appearance at least, by Monsieur le Marquis d'Esgrignon and by his friends."

"I do not know how we shall bring it about, but you shall be received."

"I want a bond of four hundred thousand francs based upon a written account drawn up of this affair, so that I may always have a pistol held at your head."

"We consent," said Chesnel, who did not yet admit that he had the hundred thousand écus about him; "but it shall be placed in the hands of a third party and returned to the family after your election and the payment."

"No, but after the marriage of my great-niece, Mademoiselle Duval, who will bring together, perhaps, some day four millions. This young woman will be formally constituted my heiress and that of my wife, you shall marry her to your young count."

"Never!" said Chesnel.

"Never?" repeated Du Croisier, intoxicated with his triumph. "Good-night."

"Imbecile that I am," thought Chesnel, "why should I hesitate before a lie to such a man?"

Du Croisier left the room, pleased at having annulled everything in the name of his offended pride, after having enjoyed the humiliation of Chesnel, after having held in the balance the destinies of the superb house in which was summed up all the aristocracy of the province, and printed the mark of his heel on the heart of the D'Esgrignons. He went up to his chamber, leaving his wife with Chesnel. In his intoxication, he saw nothing that would interfere with his victory, he believed firmly that the hundred thousand écus had been dissipated; to repay them, the house of D'Esgrignon would be obliged to sell or to mortgage its estates; in his eyes, the court of assizes was therefore inevitable. Cases of forgery can always be compromised when the sum unlawfully obtained is restored. The victims of this crime are usually wealthy people who do not desire to dishonor an imprudent man. But Du Croisier was willing to renounce his rights only for value received. He therefore went to bed thinking of the magnificent accomplishment of his hopes, either by the court of assizes or by this marriage, and it gave him pleasure to hear the voice of Chesnel lamenting with Madame du Croisier. Profoundly religious and Catholic, royalist and attached to the nobility, Madame du Croisier partook of the ideas of Chesnel with regard to the D'Esgrignons. Thus all her sentiments had just been cruelly offended. This good royalist lady had heard the howling of liberalism which, in the opinion of her spiritual director, desired the ruin of Catholicism. For her, the Left represented 1793 with the uprising and the scaffold.

"What would your uncle say, that saint who now listens to us?" exclaimed Chesnel.

Madame du Croisier replied only by great tears which rolled down her cheeks.

"You have already caused the death of a poor young man and the eternal grief of his mother," Chesnel went on, seeing how his blows told, and willing to strike to this heart to save Victurnien, "do you wish to assassinate Mademoiselle Armande, who would not survive the infamy of her house a week? Do you wish to assassinate the poor Chesnel, your old notary, who will kill the young count in his prison before he is accused, and who will kill himself so as not to be brought himself before the court of assizes as guilty of murder?"

"Enough, enough, my friend! I am capable of doing everything to suppress such an affair as this, but I have only known Monsieur du Croisier completely within the last few minutes.—To you, I can admit it! there is no resource."

"If there were one?" said Chesnel.

"I would give the half of my blood to find one," she replied, supplementing her assertion by a movement of the head which expressed a desire to succeed.

Like the First Consul, who, vanquished on the field of Marengo up to five o'clock in the evening, at six o'clock obtained a victory by the desperate attack of Desaix and by the terrible charge of Kellermann, Chesnel perceived the elements of triumph in the midst of ruin. It was necessary to be Chesnel, it was necessary to be an old notary, an old intendant, to have been junior clerk under Maître Sorbier père, it required the sudden illuminations of despair, to be thus as great as Napoléon, greater even,—this battle was not Marengo, but Waterloo, and Chesnel was determined to vanquish the Prussians as he saw them arrive.

"Madame, you whose business affairs I had charge of for twenty years, you, the honor of the bourgeoisie, as the D'Esgrignons are the honor of the nobility of this province, you must know that it now depends entirely upon you to save the house of D'Esgrignon. Answer, now,—will you allow to be dishonored the manes of your uncle, the D'Esgrignons, the poor Chesnel? Will you kill Mademoiselle Armande who is weeping? Will you redeem your wrongs by rejoicing your ancestors the intendants of the Ducs d'Alençon, by consoling the manes of your dear abbé, who, if he could issue from his coffin, would command you to do that which I ask of you on my knees?"

"What!" cried Madame du Croisier.

"Well, you see these hundred thousand écus," he said, drawing from his pocket the package of bank-notes. "Receive them, everything will be ended."

"If it is only a question of that," she replied, "and if nothing evil can result from it for my husband—"

"Nothing but good," said Chesnel. "You will spare him the eternal vengeance of hell at the cost of a small disappointment here on earth."

"He will not be compromised in any way?" she asked, looking at Chesnel.

He was able to read in the very bottom of the soul of this poor wife. Madame du Croisier hesitated between two religions, between the commandments which the Church has laid on spouses and her duties toward the throne and the altar,—she considered her husband blamable and did not venture to blame him, she would have wished to be able to save the D'Esgrignons, and wished to do nothing against her husband's interests.

"In no way," said Chesnel, "your old notary swears it to you on the Holy Scriptures—"

Chesnel had nothing left but his eternal salvation to offer to the house of D'Esgrignon, he perilled it by a horrible falsehood; but it was necessary to deceive Madame du Croisier or perish. Therefore he himself drew up and dictated to Madame du Croisier a receipt for a hundred thousand écus dated five days before the fatal bill of exchange, at a period when he recalled the fact that Du Croisier was absent, having gone to oversee some improvements on his wife's property.

"You swear to me," said Chesnel, when Madame du Croisier had the hundred thousand écus and when he held this receipt, "that you will declare before the juge d'instruction that you received this sum on the day here mentioned.

"Will not that be a falsehood?"

"An officious one."

"I could not do it without the advice of my spiritual director, Monsieur l'Abbé Couturier."

"Well," said Chesnel, "act in this affair only as he counsels you."

"I promise you to do so."

"Do not hand the money to Monsieur du Croisier till after you have appeared before the juge d'instruction."

"Yes," said she. "Alas! may God give me strength to appear before human justice for the purpose of maintaining a falsehood!"

After having kissed Madame du Croisier's hand, Chesnel straightened himself up majestically like one of the prophets painted by Raphael in the Vatican.

"The soul of your uncle thrills with joy, you have forever redeemed the wrong of having espoused the enemy of the throne and the altar."

These words produced a great effect upon the timorous soul of Madame du Croisier. It suddenly occurred to Chesnel to make sure of the Abbé Couturier, the director of her conscience. He knew with what obstinacy the devout contend for the triumph of their principles when they have once come forward for their party, he wished to engage the Church as promptly as possible in this contest by getting it on his side; he therefore went to the Hôtel d'Esgrignon, awakened Mademoiselle Armande, informed her of the events of the night, and started her on the road to the bishop's in order to bring the prelate himself on the field of battle.

"My God, Thou shouldst save the house of D'Esgrignon!" he exclaimed, as he returned homeward with slow steps. "Now, the affair becomes a judicial struggle. We have to do with men who are swayed by their passions and interests, we can obtain everything from them. This Du Croisier has taken advantage of the absence of the procureur du roi who is devoted to us, but who, since the opening of the Chambers, has been in Paris. What have they then done to inveigle the first deputy who issued the warrant on the accusation without consulting his chief? To-morrow morning, I must penetrate this mystery, study the ground, and perhaps, after having seized the thread of this conspiracy, I will return to Paris in order to secure the support of the higher powers by the hand of Madame de Maufrigneuse."

Such were the reasonings of the poor old athlete, who saw clearly, and who went to bed almost dead under the weight of so many emotions and so much fatigue. Nevertheless, before going to sleep, he surveyed carefully in his mind all the magistrates who constituted the tribunal, scrutinizing the secret aims of their ambitions, in order to determine what were his chances in this contest, and how they could be influenced. By giving a succinct form to the long examination of consciences made by Chesnel, we may perhaps furnish a picture of the provincial magistracy.

*

The judges and the officers of the crown compelled to begin their careers in the province, where the judicial ambitions are the most active, all look toward Paris at their début, all aspire to shine on that vast theatre where are tried the great political causes, where the magistracy is allied with the throbbing interests of society. But this paradise of the servants of justice admits but few of the elect, and nine tenths of the magistrates must, sooner or later, fix themselves for ever in the provinces. Thus every tribunal, every royal court in the provinces, presents two parties sharply divided,—those of the ambitious, weary of hoping, contented with the excessive consideration accorded in the provinces to the position held by the magistrates, or lulled by a tranquil life; then, that of the younger men and the real talents to whom the desire of succeeding, which no deception has modified, or whom the thirst for success constantly spurs, gives a sort of fanaticism for their priesthood. At this period, royalism animated the young magistrates against the enemies of the Bourbons. The smallest deputy dreamed of suits, desired with all his heart one of these political processes which afford such an opportunity for displaying zeal, attract the attention of the ministry and bring about the advancement of the officers of the crown. Who, among the members of the bar, was not jealous of that court in the jurisdiction of which some Bonapartist conspiracy broke out? Who did not desire to find a Caron, a Berton, to discover an armed uprising? These eager ambitions, stimulated by the great contest of parties, supported by the excuse of the welfare of the State and the necessity of monarchizing France, were clear, foreseeing, perspicacious; they formed a very efficient police, watched the population and directed them into the path of obedience from which they should not deviate. Justice, then fanaticized by the monarchical faith, repaired the wrongs of the ancient parliaments, and proceeded in close accord with religion, too ostensibly perhaps. It was then more zealous than skilful, it sinned less by Machiavelism than by the sincerity of its views, which appeared to be hostile to the general interests of the country which it was endeavoring to secure against revolutions. But, taken in its entirety, justice still contained too much of the bourgeois element, it was still too accessible to the petty passions of liberalism, it would become sooner or later constitutional, and place itself on the side of the bourgeoisie on the day of a struggle. In this great body, as in the administration, there was hypocrisy, or, rather, a spirit of imitation which leads France into the habit of always imitating the court, and of thus very innocently deceiving it.

These two kinds of judicial physiognomies existed in the tribunal in which the fate of the young D'Esgrignon was about to be decided. Monsieur le Président du Ronceret, an old judge named Blondet, there represented those magistrates resigned to being only what they are and quartered forever in their town. The young and ambitious party included Monsieur Camusot, the juge d'instruction, and Monsieur Michu, appointed assistant judge by the favor of the house of Cinq-Cygne, and who was expected on the first occasion to enter the jurisdiction of the royal court of Paris.

Protected from all danger of removal by the permanent tenure of office of the judiciary, and perceiving that he was not welcomed by the aristocracy according to the importance which he gave himself, the president Du Ronceret had sided with the bourgeoisie, giving to his disappointment the varnish of independence, without being aware that his opinions condemned him to remain president all his life. Once engaged in this road, he was conducted by the logic of things to place his hope of advancement in the triumph of Du Croisier and the party of the Left. He was no more acceptable at the prefecture than at the royal court. Obliged to be circumspect with the authorities, he was suspected by the liberals. He had thus no place in any party. Compelled to leave the electoral candidacy to Du Croisier, he saw himself without influence and played only a secondary part. The falseness of his position reacted upon his character, he was bitter and discontented. Wearied with his political ambiguity, he had secretly resolved to place himself at the head of the liberal party and to thus control Du Croisier. His conduct in the affair of the Comte d'Esgrignon was his first step in this career. He already represented admirably that bourgeoisie which confuses with its little passions the great interests of the country, whimsical in politics, to-day for and to-morrow against the party in power, which compromises everything and saves nothing, aghast at the evil which it has done and continuing to breed more, unwilling to recognize its littleness, and vexing authority while proclaiming itself its servant, at once humble and arrogant, demanding of the people a subordination which it does not grant to royalty, worried over the superiorities which it desires to bring down to its level, as if grandeur could be little, as if power could exist without strength.

This president was a tall man, thin and dry, with a receding forehead, lank chestnut hair, odd eyes, a pimpled complexion, thin, compressed lips. In his feeble voice might be heard the thick whistling of asthma. He had for wife a tall creature, solemn and ill-formed, who wore the most absurd costumes and who decked herself out excessively. The president's wife gave herself the airs of a queen, she wore the most lively colors, and never went to a ball without ornamenting her head with one of those turbans so dear to the English and which the provinces cultivate lovingly. Possessed, each of them, of four or five thousand francs of income, they enjoyed together, with the salary of the presidency, an annual sum of some twelve thousand francs. Notwithstanding their leaning toward avarice, they received once a week in order to satisfy their vanity. Faithful to the ancient manners of the city into which Du Croisier had introduced modern luxury, Monsieur and Madame du Ronceret had made no change since their marriage, in the antique mansion in which they dwelt, and which belonged to madame. This house, which had a front on the court and another on a little garden, presented to the street an old triangular and grayish gable end, pierced with a window on each story. The court and the garden were enclosed by a high wall, along which extended in the garden an alley of chestnut trees, and in the court, the servants' offices. On the street which ran along the side of the garden was an old iron railing, devoured by rust, and on the court, between two panels of the wall, was a great porte cochère surmounted by an immense shell. This shell might be seen also above the front door. Here, everything was sombre, smothered, without air. The partition wall presented grated openings like the windows of a prison. The flowers had the air of being unhappy in the little squares of this little garden, in which the passers-by could see through the railing what was going on. On the ground floor, after a great antechamber lit from the garden, the visitor entered the salon, of which one of the windows opened on the street and which had a perron with a glass door leading into the garden. The dining-room, equal in size to the salon, was on the other side of the antechamber. These three apartments were in harmony with this melancholy whole. The ceilings, all cut up by those heavy painted rafters, ornamented in the middle by a few meagre lozenges with carved rosettes, offended the eye. All the painting, in crude tones, was old and darkened by smoke. The salon, decorated with great curtains in red silk faded by the sun, was furnished with articles in wood painted white and covered with old Beauvais tapestry the colors of which were effaced. On the chimney-piece, a clock of the time of Louis XV. was placed between two extravagant branched candlesticks, the yellow candles of which were never lit except on the days on which the president's wife removed its green wrappings from an old chandelier with drops of rock crystal. Three card-tables with threadbare green cloth, and a backgammon board sufficed for the joys of the company, to whom Madame du Ronceret granted cider, cakes, chestnuts, glasses of sugar and water and orgeat prepared in her own house. She had recently adopted for every other week a service of tea set off with sufficiently pitiful pastry. Every three weeks the Du Roncerets gave a grand dinner of three courses, proclaimed throughout the city, served on detestable plate, but prepared with the science that distinguishes the cooks in the provinces. This Gargantuesque repast lasted six hours. On these occasions the president undertook to compete by a miser's abundance with the elegance of Du Croisier. Thus life and all its accessories with the president were in accord with his character and his false position; he was uneasy in his own house without knowing why, but he did not dare to go to any expense to change the state of things, too happy to put aside every year seven or eight thousand francs to provide a wealthy establishment for his son Fabien, who had no desire to become either magistrate or avocat or administrator, and whose indolence filled his father with despair. With this son the president was in rivalry with his vice-president, Monsieur Blondet, an old judge who had, long before, proposed to ally his son with the Blandureau family. These rich linen merchants had an only daughter to whom the president hoped to marry Fabien. As the marriage of Joseph Blondet depended upon his appointment to the functions of assistant judge which the old Blondet hoped to obtain by resigning, the president Du Ronceret secretly opposed the judge's attempts and worked upon the Blandureaus in an underhand way. Thus, independently of the affair of the young Comte d'Esgrignon, the Blondets would perhaps have been supplanted by the astute president, whose fortune was much superior to that of his competitor.

The victim of the machinations of this Machiavelian president, Monsieur Blondet, one of those curious figures buried in the provinces like old medals in a crypt, was at this time about sixty-seven years of age; he carried his years well, was of a tall figure and his appearance recalled the canons of the good old times. His countenance, pitted by the thousand holes of smallpox, which had deformed his nose by turning it into a drill, was not lacking in expression; it was colored all over with a uniform red and animated by two sharp little eyes, habitually sardonic, and by a certain satiric movement of his purple lips. An advocate before the Revolution, he had been appointed *accusateur public;* but he was one of the mildest of these terrible functionaries. The goodman Blondet, as he was called, had mollified the revolutionary action by acquiescing in everything and executing nothing. Compelled to imprison several nobles, he had managed to conduct their cases so slowly that he brought them to the 9th Thermidor with an address which had secured him the general esteem. Certainly, the goodman Blondet should have been president of the tribunal; but, at the period of the reorganization of the tribunals, he was set aside by Napoléon, whose aversion for the republicans appeared in the slightest details of his government. The qualification of former *accusateur public,* written on the margin opposite the name of Blondet, had caused the Emperor to ask of Cambacérès if there were not in the district some scion of an old parliamentary family to put in his place. Du Ronceret, whose father had been counsellor to the parliament, was accordingly appointed. Notwithstanding the Emperor's repugnance, the archchancellor in the interests of justice retained Blondet as a judge, saying that the old advocate was one of the strongest jurisconsults in France. The talent of the judge, his acquaintance with the ancient law and, later, with the new legislation, should have advanced him very far; but, resembling in this many great spirits, he prodigiously misprized his own judicial knowledge and occupied himself almost exclusively with a science foreign to his profession, and for which he reserved his pretensions, his time and his capacities. The goodman passionately loved horticulture, he maintained a correspondence with the most celebrated amateurs, he had the ambition to create new species, he interested himself in the discoveries of botany, he lived, in short, in the world of flowers. Like all florists, he had his predilection for a plant selected from all others, and his favorite was the *pelargonium.* The tribunal and its cases, his real life, were thus nothing in comparison with the life, fanciful and full of emotions, which the old man led, more and more enamored of his innocent sultanas. The care to be given to his garden, the gentle habits of horticulture, retained the old man in his greenhouses. Had it not been for this passion, he would have been made deputy under the Empire, he would doubtless have shone in the Corps Législatif. His marriage was another reason for his obscure life. At the age of forty, he committed the folly of espousing a young girl of eighteen, by whom he had in the first year of his marriage a son named Joseph. Three years later, Madame Blondet, then the prettiest woman in the city, inspired the prefect of the department with a passion which was terminated only by her death. She had by the prefect, to the knowledge of the whole city and even of the old Blondet himself, a second son named Émile. Madame Blondet, who could have stimulated the ambition of her husband, who could have made it triumph over his flowers, favored the judge's taste for botany, and was no more willing to leave the city than the prefect was to change his prefecture while his mistress lived. Incapable at his age of maintaining a struggle against a young wife, the magistrate consoled himself in his greenhouse, and took a very pretty serving-maid to take care of his seraglio of beauties so constantly diversified. Whilst the judge unpotted, transplanted, watered, set out, grafted, hybridized and variegated his flowers, Madame Blondet expended his property in toilets and in fashions with which to shine in the salons of the prefecture; one interest only, the education of Émile, who was certainly still related to her passion, had the power to draw her from the nourishing of this constant affection, which the city ended by admiring. This child of love was as handsome, as sprightly, as Joseph was heavy and ugly. The old judge, blinded by paternal affection, loved Joseph as much as his wife cherished Émile. During twelve years, Monsieur Blondet displayed a perfect resignation, he closed his eyes to his wife's amours while preserving a noble and worthy attitude, after the manner of the grand seigneurs of the eighteenth century; but, like all individuals with peaceful tastes, he nourished a profound hatred of his younger son. In 1818, at the death of his wife, he expelled the intruder, sending him to prosecute his law studies at Paris without any other aid than an allowance of twelve hundred francs, to which sum no cry of distress could induce him to add an obole. Had it not been for the protection of his real father, Émile Blondet would have been lost. The house of the judge is one of the prettiest in the city. Situated almost opposite to the prefecture, it has on the principal street a spruce little court, separated from the sidewalk by an old iron railing between two brick pilasters. Between each of these pilasters and the neighboring house are two other railings rising from little walls, also of brick, and breast high. This court, twenty yards wide and forty long, is divided into two clusters of flowering plants by the brick pavement which leads from the gate to the door of the house. These two clumps of flowers, carefully renewed, offer to the public admiration their triumphant bouquets at every season. From their bases sprouts a magnificent mantle of climbing plants that covers the walls of the two adjoining houses. The pilasters are enveloped in honeysuckle vines and ornamented with two terra-cotta vases, in which acclimated cactus plants present to the astonished eyes of the ignorant their monstrous leaves bristling with those prickly defences which seem to be the result of some botanic malady. The house, built of brick, the windows of which are decorated by an arched border, also of brick, presents its simple façade, enlivened by Venetian blinds of a lively green. Its glass door permits you to see, through a long corridor at the end of which is another glass door, the principal alley of a garden of about two acres in extent. The flowering clusters of this enclosure may often be seen through the windows of the salon and the dining-room, which correspond to each other like those of the corridor. On the street side, the brick has taken in the course of two centuries a tone of rust and of moss mingled with greenish tints in harmony with the freshness of the clusters and their bushes. It is impossible for the traveller who traverses the city not to fall in love with this house so graciously enclosed, flowered, moss-grown, even to its roofs, which are decorated by two chimneys in earthenware.

In addition to this old house, in which nothing had been changed for a century, the judge possessed about four thousand francs of income in lands. His vengeance, sufficiently legitimate, consisted in transferring this house, the lands, and his seat on the bench to his son Joseph, and the whole city knew his intentions. He had made a will in favor of this son, in which he took advantage of all that the Code permits in the way of allowing a father to give to one of his children to the detriment of the other. Moreover, the goodman had been saving up for the last fifteen years in order to leave to this ninny the sum necessary to pay over to his brother Émile the portion which could not be taken from him. Chased from the paternal mansion, Émile Blondet had been able to conquer a distinguished position in Paris, but one more intellectual than positive. His laziness, his indifference, his carelessness, had reduced to despair his own father, who, dismissed in one of the ministerial reactions so frequent under the Restoration, had died almost ruined, full of doubts concerning the future of a child endowed by nature with the most brilliant qualities. Émile Blondet was sustained by the friendship of a Demoiselle de Troisville, married to the Comte de Montcornet, and whom he had known before her marriage. His mother was still living at the period when the Troisvilles returned from the emigration. Madame Blondet was connected with this family by ties distant, but sufficient to introduce Émile. The poor woman foresaw the future of her son, she saw him an orphan, a thought which rendered death doubly bitter; therefore she sought protectors for him. She was able to establish an intimacy between Émile and the eldest of the Demoiselles de Troisville, whom he infinitely pleased but who could not marry him. This liaison resembled that of Paul and Virginia. Madame Blondet endeavored to give duration to this mutual affection, which might be expected to pass away as do usually these childish things, which are, in love, like the pretended little dinners of infants, by showing her son a support in the Troisville family. When, on her death-bed, Madame Blondet heard of the marriage of Mademoiselle de Troisville with General Montcornet, she sent to beg her solemnly never to abandon Émile and to be his patron in the Parisian world where she was called by the general's fortune to shine. Fortunately for him, Émile protected himself. At twenty, he made his début like a master in the literary world. His success was no less in the select society into which he was introduced by his father, who at first was able to supply the young man profusely. This precocious celebrity, the fine appearance of Émile, drew still closer perhaps the bonds of friendship which united him to the countess. Perhaps Madame de Montcornet, who had Russian blood in her veins, her mother having been a daughter of the Princess Sherbellof, would have denied the friend of her childhood poor and struggling with all his intelligence against the obstacles of Parisian and literary life; but, when there appeared the sparkling attractions of the adventurous life of Émile, their attachment became unalterable on both sides. At this moment, Blondet, whom the young D'Esgrignon had met in Paris at his first supper, was accepted as one of the luminaries of journalism. A great superiority in the political world was attributed to him, and he controlled his reputation. The goodman Blondet was completely ignorant of the power which the constitutional government had given to the journals; no one took it upon himself to inform him of a son of whom he never wished to hear; he therefore knew nothing either of this cursed son or of his power.

The integrity of the judge was equalled only by his passion for flowers, he knew only justice and botany. He received the litigants, listened to them, talked with them and showed them his flowers; he accepted from them precious seeds; but, on the bench, he became the most impartial judge in the world. His manner of proceeding was so well known that the litigants no longer came to see him but to hand him the documents that might enlighten his equity; no one sought to deceive him. His knowledge, his enlightenment, his indifference to his real talents, rendered him so indispensable to Du Ronceret that, without his matrimonial reasons, the president would still have secretly sought to thwart by all means possible the request of the old judge to resign in favor of his son; for, if the learned old man left the tribunal, the president was incapable of pronouncing a judgment. The goodman Blondet did not know that in a few hours his son Émile could bring about the accomplishment of his desires. He lived in a simplicity worthy of the heroes of Plutarch. In the evening, he examined the papers; in the morning, he took care of his flowers, and, during the day, he judged. The pretty servant maid, now as ripe and wrinkled as an Easter apple, took charge of the housekeeping, maintained with the usages and customs of a rigorous avarice. Mademoiselle Cadot always carried about her the keys of the closets and the fruit loft; she was indefatigable,—she went to the market herself, attended to the apartments and the cooking, and never failed to hear her mass in the morning. To give an idea of the life in the interior of this house, it will suffice to say that the father and the son never ate any but damaged fruit, in consequence of Mademoiselle Cadot's habit of always bringing on for dessert the most advanced ones; that the luxury of fresh bread was unknown, and that all the fasts ordained by the Church were observed. The gardener was rationed like a soldier, and constantly watched by this elderly Validé, treated with so much deference that she dined with her masters. Thus she was continually trotting to and fro between the dining-room and the kitchen during the meals. The marriage of Joseph Blondet with Mademoiselle Blandureau had been made conditional by the father and the mother of this heiress on the appointment of this poor, briefless advocate to the post of assistant judge. In the desire of rendering him capable of exercising his duties, the father killed himself in endeavoring to beat into his son's head instructions that would enable him to work by routine. The son Blondet passed almost all his evenings in the house of his intended, to which, since his return from Paris, Fabien du Ronceret had been admitted, without exciting the least alarm either in the old Blondet or the young one. The economical principles which presided over this life measured with an exactitude worthy of the "Money changer" of Gérard Dow, into which there did not enter a grain of salt too much, in which no possible profit was forgotten, yielded however to the exigencies of the greenhouse and the gardening. "The garden was monsieur's folly," said Mademoiselle Cadot, who did not consider his blind love for Joseph as a folly, with regard to this son she partook of the father's predilection,—she took care of him, mended his stockings, and would have wished to see the money spent on horticulture devoted to his use. This garden, kept in marvellous order by a single gardener, had alleys sanded with river sand, ceaselessly raked over, and on each side of which swayed the beds full of the rarest flowers. There were all the perfumes, all the colors, myriads of little pots exposed to the sun, the lizards on the walls, the hoes, the grubbing hoes, arranged in order, in short, all the apparatus of these innocent things and the ensemble of gracious productions which justify this charming passion. At the end of his greenhouse the judge had established a vast amphitheatre in which, on the benches, were seated five or six thousand pots of pelargoniums, a famous and magnificent collection which the whole city and many persons from the adjoining departments came to see when they flowered. On her passage through the city, the Empress Marie-Louise had honored this curious greenhouse with a visit, and was so greatly impressed with this sight that she spoke of it to Napoléon, and the Emperor gave the cross to the old judge. As the learned horticulturist went into no society outside of the house of Blandureau, he was ignorant of the underground proceedings of the president. Those who had been able to penetrate the intentions of Du Ronceret feared him too much to notify the inoffensive Blondets.

As to Michu, this young man, strongly protected, concerned himself much more with pleasing the women of the highest society into which he had been admitted on the recommendation of the family of Cinq-Cygne, than with the excessively simple affairs of a provincial tribunal. Rich, with about twelve thousand francs of income, he was courted by the mothers, and led a life of pleasure. He attended to his tribunal as a matter of conscience, as young men perform their collegiate duties; he voted at random, saying to everything: "Yes, my dear president." But, under this apparent indifference, he concealed the superior intelligence of a man who had studied at Paris and who had already distinguished himself as an assistant. Accustomed to consider all subjects broadly, he executed rapidly that which occupied the aged Blondet and the president for a long time, and for them he often made a résumé of questions difficult to solve. In delicate conjunctures the president and the vice-president consulted their assistant judge, they confided to him difficult problems and were always surprised at his promptness in bringing them to a solution in which the old Blondet found nothing to amend. Protected by the most scornful aristocracy, young and wealthy, the assistant judge lived outside of the intrigues and the littlenesses of the department. Indispensable at all the country parties, he gambolled with the young people, made court to the mothers, danced at the balls, and played like a financier. In short, he acquitted himself admirably in his rôle of a fashionable magistrate, without, nevertheless, compromising his dignity, which he knew how to assert at the proper time, like a man of spirit. He gave infinite pleasure by the frank manner in which he had adopted the customs of the provinces, without criticising them. Therefore, everyone made an effort to render the period of his exile supportable to him.

The procureur du roi, a magistrate of the greatest talent, but involved in the upper spheres of politics, controlled the president. Had it not been for his absence, the affair of Victurnien would not have taken place. His ability, his knowledge of affairs, would have prevented everything. The president and Du Croisier had profited by his presence in the Chamber of Deputies, where he was one of the most remarkable ministerial orators, to concoct their schemes, considering, with a certain cleverness, that justice once put in motion and the affair noised abroad, there would be no longer any remedy. In fact, in no tribunal, at this period, would the court have received without a long examination, and perhaps without referring it to the procureur général, a charge of forgery against the eldest son of one of the most noble houses in the kingdom. In similar circumstances, the officers of justice, in concert with the sovereign power, would have essayed a thousand procedures to suppress an accusation that might send an imprudent young man to the galleys. They would perhaps have done the same for a liberal family of consideration, at least if they were not too openly enemies of the throne and the altar. The reception of Du Croisier's accusation and the arrest of the young count had not, then, been easily effected. These are the methods that the president and Du Croisier had taken to attain their ends.

Monsieur Sauvager, a young royalist advocate, attained to the judicial rank of first deputy by reason of his ministerial servility, ruled in his chief's absence. It depended upon him to issue a warrant in accepting Du Croisier's accusation. Sauvager, a man without anything, without any kind of a fortune, lived on the salary of his office. Thus, the sovereign power counted entirely upon a man who had everything to expect from it. The president made the most of this situation. As soon as the document declared to be a forgery was in Du Croisier's hands, that very evening, Madame la Présidente du Ronceret, inspired by her husband, had a long conversation with Monsieur Sauvager, whose attention she called to the very uncertain career of the *standing magistracy*,—a ministerial caprice, a single fault, would destroy a man's future.

"Be a conscientious man, decide against power when it is in the wrong, and you are lost. You can," she said to him, "take advantage of your position at this moment to make a fine marriage which will place you forever beyond the reach of evil fortune, by giving you a fortune which will enable you to secure for yourself a position in the *sitting* magistracy. The moment is propitious. Monsieur du Croisier will never have any children, everyone knows why; his fortune and that of his wife will go to his niece, Mademoiselle Duval. Monsieur Duval is an ironmaster whose purse is already tolerably well filled, and his father, who is still living, has some property. The father and the son have between them a million, they will double it, aided by Du Croisier, now closely allied with the great bankers and the important manufacturers of Paris. Monsieur and Madame Duval the younger will certainly give their daughter to the man who is presented by her uncle Du Croisier, in consideration of the two fortunes which he must leave to his niece, for Du Croisier will undoubtedly formally endow his niece with the entire fortune of his wife, who has no heirs. You know the hatred of Du Croisier for the D'Esgrignons, render him a service, be his man, receive an accusation of forgery which he will deposit with you against the young D'Esgrignon, pursue the count immediately, without consulting the procureur du roi. Then, pray God that, for having proved yourself an impartial magistrate, in opposition to power, the minister dismiss you, your fortune is made! You will have a charming wife and thirty thousand francs of income as a dowry, without counting four millions in expectancy within the space of ten years."

In the course of two evenings, the first deputy was won over. The president and Monsieur Sauvager had kept the affair secret from the old judge, from the assistant judge and from the second deputy. Confident of the impartiality of Blondet in presence of the facts, the president had a majority, not counting Camusot. But everything was spoiled by the unforeseen defection of the juge d'instruction. The president wished an indictment drawn up before the procureur du roi was notified. Might not Camusot or the second deputy inform him?

Now, in explaining the inward life of the juge d'instruction Camusot, perhaps the reasons may be perceived which permitted Chesnel to consider this young magistrate as secured to the D'Esgrignons, and which had given him the hardihood to suborn him in the middle of the street. Camusot, the son of the first wife of an illustrious silk merchant of the Rue des Bourdonnais, the object of his father's ambition, had been destined for the magistracy. In marrying his wife, he had married the protection of an usher of the cabinet of the king, a protection concealed but efficacious, which had already secured him his appointment as judge, and, later, that of juge d'instruction. His father had given him in marrying him only six thousand francs of income, the fortune of his late mother, after having made all deductions to which he was entitled as husband; Mademoiselle Thirion had not brought him more than twenty thousand francs of dot. This household was acquainted with all the unhappinesses of a concealed poverty, for the appointments of a judge in the provinces do not rise above fifteen hundred francs; however, the juges d'instruction have a supplementary allowance of about a thousand francs because of the expenses and the unusual amount of labor required by their functions. Notwithstanding the fatigues attending them, these posts are sufficiently coveted, but they are revocable; for this reason Madame Camusot had scolded her husband for having revealed his opinions to the president.

Marie-Cecile-Amélie Thirion in three years of married life had been conscious of the benediction of God by the regularity of two happy accouchements, one of a daughter and one of a son; but she supplicated God to bless her no more to such an extent. But a few more benedictions, and her pecuniary embarrassment would become actual poverty. The fortune of Monsieur Camusot the father might involve a long waiting. Moreover, this rich inheritance could not give more than eight or ten thousand francs of income to the children of the merchant, who were four in number, and by two mothers. Then, when there came to be realized that which all the makers of marriages call *expectations,* would not the judge have children of his own to establish? Everyone may therefore conceive the situation of a little woman full of good sense and of resolution, like Madame Camusot; she was too conscious of the importance of a false step made by her husband in his career not to interfere in judiciary matters.

The only child of a former servitor of the king, Louis XVIII., a valet who had followed him into Italy, into Courland, into England, and whom the king had rewarded by the only place which he could fill, that of usher of his cabinet, serving quarterly, Amélie had received herself something like a reflection of the court. Thirion described to her the grand seigneurs, the ministers, the personages whom he announced, introduced, and saw passing and repassing. Brought up, as it were, at the gate of the Tuileries, this young woman had thus taken the tone of the maxims which there prevailed, and adopted the dogma of absolute obedience to power. Thus she had sagely concluded that in taking the side of the D'Esgrignons her husband would please Madame la Duchesse de Maufrigneuse, two powerful families on whose support her father might rely at an opportune moment for the king's favor. On the first opportunity Camusot might be appointed judge in the jurisdiction of Paris, then, later, at Paris itself. This promotion dreamed of, desired every moment, would bring a salary of six thousand francs, the pleasures of dwelling with her father or with the Camusots, and all the advantages of two paternal fortunes. If the adage, *Out of sight, out of mind,* is true for the greater number of women, it is especially true with regard to family sentiments and to ministerial or royal protection. In all times, those who personally serve kings do very well in their own affairs,—one is naturally interested in a man, even a valet, when one sees him every day.

Madame Camusot, who considered herself as only a bird of passage, had taken a little house in the Rue du Cygne. The city was not sufficiently a thoroughfare for the industry of furnished apartments to be established in it. This household was, moreover, not wealthy enough to live in a hotel, like Monsieur Michu. The Parisienne had then been obliged to accept the furnishings of the country. The modesty of her revenues had obliged her to take this remarkably ugly house, which, however, did not lack a certain simplicity of detail. Supported against the adjoining house in such a manner as to present its façade to the court, it had on each story only one window on the street. The court, enclosed in its width by two walls ornamented with rose bushes and privet bushes, had, at the back, opposite the house, a sort of out-house built upon two brick arches. A little door, neither gate nor porte cochère, gave entrance to this sombre mansion, rendered still more sombre by a great walnut tree planted in the middle of the court. On the ground floor, which was entered by a perron with a double flight of steps and a balustrade in iron work, very ornate but eaten by rust, there was a dining-room on the side of the street and, on the other side, the kitchen. The end of the corridor which separated these two chambers was taken up by a wooden staircase. The first story consisted of only two apartments, of which one served the magistrate for a cabinet and the other for a bedroom. The second story, a mansard, also contained two chambers, one for the cook and the other for the femme de chambre, who kept the children with her. No room in the house had a ceiling, all of them presented those white-washed rafters of which the intermediate spaces were ceiled with white plaster. The two rooms on the first floor and the dining-room below had those ceilings with contorted forms on which the woodworkers of the last century had exercised their patience. This woodwork, painted a dirty gray, presented a most melancholy aspect. The judge's cabinet was that of a provincial advocate,—a great desk and an armchair in mahogany, the library of a law student, and his shabby furniture brought from Paris. The chamber of Madame was indigenous,—it had white and blue ornaments, a carpet, one of those heteroclitic sets of furniture which seem in the style and which are simply furniture whose style has not been adopted in Paris. As to the dining-room of the ground floor, it was what such apartments are in the provinces, bare, cold, the walls covered with a damp and out-of-date paper.

It was in this shabby chamber, without any other view than that of this walnut tree, of these walls with black leafage and of the almost deserted street, that a woman, sufficiently alert and lively, accustomed to the pleasures, to the movement of Paris, passed all her days, alone the greater part of the time, or receiving wearisome and stupid visits which made her prefer her solitude to that empty cackle, in which the least sparkle of wit which she might allow herself gave rise to interminable commentaries and embittered her situation. Occupied with her children, less by inclination than to bring an interest into her almost solitary life, she could exercise her mind only on the intrigues which developed themselves around her, on the proceedings of the people of the province, on their ambitions confined within narrow circles. Thus she penetrated promptly into mysteries of which her husband did not dream. Her out-house full of wood, in which her femme de chambre was washing in soapsuds, was not that which struck her eye when, seated at the window of her chamber, she held in her hand some interrupted embroidery,—she contemplated Paris, where all is pleasure, where everything is full of life, she dreamed of its fêtes and wept to be in this cold prison of the provinces. She was in despair at living in a peaceable country, in which there never happened any conspiracy or any great affair. She saw herself resting for a long time under the shadow of this walnut tree.

Madame Camusot was a little woman, plump, fresh, blonde, adorned with a very arched forehead, with a sunken mouth, with a prominent chin, features which youth renders supportable but which would early give her the appearance of age. Her lively and intelligent eyes, which, however, expressed a little too clearly her innocent desire to succeed and the jealousy which her present inferiority caused her, shone like two lights in her commonplace face, and relieved it by a certain strength of feeling which success was later to extinguish. She expended at this period much industry upon her toilet, she invented trimmings, she embroidered them; she deliberated over her attire with her femme de chambre, whom she had brought from Paris, and thus maintained in the provinces the reputation of the Parisiennes. Her caustic wit caused her to be dreaded, she was not liked. With that subtle and investigating spirit which characterizes unoccupied women, obliged to find employment for their days, she had ultimately discovered the secret opinions of the president; consequently she had been advising Camusot for some time to declare war against him. The affair of the young count afforded an excellent opportunity. Before going to spend the evening with Monsieur du Croisier, she had not had much trouble in demonstrating to her husband that in this affair the first deputy was acting contrary to the intentions of his chiefs. Was it not the part of Camusot to make a stepping stone of this criminal process, by favoring the house of D'Esgrignon, much more powerful than Du Croisier's party?

"Sauvager will never marry Mademoiselle Duval, whom they have dangled before his eyes, he will be the dupe of those Machiavellis of the Val-Noble, to whom he is going to sacrifice his position. Camusot, this affair, so unfortunate for the D'Esgrignons and so perfidiously set on foot by the president for Du Croisier's profit, will be advantageous only to you," she had said to him on returning home.

This shrewd Parisienne had also divined the secret proceedings of the president with regard to Blandureau, and the motives which he had to defeat the efforts of the old Blondet, but she could perceive no profit in enlightening the son or the father on the peril of their situation; she enjoyed the commencement of this comedy, without suspecting of what importance might be the secret that she had discovered of the application made to the Blandureaus by Chesnel's successor in favor of Fabien du Ronceret. In case her husband's position should be menaced by the president, Madame Camusot would be able to threaten in her turn the president by calling the attention of the horticulturist to the projected rape of the flower which he proposed to transplant in his own garden.

Without having penetrated, like Madame Camusot, the methods by which Du Croisier and the president had gained the first deputy, Chesnel, in examining these divers existences and these varied interests grouped around the fleur-de-lys of the tribunal, counted upon the procureur du roi, upon Camusot, and upon Monsieur Michu. Two judges for the D'Esgrignons would paralyze everything. Finally, the notary was too well acquainted with the wishes of the old Blondet not to know that, if anything could make his integrity waver, it would concern the work of his whole life, the appointment of his son to the post of assistant judge. Thus Chesnel went to sleep full of confidence, promising himself to go and see Monsieur Blondet, to offer him the realization of the hopes which he had been so long cherishing while enlightening him as to the perfidiousness of the president Du Ronceret. After having gained the old judge, he would go to negotiate with the juge d'instruction, to whom he hoped to be able to prove, if not the innocence, at least the imprudence of Victurnien, and to reduce the affair to simply a young man's folly. Chesnel slept neither peacefully nor long; for, before daybreak, his housekeeper awoke him to present to him the most seductive personage of this history, the most adorable young man in the world, Madame la Duchesse de Maufrigneuse, who had arrived alone in a calèche, dressed like a man.

"I have come to save him or to perish with him," she said to the notary, who thought he was dreaming. "I have a hundred thousand francs which the king has given me from his privy purse to purchase the innocence of Victurnien, if his adversary can be corrupted. If we fail, I have poison to save him from everything, even the accusation. But we shall not fail. The procureur du roi, whom I have notified of what is going on, is following me; he could not come with me, he wished to receive the orders of the keeper of the seals."

Chesnel repeated for the duchess the little scene which she had played for him,—he enveloped himself in his dressing-gown and fell at her feet, which he kissed, not without asking pardon for the forgetfulness which joy caused him.

"We are saved!" he cried, while giving orders to Brigitte to prepare whatever the duchess might need after a night spent in riding post.

He made an appeal to the courage of the fair Diane, demonstrating to her the necessity of going to see the juge d'instruction at daybreak, so that no one could suspect this proceeding, and could not even suppose that the Duchesse de Maufrigneuse had come.

"Have I not a passport regularly made out?" said she, showing him a paper in which she was designated as being Monsieur le Vicomte Félix de Vandenesse, *maître des requêtes* and private secretary of the king. "Do I not know how to play my part of a man?" she went on, brushing up the front of her perruque *à la Titus* and cracking her riding-whip.

"Ah! madame la duchesse, you are an angel!" exclaimed Chesnel, with tears in his eyes.—She was destined to be always an angel, even as a man!—"Button up your redingote, wrap yourself up to the nose in your cloak, take my arm and let us hasten to Camusot's house before anyone can meet us."

"I shall then see a man whose name is Camusot?" she asked.

"And who has the nose of his name,"—*camus,* flat-nosed,—replied Chesnel.

Although he had death in his soul, the old notary judged it necessary to obey all the caprices of the duchess, to laugh when she laughed, to weep with her; but he sighed over the lightness of a woman who, even while accomplishing a great work, yet nevertheless found in it matter for jesting. What would he not have done to save the young man! While Chesnel was dressing, Madame de Maufrigneuse partook of the cup of coffee with cream which Brigitte served her, and admitted the superiority of the provincial cooks over the chefs of Paris, who disdain those little details so important for the gourmets. Thanks to the cares which were rendered necessary by her master's fondness for good living, Brigitte was able to offer the duchess an excellent collation. Chesnel and his fair companion took their way to the house of Monsieur and Madame Camusot.

"Ah! there is a Madame Camusot?" said the duchess. "The affair can be arranged."

"And so much the more so," replied Chesnel, "as madame evidently suffers ennui among us provincials; she is from Paris."

"Therefore we need not have any secrets from her?"

"You will be the judge of what will be necessary to conceal or reveal," said Chesnel humbly. "I think that she will be very much flattered to offer hospitality to the Duchesse de Maufrigneuse. In order to compromise nothing, it will doubtless be necessary for you to remain in her house until night, unless you should find it inconvenient."

"Is she agreeable, Madame Camusot?" asked the duchess with a foolish air.

"She is somewhat of a mistress in her own house," replied the notary.

"She should then interest herself in the affairs of the Palais," replied the duchess. "It is only in France, dear Monsieur Chesnel, that you see women marrying their husbands so thoroughly that they marry their functions, their business or their work. In Italy, in England, in Spain, the wives make it a point of honor to leave their husbands to struggle with their own affairs; they bring to the ignoring of them the same perseverance which our French bourgeoise women display in acquiring a knowledge of the affairs of the community. Is it not in this manner that you designate that judicially? The French women, of an incredible jealousy in matters of conjugal politics, wish to know everything. Thus, in the smallest difficulties of life in France, you feel the hand of the wife who counsels, guides, enlightens her husband. The greater number of men do not find themselves badly off because of it, truly. In England, a married man may be put in prison for twenty-four hours for debt, his wife, on his return, will make a scene of jealousy for him."

"We have reached here without having met any one at all," said Chesnel. "Madame la duchesse, you should have all the more authority here, since the father of Madame Camusot is an usher of the king's cabinet, named Thirion."

"And the king never thought of it! he thinks of nothing," she exclaimed. "Thirion introduced us, the Prince de Cadignan, Monsieur de Vandenesse, and myself! We are the masters in this house. Make all your arrangements with the husband whilst I speak to the wife."

The femme de chambre who washed, cleaned, dressed the children, introduced the two strangers into the little, fireless, front apartment.

"Go and take this card to your mistress," said the duchess in the ear of the femme de chambre, "and let no one read it but her. If you are discreet, you will be rewarded, my girl."

The femme de chambre stood as if thunderstruck on hearing this woman's voice and seeing this delightful figure of a young man.

"Awaken Monsieur Camusot," said Chesnel to her, "and tell him that I am awaiting him on an important affair."

The femme de chambre went upstairs. A few moments later, Madame Camusot in a peignoir flew down the stairs and introduced the fair stranger into her room, after having pushed Camusot in his shirt into his cabinet, with all his clothes, ordering him to dress himself and wait for her there. This theatrical stroke had been brought about by the card, on which was engraved MADAME LA DUCHESSE DE MAUFRIGNEUSE. The daughter of the usher of the king's cabinet had comprehended everything.

"Well, Monsieur Chesnel, would you not say that this house had been struck by lightning?" exclaimed the femme de chambre under her breath. "Monsieur is dressing in his cabinet, you can go up there."

"Silence concerning all this," replied the notary.

Chesnel, feeling himself supported by a great lady who had the verbal assent of the king to all the measures to be taken to save the Comte d'Esgrignon, assumed an air of authority before Camusot which was of much greater service to him than would have been the humble air which he would have taken if he had been alone and without aid.

"Monsieur," he said to him, "my words yesterday evening may have astonished you, but they were serious. The house of D'Esgrignon counts upon you to well investigate an affair from which it must issue without a stain."

"Monsieur," replied the judge, "I will not take up what there is insulting to me and derogatory to justice in your words, for, up to a certain point, your position with the house of D'Esgrignon excuses it; but—"

"Monsieur, pardon me for interrupting you," said Chesnel. "I come to say to you things which your superiors think but do not venture to avow, but which men of intelligence will divine, and you are a man of intelligence. If we suppose that the young man has acted imprudently, do you suppose that the king, that the court, that the ministry, would be flattered to see a name like that of D'Esgrignon dragged before the court of assizes? Is it to the interests of the kingdom, to the interests of the country, that the historic houses should fall? Does not equality, to-day the great word of the opposition, find a guarantee in the existence of a high aristocracy consecrated by time? Well, not only has there not been the slightest imprudence, but we are, in fact, innocents fallen into a trap."

"I am curious to know how," said the judge.

"Monsieur," resumed Chesnel, "for two years, the Sieur du Croisier has constantly allowed Monsieur le Comte d'Esgrignon to draw upon him for heavy sums. We will produce drafts for more than a hundred thousand écus, constantly made good by him and the sums for which have been remitted by me—take particular notice of this—sometimes before, sometimes after they fell due. Monsieur le Comte d'Esgrignon is prepared to present a receipt for the sum drawn by him, dated before the draft which is said to be a forgery; do you not recognize then in the accusation an act of hatred and of party spirit? is it not an odious calumny, this accusation brought by the most dangerous adversaries of the throne and the altar against the heir of an old family? There has been no more forgery in this affair than there is in my office. Summon before you Madame du Croisier, who is still ignorant of the accusation of forgery, she will declare to you that I brought the money to her, and that she kept it to hand over to her husband, then absent, who did not claim it from her. Interrogate Du Croisier on this subject,—he will tell you that he was ignorant of my remittance to Madame du Croisier.

"Monsieur," replied the juge d'instruction, "you can utter such assertions as these in the salon of Monsieur d'Esgrignon or among people who have no knowledge of affairs, they may believe them; but a juge d'instruction, unless he were an imbecile, will not believe that a wife as submissive to her husband as is Madame du Croisier is keeping at this moment in her secretary a hundred thousand écus without saying anything to her husband, or that an old notary would not have informed Monsieur du Croisier of this remittance on his return to the city."

"The old notary had gone to Paris, monsieur, to arrest this young man in his course of dissipation."

"I have not yet interrogated the Comte d'Esgrignon," resumed the judge, "his replies will enlighten my judgment."

"He is not allowed to communicate with his friends?" asked the notary.

"No," replied the judge.

"Monsieur," exclaimed Chesnel who perceived the danger, "the *examination* may be conducted for or against us; but you will choose to establish, according to Madame du Croisier's testimony, the remittance of the funds anterior to the bill of exchange, or to interrogate a poor young man inculpated who, in his trouble, may remember nothing and compromise himself. You will seek for the most credible, either a forgetfulness on the part of a woman ignorant of affairs, or a forgery committed by a D'Esgrignon."

"That is not the question at all," replied the judge, "it is a question of knowing whether Monsieur le Comte d'Esgrignon has converted the bottom of a letter addressed to him by Du Croisier into a bill of exchange."

"Eh! he could have done so," suddenly exclaimed Madame Camusot, entering quickly, followed by the fair unknown, "Monsieur Chesnel remitted the funds—"

She leaned toward her husband:

"You shall be assistant judge at Paris on the first vacancy; you are serving the king himself in this affair, I have the certainty of it, you will not be forgotten," she said to him in his ear. "In this young man you see the Duchesse de Maufrigneuse, endeavor to say that you have never seen her, and do everything for the young count, boldly."

"Messieurs," said the judge, "when the instruction shall have been concluded favorably to the young count, can I depend upon a judgment to interfere? Monsieur Chesnel and you, my dear, you know the dispositions of monsieur le président."

"Ta, ta, ta!" said Madame Camusot; "go yourself, this morning, to see Monsieur Michu, and inform him of the arrest of the young count, you will be already two against two, I will answer for it. Michu is from Paris, he is! and you know his devotion to the nobility. Like father, like son."

At this moment, Mademoiselle Cadot made her voice heard at the door, saying that she brought an urgent letter. The judge went out, then returned, reading these words:

"Monsieur the vice-president of the tribunal requests Monsieur Camusot to preside at the audience this day and the following days, so that the tribunal may be complete during the absence of monsieur le president. He presents to him his compliments."

"No *examination* in the affair D'Esgrignon!" cried Madame Camusot. "Did I not tell you, my friend, that they would do you some ill turn? The president has gone to calumniate you to the procureur général and to the president of the court. Before you can investigate the affair, you will be removed. Is that clear?"

"You will remain, monsieur!" said the duchess, "the procureur du roi will arrive, I hope, in time."

"When the procureur du roi arrives," said the little Madame Camusot in a heat, "he will find everything ended.—Yes, my dear, yes," she said, looking at her stupefied husband.—"Ah! old hypocrite of a president, you are playing your finest tricks with us, you will remember them! You wish to serve us up a trick of your trade, you shall have two prepared by the hand of your servant, Cécile-Amelie Thirion.—Poor goodman Blondet, it is fortunate for him that the president has gone about to have us dismissed, his great booby of a son shall marry Mademoiselle Blandureau. I am going to dig up the seed beds of the Père Blondet.—You, Camusot, go to see Monsieur Michu whilst madame la duchesse and I, we will go to find the old Blondet. Prepare yourself to hear it said by all the town that I have gone walking this morning with a lover."

Madame Camusot gave her arm to the duchess, and conducted her by the deserted quarters of the city so as to arrive without any unfortunate encounter at the door of the old judge. During this time Chesnel went to confer with the young count in prison, into which Camusot caused him to be secretly introduced. The cooks, the domestics and other early risers of the provinces, who saw Madame Camusot and the duchess in the byways of the town, took the young man for a lover from Paris. As Cecile-Amélie had foreseen, in the evening the news of her behavior circulated through the city and gave rise to more than one slander. Madame Camusot and her pretended lover found the old Blondet in his greenhouse; he saluted the wife of his colleague and her companion, throwing upon this charming young man a distrustful and scrutinizing look.

"I have the honor to present to you one of my husband's cousins," she said to Monsieur Blondet, indicating the duchess, "one of the most distinguished horticulturists of Paris, who is returning from Brittany, and can spend only this day with us. Monsieur has heard of your flowers and of your plants, and I have taken the liberty of coming so early in the morning."

"Ah! monsieur is a horticulturist," said the old judge.

The duchess bowed without replying.

"Here," said the judge, "is my coffee tree and my tea tree."

"Why is it, now," said Madame Camusot, "that monsieur le président has gone? I will wager that his absence has something to do with Monsieur Camusot."

"Precisely so.—Here, monsieur, is the most original cactus that exists," said he, showing in a pot a plant that had the appearance of a rattan covered with leprosy, "it comes from New Holland. You are very young, monsieur, to be a horticulturist."

"Leave your flowers, dear Monsieur Blondet," said Madame Camusot; "it is a matter concerning you, your hopes, the marriage of your son with Mademoiselle Blandureau. You are the dupe of the president."

"Bah!" said the judge with an incredulous air.

"Yes," she replied. "If you cultivated the world a little more and your flowers a little less, you would know that the dot and the hopes which you have planted, watered, cultivated, weeded, are on the point of being gathered by shrewd hands—"

"Madame!"

"Ah! no one in the city would have the courage to affront the president by warning you. I, who am not of the city, and who, thanks to this worthy young man, will soon be going to Paris, I inform you that Chesnel's successor has formally requested the hand of Claire Blandureau for the little Du Ronceret, to whom his father and his mother give fifty thousand écus. As to Fabien, he promises to have him received as an advocate in order to be made a judge."

The old judge dropped the pot which he had in his hand to show to the duchess.

"Ah! my cactus! ah! my son! Mademoiselle Blandureau!—Oh! the flower of the cactus is broken!"

"No, everything can be arranged," said Madame Camusot to him, laughing. "If you wish to see your son judge in a month from now, we are going to tell you how to go about it—"

"Monsieur, will you pass this way, you will see my pelargoniums, a magic spectacle when they are flowering—Why," said he to Madame Camusot, "do you speak to me of these affairs before your cousin?"

"Everything depends upon him," answered Madame Camusot. "The appointment of your son is forever lost if you say a word about this young man."

"Bah!"

"This young man is a flower."

"Ah!"

"It is the Duchesse de Maufrigneuse, sent here by the king to save the young D'Esgrignon, arrested yesterday in consequence of an accusation of forgery brought by Du Croisier. Madame la duchesse has the word of the keeper of the seals, he will ratify the promises which she will make us—"

"My cactus is saved!" said the judge, who was examining his precious plant.—"Go on, I am listening."

"Consult with Camusot and Michu to suppress the affair as soon as possible, and your son shall be appointed. His nomination will then arrive in plenty of time to permit you to thwart the intrigues of the Du Roncerets with the Blandureaus. Your son shall be better than assistant judge, he will succeed Monsieur Camusot in the course of the year. The procureur du roi arrives to-day; Monsieur Sauvager will doubtless be forced to give in his resignation in consequence of his conduct in this affair. My husband will show you documents at the Palais which establish the count's innocence and which prove that the forgery is a snare set by Du Croisier."

The old judge entered the Olympian circus of his six thousand pelargoniums and saluted the duchess.

"Monsieur," he said, "if that which you desire is legal, it can be arranged."

"Monsieur," replied the duchess, "send your resignation to-morrow to Monsieur Chesnel, I promise to send you in the course of the week the appointment of your son, but do not give it in until after you have heard monsieur le procureur du roi confirm my words to you. You will understand each other better among you people of the law. Only, let him know that the Duchesse de Maufrigneuse has given you her word. And silence concerning my journey here," she said.

The old judge kissed her hand, and set himself to gathering without pity his finest flowers, which he offered to her.

"What are you thinking of? give them to madame," said the duchess to him, "it is not natural to see flowers on a man who gives his arm to a pretty woman."

"Before going to the Palais," said Madame Camusot to him, "go and inform yourself from Chesnel's successor of the propositions made by him in the name of Monsieur and of Madame du Ronceret."

The old judge, stupefied at the president's duplicity, remained planted upon his two legs, at his gate, looking after the two women who departed by unfrequented streets. He saw crumbling around him the edifice so painfully constructed during ten years for his dear child. Was it possible? He suspected some ruse, and hastened to Chesnel's successor. At half-past nine, before the hearing, the vice-president Blondet, the judge Camusot and Michu presented themselves with remarkable punctuality in the council chamber, the door of which was carefully closed by the old judge when he saw enter Camusot and Michu, who came together.

"Well, monsieur le vice-président," said Michu, "Monsieur Sauvager has issued a warrant against a Comte d'Esgrignon, without consulting the procureur du roi, in order to gratify the passion of one Du Croisier, an enemy of the king's government. It is a real topsy-turvy. The president, for his part, goes off and thus prevents the examination. And we know nothing of this affair! They wish perhaps to force our hand?"

"This is the first word that I have heard of this affair," said the old judge, furious at the step taken by the president with the Blandureaus.

Chesnel's successor, the Du Ronceret's man, had been the victim of a ruse invented by the old judge in order to learn the truth, he had revealed the secret.

"It is fortunate that we speak of it to you, my dear master," said Camusot to Blondet; "otherwise, you might have renounced forever seating your son on the fleurs-de-lys, and marrying him to Mademoiselle Blandureau."

"But it is not a question of my son, or of his marriage," said the judge, "it is a question of the young Comte d'Esgrignon,—is he or is he not culpable?"

"It appears," said Michu, "that the funds have been remitted to Madame du Croisier by Chesnel; they have made a crime of a simple irregularity. The young man, according to the accusation, took the bottom of a letter on which was the signature of Du Croisier to convert it into a draft upon the Kellers."

"An imprudence!" said Camusot.

"But, if Du Croisier had received the sum, why has he complained?" said Blondet.

"He does not yet know that the sum has been remitted to his wife, or he feigns not to know it," said Camusot.

"A provincial's vengeance," said Michu.

"That has, however, the appearance to me of being a forgery," said the old Blondet, with whom no passion could obscure the clearness of the judicial conscience.

"You think so?" said Camusot. "But, in the first place, supposing the young count had not had the right to draw upon Du Croisier, there would have been no imitation of the signature. But he thought that he had this right from the notification which Chesnel had given him of the payment made by him, Chesnel."

"Well, then, where do you see a forgery?" said the old judge. "The essence of forgery, in civil cases, is to constitute a wrong done to another."

"Ah! it is clear, accepting Du Croisier's version, that the signature was appropriated in order to get the sum in spite of a forbiddance by Du Croisier to his bankers," said Camusot.

"This, messieurs," said Blondet, "appears to me to be a quibble, a trifle. You had the money, I should perhaps wait for a draft from you; but, I, Comte d'Esgrignon, I was in an urgent need, I have—come now! your accusation is only passion, revenge! In order that there should be forgery, the legislator has determined that there must be an intention to abstract a sum, to procure a profit of some kind, to which there is no legal right. There has been no forgery either in the terms of the Roman law, or in the spirit of present jurisprudence, always keeping ourselves in the civil law, for there is no question here of forgery in a public or authentic document. In private matters, forgery includes an intention to steal; but here, where is the theft? In what times are we living, messieurs? The president leaves us in order to stop an examination that should be finished! I have become acquainted with monsieur le président only to-day, but I will pay him up the arrears of my error; he will hereafter draw up his judgments himself. You should carry this out with the greatest promptness, Monsieur Camusot."

"Yes. My advice," said Michu, "is, instead of a release on bail, to get this young man out of there immediately. Everything depends upon the interrogations to be put to Du Croisier and his wife. You can summon them during the sitting, Monsieur Camusot, receive their depositions before four o'clock, make your report this evening, and we will decide the case to-morrow, before the sitting of the, court."

"While the avocats are pleading, we will arrange the proceedings to be taken," said Blondet to Camusot.

The three judges entered the court, after having assumed their robes.

At noon, Monseigneur and Mademoiselle Armande arrived at the Hôtel D'Esgrignon, where were already Chesnel and Monsieur Couturier. After a sufficiently brief conference between Madame du Croisier's director and the prelate, the priest departed immediately for the house of his penitent.

At eleven o'clock in the morning, Du Croisier received a summons which required him to appear, between one and two o'clock, in the cabinet of the juge d'instruction. He went there, a prey to some lawful suspicions. The president, incapable of foreseeing the arrival of the Duchesse de Maufrigneuse, that of the procureur du roi, or the sudden confederation of the three judges, had forgotten to trace out for Du Croisier a plan of action in case the examination should begin. Neither one nor the other of them had believed in any such celerity. Du Croisier hastened to obey the summons, in order to learn the dispositions of Monsieur Camusot. He was therefore obliged to respond. The judge addressed to him summarily, the six following interrogations:

"Did not the document charged with being a forgery bear a genuine signature?" "Had he not, before this draft, transacted business with Monsieur le Comte d'Esgrignon?" "Had not Monsieur le Comte d'Esgrignon drawn bills of exchange on him with or without notice?" "Had he not written a letter in which he authorized Monsieur d'Esgrignon to always make him his banker?" "Had not Chesnel on several occasions already liquidated his accounts?" "Had he not been absent at such a date?"

These questions were all answered affirmatively by Du Croisier. Notwithstanding his wordy explanations, the judge always brought the banker to an alternative of a yes or a no. When these questions and their answers were taken down on the *procès-verbal,* the judge ended by this overwhelming interrogation:

"Did Du Croisier know that the funds for the draft claimed to be a forgery had been deposited with him, according to a declaration made by Chesnel and a letter of advice from the said Chesnel to the Comte d'Esgrignon, five days before the date of the alleged forgery?"

This last question terrified Du Croisier. He asked for the meaning of such an interrogation, and if he were the culprit, and Monsieur le Comte d'Esgrignon the complainant? He observed that if the funds had been in his hands, he would not have made the complaint.

"Justice is being enlightened," said the judge, sending him away, not without having taken down this last observation.

"But, monsieur, the funds—"

"The funds are in your hands," said the judge.

Chesnel, also cited, appeared to explain the affair. The truth of his assertions was corroborated by the deposition of Madame du Croisier. The judge had already interrogated the Comte d'Esgrignon, who, prompted by Chesnel, produced the first letter in which Du Croisier wrote him to draw upon him without affronting him by depositing funds in advance. Then he produced a letter written by Chesnel, in which the notary notified him of the deposit of a hundred thousand écus with Monsieur du Croisier. With such evidence, the young count's innocence necessarily was established by the tribunal. When Du Croisier returned from the Palais to his house, his visage was white with wrath and on his lips trembled the light foam of a concentrated fury. He found his wife seated in the salon, at the corner of the chimney-piece, and working him a pair of slippers in tapestry; she trembled as she lifted her eyes to him, but she had taken her stand.

"Madame," he cried, stammering, "what deposition did you make before the judge? You have dishonored me, ruined me, betrayed me!"

"I have saved you, monsieur," she replied. "If you should have the honor to ally yourself one day with the D'Esgrignons by the marriage of your niece with the young count, you will owe it to my conduct to-day."

"A miracle! the she-ass of Balaam has spoken," he cried. "I shall no longer be astonished at anything. And where are the hundred thousand écus which Monsieur Camusot says are in my hands?"

"Here they are," she replied, drawing the package of bank-notes from under the cushion of her couch. "I have not committed a mortal sin in declaring that Monsieur Chesnel deposited them with me."

"In my absence?"

"You were not here."

"You swear it to me by your eternal salvation?"

"I swear it," she said in a calm voice.

"Why did you say nothing of it to me?" he asked.

"I was wrong in that," replied his wife, "but my fault will turn to your advantage. Your niece will be one day Marquise d'Esgrignon and perhaps you will be deputy, if you conduct yourself well in this deplorable affair. You have gone too far, endeavor to return."

Du Croisier walked up and down his salon a prey to a horrible agitation, and his wife awaited, in an equal agitation, the result of this promenade. Finally, Du Croisier rang.

"I shall receive no one this evening, close the great gate," he said to his valet de chambre. "To all who come, you will say that Madame and I are in the country. We will set out immediately after dinner, which you will advance a half-hour."

In the evening, all the salons, the little shopkeepers, the poor, the beggars, the nobility, the merchants, the whole city, was talking of this great piece of news,—the arrest of the Comte d'Esgrignon suspected of having committed a forgery. The Comte d'Esgrignon would go to the court of assizes, he would be condemned, branded. The greater number of those to whom the honor of the house of d'Esgrignon was dear, denied the fact. When the night fell, Chesnel went to the house of Camusot for the young unknown, whom he conducted to the Hôtel d'Esgrignon, where Mademoiselle Armande was waiting for her. The poor lady received the lovely Maufrigneuse, to whom she gave her apartment. Monseigneur the Bishop occupied that of Victurnien. When the noble Armande saw herself alone with the duchess, she threw upon her the most deplorable glance.

"You indeed owed your succor to the poor child who ruined himself for you, madame," she said, "a child for whom everybody here sacrifices himself."

The duchess had already surveyed with her woman's eye the chamber of Mademoiselle d'Esgrignon, and had seen in it the image of the life of that sublime maiden,—you would have said that it was the cell of a nun, on seeing this room, cold and bare and without any luxury. The duchess, affected in contemplating the past, the present and the future of this existence, in recognizing the incredible contrast produced by her presence there, could not retain the tears which rolled down her cheeks and served for her response.

"Ah! I am wrong, pardon me, madame la duchesse!" exclaimed the Christian woman, overcoming the aunt of Victurnien; "you were ignorant of our poverty, my nephew was incapable of confessing it to you. Moreover, on seeing you, everything may be imagined, even crime!"

Mademoiselle Armande, thin and dry, pale, but beautiful as one of those thin and severe figures which only the German painters know how to depict, had also wet eyes.

"Reassure yourself, dear angel," said the duchess finally, "he is saved."

"Yes, but honor, but his future! Chesnel has told me,—the king knows the truth."

"We will think about repairing the evil," said the duchess.

Mademoiselle Armande descended to the salon, and found the Cabinet of Antiquities full to overflowing. As much to welcome Monseigneur as to surround the Marquis d'Esgrignon, every one of the habitués had come. Chesnel, posted in the antechamber, recommended to each new arrival the most profound silence concerning the great event, so that the venerable marquis might never know anything of it. The loyal Frank was capable of killing his son or of killing Du Croisier; under these circumstances, he would have required a criminal on one side or the other. By a singular chance, the marquis, happy over the return of his son to Paris, talked more than usual about Victurnien. Victurnien was soon to be placed by the king, the king was finally occupying himself with the D'Esgrignons. Everyone, with death in his heart, exalted the good conduct of Victurnien. Mademoiselle Armande prepared the way for the sudden apparition of her nephew, by saying to her brother that Victurnien would doubtless come to see them and that he should be on the road.

"Bah!" said the marquis, standing before his chimney-piece, "let him attend to his affairs where he is, he should stay there, and not think of the joy which his old father would have in seeing him. The service of the king before everything."

The greater number of those who heard this phrase, shuddered. The law might deliver the shoulder of a D'Esgrignon to the executioner's brand! There was a moment of frightful silence. The old Marquise de Castéran could not retain a tear, which she dropped upon her rouge, while turning her head.

The next day at noon, in superb weather, the entire population in great agitation were dispersed in groups in the street which traversed the city, and there was nothing talked about but the great event. Was the young count in prison, or was he not? At this moment, the well-known tilbury of the Comte d'Esgrignon was seen descending the upper part of the Rue Saint-Blaise, and coming from the prefecture. This tilbury was driven by the count, accompanied by a charming, unknown young man, both of them gay, laughing, talking, with Bengal roses in their button-holes. It was one of those dramatic strokes which it is impossible to describe. At ten o'clock, the young count had been set at liberty by a judgment of no cause of action, clearly set forth. Du Croisier was threatened in it by a *whereas* which reserved to the Comte d'Esgrignon his rights to sue him for slander. The old Chesnel was ascending, as if by chance, the Grand'Rue, and telling everyone who would listen that Du Croisier had set the most infamous snare for the honor of the house of D'Esgrignon, and that, if he were not pursued as a slanderer, he would owe this condescension to the nobility of sentiments which animated the D'Esgrignons. On the evening of this famous day, after the Marquis d'Esgrignon had retired for the night, the young count, Mademoiselle Armande and the handsome little page who was about to depart, were alone with the chevalier, from whom the sex of this charming cavalier could not be concealed and who was the only one in the city, with the exception of the three judges and Madame Camusot, to whom the presence of the duchess was known.

"The house of D'Esgrignon is saved," said Chesnel, "but it will take it a hundred years to recover from this shock. The debts must now be paid, and you can no longer, monsieur le comte, do anything but marry an heiress."

"And take her wherever you find her," said the duchess.

"A second misalliance!" exclaimed Mademoiselle Armande.

The duchess began to laugh.

"It is better to marry than to die," said she, taking out of the pocket of her waistcoat a little flask given by the apothecary of the château of the Tuileries.

Mademoiselle Armande made a gesture of fright, the old Chesnel took the hand of the lovely Maufrigneuse and kissed it without permission.

"You are then crazy here?" the duchess went on. "You then insist upon remaining in the fifteenth century when we are in the nineteenth? My dear children, there is no longer any nobility, there is no longer anything but the aristocracy. The Code Civil of Napoléon has killed all the parchments, as the cannon had already killed feudality. You will be much more noble than you are when you have some money. Marry whom you like, Victurnien, you will ennoble your wife, this is the most solid privilege which remains to the French nobility. Did not Monsieur de Talleyrand marry Madame Grandt without compromising himself? Remember that Louis XIV. married the widow Scarron."

"He did not marry her for her money," said Mademoiselle Armande.

"If the Comtesse d'Esgrignon were the niece of one Du Croisier, would you receive her?" asked Chesnel.

"Perhaps," replied the duchess, "but the king, without any doubt, would see her with pleasure. You are not then aware of what is going on?" she said, seeing the astonishment depicted on every countenance. "Victurnien has come to Paris, he knows how things are going there. We were more powerful under Napoléon. Victurnien, marry Mademoiselle Duval, she will be Marquise d'Esgrignon quite as much as I am Duchesse de Maufrigneuse."

"Everything is lost, even honor!" said the chevalier with a gesture of despair.

"Adieu, Victurnien," said the duchess, kissing him on the forehead, "we shall see each other no more. That which is the best for you to do, is to live on your estates, the air of Paris is not good for you."

"Diane!" cried the young count in despair.

"Monsieur, you forget yourself strangely," said the duchess coldly, quitting the rôle of a man and a mistress, and becoming again not only angel, but still more, duchess, not only duchess, but the Célimène of Molière.

The Duchesse de Maufrigneuse saluted nobly these four personages, and obtained from the chevalier the last tear of admiration which he had at the service of the fair sex.

"How she resembles the Princess Goritza!" he exclaimed in an undertone.

Diane had disappeared. The crack of the postilion's whip announced to Victurnien that the beautiful romance of his first passion was ended. While in danger, Diane had still been able to see in the young count her lover; but saved, the duchess despised him for the feeble man that he was.

Six months later, Camusot was appointed assistant judge at Paris, and, later, juge d'instruction. Michu became procureur du roi. The goodman Blondet passed as counsellor to the royal court, remained there long enough to get his pension, and returned to inhabit his pretty little house. Joseph Blondet had his father's seat in the tribunal for the rest of his days, but without any chance for advancement, and was the spouse of Mademoiselle Blandureau, who to-day wearies herself in that house of brick and of flowers, as much as a carp in a basin of marble. Finally, Michu and Camusot received the cross of the Legion of Honor, and the old Blondet received that of officer. As to the first deputy of the procureur du roi, Monsieur Sauvager, he was sent to Corsica, to the great contentment of Du Croisier, who certainly did not wish to give him his niece.

Du Croisier, inspired by the president Du Ronceret, appealed from the judgment of no ground of action to the royal court, and lost. Throughout the whole department the liberals maintained that the little D'Esgrignon had committed a forgery. The royalists, on their side, recounted the horrible plots which vengeance had caused *the infamous Du Croisier* to hatch. A duel took place between Du Croisier and Victurnien. The fortune of arms was for the former contractor, who dangerously wounded the young count and maintained his words. The contest between the two parties was still more envenomed by this affair, which the liberals were constantly bringing forward. Du Croisier, always defeated after the elections, saw no chance of marrying his niece to the young count, especially after his duel.

A month after the confirmation of the judgment by the royal court, Chesnel, worn out by that horrible struggle in which his forces, moral and physical, had been shaken, died in his hour of triumph, like a faithful old hound who has been ripped up by a young wild boar. He died as happy as he could be in leaving the house as good as ruined and the young man in poverty, steeped in ennui, and without any prospect of establishing himself. This cruel thought, joined to his enfeebling, doubtless finished the poor old man. In the midst of so many ruins, overwhelmed by so many griefs, he received a great consolation,—the old marquis, solicited by his sister, restored him to all his former friendship. This great personage came into the little house of the Rue du Bercail, he seated himself at the bedside of his old servitor, all whose sacrifices were unknown to him. Chesnel rose up in his bed and recited the canticle of Simeon; the marquis permitted him to be buried in the chapel of the château, lying crosswise, and at the bottom of the pit where this, practically the last of the D'Esgrignons would come to lie himself.

Thus died one of the last representatives of that great and fine *domesticité*, a word which is often taken in an evil sense, and to which we give here its real significance in making it express the feudal attachment of the servitor to the master. This sentiment, which no longer exists but in the depths of the provinces and among some old servants of royalty, honors equally the nobility which inspires such affections and the bourgeoisie which conceives them. This noble and magnificent devotion is, to-day, impossible. The noble houses have no longer any servitors, in the same manner as there is no longer any king in France or any hereditary peers, or immovable property attached to the historic houses to perpetuate the national splendors. Chesnel was not only one of those great men unknown to private life, he was then also a great thing. Does not the continuity of his sacrifices give him something, I know-not-what, of grave and sublime? does it not surpass the heroism of munificence, which is always a momentary effort? The virtue of Chesnel belongs essentially to the classes placed between the poverty of the people and the grandeurs of the aristocracy, and which can thus unite the modest virtues of the bourgeois to the sublime thoughts of the noble, by enlightening them with the flame of a substantial instruction.

Victurnien, viewed with disfavor at court, could find there neither rich damsel nor employment. The king constantly refused to give the peerage to the D'Esgrignons, the only favor which could draw Victurnien out of his poverty. During the lifetime of his father, it was impossible to marry the young count with any bourgeois heiress, he was obliged to live shabbily in the paternal mansion with the souvenirs of his two years of Parisian splendor and aristocratic love. Dull and sorrowful, he vegetated between his father in despair, who attributed to a languishing malady the state in which he saw his son, and his aunt devoured with grief. Chesnel was no longer there. The marquis died in 1830, after having seen the king, Charles X., on his road to Nonancourt, where this grand D'Esgrignon went, followed by all the valid nobility of the Cabinet of Antiquities, to serve him and to join the meagre cortége of the vanquished monarchy. An act of courage which will seem simple enough to-day, but which the enthusiasm of the revolt then rendered sublime!

"The Gauls are triumphant!" were the last words of the marquis.

The victory of Du Croisier was then complete, for the new Marquis d'Esgrignon, a week after the death of his old father, accepted Mademoiselle Duval for his wife; she had three millions of dot, Du Croisier and his wife formally assured Mademoiselle Duval of their fortune. Du Croisier said, during the marriage ceremony, that the house of D'Esgrignon was the most honorable of all the noble houses of France. You will see every winter the Marquis d'Esgrignon, who will have one day more than one hundred thousand écus of income, in Paris, where he leads the gay life of bachelors, having nothing in common with the grand seigneurs of former times but his indifference for his wife, of whom he does not think at all."

"As to Mademoiselle d'Esgrignon," said Émile Blondet, to whom are owing the details of this history, "if she no longer resembles the celestial figure of which I had glimpses during my infancy, she is certainly, at sixty-seven, the most sorrowful and the most interesting figure of the Cabinet of Antiquities, where she is still enthroned. I saw her on the last journey which I made to my native province, in search of the papers necessary for my marriage. When my father learned that I was marrying, he remained stupefied, and recovered his speech only when I told him that I was a prefect.

"'You were born a prefect!'" he replied, smiling.

"While taking a turn about the city, I met Mademoiselle Armande, who appeared to me to be grander than ever! I seemed to see Marius amidst the ruins of Carthage. Was she not surviving her religions, her beliefs destroyed? She no longer believed but in God. Habitually sorrowful, mute, she preserved of her former beauty only the eyes of a supernatural light. When I saw her going to mass, her book in her hand, I could not refrain from thinking that she asked God to withdraw her from this world."

Aux Jardies, July, 1837.

9 781396 322310